VAMPIRES *of* EDEN

BOOK ONE • OLIVER

KARLA NIKOLE PUBLISHING

VAMPIRES *of* EDEN

KARLA NIKOLE

KARLA NIKOLE PUBLISHING

First Karla Nikole Publishing Edition, December 2023

This is a work of fiction. All names, characters and incidents are the product of the author's imagination and are used fictitiously. Any resemblance to actual persons, living or dead, or events is entirely coincidental.

ISBN: 979-8-218-29826-5 (paperback)

ISBN: 979-8-218-30770-7 (ebook)

Library of Congress Control Number: 2023920439

Cover illustration by Thander Lin

Contact@LoreAndLust.com

www.LoreAndLust.com

Printed in the United States of America

10 9 8 7 6 5 4 3 2 1

*For anyone who feels out of place in an antiquated society.
You are valid.*

Dearest reader, this book contains instances of violence, verbal and emotional abuse, as well as some mild but uncomfortable moments of non-consent.

Chapter One

I can't breathe.

My chest is tight and it feels as if my heart has stopped.

Why is he like this? Why does *everything* have to be so hard?

"A-are you joking?" I ask, panicked and frozen with my mobile phone clutched in my palm. "Right now?"

"Right now," Camille parrots. Her eyes are filled with remorse and empathy, as if she hates being the bearer of bad news. The herald of Lord Blakeley's ill will. "He's asked that you go—"

I turn and run. Unthinking as anxiety fuels and propels my legs forward. The rose garden is a blur around me—a smeared palette of green brush dotted with pink and white. Five minutes ago, I was carelessly reveling in the colors and life pulsating around me. The warmth of the sun on my face and arms as I crouched and observed a honeybee collecting pollen through the artful eye of my phone.

All of that feels like a dream. Because the nightmare that is my existence has returned to the forefront. Like some cruel, antagonistic reminder that I can never truly be happy. Maybe I don't deserve happiness?

I push through the heavy wooden door that leads back into

the castle. The cold air clutches my arms and raises goosebumps across my skin. Sixteenth-century stone walls are impermeable to warmth—an unassailable foe to the late-summer sun in a cloudless sky.

The door echoes loudly as it slams shut. My eyes have barely adjusted to the drastic change in light before I'm running again, down a long hallway, then up a narrow flight of stairs until I hit a set of double doors. I burst through and am showered in light once more because of the arched windows on either side of the curtain wall. This open passage is the singular link between my tower and the rest of the castle.

The sunlight blinks as I pass amid bright rays and shadows cast from the arches, like a dizzying kaleidoscope of day and night. Another pair of doors at the end lead me back into cold and dank air. Into the familiar gray and colorless corridor that feels more like a prison than a home.

There's nothing beautiful or inspiring here.

A discolored family coat of arms made from wood and metal hangs high above my head. At the bottom of the steps leading to my room, a portrait of an ancestor long deceased peers down at me—proud and disapproving. A true and undeniable predecessor of Lord Blakeley if ever there was one.

I pass the empty guest room across from the disturbing painting and take the spiral stairs two at a time. My heart beats wildly in my chest as I climb, hoping and praying that Camille has made a mistake. That this is all some kind of mean-spirited joke, even though I know she would never do something like that.

Any notion of hope is dispelled when I hear voices and commotion. I round the final corner and see Lana and Kelvin carrying large crates overflowing with recognizable items. The aluminum legs of my tripod, stacks of books and small boxes of film. Benjamin exits my room holding the backpack in which I keep my compact camera and laptop equipment for uploading.

"Wait—Just hold on a second!"

Lana and Kelvin nervously look away as they pass. Ben

winces, clenching his teeth as he follows the other two down the stairs. I rush toward my room, but stop dead. Without warning, Hudson fills the entire frame, making me gasp in surprise and stumble backward.

Tall and imposing, Lord Blakeley's primary manservant blocks the entrance like a brick wall in his clean, well-tailored uniform. He's broad-shouldered and bulky with flawless dark skin.

"Lord Blakeley has ordered that all of your photography equipment be confiscated until further notice," he announces with expressionless hazel eyes. "Including your mobile device."

"Hudson, *please*—this is all I have. You know that I... I already apologized for—"

"The device, your grace." His gaze lowers to my right hand, where I'm clutching my phone. He exhales an audible sigh. "The order has been given. Please don't make me take it from you."

We stand in silence, surrounded by stone. The cold atmosphere penetrates my skin, oppressing and weighted with misery. Without speaking, I lift my arm, palm up, and offer the phone.

Gently, he takes it from my hand. "Thank you, your grace." He walks, bypassing me as I stand, unmoving. Gutted and small. Powerless, as always. Hudson disappears, but his heavy footfalls echo in staccato as he descends the steps behind me.

Hollowed, I walk into my room. The circular space is well lit because the curtains are drawn over the east- and west-facing windows. Dust motes float along an invisible air current and there isn't a single sound.

My stomach drops.

All of the shelves are empty. The second-hand photography books I've scavenged over the years and treasured knickknacks—a porcelain elephant from Thailand gifted to me by my former tutor and my first classic instant camera—all vanished. My desk is wiped clean as well. No laptop, compact camera or chargers. No tripod standing in the corner or backpack hanging from the hook on the wall.

Disbelief sweeps through me as I slowly sit down on the ottoman at the end of my bed. Breathing, I lower and place my head in my palms, then close my eyes.

The silence engulfs me, as if someone has set my life and very being to mute.

"You're okay," I whisper. "It's okay..."

Alone, isolated, I repeat this mantra over and over as I sit in the barren room. I don't move. The sun shifts, sluggishly dipping below the horizon and casting the space into night and shadows.

Eventually, Camille is at my side. I don't know how long I've been sitting, but when I try to move, my legs are numb.

"Lord Blakeley is expecting you at dinner tonight," she says, standing over me. "It's the last dinner before the bonding festivities begin this weekend..."

I shake my head. "I'm not hungry."

"But he's expecting you. The viscount as well—"

"Camille, look around." Shifting to my knees, I crawl back toward the headboard, then drop down onto my stomach and lie against the pillow with my eyes closed. "I said that I was sorry. I begged for his forgiveness, but he still took everything. How can I go to dinner and pretend like I'm fine? We don't even need to eat food this often. It's ridiculous."

How far can you push someone before they snap? Before all the restrictions, punishments and admonishments backfire and all that's left is a hurting pile of ashes?

"Your grace, it could always be worse... Remember Thomas."

My eyes blink open. Those two words pulsate in my ears like a warning signal.

Remember Thomas.

I don't say anything, but I lie against the bed, heart racing. Frightening, forgotten images of my elder brother flash to the forefront of my mind—his skin covered in ugly scabs. His body emaciated and his spirit broken.

To this day, he is an empty shell of the vampire he used to be.

"Sasha will be here tomorrow," Camille adds, hopeful and much less cryptic. "Both Lord Blakeley and the viscount have permitted her to visit with you prior to the festivities, but if you refuse to go to dinner, I think that will be canceled, and inevitably, we'll both be in trouble..."

Exhaling, I push myself upright. The situation is already bad enough without dragging Camille into it. She shouldn't be exposed to the wrath of Lord Blakeley because I'm feeling sorry for myself. That isn't fair to her.

"Alright," I say, rubbing a palm down my face. "I'll go."

She nods, turning toward the closet. "You should take a shower, and I'll lay something out for you. I'll be waiting outside."

I stand, then drag myself into the bathroom. How am I going to get through this evening—no, through this entire circus? Smiling and faking my way through weeks of celebratory dinners, local tours and events.

The first mating attempt with Alexander. God...

"I know there's a lot going on right now," Camille says, popping out of the closet with pre-pressed and ironed clothing draped over her arm. She walks with efficiency toward the bed. "But don't forget that you're sitting in with the viscount during his meeting with the Italian dignitary next week. And the designer will be here on Monday."

Confused, I pause in the doorframe to the bathroom and glance over my shoulder. "The what? What kind of designer?"

"We've talked about this, your grace—he's coming to make custom suits for your and Alexander's wedding. Now, hurry, please?" She stalks toward the bedroom door. As she leaves, she gently closes it behind her.

I shake my head. I have no idea what she's talking about.

~

The small dining room is dimly lit when I push open one of the double doors and slip through the gap. It's quiet. Like the calm before the storm. We use this space for immediate family members, saving the larger, more grandiose dining rooms of the castle to impress visiting lords, ladies and dignitaries. Tonight, there are only three of us. Me, Lord Blakeley and the viscount. My purebred vampire fathers.

One is domineering, prideful and insatiable in his yearning for respect, status and validation. This strange, inherent need of his covers us like a virus. An infectious ailment that steadily deteriorates and worsens the quality of all our lives.

The other is innocuous. Not unkind, but complicit and culpable by silence—always standing idly by as a witness to the harm being done.

My fathers... don't like me at all. No matter how hard I've tried to be what they want me to be, and do what they want me to do, I'm never quite good enough. Somehow, I'm always wrong. A misfit.

It's exhausting. Living underneath the weight of their constant disappointment.

Love is completely off the table. As I've grown older, I've come to the painful realization that my existence is for functional purposes only. No one loves a broom or a shovel.

"Why have you kept us waiting?" Lord Blakeley's stormy-gray eyes are emotionless as I approach the table and take my seat. A pair of bronze Gothic candelabras line the center of the white tablecloth. The light from the candles dances and casts ominous shadows across his stern face.

"I apologize," I say reflexively with my head bowed.

"The season of your bonding ceremony has finally arrived," Lord Blakeley goes on. It's as if my body is physically shrinking beneath the heft of his aggravated voice and gaze. "We have been anticipating this moment for centuries, Oliver. *I* have been yearning for this pivotal ascent in our clan's history. It feels as if you are singularly determined to ruin it. To throw everything away."

"I-I'm not," I say, shaking my head and keeping my gaze down. "I'm sorry."

"Stop sputtering, and do not be late this weekend—to *anything*. Not a single event. Do not disappear and do not wander off. You will not take a single picture and you will *not* be fantasizing or lost in your own ridiculous, silly thoughts. From Sunday and until the completion of this ritual next month, Alexander should be your primary focus at all times—have I made myself clear?"

"Yes, my lord." Anxious, I clench my palms into fists against my lap. I close my eyes, willing this moment to be over. Wishing that I could be somewhere, anywhere else but at this table.

"I expect great things from you and this arrangement. Do not disappoint me."

A small bell chimes—the cue from the viscount to begin dinner service. It is also the signal that my admonishment is finished. For now.

Members of the waitstaff enter the room. Their white shirts are a stark contrast to the dusky, navy and silver damask wallpaper surrounding us. Soon, there's the unmistakable *clink* of glasses and plates being set on the table. My ears detect liquid sloshing as it's poured into glasses.

"Oliver?"

Cautiously, I glance up at the sound of the viscount's voice. His prominent blue eyes meet mine, searching. They almost glow, contrasted with the warmth of his tawny, maple-brown skin. A trait that's emblematic of his ancestral southern roots. "I confirmed our meeting next week with Dignitary Garibaldi. Will you still join me? You seemed excited about the opportunity to speak in Italian with her."

I nod and speak slowly, careful not to stutter. "Yes, I will. Of course." My eyes flicker over to Lord Blakeley. There's less hostility in his gaze, but his expression is apathetic. Unimpressed.

We eat in silence. I stuff down as much as I can. As much as my nerves will allow, because I don't want to be chastised for not cleaning my plate.

When dinner is over, I'm allowed to return to my half-empty room in my isolated tower. Everything that I forced down comes back up.

Eventually, I crawl into bed. When my body stops shaking, I fall into a restless and shallow sleep.

Chapter Two

"I heard that Lord Heartless has hired a designer for your wedding."

The next day, a book of photographic techniques rests heavily in my lap. *The Negative* by Ansel Adams. It is the only item to have survived the security raid of my room. The last time I looked at it, about a month ago, I was sitting on the floor and had absently slid it under the bed when I was finished.

My sister, Sasha, is lying on her stomach against the bed, facing me. She's propped up on her elbows and has her chin resting in her palms. The lower half of her body is cast in a square of white light from the afternoon sun beaming through the window. It covers her like an incandescent blanket.

I'm not sure how to respond to her statement. It isn't a question, so I shrug and shake my head. Confused.

"*Ollie*," she says, smirking, "he didn't hire a damn designer for my wedding. Or for Thomas when he got married. Lord Heartless really wants to show off because his special baby boy is about to make all our ancestors' dreams come true. It's going to be the affair to end all affairs—an extravaganza!"

For as long as I can remember, she's referred to our parents as

"Lord Heartless" and "Viscount Pointless." Both designations are a bit cruel, but not untrue.

Lifting my head from the book once more, I sigh as I stare at her, vacantly. I don't say anything, because she knows better. I don't understand her intention.

She sits upright, shaking her head. "Oh, boy—"

"Sasha, I couldn't care less about all of this and you know it. Having 'influence' and sitting on Eden's governing board. Our family being part of the Royal Order. It's... a silly, antiquated game of titles and I'm just a pawn in Lord Blakeley's ambitions. We all are."

My heart pulses in my ears as the room falls silent. Most days, I keep my feelings locked inside and do what they ask of me. I don't say these things. Instead, I stay quiet, obedient and polite.

But as we draw closer to the end... to this arranged marriage that I've been groomed for since I was a child for the sake of Lord Blakeley's aspirations and dreams... it's getting harder to comply.

Lord Blakeley is becoming even more strict and hostile, and I'm depleted. I'm so tired of operating under these bizarre and old-fashioned rules.

Sasha narrows her eyes. Her hand darts out and pokes the arch of my foot through my sock. The quick sensation makes me jump and I pull my legs in and away from her.

"You're so sad, Ollie. You only make things more miserable for yourself by thinking this way."

"But, isn't it the truth?"

"Yes," she says. "It is the truth. You're right. This is our circumstance. This is our life. So, why not try to make the best of it? We have to work with the materials that are in front of us, you know? Being depressed and resentful doesn't help anything."

Frustrated, I rub a palm against my scalp and muss my hair. "Sash, there's nothing good about this situation. Look around you. Do you see what he did?" Exhaling, I drop my hand. Sasha stares back at me with blueish, heather-gray irises. They're almost the same color as my eyes, except mine more closely mirror the bright blue of the viscount's.

"Camille told me about this," she says softly. "I'm sorry it's gone this far. You took the pictures down and closed your social media account, right?"

"Yes."

She nods empathetically, then glances around my room and toward the barren shelves between the windows. The empty desk in the corner. "This feels excessive—even for him. He took your phone, too?"

Closing my eyes, I lie back against the headboard. The wood is hard, ornately carved and, therefore, uncomfortable. "He did. From today onward, my sole purpose in life is to please His Royal Highness Prince Alexander Kendrick, and to ensure that the Blakeley Clan is finally designated as a Royal House of Eden. That we become one of the Five Major Houses governing our aristocracy since the inception of the peace treaty and the end of the vampire wars."

This rhetoric has been drilled into my brain for as far back as I can remember.

Major Houses.

Royal Order and Governing Board.

Peace Treaties and Historical Records.

All capital letters. All integral to the systemic culture of our society. It's been reiterated to me by tutors, relatives and servants. At society parties and in a particularly ostentatious fashion at the Annual Eden Spring Fête.

Above all, it has been emphasized by Lord Blakeley. Privately and adamantly.

Sasha shifts to sit upright, her teeth clenched. "Speaking of 'pleasing Prince Alexander,' it's scheduled for tomorrow night, isn't it? Your first mating attempt?"

I exhale, my shoulders slumping with dead weight. I do not want to talk about this because it's mortifying. The heat of embarrassment rushes up to my neck and cheeks. I close the book in my lap since I can't focus on it anyway. "Yes," I groan.

"How are you feeling about it?"

I rub my palms against my face. "Like I hate my life."

"Well, that's baseline for you. The royal council won't expect you to bond right away. Everyone knows that it takes a lot of time, so don't feel too pressured."

Dropping my hands, I meet her eyes, incredulous. "Don't feel pressured? Everything about this situation is pressured. How can I not feel stressed about a group of old and snobbish purebreds watching me have sex for the first time—and with a vampire that I have nothing in common with. That I have no chemistry—"

"Oh, come on, Ollie. You and Alexander have loads in common. You're the same age, you're both the youngest in your households... you're the same species—"

"Wow."

"No, but seriously. You've known him for fifteen years!"

"And we've never once spent an iota of time alone together— is that natural?" I ask as the anxiety sits heavily in my chest. "All of our interactions have been supervised, scheduled and planned. Rehearsed and with Lord Heartless breathing down my neck to be on my best and most docile behavior. There is *nothing* tangible or remarkable between us and I just..."

I pause, overwhelmed because my life is truly spiraling out of control.

The things I dream about—those ridiculous and silly thoughts that Lord Blakeley accuses me of—they rise up within me now and I have to let them out. Even though Sasha has heard this speech at least a thousand times, I can't help myself.

"There are places—communities and aristocracies in the world—that don't do this stuff anymore," I say, lifting my palm to the top of my head and closing my eyes. Trying to rein in the sadness and injustice crushing my heart. "Most have stopped, because this system is invasive and outdated. They let vampires choose their mates freely. Not because of politics, treaties or power. Not anymore. They do it because their aura speaks to them or their eyes alight. I feel nothing like that for Alexander—none of us who are wrapped up in this charade ever do! And I... I don't want this, Sash. I *don't want* this."

"I know..." My sister sits up and reaches out, taking hold of my free hand near my thigh. "I know."

The room is silent, the sun shining brightly through the windows at a golden slant. In the eastern wing of the castle, where my room is located, it's always quiet.

I was relocated here around the age of ten. At the time, my much older manservant was having trouble keeping track of me. In the main estate, there are too many corridors, rooms and exits that lead out into the greater gardens and I had a habit of escaping —usually to the woods and lavender fields. On one too many occasions, my whereabouts were unknown. And so, I've been confined to this tower ever since.

Twelve years. One way in and one way out.

"Is it preposterous to want freedom?" I ask, opening my eyes and sincerely meeting Sasha's gaze. "To want to learn and discover, and to maybe eventually bond with someone because I feel drawn to them in my nature and they reciprocate these feelings? Not because vampires are forcing me to do it for political gain but because my eyes alight for them. Lots of purebred vampires live that life. In the modern era, it's more natural—"

"Yes, it's natural for some, but not for us." She exhales a heavy sigh, and I can see it. I've pushed her too far. "What we do... The rules of our aristocracy are important, Oliver. If the Five Major Houses hadn't signed the Peace Treaty of Eden, we—"

"We wouldn't exist today. We would have killed each other in the clan wars, and we'd all be dead. Extinct as a race." I shake my head. "Well, I'd rather be, honestly. For all the good it's done."

Sasha lets go of my hand and stands up from the bed. Incensed. "Well, that was a shit thing to say—you selfish little vampire. One minute I feel bad that Lord Blakeley treats you like a child, then the next, you fit the bill, don't you?"

Ignoring the insult, I watch her carefully. "Have your eyes ever alighted for Elaine? Or for anyone? Have you ever felt the pull in your nature for another vampire?"

Sasha's face hardens as she looks away. "Is one vampire's passion and whimsy worth starting a war? Potentially sacrificing an entire race of purebreds?"

I frown, folding my arms. "That's a slippery slope. I don't think I'm capable of single-handedly dismantling centuries-old doctrine by having freedom in my life. I don't have that kind of power—"

"But *you do*. Centuries ago, five clans almost tore this aristocracy apart. This peace treaty and what we do now is the only thing that stopped the fighting and killing. It was the only way to balance and share the power. Sacrifices have to be made for the greater good, and you're part of that, Oliver. Full stop."

I hate it when she lectures me. It's always like this. Sasha understanding and commiserating with me, but only up until a point. "I know it's important," I say, folding my legs and feeling guarded. "I don't need a speech about history and responsibility —you sound just like him right now. I apologize for what I said, okay? I'm sorry. It won't happen again."

Sasha steps back, blinking as if I've just slapped her. "I—No. That's not... Listen—"

"It's fine, Sash. You're right. I'm sorry. I'm selfish and silly and I need to grow up." I take a breath, but my chest feels heavy. Hardened, like it's stuffed with rocks. I bite the inside of my cheek.

This moment feels like dinner last night. Me, being rebuked because I'm lacking. Because I'm screwing up yet again and not subscribing to the system. Maybe she's right? Maybe it is time that I faced reality and let go of these passions and whimsies that threaten to wipe out my entire aristocracy.

The light in my room shifts as the sun dips behind a cloud. Sasha watches me. Her expression is creased and downcast, as if

I've said something hurtful to her, even though I don't think I have.

After a long moment, she picks her bag up from the ottoman at the end of my bed and digs inside. Soon, she pulls out a square box and sets it just in front of my folded legs. Then, she produces another, smaller one, setting them side by side.

"He shouldn't have taken all your devices and equipment away," she says. "That was immature of him. The pictures that you took and posted were fantastic, and we *should* do better in supporting our lower-ranked kin. Well done."

"Thank you, but..." I glance at the packaging before gently pushing the boxes back toward her. "If anyone finds out that I have this, I'll just be in more trouble." The first box is a miniature hybrid instant camera. Black with rose-gold trimmings. Lovely. The second, smaller box is a pack of instant film because it's a niche camera.

She sighs, shaking her head. "Ollie... I always want you to be yourself with me. I don't want you to be submissive and withdrawn all the time—I really love that you think differently from all of us and have these creative aspirations. I'm sorry that I scolded you. But I do think that you need to accept reality, because there is no escaping this. The ceremony is real and it's happening next month. In the meantime, though, find joy in the tangible things?"

"Like... what?"

"Use the camera. It's small, so you can hide it if someone comes around. And... Alexander is a little too perfect-y and blonde for my taste, but I really believe that he genuinely likes you? He specifically chose you. Maybe the two of you will have 'chemistry' once everyone's eyes are no longer watching and dissecting your every move?"

"Sure." I nod. "Or maybe it'll get worse."

Sasha rolls her eyes. "You're so negative. Listen, since you're relocating to Central Eden to be with Alexander and it's his realm, he'll oversee all the boring stuff. You'll mostly just be like... hm... arm candy?"

I blink, confused. "Is this supposed to comfort me?"

"Well, yes, a little. You won't need to be deeply embroiled in the politics of Eden. You'll just have a seat beside him while he does all the work. That's how it is with Elaine and me. I play my part when I'm needed—you know, make sure my hair and appearance are just so, and that I'm well versed on whatever relevant topics or guests. It's easy."

"It sounds empty."

"It isn't empty. Having a Blakeley on the Royal Governing Board and finally represented within the Eden Historical Records will be enough to make Lord Heartless and all our dead ancestors proud. You're fulfilling a centuries-long ambition!"

I really... don't have anything else to say. When I stare unmoving in the silence for a little too long, she shrugs.

"Alright then," she concedes. "Look forward to meeting the designer? I researched him online and he's really amazing. It's impressive that Lord Heartless is going all out for your wedding."

I squint, considering. "Can we afford this? Wouldn't it have been better to put more electrical sockets in the library so we don't have to read by candlelight anymore?"

"His name is Aries, I think?" Sasha goes on, ignoring me. "Ask him about his travels and Italy. Maybe you can live vicariously through him?"

I'm not interested in living vicariously through some random vampire. Or custom-made clothes that we definitely cannot afford. Or even Prince Alexander and this month-long ritual leading up to a forced wedding and being his "arm candy."

But I know that she's trying to comfort me in her own way. So, I smile politely with my hands clasped in my lap. "I will. Thanks, Sasha."

Hesitating, she nods, turns and walks toward the door. She grabs the handle and speaks with her back toward me. "You're being fake as hell."

"I-I'm not."

"You are. You're giving me that false 'I'm a well-behaved and compliant vampire' voice and smile that you do for Lord Blakeley." She turns, still holding the handle but with her arm folded behind her back as she leans against the door. "To answer your earlier question, no, my eyes have never alighted for Elaine... obviously. It's been two years, and we still can't even manage to link our natures properly, can we? No bond in sight."

She sighs, glancing up toward the sunlight ricocheting off the ceiling from the window. "But I have felt the pull once... that natural desire you mentioned. Father took me to my last Global Vampire Summit when I was sixteen. This was before Lord Heartless forbade any more trips like that, and also before Father buckled to his every ridiculous demand and became Pointless.

"Anyway, there was an Ethiopian vampire there with her mother, a purebred from Addis. Our gazes met from across the lobby and it felt like... like fire was racing up my spine. It was a passing moment, but I've never forgotten it."

A gentle pause like a heartbeat or two passes between us, and I can visualize the scene she's painted. It gives me second-hand butterflies in my stomach. "That's special," I tell her, softening and relaxing my shoulders. "You're lucky to know that feeling. I never will."

Sasha turns, pulls the door open, then winks back at me. "You don't know that, Oliver. It's over for me, but I have hope for you."

lexander Kendrick is arrogant. We have nothing in common, and where everything that I do and say is utterly wrong in the eyes of my fathers and the vampires around me, Alexander's very existence is perfection to society at large.

We've been engaged since we were seven, which was when he decided that I would eventually be his mate after we came of age. I had nothing to do with this decision and my opinion was not considered. Lord Blakeley eagerly accepted his family's proposal on my behalf... Before I even understood what a proposal was.

When the wealthy and beautiful purebred prince from the most prominent royal house in Eden asks for your son's hand in marriage, there is no hesitating. Especially if your son is from a family that's broadly deemed as unworthy of such a coveted honor. A child born of a vampire clan that's regarded as second tier, at best.

"There's a quote from Alexander circulating in the news recently," Lord Blakeley announces proudly. "He's 'extremely excited' about the upcoming ceremony. Were you aware?"

Lord Blakeley sits beside me in the drawing room, impeccably dressed and glancing down from the corners of his steely eyes.

Somehow, I wasn't blessed with his or the viscount's long legs and general vertical prowess. Everyone in my immediate family is tall, and I'm shorter than both Thomas and Sasha. Truly, I'm the runt of the litter.

It's as if fate was having a laugh while designing my life, but with this, and in my humble opinion, she took it a step too far.

How would I know about any quotes circulating in the news when all of my electronic devices have been confiscated? I'm sure Alexander never experiences this type of rudimentary punishment. He always says and does the right things, doesn't he? Because he's the model vampire prince.

Things like "problem solving" are bad in our culture. Being curious, questioning or challenging norms. Suggesting tangible change in the social structure makes you a miscreant.

"I hadn't heard," I respond flatly. "That's nice."

"Would you please exhibit a little more... zeal, when Prince Alexander and Lord Kendrick arrive? Today is the first occasion where the two of you are permitted to be alone together as adults. This meeting is very important, Oliver, as it sets the tone for our arrangement within the grander realm of Central Eden. Can I rest assured that you will be accommodating of his highness? And that you'll keep your controversial opinions to yourself?"

"Yes, Lord Blakeley."

He nods, shifting his gaze toward the large stone fireplace, where the hearth is empty. "This will be the first time in our clan's history that we will have a place within the Royal Order. Finally, we will exert true, influential power within Eden's aristocracy." His voice sings with a familiar pride, interlaced with hope and ambition.

I take a deep breath and close my eyes as I blow it out. Here we go.

"Blakeley House will reign in the south, and through this bonding, we will be directly connected with the most powerful family in Eden. What's more, Alexander specifically chose *you*. Let's not tarnish a situation that is heavily tipped in our favor."

Knowing the appropriate response to this speech, I nod. "I understand." When I swallow, it goes down hard. This pressure is unbearable.

Silence falls between us and I breathe slowly, trying to stay calm so that I don't exacerbate the perpetual knot of angst in my chest. Weirdly, I sense Lord Blakeley looking at me. When I glance up, I meet his eyes. "Y-yes? Is something the matter?" He probably doesn't like the suit my maidservant has chosen for me, or there's a hair out of place on my head.

"Stop sputtering…" He surprises me when he smiles. "I have always felt that Winston's handsome features have inexplicably settled the most gracefully within your face. You are striking, my son. Perhaps this is why Alexander chose you? I did not hesitate in accepting his family's offer, but you should know that he was not the only one to seek your hand."

Well, this definitely corroborates Sasha's prediction of my being "arm candy" for the rest of my life. I guess this is a compliment? I'm not used to him saying anything remotely kind to me, so I rub the back of my neck and nod.

He smirks. "Don't tell your brother or sister that I said this to you."

A loud knock at the double doors makes me jump in my seat. My hands tremble as I grip my thighs. Perceiving my stress, Lord Blakeley rolls his eyes.

"Come," he commands, then stands perfectly straight. Stiffly, I follow his lead as the doors spring open.

Hudson is there, announcing the arrival of Alexander and his father, Lord Kendrick. The two vampires enter the room, distinctly different but somehow similar.

Lord Ansväd Kendrick hails from the northern mountains, where the vampires are built like Vikings of the past—pale, domineering and almost always blonde. He isn't especially tall, but he is wide and square with a commanding presence in his tailored suit.

Standing a whole head above his father, Alexander is dressed smartly, as always. Modern, and his façade is more richly colored by comparison. Where Ansväd's neat ponytail is an icy, almost platinum blonde, Alexander's hair is short, stylish and the color of buttery sunlight.

I force a genial smile and bow while the two older vampires greet each other in boisterous approval, embracing warmly. Alexander grins at me with his perfect teeth, openly pleased, as if there's a television camera filming all of this.

"Master Oliver Blakeley—how wonderful to see you again!" Lord Kendrick releases my father and comes over to shake my hand with both of his.

I bow politely while gripping his palms. "Hello, your highness. It's a pleasure to see you as well."

He stands back, lightheartedly assessing. "Have you grown even taller since the last time we met?"

I... definitely have not. This feels like a running joke between us and he says it to me every time. Whether he's being antagonistic or not, I can't discern. I shrug, smiling nervously. "Maybe?"

"Hm, are you working on any more scathing articles or posts? It seems as if there's always something interesting brewing in that clever head of yours."

"He is not, I assure you." Lord Blakeley pats our guest on the back. His tone is light, but there's a hard edge in his expression that's unmistakable. "Oliver's attention is centered on the upcoming ceremony and subsequent mating rituals. I was delighted to see Alexander expressing his enthusiasm in the news."

Alexander's gaze is cast down to his expensive oxfords. But then, he lifts his golden, maple-brown eyes demurely. "We've been waiting fifteen years for this event. I'm thrilled that Oliver and I can finally be together. I'm ready to be bonded with him."

Distressed, flustered, I squeeze my clasped hands as I hold them in front of me. Both lords nod approvingly at the mushy and resolute statement.

Suddenly, everyone's focus is on me. Like we're acting in a stage play and I've missed my line. "M-me too. I'm very excited."

Lord Blakeley narrows his eyes in disapproval for a split second, and I realize that I've stammered again. God. I'm already screwing this up.

There is an entity, a rare space phenomenon where no electro-magnetic radiation, matter or substance of any kind can escape from it. It is called a black hole. At this precise moment, I sincerely wish that one would open up in the center of my chest, then proceed to suck me into it, wholly and completely, so that I no longer exist.

Lord Kendrick smiles warmly, breezing past my awkwardness. "Shall we allow our young vampires some time alone in preparation for the first ritual tonight?"

Lord Blakeley's disapproving look is still in place as he regards me. "Of course. Oliver, I trust you will make certain that our guest is comfortable?"

"Yes, Lord Blakeley." When the two older vampires have gone and the door is closed, I gesture toward a tufted armchair. "Um, please make yourself com—"

Alexander plops down in a huff, then leans back and content-edly gaps his long legs. "*God*, we're finally alone! No goddamn supervision or cranky, strict vampires hovering over us. It's taken forever to get here, yeah?" He stares brightly, as if we're old pals. But I've missed that memo. I was absent during an entire hypo-thetical stretch of meaningful interactions that led us to this level of candor.

Not knowing how to respond, I slowly sink down into my armchair. A small round end table sits between us with a tray of tea, sugar and milk. Silently, I pick up the tea pot and pour.

Looking me over, he scoffs, grinning. "You haven't changed at all through the years. Still uptight. Still a big nerd. It's a relief though, honestly. I'm really glad... And your eyes have gotten even prettier—like the skies above a clear, placid lake. And those lips? Perfectly kissable."

I set the teacup and saucer over to his side of the table, inten-tionally breathing to stop my hands from trembling so I don't spill. If I make a mess in front of Alexander and Lord Blakeley finds out about it, I'll be scolded all night. Maybe for eternity.

"I've always had this image of you, Ollie," he says, charging on with his monologue. He casually runs his fingers up and through the swoop of his stylishly coiffed hair "Do you know what you're like? A wild horse. A small one, though, since you're not very tall. Anyway, you had so much to say when we first met—I mean, you would *not* shut up. And I thought to myself, 'Ah, they'll try to break this one. He's too independent. Too many thoughts in his head.'"

Alexander taps his temple with two fingers, as if he needs to clarify anatomically where the head and brain are located. "But then you posted those smashing photos at Evanshire and I exhaled in relief. Seems they haven't broken my little pony yet. Thank goodness!"

He nods to himself, satisfied, so I pick up my tea and take a sip. After a moment, though, Alexander leans over the arm of the chair. "You're not going to say anything to me? We're finally alone together."

I swallow, breathe, and speak slowly. "There's milk and sugar on the tray, if you like."

"C'mon, Ollie. Drop the façade already and *talk* to me—we don't have to be perfectly behaved anymore! After all these years, we haven't got a single chaperone or housemaid, butler, guard or nanny hovering over us. We don't need to be on our best 'pure-bred prince' behavior right now."

We stare at each other in an awkward moment. His face is full of expectancy and I... I don't know what he wants me to say? My initial thought is that "we" aren't a prince. *He* is. Maybe this situation is a breezy joke for him, because his privilege and status at the top of the purebred vampire food chain allow for that.

For me, though? It's a nightmare. It always has been.

"What would you like me to say... when you've called me an uptight, short nerd horse within five minutes of us being alone together?" I ask honestly.

He laughs loudly, rocking back into his chair. "It's just jokes, my love. I don't mean anything by it! What did your father do to you after that article dropped in the *Metro Press*, and with your photographs? Your social media account disappeared afterward. Did he make you delete it?"

I don't care much for social media, but we have been strongly advised by our PR representatives that it's a good way to make our family seem more "relatable" given the upcoming ceremonies.

I live isolated in a stone tower within a centuries-old castle with one hundred acres of land, its own river and lavender field. What's "relatable" about that?

Occasionally, I post random photos I've taken online. Some interesting cloud formations, a plant or remarkable flower I've come across on my walks. A few selfies with Sash. Only once, I posted a series of contrasting photos that I took during a visit to one of the local villages.

This is what got my room raided.

Alexander likes and comments on everything that I post, and his comments get more likes than my stupid posts. It's always some clichéd declaration, like "You're so talented!" or "I love this shot of you."

"My mother was livid about that article and those photos," Alexander goes on in my absorbed silence. "She even suggested calling off our arrangement. It was an empty threat, though, and my father and me talked her out of it. Not an easy feat, but we did it. Teamwork, eh?"

He finally stops talking for five seconds and reaches over for his tea. I sigh. I wish Lady Kendrick would have called this off. Please, ma'am, do me the honor.

"You're probably thinking that it would have been nice if this was called off," Alexander says, peeking over the rim of his cup. "But trust me, Ollie, when I tell you that your elder father would *not* be pleased with that outcome."

How the hell does he know what I'm thinking? I clear my

throat, brushing past his odd but precise observation. "C-can we discuss tonight, please?"

"Mm, right." Alexander turns, sets his cup down on the table and leans on the armrest to stare directly into my face. "Have you ever had sex before? And with a man?"

God in heaven. "*No.* We're supposed to have waited, as part of the agreement."

He scoffs. "Nobody actually does that—wait, you really haven't had sex ever? Not with a servant or anything behind your parents' back?"

I exhale and face forward. Have I mentioned that I hate my life?

"Amazing... Oliver James Blakeley, you're so pure. Too good for this world. I don't know what to do with you."

Allegedly, I am an uptight, short and *pure* nerd horse.

But I wish that I was a professional photographer of some sort. An apprentice? Or that I could take proper classes instead of always researching everything on the Internet. Lately, and before it was confiscated, I'd been reading a book about shooting with 35 mm and single-lens reflex cameras. It would be so incredible to travel somewhere beautiful and historical like Italy and take—

"Hello? Are you with me, my love?"

Looking into his face, I'm forced back to reality. "Yes."

He tilts his head, observing me with his large golden-brown eyes as if I'm some strange creature. "I wish I could know what goes on in that gorgeous head of yours. All sorts of things, I'd bet. Anyway, tonight. The council will watch us the first two or three times we mate, or at least until they feel we're genuinely making a connection."

Alexander talks about this as if it's totally natural. As if it isn't a big deal that the two of us—who have never even been alone together until this very moment—are expected to have sex, in front of other vampires. Tonight.

The thought alone makes me want to curl into myself and disappear, but he's so matter-of-fact about it.

"What does 'genuinely make a connection' mean?" I ask. I have to try to get on board with this. Sasha is right. There's no other choice.

"You know, like, we're enjoying the act. One or both of us orgasms—huge bonus points if our eyes mutually alight or our auras flare out. We don't have to bond tonight and through these trials. They just want to be sure the chemistry is there. I've heard that it's best if we put on a wild show, and then they won't have to watch us again."

Wild? I lift and rub my palms against my face because I cannot fathom this situation. My hands are trembling again. God help me.

"You've never had sex, but, Ollie... have you ever been in love? Or do you have strong feelings for someone?" Alexander's gaze is intense, or, like, hopeful? It's unbelievably nerve-racking—all of these very personal questions and his bright molten eyes. It feels as if he's been laser focused on me from the moment he entered this room.

I'm about to tell him no—because with whom or where would I ever be allowed the space or freedom of will to feel something like love? To experience anything aside from pressure, reprimand and stress?

But he holds up his palms, smiling and shaking his head. "Wait! Don't answer that. Listen, just... we have to fake it, okay? If we can give them a show, the hardest part is over and we can relax. Do you get me? I'll lead tonight. We won't do anything too advanced. Just, try to focus on me, yeah? Let's enjoy each other?"

I'm seconds away from hyperventilating. I'm dreading this. For fifteen years I've been dreading this night, and already I have never felt more exposed and mortified in my entire existence. Is it possible to die of embarrassment? I really, really hope so.

"Should we feed?" he asks, wiggling his eyebrows. "May as well—or we could wait until tonight?"

Resigned, nodding, I pull up the sleeve of my blazer and start unbuttoning my shirt at the wrist. Once I have that rolled up, I offer my palm to Alexander, because now or tonight makes no difference to me.

He takes hold of my hand, but his nose is upturned. "I'm glad we'll be done with this childish hand-feeding shit soon. Christ, I'm over this." His fangs elongate into sharp white points just as he bites into my flesh.

As he feeds, I look away from him, pretending like my arm is no longer a meaningful appendage on my body. Closing my eyes, I calm myself by imagining that I'm in some far-off, distant land. An exciting place where I have a new, completely different life from the situation I'm in now.

Alone, just me and my camera.

Chapter Four

When I open my eyes the next morning, I find that I did not die from embarrassment.

Shame. I definitely wish that I had.

I haven't died, but I immediately recall being scolded by Alexander for my blatant lack of enthusiasm during our performance. Also, the name "cold fish" has been added to the ever-growing list of his descriptors for me.

Last night was paralyzing. From the moment we walked into the veiled bedroom filled with burning tapered candles, my blood froze in my veins and I could barely move or think. Our fathers and his mother were seated in the perimeter like formless shadows, along with other high-ranking elders from the Royal Order —a ghastly room specifically made for this bizarre, ancient and voyeuristic activity. I couldn't see their faces behind the gauzy curtains, but I could feel them there. All of them. Silent and concentrating on us.

We had to undress and situate ourselves atop the huge four-poster bed. Then Alexander was just *on* me. Kissing and stroking his hands across every inch of my skin. It felt like he'd morphed into an octopus at some point because I couldn't keep track of anything, and all I wanted was for it to be over as quickly as possible.

Yesterday was the most uncomfortable and horrific experience of my life. I think, maybe I'm not made for this world? The one I currently reside in. There must have been some mistake along the way, where I was born and dumped into the wrong family. Or maybe I'm the wrong rank? Maybe I should have been born as a first- or second-generation vampire—with remnants of human DNA in my bloodline and therefore less responsibility to the aristocracy at large.

These things that are expected of me as a purebred... things that are considered natural to my "flawless, vampiric station" but feel painfully unnatural. I don't know how to cope, and I don't know who to talk to about it.

Usually, I would try talking to Sasha, because she's the only vampire in my life that kind of accepts me. But she scolded me the last time I tried, didn't she?

Lord Blakeley is out of the question, and the viscount is never alone. I can't ever talk to him about anything without an audience of servants surrounding us. It's as if he's always under surveillance, too.

Poor Thomas is like the walking dead ever since the incident. Beyond basic greetings, we haven't spoken since I was a teenager.

"Lord Blakeley and the viscount are expecting you for breakfast, but first, you're scheduled to meet with the designer for your measurements."

Camille, my maidservant and handler, briskly walks in and out of my closet. I like her a lot. She gives me space and doesn't try to follow me every minute of every single day like my last handler did. Patrick—an ancient vamp who'd been serving our family for centuries. He retired when I turned sixteen. I don't miss him.

Dragging my body upright, I rub my face as I sit in the bed, still in my pajamas. Camille tosses multiple combinations of slacks, sweaters and shirts onto the large ottoman at the end of my mattress.

"The banquet tonight starts at seven, so you have a little free time today," she goes on, winking as she passes. "I'll have a suit ready and laid out for you."

I scratch the back of my head, eternally grateful. "Thank you so much, Camille." Free time is perfect, because what I truly want is to hide all day. After last night's gross humiliation, I need some time to myself. To be alone and in my own skin.

When I take a deep breath and stretch my arms up, I smell and sense something new. Someone?

I sit still, processing. New vampires come and go within our estate all the time. I always notice, but it never registers as anything particularly pleasant. It's just background noise—like birds singing or the hum of a car passing.

This scent registers differently. It commands my attention.

"As soon as you're dressed, I'll take you downstairs to where they've set up the designer's studio. His name is Aries Moralis."

I tilt my head in confusion. "Why is his studio set up over here? Why not the main house?"

"The main house will be full between the dignitaries and families from Central Eden and the Italian representative. Plus, he'll be working on your suit and Alexander's, primarily, so it makes sense, proximity-wise."

Sighing, I crawl to the edge of the bed and stand upright. It doesn't matter.

"I'll be waiting outside?" she goes on.

"Sure. Just give me a minute."

"Great." Camille turns, hesitates, then flips back. "Your grace... you didn't need to give me flowers."

"Lord Blakeley shouldn't have yelled at you like that. Posting those photographs was my decision. I'm very sorry that you got in trouble. I don't mean to make things difficult for you."

Grinning, she bows. "You're too kind. The flowers were arranged beautifully. And—oh! Alexander has requested to escort you to dinner tonight."

I freeze mid-step. "C-can I decline?" I do not want to see him until I absolutely have to.

"I would advise you to accept, your grace. Naturally, Lord Blakeley will be displeased... and you'll end up picking more flowers for me."

Groaning, I walk into the bathroom. "Fine." Isn't it enough that we'll be sitting together all night? I suppose he needs the five extra minutes to walk with me to the great hall so that he can come up with new insults. Yet another vampire to admonish me and point out everything that I'm doing wrong.

After I've dressed, Camille precedes me down the spiral stone steps and toward the only guest chamber in the east tower. This is where they've set the designer up to work for the next month. The room is located just at the landing, and the entrance is marked by an ornate rosewood door.

This guest room is smaller than mine, which, to me, makes it cozier. I wanted this room because it feels tucked away, at least? Intimate—and in the afternoons, the lighting is just right. But I was told it wasn't appropriate for my station. So, I have the very large and empty room in the tower, up the spiral staircase that overlooks the lake, which isn't dramatic at all.

Camille dictates my schedule for the rest of the week as we walk, but I am completely focused on this new scent. When I woke up this morning, it immediately called to me—subtle and calm, like a warm whisper. But now, it's thick as I breathe in, and my nature is shifting inside me in ways it *never* has.

It's as if... I've been starved for something, and I'm finally going to be fed. I don't know what this means, but everything in my body is electrified and I have goosebumps on my arms underneath my sweater.

"The designer—Mr. Moralis—arrived this morning," Camille says, glancing over her shoulder as we approach the door. "He's kind, professional and he's dressed all sorts of vampire politicians over the past several decades. It's no wonder Lord Blakeley requested him for your wedding."

"He sounds expensive." My heart is beating three times its normal speed, and the warmth of my vampiric energy is quietly snaking up my spine. Suppressing it is taking much more effort than I'm accustomed to. Usually, I don't need to suppress it at all because it's always dormant and lifeless.

"He is first-generation. His purebred mother hailed from a moderately old bloodline out of Greece—Mykonos, to be exact. He grew up there, but his father was Albanian. They mated through an arrangement between their families. Both of his parents are deceased."

"How old is he?" God, my hands are starting to shake.

"Ninety-five." Camille knocks twice on the heavy door, waits for a response, then pushes it open. The unique, alluring essence hits me full on. I gasp and step back. It literally takes my breath away.

The sensation is like... nightfall in early summer, when the wind carries the scent of the jasmine vines. Sometimes, if my schedule has a large enough gap, I take a long walk away from the castle, past the pageantry of the rose gardens, porcelain fountains and manicured hedges.

I trek out to where the woods are thick. Pristine and wild. It's a different world there, and when the sun sets, firelight glows between the trees. In that space, I'm free from the burden of time and place. From the chains and irons of monarchy and purebred responsibility.

What is happening right now?

We walk into the room and the designer is there. He's unpacking something, but then quickly stands and turns to face us. He blinks, taking me in before his face shifts into something like a cool mask as he bows, smooth and unaffected. It is the subtlest of actions, but I notice it as I stare at him with my mouth open and every nerve in my body standing on end.

"Your grace. It's a pleasure to meet you."

Wow. Even his voice is smooth and velvety to my ears. Like coffee liqueur and hot chocolate.

"Mr. Moralis, this is Master Oliver James Blakeley, second son of the Blakeley Clan." Camille steps aside, lifting her hand in a formal gesture. "You'll be primarily working with his grace in preparation for and up through the ceremony, as well as his fiancé, Prince Alexander Ethan Kendrick. I believe Lord Blakeley has given you specific direction with regard to the style of their suits?"

"Yes, he has." The designer stands straight, but flickers his gaze to Camille, avoiding direct eye contact with me. It's for the best, though, because I honestly cannot look away from him.

He has very long legs, which makes him tower over both me and Camille by at least half of a foot. His dark hair is thick, elegantly wavy but cut short, and his skin is warm like sunlit honey. A neatly trimmed beard graces his jawline, chin and full lips, and he is simply...

I have never felt this attracted to another creature. My nature is practically doing somersaults. The sensation heats up my entire body. Astonishing.

Camille flips her wrist up to check her watch. "Is thirty minutes enough time to take his grace's initial measurements? Lord Blakeley and the viscount are expecting the young master for breakfast shortly."

He smiles hospitably. "Of course. Absolutely, I'll do my best."

Turning, Camille walks toward the door. "If you don't finish, no need to worry. We can make time before the banquet tonight —which you are welcome to attend. Did Lord Blakeley mention this?"

"He did, which was very kind. Thank you."

"Perfect. Your grace, I'll return shortly to escort you to breakfast." Camille leaves, closing the door behind her, and I grind my teeth. Am I a child? I'm twenty-two years old. I don't need her or anyone to pick me up and drop me off from room to room. Humiliating.

When I whip my head toward the designer... Aries... he's

standing with his back to me. What a lovely name. It sounds like a celestial being with wings that dwells within the summer skies. Something beautiful that soars among the sculpted clouds and shooting stars.

He's moved toward a table against the wall and is looking over the various odds and ends sprawled there. "Would you please remove your sweater, your grace?"

I start, then swallow hard and grab the hem of my sweater to pull it over my head. While he isn't looking, I briskly and self-consciously run my free hand through my hair to quell it. I'm suddenly very grateful the viscount suggested that I get it cut before the first bonding attempt last night.

"Do you have anything in your pockets? A wallet or phone, perhaps? You'll need to remove those as well. And your belt." Busily, he gathers things as he scans the table. What I really want is for him to turn around and look at me. I don't know why, but I *need* him to.

"Your grace?" He shifts his head to the side.

"I-I don't have a phone." Lord Heartless took it from me as punishment. And what would I need a wallet for? I'm not allowed to leave the estate on my own.

God, I feel like I'm standing on a tightrope. Or as if I'm a literal rubber band stretched to its limit and seconds away from snapping. Aries finally turns and walks forward with a tape measure draped around the back of his neck. A pencil and small notebook are in his hands.

He's dressed casually but impeccably—light-colored trousers and a white cable-knit sweater layered over a sapphire patterned shirt that emphasizes his eyes, which I now realize are deep blue. Haunting. The color of midnight when a full moon illuminates the expanse.

"You don't have a phone?" He raises a dark eyebrow as he approaches, but he's looking down at his watch, not at me.

"I'm not allowed to have one at the moment." I don't know why I'm telling him this. He doesn't need to know.

Aries nods, letting the odd statement hang between us as he gestures and looks past me. "Your grace, would you please step up on the platform behind you?" I turn, and there is indeed a new and elaborate vanity assembled along the back wall. A tall three-paneled mirror frames the mahogany stage. This wasn't here before, nor the worktable with all of his tailor-y things on it. They must have outfitted the room to his specifications.

My heart pounds in my ears as I step up onto the stage like he's asked. I turn around to face him, simultaneously wanting to watch him and hoping to finally catch his gaze.

"You forgot your belt," he says, staring down at my buckle.

"Ah—I-I'm so sorry."

Smoothly, he takes the bunched-up sweater from my grip, then waits as I fumble over my belt with shaky hands. I'm such an idiot. I require an escort from room to room, I don't have a phone and now, I can barely undress myself.

When I slide the material from around my waist, he takes it and walks over to a bench. He neatly folds my sweater and lays the belt beside it.

Aries flips his notebook open as he walks back, writing something down, focused. But before he has a chance to ask another question, I realize I haven't even properly greeted him. I'm just stammering and awkward and half listening to what he's saying because I'm so consumed by him and this feeling.

When he's in front of me again, we're the same height because of the lifted stage. I quickly run my fingers through the top of my hair and take a deep breath. "Hi..."

Finally, he looks up. His rich, cobalt-blue eyes meet mine, and the moment is just... static. Heavenly.

He grins. "Hello."

"It's nice to meet you."

"And you as well. Are we alright, your grace?"

I nod, staring helplessly. "Yes... I think so."

He lowers his gaze, focusing on his notebook again, but he's still smiling. "Good. Will you lift your arms for me?"

"What?"

"Your arms. Straight out. I'll measure your chest first."

"Oh, right, sure." I lift my arms and he swiftly pulls the tape measure from his neck, reaches behind me in a pseudo hug and wraps the thin strip around so that it rests just underneath my armpits. As he moves, his scent fans out and over me. My breath is short and my heart is so loud in my ears that I'm worried he can hear it as well.

"Relax your shoulders, please?"

"I'm sorry."

"You're alright, just take a deep breath and let everything drop. You're a little too tense."

I inhale deep, which only intensifies his wonderful scent in my nostrils, but I do what he says, suppressing my nature and its extreme reaction to him in the process. Is this... Is what I'm feeling completely one-sided? Does he not feel this at all?

The moment I relax, Aries moves with lightning speed, smoothly taking measurements of my chest and stomach—setting the tape lightly against the material of my clothes, then writing down his findings. When he reaches back and around my butt to measure my hips, I stiffen again and he pauses, flickering his eyes up. "If I'm making you uncomfortable, I can instruct a servant to do this—"

"N-no. That won't be necessary, I'm sorry. I just—" I freeze.

What do I say? That I haven't ever been attracted to someone like this? That I don't even know him, but somehow feel as if I do, and that his very presence and scent comfort me? I cannot say any of that, obviously, so I rub my palm down my face, shaking my head.

Delicately, Aries wraps the tape against my hips again, barely touching my body. His voice is low. "Your bonding ceremony is next month."

"Yes."

He whips the tape from around me, then writes in his notebook. "You must be excited?"

"No."

My eyes widen, and he looks up, blinking. But like before, the moment is brief, and his poker face is back on before I can register his reaction.

"Would you turn, please? I need to do your shoulders and back."

I do as he's asked, still beside myself from my sudden and unwarranted transparency. What the hell am I thinking? It would be so easy for him to take that answer to the newspapers, and Lord Blakeley would have a literal meltdown from the fallout: *Youngest Blakeley Prince is Decidedly Not Excited for Upcoming Nuptials to Central Eden's Vampire Prince Heartthrob. A Tailor Tells All Exclusive.*

Somehow, though, I know he won't do that.

Aries is swift and silent as he finishes my measurements, trailing the tape down my spine, the length of my arms and legs, around my waist and up the curve of my crotch. I stiffen like before, but he doesn't stop this time, and it very much feels as if he's trying to hurry up and get this over with.

When he's finished, he goes over to the bench to retrieve my belt and sweater. "We should be all set," he says, walking back and handing me my things. "If I need anything specific, I'll send a servant to do my bidding."

Panicked, I shake my head. "I can come here if you need me to. I don't mind, and it's what Lord Blakeley wanted. I'm sorry if I've been awkward. I don't mean to make you uncomfortable..." I pull my sweater over my head. He probably thinks I'm some young and ridiculous creature. Maybe I am.

With my sweater on, I sigh and drop my shoulders. Aries watches me with hooded lids and I marvel at his long dark eyelashes. His rare gemstone irises. "If you don't mind my saying, you seem to apologize quite a bit for an Eden purebred of ancient blood."

This makes me chuckle. "Given time, you'll find that I am a *very* poor excuse for an Eden purebred."

"I doubt that." He takes a step back, then offers a shallow bow. "Thank you, your grace. We're all finished for now."

Threading my belt, I step down from the platform. "Will you... be attending the banquet tonight?"

"It's difficult for me to resist the extravagance of a royal banquet, but I'm not sure. I have a lot of work to do."

I nod, considering as I finish securing the buckle. "Yes, of course... but I-I do hope that you can make it."

Aries blinks. His expression is suddenly unreadable. "Is this a formal command, your grace? As my superior?"

I draw back, mortified. "*No.* No, not at all! I don't—I would never. I just—" There's a knock at the door, and as Camille enters, I realize my face is hot from embarrassment. Flustered, I look back at Aries and speak in a rushed whisper.

"Please forget I said that. I'm sorry." I don't wait for a response, because I've made a fool out of myself two days in a row now. It's enough.

"Your grace?" Camille calls after me as I pass her in the doorway. I know where the breakfast room is. I don't need an escort.

Chapter Five

Later in the evening, Alexander is at my side as we walk toward the great hall. Thankfully, he isn't berating me over the ritual that we had last night.

"The council won't watch us mate again until the night of our formal ceremony." Alexander is dressed to the nines with his sunshine-blonde hair swept back. His chin is naturally lifted—like a vampire that's never once been challenged or rebuked. As if the angels in heaven started singing on the day he was born and they haven't stopped since.

He's also taller than me, but not towering like Aries. The deficit between Alexander and me is probably just a few inches, but it's obvious that he takes great pride in this.

"I assured everyone that we were nervous," he goes on. "We've barely been able to spend time alone together, so we need the next four weeks to get better acquainted. They seemed to understand, so I think we're in the clear for now."

I'm extremely relieved to hear this, honestly. At the very least, I won't be subjected to that specific brand of torture and humiliation again for another month. Maybe by then I can figure out how to fake it better so it can be the last time?

This... is my life, whether I want it or not. I should start figuring out how to adapt, like Sasha says.

It feels all wrong, though. On some visceral level.

"That's good." I breathe, relaxing just a little. "I'm happy to hear that."

Alexander flips so that he's walking backward but directly in front of me. "I knew you would be. So... what should we do for the next four weeks to 'better acquaint' ourselves?" He wiggles his eyebrows, grinning.

Is he being serious? I can't ever tell if he's joking or not. It feels like Alexander is always putting on a show, but there's no audience right now. I'm confused. "Um... well, there's a path I like to walk out past the gardens—through the woods. It leads to a field of lavender. We could go there and talk? The bloom is drying out since it's so late in summer, but it's still nice. Or I could show you the greenhouses where I take a lot of photos? The great library on the southern side of the estate is also very nice."

These are some of my favorite places to hide away. Sharing them with him would be strange, but maybe it will help?

He puffs a breath and turns so that he's walking beside me again. He doesn't say anything.

"What is it?" I ask.

"You're such a nerd. I'm not talking about looking at flowers or going to boring libraries. We're past all that! We need physical practice for the mating ritual, Ollie. I was thinking we should spend time together in your room."

"We are distinctly not supposed to do that—"

"*Everyone* cheats like this. It's how we work the system. How else are we going to get past this? You're being a cold fish again."

"I really dislike it when you call me that. Please don't."

Alexander frowns. "Well then, stop being a cold fish. Lighten up already!"

The two waitstaff standing outside the banquet doors pull them open as we approach. Inside, there's a sea of vampires elegantly dressed and milling around—a myriad of muted auras and energies radiates in the atmosphere. The Gothic-style room is warmly lit with sparkling oversized crystal chandeliers hanging from the ceiling. It is a vibrant scene brimming with activity.

"Take my arm, please." Alexander bends his elbow so that his arm is in the shape of a triangle, then waits for me to slip my hand through. I hesitate, though, because I'm suddenly feeling contrary. Why is he so dismissive when I speak? Just like Lord Blakeley.

"*Oliver.*" He's smiling through clenched teeth because people are watching us. Not people. Vampires. Other purebreds and high-ranked creatures from my realm and Central Eden, looking on expectantly at the latest politically arranged couple. A highly anticipated union between two realms.

Buckling to the immense pressure, I slip my arm into his, but I don't smile. I'm a vampire. Smiling is superfluous.

We walk forward, greeting and nodding, stopping occasionally for snippets of trite conversation and congratulations on our upcoming union. Many express that we are an attractive couple. Alexander likes this particular compliment, because his smile widens every time and his golden-brown irises seem to light up.

I am arm candy incarnate. Sasha was right. It isn't a hard job at all.

The night goes on like this. Later, I sit at a grandiose table with my and Alexander's families at the head of the room, and in every way, I shut myself off. I am polite and smile when I am expected to do so. I laugh when it's appropriate. Alexander leans into my side, so close that it feels and probably looks like he's about to kiss my cheek—a candid, intimate moment between the excited young couple. But he whispers that everything is going brilliantly. I'm doing a great job. I grin, because I guess I should. When he leans away, I'm relieved.

I hate my life.

After the second course has been served and I am internally contemplating the true likelihood of spontaneous combustion (is there something I can do to promote this phenomenon? Something I should eat more or less of?), a particular scent wafts against my skin and shifts my attention toward the double doors we entered through earlier.

Everything aligns—the lighting, the spacing between the members of the crowded room and the tables and chairs—it all shifts, just right, as if by magic, and my gaze instantly finds him.

Aries enters the banquet hall, marvelously dressed in a teal suit. The color is dark, but warm enough to make him stand out against the sea of boring black and gray. He strides forward, but then his midnight eyes meet mine and he stops dead.

I inhale a breath, because my nature is speaking to me again, telling me that we like him. Yes, we like the way he looks—particularly in this beautiful suit—but we like more than that, even though I don't quite understand what that means. Regardless, my energy bubbles up inside, and we can't look away from each other. Aries and I are locked in the magnetic tension of this isolated moment.

For the first time in my life, I feel the burn of my nature climbing up my spine, to my brain and up to my eyes. It's so strong, I can't breathe.

"Ollie? What are you staring at?"

The sound of Alexander's voice severs the hypnotic trance. Swallowing hard, I blink and force my energy down. God help me. It suddenly had a mind of its own. I look over at Alexander, and his brow is creased in confusion.

I shake my head, breathing. "I—Nothing. I wasn't..." I look back out into the crowd. Aries is gone. He's still on the grounds, of course. I can sense him. But the intensity of his scent and energy has dissipated—drifted away so that it's a gentle hum in the distance.

"Why did you fan your energy out?" Alexander asks.

"Did I? I didn't mean for it to." I rub a palm against my forehead. Wow. I have to rein this in. It caught me off guard and I'm not accustomed to feeling like this at all.

Alexander sits back slightly. "But what triggered it? Why would you—"

"Please just drop it? I wasn't paying attention, alright? I'm *sorry*." I exhale a breath, calming my heart rate. I wish I could leave and go find him. I just... I want to talk to him.

"You don't need to be sorry," Alexander says. He turns forward and grabs his fork as he smiles. "It was lovely. I wish... that you would do it more often. That's all." I glance down at his plate and it's messy. Like the food has been pushed around to look as if it's being eaten but it hasn't really. I suspect that not a single vampire will chastise him for that.

The way our eyes locked, even from across the room... Could Aries possibly feel the same way about me?

After an eternity, dinner finally ends. A visiting purebred from London corners Alexander, trapping him in a long-winded conversation about the recent demand increases in exports, so I bid them both goodnight and sneak away.

It's a long walk back to my wing of the castle grounds (which I am fully capable of traversing alone). I take the outside pathways for some much-needed fresh air.

In an unexpected turn of events, I don't hate my life at this exact moment. I lift my chin, taking in the cool nighttime breeze underneath the infinite sea of blackness overhead. The stars are bright specks of light and the crescent moon glows hazily. It's still technically summer, but I can smell autumn hovering at the edges— threatening to jump in and take over like a game of double Dutch.

My eyes almost alighted.

My aura responded to someone today. *Twice.*

These moments, albeit brief and arguably very awkward... I don't know if I've ever felt so alive. I know what Sasha meant now —how she never forgot that Ethiopian dignitary. How could she?

How could anyone forget the sensation of their blood rushing like scorching, sparkling champagne inside of them? Your energy threatening to swell and break free from your body, reaching for someone you might truly and deeply desire if you allow yourself to submit to it.

There are no words to accurately describe the euphoria and ecstasy. The smallest hint makes me feel like I'm walking on air, which is a lovely change from my normal existence of being crushed between two concrete slabs.

When I arrive at my wing, it's silent. I have to pass Aries's door in order to climb the spiral stairs to my room in the tower.

Honestly? I'm looking forward to it. I acknowledge that my behavior is quite questionable right now, but I want to smell him as I go by. Nothing more. Just a nice, healthy inhale as I pass.

I approach, knowing he's inside because one, I do indeed sense him, and two, the lights are on underneath his door. Slowing my stride, I relax my aura and breathe in to indulge a little. It's truly wonderful, and the fizzy sensation in my core immediately kicks up again.

The door whips open and I start and stumble backward until my spine hits the opposite wall. It's like my breath and heart have been snatched from my body as I stand pressed against the stone, gasping and wide-eyed.

Aries looms in the doorway, unsmiling as he stares down at me. He's still in his stylish teal suit. It's even more striking up close, but that's beside the point.

"Can we please talk, your grace?" he asks. "May I have a moment of your time?"

Shaken, I nod and stand straight. "Yes. Sure." My heart is back inside me, but shoved into my throat as Aries pulls the door open wider. Nervous, I push up from the wall and timidly step past him into the room.

Chapter Six

The large sconces adorning the stone walls in Aries's room burn brightly with real candlelight, drenching the space in a soft yellow glow. He's been busy, because there are raw materials draped on male dress forms. His worktable is messier than it was this morning.

Hearing the door close, I turn toward him. He stands with his back pressed against the rosewood. "Permission to speak frankly, your grace?"

"Please... and you don't need to add an honorific every time you talk to me. You can call me Oliver, if you'd like."

He shakes his head. "No, I cannot. What *is* this? What are you doing?"

"What do you mean?"

"What do I mean? I mean you, telling me that I don't need to use honorifics, even though you are a purebred in an infamously strict aristocracy that shuns any and all vampires beneath your bloodline. You, watching me and fidgeting—staring from across a crowded room and fanning your aura out toward me. *You,* standing outside my room in the middle of the night."

Blinking, I run my fingers into the top of my hair. God. I sound crazy—like an actual stalker. I take a breath because my pulse is beating in my ears. "I don't mean to do those things, I really just..."

How do I explain myself without explaining myself? Without sounding like the pathetic, sheltered and awkward loser that I am?

At my hesitation, Aries cuts in. "You are a purebred of ancient blood."

I nod, uncomfortable. "I... know that."

"And you're getting married to the Royal Prince of Central Eden in a month."

"I *know*. You don't need to tell me those things."

"I apologize, your grace, but apparently, I do, because you are brazenly coming on to me from across a crowded room full of rigid dignitaries, and while you sit beside your fiancé. What are you thinking, exactly? What is your objective?"

Coming on to him? My throat is tight as I rub my palms against my face. An intense heat rushes up my neck. "I don't have an objective! I just—" I drop my hands and look at him.

What do I say?

Aries watches carefully. His square shoulders rise and fall in a breath. He straightens his spine. "Your grace, while I'm very flattered, I... don't appreciate being manipulated, or subjugated by your power without my consent. Please don't ever force your aura on me. And if you're thinking that you'd like to take liberties with the hired help before you're officially bonded, my apologies, but I don't engage in those sorts—"

"Oh for God's sake—*no*, it's nothing like that!" The weight of his words and how I look from his perspective crashes down on me. Depleted, I sit on the edge of his bed.

This is what comes from living a sheltered life. From being escorted to various rooms within your own home and having your books and electronics taken away as punishment for producing tangible thoughts. From being painfully secluded and unable to experience the world.

After taking a deep breath in, I blow it out. These truths are humiliating, so I stare down at my feet to avoid his direct gaze. "I-I would never force my aura onto you or subjugate you. I'm not making excuses, but I... My existence is very sterile. I don't leave the estate without multiple escorts and my schedule is planned out for me every day. I'm not allowed to do anything or go anywhere or meet anyone of my own will, so I..."

Gripping the edge of the mattress in my palms, I take another breath. "When I met you, I felt something in my nature. Organically and for the first time in my life. But I was sloppy in controlling myself. I sincerely apologize for my behavior today. And I— I'll make sure to do better going forward. Thank you for telling me honestly like this."

There it is. I'm a naïve idiot. My only hope now is that he doesn't complain to Lord Blakeley. That would be devastating. I can't imagine what he'd do to me.

Standing from the bed, I walk forward, refusing to look at him as I pass.

"Why don't you have a phone?" he asks, surprising me. "You used to have a social media account, didn't you?"

Hesitating, I meet his gaze. "I did. But Lord Blakeley confiscated it. How... did you know I had an account?"

"Because I research my clients before accepting a job. Why did he take it, if I may ask?"

I rub my palm against the back of my neck. "He was upset about some photos that I took."

"The ones from the Evanshire Summer Fête with the derelict houses and abhorrent living conditions for ranked vampires?"

My heart skips as I suck in a breath. "You saw them? I thought he had them taken down?"

"Indeed, he did." Aries turns, then walks over to the bench on the adjacent wall. He sits, and I can't help but admire his perfect posture as he casually folds his arms. "But nothing online ever really disappears, does it? Several international news outlets republished those photos with corresponding articles. Did they not ask for your permission?"

This surprises me, and I shake my head. "No, but I... They wouldn't have been able to reach me."

"They credited you, regardless. I also found the scathing editorial essay that you wrote for the *Eden Gazette* several years ago."

Lifting a palm, I want to clarify. "I-I didn't write that for the *Gazette*, technically. My tutor at the time took me on a trip to the Eden Museum of Art History and asked me to write a report about it afterward. So, I did, and, well... she secretly submitted it to the paper." After which, she was promptly and forever banished from the Eden aristocracy.

She's in Thailand now. I envy her.

"I can certainly see why she would. It was thoughtful and unprecedented—especially from the mind of a young Eden pure-bred. A quality exposé on pilfered art. And the photos you took at the summer fête spoke volumes toward the inequalities between purebreds and ranked vampires across your aristocracy. It was a narrative both haunting and poignant."

Wow. "Thank you very much for saying that."

"May I ask how you acquired those shots?"

I think back to that hot summer day. A rare moment when there was enough chaos for me to slip away and be alone while outside of the castle. "Evanshire was having their annual summer fête—which the Akuffo Clan throws a bunch of money into once a year for the sake of showing off to the other, lesser purebred families, like ours..."

In talking about this, the usual, frustrated feelings boil over. I shouldn't be frank with him, but I can't dance around this topic and play ignorant like everyone else does. It drives me crazy. "There were champagne and wine fountains set up in the old town center—*huge* ones, continuously flowing with real alcohol! They'd hired and flown in chefs from Italy, France and Spain to make specialty cuisine. It was ridiculous, especially considering we don't even need to eat to survive as purebreds. It felt lavish and wasteful, so I decided to wander through the outskirts of the town.

"Beyond the city center, the houses and buildings were practically falling apart. The contrast was awful. I met a local vampire while I was walking—Roland, and he was really kind. He told me that he was working on rehabbing one of the houses. I asked if I could see it. He said yes, and I took photos along the way."

I shrug, because the rest is history.

Aries's midnight-blue eyes consider me as he sits with his long legs crossed at the knees and his arms still folded. "Your caption, 'A Tale of Two Evanshires,' did you write that as well?"

"I did. It felt like two different places. One for the purpose of impressing Eden's 'elite purebreds,' and the other, a village in ruins. Vampires actually live there, and it shouldn't look that way."

"Why bring attention to the living conditions of those vampires?" Aries asks, unblinking. "They're ranked beneath you. They don't matter—"

"They *do* matter." I disagree, raising my voice. Heat flushes against my cheeks. "How can you say that? The way we treat ranked vampires here is... it's horrendous. Disgusting. All of Eden's wealth and prosperity is wrapped up in old, purebred families. There's almost no trickle-down for our villages. We leech off of their hard work, and there are no opportunities aside from servitude for any vampire with an iota of human lineage. It's like we refuse to acknowledge anyone we deem as 'lesser' or 'not full-blooded.'"

I've worked myself up. I shouldn't be saying these things out loud. This line of thinking is what always gets me in trouble. An unwelcome perspective among my family and peers.

Aries unfolds his arms and leans back against the bench with his palms. The corner of his mouth lifts in a grin. "You speak passionately for someone who benefits from the very system that you rebuke. For a vampire who holds the power."

I shake my head. "I don't have any power. I'm just an instrument. A spineless pawn on Lord Blakeley's chess board."

Blinking, I pause, because I'm suddenly having an out-of-body experience. Why am I being this straightforward with a total stranger? Saying things that I don't even express with Sasha. Things that could lead to consequences I can't even imagine... like whatever Lord Blakeley did to Thomas that forever changed him.

The tension between us is thick and the air feels too hot. I'm about to apologize for being so forthright and beg for confidentiality when his entire expression changes. His rich eyes brighten, his brow relaxes. He chuckles.

"My apologies, your grace," he says. "All of this is just so... surprising."

"W-why?" I ask, startled.

"Well, you are a purebred vampire rooted in one of the coldest, most rigid and archaic aristocracies in the world, and yet your opinions are so... empathetic and progressive. It's unexpected."

I scratch my head, frowning and feeling thrown off balance. "Um, thanks?"

"Please, I mean no offense," he says, resting a hand against his chest, atop the beautiful dress shirt beneath his jacket. "It is a compliment. You should know that there has been some buzz about you in the greater international vampire community."

Wait, what? Did I mishear him? "About *me*?"

"Yes, about you. Between the critical essay you wrote and those moving photographs, some believe that there might be hope for Eden in joining the rest of the modern vampire community. That at least someone within these ancient walls has some semblance of the outside world. Congratulations."

It is... unbelievable that anything I've done could matter to someone. To anyone. Me, stuffed inside this castle and with my mediocre photography skills.

"And anyway, I shouldn't throw stones," Aries continues in my marveled silence. "The vampires of Greece are a lot like yours here in Eden. The truth is, I am a product of a similar environment."

"Are you?" I ask. Excitement bubbles inside my chest because this feels like a dream. Casually conversing with someone about something—*anything*—outside of treaties, bonding ceremonies and responsibilities. It's so refreshing. Delightful. "Camille told me that you're from Mykonos?"

"Yes, but I am always traveling. I never go back to my homeland."

"Why not?"

There's a slight pause where Aries considers. As if he isn't sure that he wants to answer my question. He folds his arms and exhales a breath. "Because it's an uncomfortable environment. Too oppressive and inflexible. I find it difficult to be myself there and... I've always felt wildly out of place—as if I don't belong. When I travel to other places, I'm free."

I stare at him in awe. "I understand. Perfectly."

This moment and his words sink into my skin, deeply caressing my soul like a warm, luxuriant oil. It gives me goosebumps. Finally, someone who speaks my language. Someone who feels the same way that I do. Maybe I'm not just weird, wrong or a selfish brat?

"I wish that I could travel," I say quietly. "I would give anything to leave here."

"Hm, but you're marrying the Prince of Eden in a month."

It's as if he's thrown a cold wet blanket over my head. I'm jolted out of the short-lived and rosy trance of our conversation.

"Yes, I am." Awkwardly, I step backward toward the door. "I'm very sorry for making you uncomfortable. That was never my intention."

He stands from the bench and walks with me. "I accept your apology. And thank you for the candid discussion. I'm glad that we could be honest about this." He opens the door and I step over the threshold.

In the hallway, I stop. My hands are shaking again because I'm nervous, but I want to take a chance. Cautiously, I turn to face him. "I don't mind honest conversation. Really. It was nice talking to you. I-I would like to talk more—if you're available. But it's completely up to you! Whatever you want. No pressure at all." I rub the back of my neck because I'm one hundred percent certain that I sound like an idiot.

Aries crinkles his brow in confusion. "Forgive me for possibly stating the obvious, but... you do realize that I'm first-generation, don't you? Only my mother was purebred."

"Yes, of course. Why?"

"This doesn't bother you? To speak casually like this, with me?"

Now I'm confused. "No. Why would it?"

He pauses, tall and working his jaw. Assessing me and making some decision in his mind. "Hm... alright. I look forward to working with you. Goodnight, your grace."

"You can just call me Oliver?"

"I cannot. If someone overheard me casually calling you by your first name, they'd think that I'd forgotten my place and would swiftly create a new home for me in the dungeons that I'm sure are still in existence underneath this castle."

I hear what he's saying, but... "No one is around—"

"*Your grace*, are we alright? Are we not on the same page?"

"Yes, okay, okay—we are. I'm sorry. Goodnight." I nod, conceding as I turn, but Aries grins with his beautiful lips as he closes the door.

The funny thing is, I'm smiling, too, as I walk up the stairs to my room. Even after I've showered and changed into my pajamas and am lying in bed, I'm still grinning like crazy.

Chapter Seven

There's a soft knock at my bedroom door early the next morning. Opening my eyes, I lie still in bed and take a deep breath to sense the vampire on the other side.

It's Alexander.

No, thank you.

I turn over and nestle down, staying silent.

But then the door creaks open and I bolt upright. "*Hey.*"

"Good morning, my love."

"What's good about it? I didn't give you permission to come in."

"Mm, it smells like Oliver amplified in here. It's yummy." He pushes the door closed behind him and swaggers over to my bed. "Why didn't you answer me? You're awake."

"I am now." I frown as he sits on the edge of the mattress. Why does everything about him grate on me? "You have a lot to learn about respecting boundaries."

His expression is unbothered. "That's our problem—you and all your boundaries." He pokes my thigh through the duvet, and I jump and scoot away. He frowns. "You're my mate, Ollie."

"I am not. Not yet. Nothing is official—"

"Oh, it's official. We're locked into this through literal

53

contracts and social obligation. I want us to have a genuine bond, Oliver James Blakeley. Not a fake one—like Sasha's, where everyone just turns a blind eye and pretends. I want us to be *real*. And my mother won't accept anything less."

Perfect, exactly what I need. More pressure. I push the duvet down and draw my legs up to fold them as I sit back against the headboard. Welp, this day is off to a horrendous start.

"What turned you on last night?" he asks. His voice is suddenly softer. "Tell me."

Rubbing my eyes with my fingertips, I sigh, then run my hands up and through my messy bedhead. Who just walks into someone's room like this uninvited? "Nothing. I told you, I wasn't paying attention."

The bed shifts as Alexander scoots closer and rests his palms on either side of my hips so that I'm trapped. He's too close to my face, so I draw back and away. "Don't—"

"Maybe you should not pay attention more often?"

"You're not supposed to be in here like this," I say, turning my head to the side.

"We need to practice. We could start with kissing, at least? You don't seem to have much experience in that area, either. Can I kiss you?"

"*No.*" My face is hot yet again, so I shove him. He falls onto his back as I climb off the bed. When I'm standing, I turn and face him. "Telling me that I don't have much experience doesn't help. It doesn't make me feel good—or very inclined to practice anything with you."

Still lying on his back, he drops his head to the side to look at me. "I think I just enjoy getting a rise out of you. Making you all flustered and cute like this."

"Well, great. That's healthy."

Alexander turns his head to gaze up at the ceiling. "This is the only authentic part of yourself that you show me. Otherwise, you're always set to purebred robot mode, aren't you? Pretending like you're hollowed out to appease your parents. But it's a façade.

There's still a fire burning inside of you, Ollie. You try to hide, but I can feel it... I wish you'd be honest with me."

My chest tightens for some reason. Be honest with him? About what? About how I hate my life? How bonding with him is the absolute last thing that I want—that I'd rather be stranded on a deserted island, slowly starving to death, because at least then I'd truly be free for a little while before I died? Give me a break.

A phone rings. Since I don't have one, I assume that it's Alexander's. I'm right, because he lifts his hips from the bed, reaches into the pocket of his chinos and pulls out a sleek silver smartphone. He looks at the screen, groans, then swipes it before bringing it to his ear and smiling.

"Good morning, Mother, I'm just out for a walk... Yes, of course I can. I'm on my way." After he hangs up, he sighs and drops his arms in a dramatic fashion, then closes his eyes. For once, it doesn't seem like he's playing up to the invisible audience and cameras.

"Let me guess," he says. "You're not joining us on the hunt this week, are you?"

"Nope." I don't have many successes in life, but this is one. I detest the hunts, and after many years of making everyone miserable with unsolicited strong opinions, facts and statistics, I have been henceforth and forevermore excused from them.

"That's lonely." Alexander hops up from the bed and I fold my arms in case he decides to get in my face again. He walks backward to the door. "If you're not coming on the trip, I don't think we'll be alone again until later this week. Sad."

"I think you'll be totally fine."

"Do you?" He turns and opens the door. "Have a lovely day, my sweet Prince Ollie."

"I'm not a prince."

"But you will be. *My* prince."

"Weren't you leaving?"

Alexander chuckles as the door softly closes. Is this funny to him? Am I a joke for his amusement?

With Alexander gone, I relax my shoulders, then stretch my arms up, trying to shake off the residual tension and stress that his presence creates in my body. Standing still for a moment, the sunshine streams in from the windows, warming my face. Breathing in, I can sense Aries's wonderful oak and jasmine essence.

I told him that I wouldn't be a creep anymore—and I won't. But I can feel that he's not in his room. He's out somewhere on the grounds, a little far from here.

Our conversation last night started off rough, which I accept full responsibility for. But by the end, it felt nice. Easy. Like when Sash and I talk, but even more candid than that.

With my sister, I know there's a certain extent to which I can be honest. Depending on the day, the figurative line is farther out, or very tight. The last time we talked, it was tight. She shut me down and I was lectured pretty quickly.

I probably shouldn't even be thinking about this, but I wonder where that line is with Aries?

There are also layers to consider. More complicated ones that don't necessarily exist between Sash and me. He asked if I was comfortable talking with him as a first-generation, which was strange. He also called himself the "hired help" and me his "superior." The former is technically, factually true, but the latter is only a matter of accepted social constructs.

Aries is older than me and undoubtedly more experienced in life. However, within the Eden aristocracy, there have been many formal pairings where two vampires have not been the same age. Lord Ashford is twenty years older than my brother, Thomas, and even Lord Blakeley is the viscount's senior by forty years. I would go so far as to say that couplings like mine and Alexander's— where two vampires are the same age—are rare.

Purebreds are always arranged with other purebreds. That much can't be denied. A purebred being mated with a first-gen is normalized in the modern era. I've seen countless examples online and across international communities.

Within Eden, though? It's unheard of. Forbidden.

Even still, Aries is indisputably talented and well traveled. Forthright, charming and probably street smart. If I disregard these paradigms surrounding the differences between our rank and age, are they still valid? Do I *have* to acknowledge them?

And, more importantly, could he let go of them? Is my being able to let go a result of my privilege? Purebreds make the rules, so to speak. As such, we can also break or change them according to our preferences.

This thought pattern definitely does not matter, given my circumstance. But I like to think about these things. I'm curious about the underlying contexts—what's happening in the roots that's impacting the trees, and what's more, the soil surrounding the roots. Things are never neatly black and white like everyone wants. There's so much gray to consider. I like to examine the gray.

This kind of thinking is what gets me in trouble.

My day officially starts with breakfast. This event is more private compared with last night's ostentatious affair. Only Alexander, his mother and father, me, Sasha, the viscount and Lord Blakeley are in attendance.

Lord Blakeley is excited about the hunt and unashamedly boasts about all the preparations that have been made (things we definitely cannot afford financially). Alexander's mother, Lady Victoria Kendrick, chimes in enthusiastically while Lord Kendrick nods politely. Alexander stays uncharacteristically quiet, pushing food around on his plate and occasionally picking at the fruit platter in the center of the table. The viscount, Sasha and me exchange glances, and I smile. The three of us hate the hunts.

Alexander's family fortune is centered in arts and entertainment. Lord Kendrick is a classical music aficionado and owns several prominent theaters across the whole of Europe. The fact that his wealth and influence extend beyond Eden is telling, because most families, like mine, are restricted to this island bubble.

The Royal Eden Opera House—the largest and most famous theater in Central Eden—attracts artists and musicians from all over the world and serves as our most important window to the outside. I saw an Italian opera there once and fell in love with the language and culture, even though I've never been.

Alexander has, though. Multiple times. He's allowed to go anywhere he wants.

My family's revenue is not nearly as lucrative or glamorous. This castle and its land have been passed down through the generations, and we live off of the taxes and rent paid to us by lower-ranked families who farm and live here. Once upon a time, there were many families and the land yielded an abundance of resources.

Over the past several years, though, many first-, second- and third-ranked vampire families have fled our realm in search of better lives. As a result, we barely scrape by. There are parts of this castle that are uninhabitable because we do not have the money for the upkeep.

But my marriage and bonding with Alexander is supposed to change all of that. Not only will we have a seat on the Governing Board of the Royal Order, the Blakeley Clan will finally be elevated to royal status and given Alexander's extraordinary dowry —a gratuitous lump sum of money.

Lucky me, I guess? Or so they say.

Immediately following breakfast, the viscount and me have plans to leave the estate for a social visit in the village of St. Cyan. It's nothing special. He asked me if I wanted to get some air and visit his sister. I like her and she's kind, so I agreed.

As I leave the breakfast room, though, Sasha grabs my arm and pulls me in close. She waits until everyone else passes us, then whispers, "What's up with you?"

"What do you mean?"

"I don't know..." She narrows her eyes as she holds my wrist. "You're *smiling*."

This makes me chuckle. "Is that so abnormal?"

"Hell yes, it is. I haven't seen you smile in months. And Camille told me you fanned your aura out at the banquet last night. Are you getting on well with Alexander now?"

Good God. Sucking in a breath, I draw back. "I—That was just an accident. It wasn't anything. Tell Camille to mind her business."

"*You* are her business. And how was it an 'accident'? As far as I know, you haven't ever—"

"Sasha, dear, please unhand your brother," the viscount calls from over his shoulder. "We need to leave."

"Yes, Father. Sorry." Sasha offers a quick nod and does as she's told. But she points at me in a dramatic gesture to suggest that we're not finished with this topic. I shrug as I walk forward. I definitely need to be more careful.

After returning to the estate, I have the rest of the evening to myself. In fact, with the hunt officially started, I have quite a bit of free time over the week, which I am thrilled about. The weather today has been beautiful. With the sun hanging low in the partly cloudy sky, I decide to take a walk to my favorite place.

Navigating through the hedge maze and toward the rose garden, my mind wanders. Was the strength of my aura so profound? It's not as if everyone in the room noticed... at least, I don't think they did? Aries noticed because our eyes met. His attention was singularly focused on me, and mine on him. It's Camille's job to focus on me, so I'm not too surprised that she noticed. And as for Alexander, well... who knows what motivates him?

My body and nature responded to Aries's presence, but I have no way of knowing how strongly it registers externally. I'll have to keep a tight hold on it going forward. Letting it unfurl was incredible—if only for a brief moment. I've never felt anything so primeval and authentic before. Like a tiny stream from the depth of life energy inside of me came rushing out in joyous manifestation.

The center of the rose garden is just ahead. I can hear the large marble fountain spouting and splashing water. Another thing that must be costing us unnecessary money, but of course, Lord Blakeley wants to show off for our visitors.

I have sensed Aries's presence more the farther along that I've walked. However, in my sincere effort to not be a vampire stalker, I've been largely ignoring it. When I round the corner and enter the wide-open space with the fountain, he's there, sitting on a nearby bench.

Immediately, our eyes lock and the garden feels suspended in time. Hovering and insulated, just like the moment in the banquet hall last night. Now, though, I clamp down on my nature as I walk forward. He's holding what looks like a large sketchpad and a pencil. There's a fancy brown leather case full of colored pencils on the seat beside him.

I smile. "Hi."

"Hello, your grace. What brings you out here?"

"I'm just out for a walk. And you?"

He sighs, setting his sketch pad flat against his thighs. "Seeking inspiration."

Taking in his demeanor, I tilt my head. "No luck?"

"Well, the castle grounds are unquestionably beautiful, but a little..."

"Ostentatious?" I offer. "Unimaginative? Stiff?"

Aries's brow furrows as he grins. His face is so wonderfully expressive. Much more so than what I'm accustomed to and compared with the vampires I usually encounter. "You've given this some thought?" he asks.

"I have. Do you..." I stop, nervous and twisting my hands as I consider. I don't know how to do this, but... something inside is urging me to try. I take a deep breath. "Would you like to walk with me? There's a place in the woods just beyond the manicured gardens that's beautiful at sunset. I'm headed there now. No pressure, of course! I don't mean to interrupt you."

The question is out there. Even still, I don't want him to feel obligated to say yes just because I'm the purebred son of the person who hired him.

He regards me for a brief moment—assessing. Making some internal decision. Slowly, he stands from the marble bench and closes his sketchpad. He wraps up his pencils in the fancy leather holder. "Yes," he says. "Thank you. I'd love to see it."

I can't suppress my smile, but I stifle my energy as it swirls like fire inside of my core.

He said *yes*.

Chapter Eight

"It's just a five-minute walk," I tell him, quelling my nature as he trails behind. He said yes...

I'm embarrassingly excited—like when Sasha gave me my first higher-quality camera. Receiving a point-and-shoot was great, but I wasn't exhilarated like I am right now. This is a new kind of thrill.

We move past another long row of thick bushes full of glossy green leaves. Bursts of white flowers litter the brush and are clustered together like powder puffs. I glance over my shoulder. "What do you need inspiration for? If I may ask?"

"My next assignment is with a small theater in New York. I have a friend who wants to take me under her wing as she works on a contemporary production of Shakespeare's *A Midsummer Night's Dream*. I've been desperately wanting to get into costume design, but it's difficult without the right connections. This could be a great opportunity for me."

"That sounds incredible. Congratulations."

"It is fortunate. However... while this very old castle definitely reminds me of Shakespearean times, something about its abundance of sixteenth-century portraiture, stone walls and turrets is ironically stifling my creativity."

I chuckle. "Not surprising. We're not really about free thinking and creative expression around here. We're more about oppression and *de*pression. That's our specialty."

Aries laughs brightly as we step into the thicket of trees bordering the garden. His laugh sounds like it comes from deep within his belly—organically and from his very soul. My heart flutters because talking with him feels so easy. Almost calming.

The sun is fading, causing the light around us to glow in hues of gold and reddish pink. I walk a little faster because I don't want to miss the sunset. Aries increases his pace as he follows.

"Do you come out here often, your grace?" he asks.

"Whenever I have free time. It's isolated, so it's peaceful. This... might sound silly, but this area feels undisturbed by time and artificial influence. It's like being in a different place altogether."

I wait for him to tell me that I'm an idiot because it's such an odd thing to say. That I sound childish and I should "grow up."

"It's not silly at all," he says. "I understand what you mean. Plus, the trees here are likely very old. They've seen many things."

"Exactly!" I beam. "Can you imagine the stories they'd tell? Like, 'If these walls could talk.'"

"Possibly. I think most of the stories would be about squirrels and ticks, though. Or the atrocities of vampire wars."

"Well, the conflicts primarily occurred near and around Central Eden, so our trees would mostly have stories about nature. Rants about birds shitting on them and bugs crawling up their bark."

We both snicker as we walk and the sound of our laughter echoes. The wind sweeps through the leaves overhead, and the aroma of the drying lavender field in combination with this inexplicable vampire behind me is glorious.

I've never experienced a moment like this—where everything feels soft and shimmery. Cozy and insulated.

Maybe I did when I was little? When we were younger, me and Sasha would sit huddled together by the fire in winter and read stories. The castle is especially harsh in colder months, with its stone walls that seemingly absorb all of the frost but none of the sun. Those moments with my sister were lovely in their own way—the sense of wonder and joy glowing within me, interlaced with physical safety.

This moment is... similar, but very different.

Near the end of the path, there's a small wooden chest tucked behind a tree. I step off the trail, pull the bolt key from my pocket and proceed to open the lid.

"What, pray tell, is this?" Aries asks from behind.

"Camille had the gardeners put wood-chips and a chest along this path since I'm out here fairly often in the summer months. It has all my things in it, so I don't have to carry them from the castle every time. At first, I was annoyed that she was spying on me, but it actually comes in handy."

When the top is unlocked and lifted, I wrestle a large quilt from inside and tuck it under my arm.

"Is she always spying on you? This is a normal aspect of your life?"

Chuckling, I stand straight. "Not always. She just... pays close attention to my needs? I'll be running out of pages in my journal and a new one will show up on my desk. Or my favorite sweater will start to have one too many lint balls. The next time I pull it out of the closet, I'll find that it's been mended. Sometimes, if I'm very stressed, my schedule will magically open up and I'll have an afternoon to myself."

"Sounds very nice. I wish I had someone like that to help me." He steps forward in the direction of the clearing and I'm suddenly worried that I sound boastful. Like a spoiled little purebred who wants for nothing.

"I'm not bragging," I blurt. "I'm just explaining what she does."

"I didn't think you were, your grace. You don't need to clarify."

Following him, I sigh, really wishing that he would say my

actual name. What would it sound like mingled between his full lips and riding on the invisible flow of his velvety, charming voice?

I bet it would sound nice.

God, I'm out of my mind. Where do I find the nerve—the audacity—to even think this way about this man? With what guts?

The scene before us is brilliant. A beautiful, expansive field layered with colors and textures as if it were hand-painted, like a Monet or Pissarro. Sunset-pink and deep purplish clouds hang listless and soft against a pale blue horizon. The lavender fields reach as far west as my eyes can see. Aside from the occasional rustling of the breeze within the trees and brush, it's quiet. Crickets chirp in a restrained start to their nighttime chorus.

There's a strip of grass in between where the woods end and the fields begin, like the dividing line between two worlds. I unfold the blanket to lay it flat. Aries puts his sketchpad and pencils aside and helps me straighten it. Soon, we're both seated and looking outward, him with one leg folded and the other drawn up. His pad rests at an angle on his thigh. I sit in lotus position, but lean and relax back against my palms.

A contented silence falls over us while we watch the sun paint the sky in different watercolor hues. Leisurely, it descends beneath the horizon. The air is gentle and cool. That same fizzy feeling is warm and pleasing within me—like a low-burning, self-made fire in my belly and spine. It's wonderful, but I'm a little nervous because I want to keep it under control.

Aries moves his colored pencil across the sketchpad in swift strokes, alternating between glancing up at the landscape and then focusing on his drawing. I want to look at him and what he's doing so badly. Partly because I'm curious and fascinated—a creative individual, a true artist, is designing right beside me and I've never witnessed anything like this before.

And of course, the part of me that is unquestionably enamored with him wants to look, too. I want to take in the details of him and inscribe them to my memory. The elegant wave of his richly brown hair, the golden undertones of his skin and the width of his shoulders. The heavy thickness of his dark lashes and his perfectly trimmed beard lining his jaw.

Someday, when someone asks me if I've ever truly felt the pull of my nature, I want to recall this vampire to my mind—to remember him and imagine what could have been given a different situation. A different life.

"You were right."

Inhaling sharply, I turn to look directly at him. "About?"

"This place is beautiful. Truly inspiring."

Drawing my knees up, I wrap my arms around them to make myself comfortable. "I'm glad that you like it. Do you usually take inspiration from landscapes? Or the outdoors?"

"For me, inspiration blooms from many sources." He closes the cover of his sketchpad and places it aside. "At times it can be the outdoors—sometimes it's a song or a poignant lyric. It could be a person, a moment or an emotion. I've also been inspired by other artists. I never know when something will move me, but it always comes."

I nod, processing. "Is there a particular source that moves you the most? Or the best?"

"People," he says, meeting my gaze and smiling warmly. "Especially those with a dynamic and colorful spirit. A vibrant, bold essence. They become my muse. I enjoy those situations the most —the complexities and layers that I'm able to explore."

Breaking his gaze, I glance out toward the darkening landscape and take another breath to calm my heartbeat.

How incredible would it feel to be someone's muse? To stir another person so deeply that they're driven to create something beautiful simply because of you. I have no realistic chance of ever becoming anyone's muse. Even if I did, what the hell would they create?

A clown suit. Not even a colorful one fit for dazzling a circus audience. Something sad and monochromatic, like for a mime. A small mime costume.

"What about you?" Aries asks, interrupting my self-deprecating thoughts. "What are you inspired by, your grace?"

"Me?" I blink. "Oh, I-I don't know, really. I'm not allowed to be inspired."

Aries laughs. "Inspiration is not something to be controlled. Plus, the way you speak about the treatment of ranked vampires... and those photographs that you took in Evanshire, they seem deeply inspired to me? As if the eyes behind the camera felt and captured the injustice and barrenness in that circumstance. The heartbreak."

Every time he mentions that he's seen my photos, tiny butterflies take up residence in my chest and abdomen. I lift one hand to rub my fingers against my scalp. "Yeah, I... well, that situation resulted in a stern reprimand from Lord Blakeley. I think I'm only allowed to be inspired by and about my fiancé. He's very pushy about that."

"I see. Well, are you?"

"Am I what?"

"Inspired by your fiancé."

I scoff. "Not at all."

Leaning back on his palms, Aries lifts his head to the sky. I look up, too. Emergent stars are dotted and gently twinkling above us.

"That's too bad," Aries says, his voice low and cautious. "It seems like they're grossly undervaluing a hidden talent."

Him saying this... I don't know how to explain it, but it comforts me. It's like, ah, someone finally agrees that I'm not totally inadequate. That maybe I'm not just meant to be arm candy, or to ensure that Prince Alexander Ethan Kendrick is comfortable and pleased for the sake of our family, economy and reputation.

My fate is inevitable. Despite the sadness in this understanding, I smile, allowing myself to look at him once more. "Thank you for saying that."

"You're welcome—although, I don't think I've said anything that wasn't obvious?"

"Well, you'd be surprised."

"Hm, I suppose." Aries sits straight, rolling his shoulders. "Thank you for not beheading me for saying it."

I draw back, frowning. "What? Who does that? We don't do that... not anymore."

Pushing up to his feet, he laughs. "There are all sorts of curious rumors about the Eden aristocracy. I definitely didn't come here to lose any limbs, so I think that I should be careful."

"You don't need to," I assure him. "Nobody here does corporal punishment anymore—just banishments or fines. And anyway, I don't have the authority to ban or fine anyone. And I wouldn't do that to you. I... I would never repeat what we talk about. I promise." I'm leaning on the blanket and looking up at him because I want him to believe me. Finally talking to someone this way—freely and openly, honestly—I wouldn't jeopardize it for anything.

He smiles, then looks off and into the fields. He's a shadowy figure with the sun gone. A strong presence with soft outlines. The subtle warmth of his energy pulses with the scent of oak and jasmine. Although I can't see him perfectly with my physical eyes, I can feel every inch of him through the undeniable spark flowing between us.

After a moment of pause, he speaks. "You are not what I was expecting."

I swallow hard, absorbed. "In a good way?"

"Perhaps. I think we should go back to the estate? I wouldn't want to cause a stir because the youngest master of Blakeley House has gone missing, only to be found in the woods with the hired help."

My shoulders drop because it's like a cold wet towel has been dropped over me again. Sighing, I stand up to collect the blanket. Aries grabs his sketchpad and pencil case.

I speak quietly. "I wish you wouldn't say that."

"It is the truth. It's good to be reminded of the facts."

"Not facts," I reason, folding the blanket. "It's perspective. Your perspective."

He bends and picks up the long edge, handing it to me. "I regret to inform you that *my* perspective is the popular one. The one likely held by the overwhelming majority of the inhabitants of this castle."

"Right." With the blanket in my arms, I move back into the woods and toward the chest.

"What's your perspective, then?" Aries asks, coming up behind me as I stuff the blanket inside. Once I've closed the lid and locked it, I turn to face him.

"That I'm just me—sitting outside on a perfect evening, in my favorite place, and with a vampire that... that I find truly fascinating. Not like anyone I've ever met before. Talking candidly, which I never have the opportunity to do." I exhale, then walk past him toward the main path.

"But I understand your perspective," I go on. "It's the right one. I'm sorry."

"You don't need to be sorry—you apologize in *excess*. Do you realize this?"

I keep moving because I feel like an idiot yet again. "Well, it's my default because I find that I'm always the one who's wrong. About what I think, the way I feel, what I say. Everyone is constantly reminding me, so it's just easier to apologize—"

His fingers lace and close around my wrist, stopping me in the middle of the path as he steps ahead to cut me off. The physical contact fiercely stirs my nature, catching me off guard with a flash of heat shooting up my arm, to my chest and up toward my brain. I gasp from the shock of it as I look into his eyes.

He snatches his hand back, pulling away as if my skin is on fire. Our eyes lock in an odd moment of enigmatic silence. He takes a breath and shakes his head, breaking the tense stillness. "*Please* stop apologizing, your grace. I—I'm not chastising you. We're simply talking and exchanging ideas. I'm enjoying this, and your opinions are... very interesting, given your circumstance and upbringing."

The hot, fizzy sensation inside blooms, leaving me breathless as it rushes full force to my face. Aries's remarkable eyes widen in surprise as he stares at me.

My irises tingle and warm in a way that they never have. Before I know it, there's a feeling like fire there. All-consuming. I shut my eyes tightly and step away from him.

I can't believe this is happening.

Just when I didn't think this situation could get any worse, here we are.

Chapter Nine

T he woods are motionless and heavy. But then, a cool breeze ruffles my hair and the surrounding leaves. It does nothing to quell the heat radiating in my cheeks and down my neck. The unrelenting burn of light behind my irises.

My eyes have alighted. God.

Someone, please help me.

"Ah, c-could you—just go on ahead, back to the castle, I mean. Please? I'm so sorry for—*Shit.*" I stand with my back toward Aries, wholly and completely ashamed. Every inch of my flesh is pulled taut with humiliation, stress and arousal. I take a deep breath and try again. "I'm going to stay out here for a little while longer."

Aries has clearly stated that he's not interested in my awkward purebred affections. And yet, here I am with my eyes alighted. The most obvious outward sign of affection possible for a vampire aside from radiating my aura. At least I've managed to keep that under control, for whatever it's worth.

He's silent, so I'm hoping that he'll have the decency to walk away and act like this never happened. I'm praying for it.

To my fear and disgrace, he takes a step closer.

"Forgive me if I'm being presumptuous," he says. His voice is low against the backdrop of the night wind rustling the foliage. "But is this the first time that your eyes have alighted, your grace?"

What a disaster. I can't even speak as I rub my palms against my face. The heat is unyielding and bright. My skin is coated in goosebumps.

"Oliver?"

The sound of my name on his lips sends a flash of lightning down my spine. "Y-yes?"

"Will you face me?"

Steeling myself, I turn my head to the side slightly, only to glance at him. "I... I really don't mean to make you uncomfortable—"

"I know. Just turn around, please?"

This is humiliating, but... he isn't leaving. Us standing here in the dark with me trying to hide isn't helping. So, I take a deep breath, then turn, looking off and avoiding direct eye contact.

He takes another step forward and speaks softly. "Is this the first time?"

"Yes. But I'm alright. I promise that I'm in control—you have nothing to worry about." I'm inclined to apologize again, but since he's brought this apparently excessive habit to my attention, I hesitate.

He steps even closer. His smooth, comforting voice is like a serenade. "The first time our eyes alight for someone is an important moment in our lives." Aries stands directly in front of me. Over me. I'm still avoiding his gaze—that is, until he reaches down and takes hold of both my wrists in his palms. The move surprises me, so I lift my head. His smile is patient. Truly compassionate.

"The way we feel, and the response that we receive when it happens, sets the tone for how we perceive intimacy, and our deeper sense of trust in romantic situations. You are not making me uncomfortable... Oliver. Your eyes are beautiful. I am honored."

A new type of heat rushes up my neck and face. Not derived of shame, like usual. But of pleasure. Wanting.

The part of me that's always humiliated is still there. Lurking like a spiteful entity in the shadows. It tells me that I'm being stupid—that I don't deserve this kindness. That I am worthless beyond my obligations.

But I don't want to listen to that part of myself. Not right now. I look into his eyes. "Thank you, Aries."

"You don't need to thank me. You're stunning."

I nod, taking a breath. Am I having another out-of-body experience? Aries and I are standing on a path in the woods under the starry sky. My eyes have alighted and he's called me stunning. I'm going to wake up from this dream at any moment.

"What color are they?" I think I know, but I want to confirm.

"Silver," he says. "Tinged with a subtle, ethereal and pale blue. Does this hue run consistent within your bloodline?"

"On Lord Blakeley's side. The viscount's family line is pure blue. I wasn't sure how I'd turn out."

Aries slides his hands down to clasp my palms. I open my hands, welcoming the gesture. When we're joined, he squeezes. "You're perfect," he says. "Silver suits you. Sharp and resilient."

I don't think I'm resilient in any way, shape or form, but his hands are warm around mine. I look down at them fastened together because I want to record everything about this moment and how light I feel. Blissful. "Thank you," I tell him again, because I don't know what else to say.

"Master Blakeley?"

Camille's voice echoes through the trees. I tense, panicking, but Aries holds my hands more firmly, grounding me.

"Oliver," he says, unruffled and commanding my attention. "Close your eyes and take deep breaths. Concentrate on stifling the warmth inside. Cooling it. Imagine something cold and calming falling over you—snowflakes drifting over your head and snuffing it out. Can you do that for me?"

I nod and close my eyes, taking a deep breath in and blowing it out. I do this a couple of times, imagining large soft snowflakes falling all around us. Gently, Aries lets go of my hands. His long fingertips slide against the undersides of my palms.

The heat and intensity of my stifled energy fades, evenly dispersing itself throughout my body. I'm so focused on the task and the surprisingly soothing sensation of it that Camille's voice startles me.

"Your grace?"

I jump as my eyes spring open. Thankfully, the burn is gone. "Y-yes? What is it?"

"What on earth are you doing? You're late for dinner." She turns, looking around. "Are you alone out here?"

Flickering my eyes to the left and right, Aries is gone. I feel him fairly close, but he's nowhere in sight. I run my fingers through the top of my hair. "I was just out by the fields. Since I had some free time."

Camille regards me for a moment. Almost suspiciously. I'm about to ask her if something is wrong, but she nods and turns. "Please be careful out here at night, your grace. The viscount is waiting for you. We should hurry."

I follow her without argument. I'm walking, but it feels like I'm floating. Images of Aries swirl and dance in my mind. His distinguished demeanor and handsome features backdropped against the moonlit shadows of the woods. Our hands clasped in the warmth and power of his grip.

I'm walking, but my heart is vibrant and alive. I want to hold on to this feeling forever.

"Non ha mai visitato l'Italia? È davvero un peccato! Lei parla italiano così bene."

You've never been to Italy? That's a shame, because you speak Italian so well.

"Grazie per i complimenti, signora," I say, smiling. "Spero

davvero di poter visitare l'Italia un giorno... Mi piacerebbe viaggiare in tanti posti diversi nel mondo."

The next morning, I start my day by having breakfast with the viscount and the purebred dignitary from Italy. She's an old friend of his, and it's largely a softball conversation with the two of them reminiscing. I'm able to practice my language skills, which is really nice. But I'm not sure why the viscount wanted me here? I'm definitely not angry about it, and it isn't the worst part of my day by any means.

Because that comes later.

Following breakfast, I travel beyond the castle walls to have tea with Her Ladyship of Wiltshire—my aunt. This meeting largely consists of me listening to my aunt complain about Lord Blakeley (her brother) and how she should receive a generous portion of Alexander's dowry after the wedding because she's *family*, after all.

She also complains about the decreasing number of purebred couplings across the world and how our race is being "bastardized." When I try to correct her harmful rhetoric, she brushes me off and says that I'm, quote, "much too young to truly understand," and how "it wasn't like this in the old days."

I give up as Lady Wiltshire goes on. Next, she spends an uncomfortable amount of time gossiping about some purebred named Leoni who's been exiled from a prominent family in eastern Eden. Banishments are a big deal, but not uncommon. Especially in the modern era, which is what my aunt seems to take issue with.

"We're too soft on this younger generation," she complains, lifting her tea and plate from the table, which is covered with an elaborate spread of sandwiches, cakes and fruit. Neither of us needs this much food.

"These shameful circumstances will repeat themselves until the day we reinstate corporal punishments and extensive prison sentences," she continues. "Only then will this defiant behavior cease. Vampires in *my* day held fast to their responsibilities, because we understood the consequences of our actions. Vampires your age don't even care. They misbehave and are practically rewarded!"

"What did Leoni do to be banished?" I ask.

She huffs in distaste, then takes a sip of her tea before answering. "I don't know. The eastern families are being irksomely tight-lipped about it."

"So... you don't know what happened, exactly, but you're certain she's in the wrong?"

"Absolutely. It's always the same. You young purebreds today have no sense of pride. No honor or loyalty to your ancestors. The contract with the Resinworth Clan of the west has been dissolved because of her. It's a disaster."

I sigh. Our ancestors fought and almost decimated our race over a few yards of land and some ill-conceived notion of power. And now, subsequent generations are imprisoned in a kind of legalistic, heartless merry-go-round of arranged marriages for the purpose of maintaining peace and civility.

What's honorable about that? Why should I be proud?

This meeting will make Lord Blakeley happy, because he detests his younger sister and avoids her at all costs. Sending me for a visit means that he can dodge a hypothetical bullet by shoving me in its path instead.

For once, though, I don't mind. What carries me through this particular day is a unique warmth in my heart, like a lamplight glowing inside my chest. Outwardly, I am invoking my purebred robot, as Alexander calls it. I nod when I am expected to and smile when it's necessary.

But inside, I'm floating in a cloud of rosy memories. Stolen moments within the trees, standing hand in hand with the gentlest, most emotionally intelligent and mature vampire that I have ever met.

Could Aries ever feel this way about me? Is it possible that something deep within him might be stirred by our interactions? By the cautious touch of our hands, or those brief instances where our eyes meet and everything around us ceases to exist?

It's ludicrous to wonder, but I do.

When I return to the castle, Camille is waiting for me in the front entryway. I never let her come with me to my aunt's estate. Camille is second-generation—two generations removed from her purebred ancestry. The last thing I want is to give my aunt an innocent target for her unfounded disgust.

"I have good news, Master Blakeley." She follows me as our footsteps clack against the marble flooring.

"Yes?"

"I have a new phone for you. Lord Blakeley is reinstating your use of electronic devices... well, only this particular device."

"What about my cameras and equipment?"

"No, unfortunately."

For God's sake. I turn, glancing at her as we move. She beams, hopeful as she holds out the new phone in her palm. I don't take it because I'm confused. "Why just this?"

"Well, I believe Prince Alexander spoke on your behalf. Since they're away on the hunt, he complained about not having a way to contact you. As such, Lord Blakeley approved this device."

Doubtful, I take the phone from her and stop in the middle of the hallway. The ceiling is high above us and the stone walls are covered in dusty tapestries and old portraits of my dead relatives who could never have fathomed something like a smartphone.

I look at the screen. What's immediately apparent is that there are no apps—not any of the ones I typically use, anyway. Only the notes, call and messaging apps are loaded. The latter already has a small red circle with the number one.

Opening the app, there's a message from Alexander. I swipe over to look at the contacts. Alexander and Camille. No one else. Not even Sash.

"What *is* this?" I ask her. "What happened to my real phone?"

"Your father agreed to Alexander's request, albeit with a few stipulations. He said that focusing on the upcoming ceremony and Alexander takes precedence above all else. No other distractions. Generally, I feel this is a positive turn?"

This is not a positive turn. This is a dog's leash. I stick the device in the pocket of my slacks and continue walking toward my wing of the estate. "Thank you, Camille." It isn't her fault, so I won't be crabby with her.

"Of course—and please respond to Alexander soon. He wants to confirm that I've delivered it."

"Sure. My schedule is clear until dinner, yes?" I just want to go to my room and be alone for a while. I need to recharge before everyone returns to the castle tomorrow evening and I'm forced to smile through another banquet.

"Yes, but Mister Moralis has asked that you stop by his studio sometime before dinner. He has fabrics for you to approve."

This is a positive turn. "Will do. You don't need to walk me there. I know the way. And I won't be late for dinner tonight. I promise."

She stops while I continue forward. "Thank you, your grace."

"Enjoy your afternoon," I call over my shoulder. My pace hastens as I walk. I'm stopping myself from breaking into a full-on jog, because that would be ridiculous.

Chapter Ten

When I get to Aries's room, the rosewood door is open. I knock anyway, then wait.

"Come in."

Stepping across the threshold, I marvel. Truly, this room is superior to mine. It has two large windows, but one is nearly covered in ivy, so it creates a moody green glow when the sun is bright like it is today. The other window offers a direct view of the glittery lake.

"Hi, Camille said that you wanted to see me?" Being in his presence and breathing his scent, the butterflies within my chest spring to life. I think that I should be ashamed about yesterday and my insane behavior, but... I'm okay.

Logically, I should be repentant. But the way Aries spoke to me—the things he said and the way he held my hands—it's given me a sense of comfort. Reassurance.

He smiles. His rich irises are warm and soft. "I did. Good afternoon, your grace."

I pause, thwarted. "We... we're back to 'your grace'? You called me Oliver last night."

Aries's eyes widen and he leans to look past me. His voice is low but urgent. "Did you come here alone?"

"Yes."

His shoulders relax and he exhales, running a palm down his face. "I have this sneaking suspicion that you truly *want* me to lose my head."

"We don't do that… anymore. And I would never put you in danger. I won't repeat our conversations."

His hand drops from his face. "But it isn't just about us talking, is it, my young lord? It's about more than that and you know it."

The heat inside rushes up, making my nature twist in my stomach. I stamp it down, but I can't do anything about the flush in my cheeks. "I don't want anything from you, I promise."

"Your reaction last night suggests otherwise."

"I know—but just ignore that." I wave a hand. "I swear I'm alright. And thank you… for making it a nice memory."

He turns, glancing at me as he stalks toward the table. A beguiling smile graces his mouth. "It's my pleasure. I have fabrics for you to choose. Come here, please?"

Nodding, I take a few steps to stand at his side. I don't want anything from him, but I… I wish I could have something. A little more of him. For us to be closer.

That's impossible. I know it, so I shouldn't bother entertaining myself with questions of how he might feel about me. If this is one-sided, or if there's something within him that responds to me, too?

I wonder… what color do his eyes alight when he's aroused? How would it feel to touch him? Or maybe, to have my lips pressed against his beautiful full ones in a kiss?

God. What does he taste like? His mouth, his skin and his blood. What would it be like to fall in love with him? To allow myself to submit to this remarkable feeling humming inside me. I've never thought about another vampire this way, and it's truly—

"Oliver?"

"Yes?" Sucking in a breath, I clench my eyes shut because the same burn from last night is threatening to spark my irises. I've really let my mind wander too far for anyone's good. Quickly, I imagine the snow. Huge white tufts falling all around.

"Are we alright?"

I exhale. "Yes. I'm here."

"You'll need to open your eyes to choose."

"Right." Cautiously, I peek one eye open. I'm okay. Marginally in control. I roll my shoulders and scan the table.

Aries launches into an expert presentation on the swatches of fabric laid out before us. Lord Blakeley has explicitly told him nothing too flashy, but the design is largely in Aries's capable hands. Words like Pima, Oxford, Swiss and Egyptian cotton fly past me, and more names for the color blue than I ever thought imaginable: spruce, Aegean, azure and cerulean. Some are darker and some lighter, but other than that, I honestly have no clue.

When Aries finishes his impressive explanation, he rests his hands on his hips. "So, do you have any particular preferences?"

I look down at the table for a long moment, then look back at him. "Um, I like the blue ones."

"They're all blue."

I point. "This one looks gray."

"It's blue."

"Listen, I have no sense of color or fashion. Camille literally picks out all of my clothes for me, every day. You're always dressed very smartly, so I trust in whatever you decide."

He folds his arms, smirking. "I can, of course. But since this is your wedding, your father thought you might like to have some say in the details of your ensemble?"

I shouldn't say what I'm about to say, but the words break free from my mouth like the pop of a soap bubble. "I don't care about my 'wedding day' or any of the details that go along with it. None of this is my choice. Lord Blakeley giving me charge over a narrow spectrum of blue fabrics is a cruel joke."

How dare he tell Aries that it's my choice—like throwing an abused dog a tiny, half-eaten bone. Utterly insane.

When I've calmed myself, I notice the silence in the room and look at Aries.

"You've mentioned this before," he says gently, almost whispering. "Forgive me for prying, but you don't care for Alexander?"

"I don't."

"He seems very fond of you when he speaks of you in the media."

"Alexander puts on a show and says whatever everyone expects him to say. There's no truth to it." I almost add that he antagonizes me, and that his list of insults to demean and belittle my character is always growing. But it feels as if I'll only be disparaging myself by disclosing it.

Aries bends and pulls out a stool from underneath the table we're standing at. He gestures, and I see that there's a second one underneath. "Is he cruel to you?" he asks, sitting atop the round surface.

"Well, he isn't kind." I keep it simple as I take the seat beside him. Aries's feet are placed firmly on the floor because of his ridiculously long legs. I'm insecure about my height, so I bend my knees. I rest my feet on the wooden bar a few inches from the bottom of the stool and straighten my spine.

"I envy you," I tell him. "Your freedom to pursue what you want—to travel and meet new people. You don't have anyone forcing and constantly pressuring you to do intrusive, humiliating things for the 'greater good.' I often fantasize about true independence and how it must feel."

"It wasn't always like this for me. The first thirty years of my life were similar to yours—with my grandfather controlling my every move after my mother and father died. He dictated where I went, what I did, who I slept with and drank from. It was miserable."

Drawing back, I blink. "Really? How did you escape?"

"He died." Aries shrugs, matter-of-fact. "He was ancient. I hadn't bonded with my assigned mate, so we talked it over and decided to go our separate ways. It was very healthy. I was lucky to have her, I think."

I nod, vaguely considering whether I'm capable of instigating Lord Blakeley's untimely demise. I'm not, of course. And even if he did die, there's a long succession of purebreds who would then presume authority over me, starting with the viscount.

Ironically, being married to Alexander is likely the easiest way to gain some semblance of freedom. I'll be taken off the leash, but still very much inside my kennel and with a new master.

"After my mating arrangement was dissolved," Aries continues, "I left my hometown and started this career. I've never once looked back."

"You had an arranged bond, too?"

"I did."

"But you didn't love her? You walked away?" I have so many questions. What unfortunate creature lost Aries Moralis? This elegant and benevolent vampire in all his jasmine and oak glory. His infinitely long legs and cobalt-blue eyes.

God. The poor sap.

Aries folds his arms. "No, I didn't love her romantically. And she didn't love me in that way, either. The two of us had a companionable relationship, but we felt more like comrades in arms than lovers. True friends. I keep in touch with her even now. Both of us were unfortunate subjects under the constant control of emotionally, sometimes physically abusive purebreds. So, we often banded together in support of one another."

I'm listening, but something in my mind clicks. Aries was abused by his grandfather—a purebred. I swallow hard, suddenly terrified that I've been triggering him all this time with my ridiculous, uncontrolled affections. How selfish have I been?

"I'm sorry," I tell him. "For what you've been through. I've probably added to the pile with my gross behavior."

"Not gross." Grinning, he leans with his elbow on the table, cradling his square chin in his palm. "I thought I asked you to stop apologizing?"

I scratch the top of my head. "This time it feels valid, though."

He huffs in a little laugh that makes me smile. His gaze lands on the swatches of material on the table. "I believe... that you're teaching me something important, Oliver."

Whenever he says my name, my stomach turns a flip and warms. "What am I teaching you?"

Aries sighs. "Perhaps that torment comes in many forms. That even a purebred in one of the wealthiest, oldest aristocracies in the world can suffer under the hand of another."

"There are definitely vampires worse off than me. I'm just being selfish, immature and spoiled—"

"That isn't the point. You shouldn't measure and compare the legitimacy of your pain against someone else's. Abuse is abuse. You aren't allowed to live of your own accord or interact with vampires of your choosing. You apologize for everything because you've been taught that your thoughts and feelings aren't valid, but that's wrong..." He pauses, suddenly meeting my gaze. "You are valid."

Clenching my palms in my lap, I take a breath, because this exchange has turned surprisingly intimate. Aries and I keep tumbling into these candid, insulated alcoves of conversation and I've never experienced this with another vampire. I've tried with Sasha, but she always stops me. I hit the line, and she tells me to get over myself and grow up.

But he's telling me that my feelings are legitimate. That I'm valid. I don't think anyone has ever said that to me before.

A loud ding makes me jump and I almost fall off the stool. Aries casually glances down at my pocket. "The young lord is dinging."

"Um, yeah."

"Are you part vampire and part bell?"

"Not that I know of?" I chuckle, shifting and pulling the new device out of my pocket. I'd already forgotten about it. When I look at the screen, there's a new message from Alexander telling me not to ignore him.

"I thought you didn't have a phone?" Aries says.

"I didn't. Camille handed this to me just before I walked in here." I lift my hip and shove it back into my pocket.

"You don't seem too thrilled about it."

"I only have it because Alexander told Lord Blakeley that he wanted to message me while they're all on the hunt. It's just... another way for them to control my actions even though they're not here."

"Hm..." Aries adjusts his spire, then rolls his shoulders. I absently notice a tiny dark mole just underneath his ear. "Well, if you're comfortable with it," he goes on, "I could message you directly when I need you to come down here for a fitting. Of course, I can keep going through Camille. But since you have a contact method now—"

"Yes, you absolutely could!" My back straightens and I've basically perked up like a meerkat. Aries grins at me, so I hunch down a bit. "I mean, I think that would work fine, if you're comfortable."

He lifts his open palm toward me. "May I?"

Confused, I look down at his hand, then instinctively place my palm in his. It's so warm and the same fiery sensation tingles up the length of my arm. He bites his bottom lip and wraps his long fingers around mine. Squeezing. "Your phone, Oliver. May I have your phone?"

"Oh *God*." I slip my hand from his, shaking my head and pulling the mobile from my pocket. What the hell is wrong with me? Such a disaster. I hand him the phone. "I'm so sorry."

"We've talked about that," he says, taking it from me and swiftly moving to the contacts app to add his info.

"Right, sor—hmm." I run my fingers into the top of my hair. I'm done for today. The brain shop is officially closed.

I hear muffled buzzing and Aries slides his own phone from

his pocket as he hands mine back. "I've got you," he says, staring at the screen. I sigh, simply watching him because I'm a failure with words at the moment. "I'll pick out the fabrics for your suit. I'll make you look fantastic. Don't worry."

"I'm not worried."

He chuckles. "Because you do not care."

"No. Because I trust you."

Aries lifts his head. Suddenly, I don't feel quite as wrong in my own skin. Or stupid, or embarrassed or any of the other emotions I always carry around. His words and presence are like a magic spell that's been cast over my mind and heart, making me a little lighter.

He's practically a stranger. I've only known him for a few days, but... I feel comfortable with him. Accepted and maybe even understood in ways that I never have.

Something in Aries's gaze shifts. Darkens. "Why do you trust me?"

"Because I... just do."

"You should be more careful with your words, young lord." Aries stands tall from his stool. His scrutiny is penetrating. "I might misinterpret your intentions."

Nervously, I look down at the phone gripped in my lap. "I-I don't have any intentions, I promise." Maybe in a parallel universe, I'd have the necessary confidence to intentionally pursue a debonair and sophisticated vampire like Aries. In this life? Absolutely not.

I glance up and am instantly caught in the silent pull of his midnight eyes. My breath catches in my throat as we stare at each other, frozen in this unexpected moment.

Can he feel this frisson sparking between us? Is it just me?

Aries raises an eyebrow. "You're a dangerous creature, Oliver James Blakeley."

My eyes widen in surprise. "Me? Dangerous? No way. I'm the least threatening vampire you'll probably ever encounter."

He shakes his head, pulling his gaze from me as he walks toward the door. "On the contrary, you might be the most dangerous purebred that I've ever met."

Chapter Eleven

S itting upright in bed, I stare at Alexander's text messages and consider my response.

[Hello my love.]
[I can't wait to see you later tonight.]

A simple "Me too" feels adequate without encouraging further conversation. It's a bit cold, though, which might lead to some name-calling. I'd definitely like to avoid that. I type out my response and hit send.

[Hello. Me too.]

His next message pops up right away.

[Liar.]

I sigh, massaging the back of my neck as a barrage of texts funnel into our chat.

[We need to practice, sweet Prince Ollie.]

[Let me come to your room tonight after dinner?]
[You need to get more comfortable with sex.]
[You were too rigid that first time.]
[We have to be convincing.]

Dropping the phone, I groan loudly. Here's the thing—even if we're rigid and awkward, *no one* is going to call off this arrangement.

First, actual contracts and business arrangements between my clan and his are already being made in anticipation of our union. Second, Sasha and Elaine still haven't properly bonded, but they're expected to stay together and keep trying—to maintain appearances for the sake of peace and civilization or whatever.

This pressure is unnecessary.

I type out a message, plain and simple.

[I don't want you in my room.]

He replies instantly.

[You have to get more comfortable with intimacy.]
[And with me.]

I shake my head. Having conversations with him is like talking to a parrot that only says one phrase over and over again.

[Enjoy the hunt, Alexander.]

I shove the phone underneath my pillow and collapse back against the mattress. I don't understand Alexander at all. He's so keen to have sex with a vampire that he has zero compatibility with. Wasn't our first bonding attempt dreadful enough?

I've known him since I was a child. We've met regularly for feedings since we were twelve, and still, we have no genuine chemistry. Our interactions have always been heavily supervised, which may have hindered any possibility for an authentic connection.

But every time I suggest an activity where we could potentially dig deeper, I'm slapped with some rudimentary label like we're children: Nerd. Boring. Cold fish. Horse.

What am I supposed to do?

My phone dings loudly and I start. I don't want to look at it, but because I'm like a trained animal, I slip my hand underneath the pillow while I'm still on my back, take a deep breath and bring it to my face.

I smile. It's Aries.

[Good morning. Do you have some free time in your
schedule today?]

My body tingles as I stare at the screen and scoot upright. Speaking of chemistry, my nature sparks and warms from the simple thought of him—like an entire galaxy of shooting stars, fiery comets and illustrious moons suddenly reside within me.

[Good morning, I think I do. Why?]

[I've draped the muslin for your jacket, so I'd like to check
the fit.]

[Sure. What time works best for you?]

There's a pause on his end as I wait. After a moment, his response comes.

[Whatever time is best for you, your grace. You're the
busy one. I'm here to accommodate you.]

I'm almost put out by the formal title, but he adds a winking emoji at the end to soften it.

[Not busy. More like being held hostage. I'll let you know when I can plan my escape?]

[I look forward to it.]

My smile widens. Does he really? I'm not sure. He's just trying to do his job. I should let him and stop overcomplicating things. I'll definitely behave myself today.

~

"Holy shit—they do it without even asking?" I am definitely not behaving myself today.

Aries sits beside me on his stool again, stylish in a black-and-white paisley-patterned dress shirt layered underneath a royal-purple sweater. Dark ankle-length slacks. The epitome of elegant but eye-catching. Tasteful but bold.

He's threading the stitching along the shoulder of a jacket. "Sometimes. I had one stick her fingers into my hair when I was riding on a train in Beijing. Not all humans do this, but some absolutely take liberties. As if we're strange creatures that exist for their own amusement and curiosities."

Amazed, I fold my arms. "Humans seem strange to me. I'm interested in a lot of things, but I'm more afraid of them than anything else."

"They're not like that all the time," Aries says. "It depends on where you travel."

"Camille told me that you were in Italy before you came here?"

Aries had stuck the back end of the needle between his lips to fluff out the garment. He takes it out of his mouth. "Yes. I went to visit an old friend of mine in Milan."

"Oh? Under Giovanni Bianchi's realm?"

"Yes, although I've never met him. After my assignment in

New York is finished, I'll visit Japan to meet up with another friend."

"What is Japan like? I've always wanted to travel there."

Aries rests the jacket in his lap, considering. "Hm... you've asked a broad question. What stands out for me is that Japan has a lot of distinct sounds."

"Sounds?"

"Yes. Unique dings and bells assigned to menial, everyday tasks like entering a convenience store or stepping onto an elevator. Endless announcements—'The train will arrive soon' and 'There's a special sale on mackerel today' or 'Please don't forget your belongings.' And cheerful jingles *everywhere*. They ring out at pedestrian crosswalks, in electronics stores... through entire PA systems of some cities to mark the end of a workday. It's a very peaceful but melodious country where everything has its place. It's an interesting experience."

I try to imagine what he's describing. It's always quiet around me, so it's slightly difficult. "It sounds fascinating."

"It is. Call me clichéd, but springtime is the best."

"In what way?"

"Cherry blossom season," Aries says, smiling. Dramatically, he lifts a hand and swipes the air as if he's painting a fanciful picture with his palm. "In the spring, the landscape is inundated with cherry blossom trees. They're everywhere, clustered and floating blissfully like soft pink clouds. I can have a beer and bento underneath the ethereal canopy and the temperature outside is perfect. In some places, they light the trees up at night, so the blossoms practically glow.

"That's my favorite. Plus, the experience is fleeting. You might only get two solid weeks of bloom, so something in it feels enchanting. It's a beautiful reminder that one's life should not be taken for granted."

I haven't been there, obviously, but I know what he's talking about because I've seen images on the Internet (back when I had apps to do such dangerous things).

The scene appears in my mind—a dark blue sky set against rows of soft pink cherry blossom trees illuminated by white lanterns. I imagine the sound of the breeze interspersed with laughter. Petals swirling and falling, gently landing on blankets and shoulders.

This situation with Aries feels the same way. Fleeting. Something unique that I shouldn't take for granted. "It sounds wonderful," I tell him. "I wish I could experience it."

He stands with the jacket muslin, setting the needle and thread on the table. "Maybe you can, someday? You could have business there, or perhaps a vacation with your mate?"

I scrunch my nose, tapping into my fantasy mind. "Maybe by myself? And you and I can have a beer together in your favorite spot under the cherry blossoms, since I showed you my favorite hiding place near the lavender field?"

He raises an eyebrow. "I don't think that's a good idea."

"Why not?"

"You know why not, Oliver."

With my arms still folded, I look out the ivy-covered window. "I don't." Does he think I can't control myself? I haven't let my aura radiate at all since the banquet a week ago. I promised him that I would restrain my weird behaviors and I meant it.

"Come to the stage, please, so you can try this on in the mirror."

Standing up from the stool, I decide to stifle my irrational indignation about his not wanting to have a hypothetical beer with me. As I move, I try to reassure him. "You don't need to worry. Listen—I've got this under control."

After stepping up onto the stage, I turn and face him. He breathes out and I get a puff of jasmine directly in my face since we're suddenly the same height. The sensation makes me gasp.

"Have you considered that you're not the one I'm worried about?" He flashes a cool smile as he fluffs out the jacket once more.

A hopeful thought floats to the top of my consciousness. Is...

he worried about controlling himself? With *me*? I open my mouth to ask, but he lifts the jacket between us and cuts me off.

"Turn around, please?"

"S-sure..." I face the mirror, watching the reflection of him while he holds the jacket up. We're quiet as I slip my arms into it, but my heart thrums in my chest. I've been a blustering and ridiculous mess ever since I first laid eyes on him, but... does he find me attractive?

He's been polite, but largely unresponsive—like no part of his nature is even the slightest bit interested in mine. I'm assuming his kindness toward me is more out of pity than any actual attraction. Or more like he's being paid very well by Lord Blakeley, so he should humor his naïve and horny son.

With the mock jacket on, Aries caresses his palms across my shoulders, smoothing out the fabric. "What do we think?" he asks, his tone businesslike as he slides his hands down my arms. "Is the fit comfortable? Too snug?"

The heat of my nature swirls inside my belly. I take a breath to stifle it, but I can already feel the warmth behind my eyes. "I-it's fine. I'm comfortable."

In the mirror's reflection, he winks, running his hand down my back to flatten the material and simultaneously exerting a gentle pressure down my spine. He pulls at the hem. "You don't care."

"I do! But I..." It's over. I've successfully managed to stifle my aura, but my eyes have alighted. I close them and sigh. Humiliating.

"Turn for me?" Aries asks, taking a step back.

Reluctantly, I turn, then slowly open my eyes. I look away. "Sorry."

"Did you not *just* tell me two minutes ago that you had this under control?"

"Well... two minutes ago, I did."

His smile is amused as he steps into me and adjusts the collar.

My pulse rings in my ears from his closeness and scent. From the wry upturn of his beautiful lips.

"Learning to suppress the burn behind your irises takes time," he says with his voice low. "You're very young, Oliver. You don't need to be sorry."

"I'm not 'very young.' I'm twenty-two—I'm of bonding age." Internally, I cringe because defending myself only makes me sound more immature.

Aries chuckles through his nose while tugging and adjusting the fabric. "You seem to forget that I'm first-generation—and that I'm almost five times your age."

"I haven't forgotten, but... I already told you that rank doesn't matter to me. And you're not even a hundred." I wait, but Aries doesn't say anything as he examines the jacket, as if the conversation is finished. "You've learned to suppress your eyes alighting?" I ask, because I don't want this exchange to end.

"I have," he confirms. "Because I'm old."

"You are not." He isn't old. By vampire standards, we don't even register as properly mature until we're one hundred. "Old" vampires have been alive for at least two and a half centuries. His countenance and demeanor are nothing like that, so I assume his point is that he's old in juxtaposition to me.

I disagree.

"We're both young," I protest. "Just... you're farther ahead of me on the young scale. You've been young longer."

"Oh my," he laughs. "I've never heard an interpretation quite like that before."

"Plus, you're well-traveled and I've never left Eden. You have an unfair advantage." Undeniably, Aries carries himself with the confidence of someone who knows how to navigate the world. It's obvious that he's proficient in engaging with people from all walks of life—kings and queens of entire nations. Artists, servants and skilled tradespeople alike.

I imagine that he's like a charming chameleon. Always

changing his colors and fitting in perfectly regardless of his surroundings.

Aries pauses and stands straight. His dark brows are crinkled. "What are you making a case for, exactly? What's your intention with this argument?"

That makes me flounder, because my intention is quite obvious as I stand here—debating that the difference in our age is irrelevant to me while I simultaneously stare at him with my irises burning. "I-I don't... I'm not sure." Such a train-wreck.

"Right." Aries tilts his head. "You do seem easily sparked? What have I done to warrant this lovely response? I'm just standing here."

"You're rubbing your hands all over me."

"I was smoothing out the fabric."

"Semantics."

We both laugh in a hushed, breathy sound in the quiet room. This conversation is making me feel a little brazen. My feelings are undeniably exposed in my glowing eyes, so I... I decide to ask the question.

"Aries, do you... Am I appealing to you, at all?" The question slips out, almost like a whisper. Once I've said it, I fold my lips together in regret—as if I didn't mean to let the words escape and I should try to take them back.

"Does it matter?" he asks quietly. "Given the circumstance."

"It does," I decide. "It matters a great deal to me... I would like to know how you feel." He's even more handsome up close like this. I let my gaze fall to the fullness of his lips, perfectly framed by his neat beard. I catch myself when his mouth quirks up into another beautiful smile.

"Yes," he admits freely. "Your scent is exceptionally fragrant to my senses. And you're dangerously endearing."

"That... that's not terrible, right? A little oxymoronic but..." I take another breath to quell the heat behind my eyes. It doesn't work. Everything inside of me feels as if it wants to pop like a fire-cracker.

I suck in my bottom lip and look away, but then he reaches, slipping his palms into mine so that our hands are clasped between us. He squeezes and I grip him back. His hands are warm. Firm but also soft, somehow.

"What do you want from me, Oliver?"

I shake my head. "I don't want anything—"

"Your behavior toward me keeps suggesting otherwise."

"Then just ignore my behavior. I don't have experience with anything because I rarely leave the estate, so I'm not good at controlling my nature... I'm alright. I promise." I don't want him to feel obligated, or like I'm pushing him.

There's a pause where the light of the room shifts behind the glowing ivy draping the window. It darkens, likely from a passing cloud.

"What if... I don't ignore you, and you're honest with me about what you want?"

He pulls, just the gentlest tug, and it makes our foreheads touch. Skin to skin. The fragrant heat of him consumes me, and my whole body feels as if it's on fire. God. I don't even know how to tell him or what to say, but...

"Wh-what can I have?" I whisper, lifting my head a little to see him. He smirks in that way where I know he's pleased with something I've said. I haven't known Aries long, but I notice his different smiles. The varying depths and intentions behind them.

Aries brushes his nose into me. My heart is so light that I might fly away—just levitate right up and off of this stage.

"Hm, I do like that answer," he whispers. "Very much. You make me nervous, Oliver Blakeley, but you keep surprising me. I'm not sure what to make of you."

"Why do I make you nervous?" I ask, matching his hushed tone, completely absorbed in his presence and nearness. His earthy, delicious scent and the warmth and firmness of his hands. I close my glowing eyes and I can sense my nature bubbling and swelling with joy.

Aries tilts his head, then softly, his lips touch mine. My shoulders tense as I inhale. He pulls back, noting my hesitation and looking into my eyes. "No?"

"*Yes*, but... I don't know how to kiss." My palms clench his hands at the mortifying confession. "Well—it's like, I'm not good at it. Or anything like this, honestly."

I'm anxious as words like "cold fish," "nerd" and "stiff" slam to the forefront of my brain despite the rosy-pink cloud of desire and excitement I feel for this vampire.

I want to kiss him—to at least try—but I don't want him to be disappointed.

Aries lifts his hands to cradle my head, lacing his fingers in my hair with his thumbs cupping my ears. The heat of his palms against my skin is divine. "I don't believe you." He bumps my nose again. "Just... move with me, slowly. Taste me."

My cock stiffens at that. I would definitely, absolutely love to taste him. Every bit of him. Inside and out.

As I nod, he brings me to his mouth once more. His lips are parted as we connect, so I part mine a little as well. His are so full and soft, and they playfully dip between mine as he moves. My heart is in my throat and I'm insanely nervous, but I really like this. So much.

Carefully, I move with him, taking a chance and sliding my tongue forward to taste his bottom lip. The second time I do it, our tongues touch and it surprises me. I gasp, and when my mouth opens wider, he glides his tongue against mine and I swear my mind ascends to a higher plane of existence. The sensation is warm, wet and perfect.

My shoulders drop. I relax, and as I kiss him, I realize that he tastes like the woods. When the air is clean and I can smell the flowers floating on the breeze. He tastes like summer, sunshine and freedom. Lazy, peaceful days and reading in the shade. I don't know how, but all these sensations overwhelm me as I relax and our mouths dance in a new rhythm I've never known.

The movement and flow between us feels completely natural. Innate.

Aries's hands hold my head captive. The kiss is getting so deep that I'm losing my grip on my nature. It's swirling, telling me it wants to be free and radiate outward—to let this vampire know that we want him.

Only him. He is my choice.

My palms rest at his hips, and I want to slide them up his spine and truly let go, but he pulls away from the kiss. Breathless, surprised, my eyes are still burning like fire when I open them.

"You lied to me," he says, brushing his lips against mine. He tilts his head and kisses my cheek. "You're very good at this."

My heart pounds hard in my chest and my nature feels electrified. I can barely speak but I want to kiss him again. I want more. "I have been told otherwise."

"They were wrong." He lifts his head and stares into my eyes for a long moment. Watching. Examining.

Then, he sighs, blinking as if he's awakened from a dream as he steps back. "I should not do this with you. We can't do this."

Chapter Twelve

"**W**e can't do this."

The searing heat behind my irises fades out. The sudden seriousness in Aries's tone sobers my mind and body.

"Why?" The question comes out timidly. I'm not even sure what he means by "this." Kissing? Talking candidly and being alone together?

"Why?" he repeats, and there's an incredulous edge to his voice that makes me nervous. "Let's run down the list, shall we, my young lord? You're an Eden purebred—engaged to be married to a literal prince in less than a month. And yet, your eyes keep alighting for me. You are discreetly seducing me even though, by all accounts, I am 'beneath' you and there's no future between us. There's no chance for anything other than a quick thrill before your wedding day. Is that what you want from me?"

The dark, twisted miasma of shame coils itself around my ribcage and slinks into my throat, making it harder to breathe. How could I be so stupid?

I step back, shaking my head. "I'm not trying to—I'm so sorry I—"

"*No*, Oliver." Aries reaches out and takes hold of my wrists to pull me back into his space. His grip is firm as he looks into my eyes. "An apology isn't what I want. What I need is an honest conversation. Because if I give in to you... if I submit to the seduction of your nature, I'm the one who will be hurt in the long run. *I'm* the one who will suffer."

He breathes in, slowly working his jaw. "I have to decide if I'm comfortable with that."

The miasma is still there, waiting to jump in and tell me that I'm an idiot. That I'm undeserving and preposterous for even desiring Aries this way and somehow instigating this situation.

But I focus on his dark eyes staring back at me and the intensity there. The honesty. I keep the shame at bay because I want to understand. There's no time for it right now. Listening is more important. "What do you mean? Why would you suffer?"

Softly, Aries slips his palms into mine and clasps our hands. "You have no idea, do you? The impact that you can potentially have on me as a purebred..." He chuckles, as if he's beside himself. "Of course you don't. Why would you?"

"I don't understand," I say truthfully. This situation is uncomfortable. I'm anxious and something inside of me wants to run away from this moment and hide, but I won't. "Will you please explain what you mean?"

His expression relaxes as he examines me for several more beats—quietly contemplating in his familiar way. "Come here," he says. With one hand still clasped in mine, he pulls me from the stage and toward the bench just beside the dressing stand. When we're seated and holding hands, he shifts his body in my direction.

"As a purebred, you know that the allure of your aura is exceptionally powerful, yes? That your very being is steeped in the ancient and supernatural roots of our ancestors."

"Yes, I know," I confirm, focused on his words but also marveling at the warmth radiating between our clasped palms. The wonderful, electrified feeling racing up my arm.

"Your desire... that mesmerizing power within you swells outward and calls to me—especially as a first-generation vampire.

If I consent to your wishes, my purebred roots will cling to you. If I'm not careful, my biology might be forever altered by our encounter. I could develop an addictive need for your profound essence—to feel and be in the presence of it. Or worse, an insatiable thirst for your blood."

I listen, and it seems strange that I wouldn't already know this about myself. How the strength of my purebred lifeblood could alter another vampire's biology. That I could be addictive in nature. "I didn't know about this," I say. "But I would never use my power to manipulate or harm you."

Aries squeezes my palm. "I know that you wouldn't. I can feel it in the sweet warmth of your essence and when you kissed me. But the shift within my biology could happen naturally from being overexposed to you, romantically and intimately. I don't know where the line is, so it's a gamble for me. Especially since..." He pauses and lifts his free hand to run it through the back of his thick waves.

"Since what?" I prompt. Over and over, Aries grapples with these moments of internal conflict and I see them outwardly. Given the situation, he doesn't know how much he can trust me, or to what extent he should reveal himself and his inner thoughts.

I want to reassure him. "I won't repeat anything that's said between us, Aries. Please tell me?"

He drops his hand into his lap. "Thank you, but, surprisingly, that isn't my primary concern... I have never been romantically entangled with a purebred before. Nor have I been exposed to a purebred's raw essence—let alone tasted their blood."

Blinking, I sit straighter because I'm shocked by his confession. "Really?"

"Yes, really."

"But... how can that be?" Aries is a liberated vampire. Suave and well traveled. It's unfathomable to me that I would be his first anything.

"Because it simply is," he says. "My chosen mate before I came of age was also first-generation. Once I was released from that commitment, I exclusively engaged with my own kind because, well... purebreds are intoxicating to ranked vampires, but also dangerous.

"In my present state, I can feed from another first-gen vampire—second-gen or even third. Traveling as much as I do and without a dedicated mate or feeding source, having this breadth of options is essential to my health and autonomy.

"But if I'm romantically exposed to and hooked on a pure-bred's essence, my palate will change. My body will crave that powerful essence and nothing else will satisfy me. Have I explained myself clearly?"

I nod. Both ends of the feeding spectrum are dangerous for him. Purebreds are so potent that we're addictive. But human blood would undoubtedly make him sick, fragile and unable to day-walk. No ranked vampire can drink human blood and retain their health and vitality. I do know that much. Everyone does.

"You have," I confirm. "And... purebreds don't easily offer their blood, do they? In Eden, we have to sign business and marriage contracts before we exchange blood."

Aries chuckles. "Yes, you Eden vampires are, as usual, the most extreme with your cultural practices. However, even beyond your island, purebred blood is difficult to acquire and I... do not wish to be in that position. Being addicted to you but not having you. Constantly endeavoring to replace you and find my next fix."

He lifts our hands and kisses the top of my knuckles. His eyes flicker up and he grins. "You are lovely, though. An unforeseen and overwhelming temptation."

Me? A temptation? That's hard to believe.

I watch as he presses his lips to my hand once more, feeling a strange mix of heat, yearning and melancholy. Overall, though, I'm grateful. It's amazing that the two of us can have an open conversation about an important topic. It feels adult and honest. An overdue experience in my life.

It's as if I've entered a new dimension where I'm allowed to be forthright and curious. I don't need to feel apprehensive, because

I'll be met with compassion and patience. With genuine answers to my questions.

The castle and its stone walls encapsulate us. Everything has fallen silent. Hushed, as if only the two of us exist within this space. Within our own world.

I swallow, steeling myself and speaking slowly with an assurance and calm that feels new for me, but very good. "Earlier, you asked me what I wanted from you."

"I did."

"Well, I don't want to hurt you. I don't want you to be addicted to me or to suffer because of my selfish desires, but... is this okay? How we are now, speaking candidly. May I have this much? And I promise I won't release my aura in your presence again. I'll be careful to keep you safe."

Aries flips my hand within his and urges my palm open. I uncurl my fingers. He litters the lines and grooves with the softest kisses as he inhales. The sight and feel of him pushing his lips against my flesh over and over makes me squirm against the bench. Heat churns in my groin and up my spine. "Um, Aries?"

"Maybe," he says in between kisses.

"Maybe?"

"Mm. In spite of everything, I'm not sure how well I can behave myself when you are this clever, unassuming and sweet. Your ethereal eyes are the color of the Mediterranean Sea and you smell like something I want to devour. I should not indulge in this, and yet, you are the perfect storm, Oliver. As if you were uniquely cultivated for my undoing."

I suck in a breath, because a magnificent bloom occurs within me like a sudden burst of spring. Euphoria and delight. He thinks I'm clever? No one has ever said things like this to me before. Not in this way—laced with affection and desire.

Abruptly, he stops and lowers our hands so that they're clasped in the narrow space between our hips against the bench. He blows out a breath. "We'll get through this without any regrets, yes? We're on the same page now. We have an understanding?"

Nodding, I squeeze his hand. "Yes. Thank you for being honest with me."

I respect his concerns. They're paramount, and what right do I have to jeopardize his health and well-being? To potentially ruin the freedom and autonomy from which he thrives.

I understand his fears, but simultaneously, if he decided that he wanted me... I would not deny him. Deep inside, my nature tells me that it's impossible because he is my choice. I've made very few choices across the span of my life, but this one is irrefutable and I want to do everything with him.

Whatever he'll give me. Whatever is possible.

Later in the evening, Alexander sits beside me at another banquet. My father and all the other members of the hunt have returned, so we're celebrating and eating the game they've caught... which I find completely off-putting.

Alexander is strangely subdued as he talks quietly with his father. I'm not listening closely enough to hear what they're saying because eavesdropping feels a little rude. Regardless, I appreciate being left alone, because I'm able to retreat into my own mind. The sensation is like shrouding myself in a soft, insulated and fluffy cloud where I can replay the memories of Aries kissing me.

We *kissed*. I never thought I cared much for kissing, or any kind of physical intimacy. I've always felt a little like an island—a vampire isolated unto myself until forced to commingle with Mr. Perfect Purebred here beside me.

But kissing Aries was so... consuming. Hesitant, but deeply fulfilling. He didn't kiss me like Alexander does, like a wild animal that's found its first bit of flesh after scavenging across a winter tundra for months on end. Aries kissed me like a butterfly trying to find a safe place to land—gentle touches to my lips interspersed with curious slips of his tongue.

My skin tingled all over and felt hot. But *good*. It was exciting and inconceivable. I don't think he'd be willing to do that with me again, given everything he's worried about, but I'd really love to—

"Did you hear what I said?"

I glance to the side, meeting Alexander's golden-brown gaze. "No, sorry. What is it?"

He frowns. "You seem out of it today, my love. I said, I'm going to meet the designer tomorrow. What's his name? Eric or something?"

"It's Aries."

"Right. I'm getting my measurements done. Come with? Since there'll be a third person in the room, does that meet your guidelines for us spending time together?"

Playfully, he bats his eyelids. I don't want to be in the same room with Alexander and Aries. Like simultaneously having a nightmare and the sweetest dream. My head will probably explode.

"Well?" Alexander presses.

"Sure. What time?"

"After breakfast. We can walk over together?"

I nod. "Okay."

My senses spark like a match being struck. Intuitively, I look toward the entryway of the banquet hall. Speak of the angel. Aries is there, moving through the crowd toward his designated seat with the air and confidence of a king. He catches my eye like before, but I'm in control now, so when he winks at me—the tiniest blink of a gesture—I smile.

"What are you smiling about?"

I turn. Alexander is watching me yet again. Good lord. "It's nothing!"

"It's something." He grins, shifting his body and giving me his full attention. "You've been... I don't know, quiet? Content?

Ever since we got back earlier. Less prickly. What's making you smile?"

Helplessly, my face warms as I look forward. A heated flush splotches my cheeks and I don't know what to say. Alexander slides his hand over mine where it rests on my thigh underneath the table, making me jump.

"Are you finally warming up to this situation, Oliver? To me?"

I can't look at him. And I can't lie. I do lie, though. All the time. I'm always hiding my feelings and keeping my true thoughts hidden. Lies of omission. But I've been taught that those kinds of lies serve a greater purpose. For the good of society and responsibility.

Lying right now feels sinister, somehow. Cruel in an intentional way that I'm not accustomed to, because I'm hiding something tangible. Something selfish.

"Can... can we just eat dinner, please? People are watching us."

Alexander smirks. "Let them watch." He leans in and presses a quick kiss to my cheek. I'm put off by the spontaneity of it, but I try hard to fix my face and not let it show.

Alexander sees right through it. "Oh, he did *not* like that."

"Please don't do that," I tell him, my voice urgent but low. So humiliating.

"We have to try again in three weeks, Ollie. Get used to me already." He squeezes my hand, then lets it go. I want to reach up and wipe my cheek, but I don't.

Through the rest of dinner, I sit calmly, offering the expected and desired appearance of Alexander's submissive arm candy mate that he's explicitly chosen because he has the power to do so. That he happily litters with kisses and affection whenever he pleases.

I hate this.

∼

"Well, you certainly are as impressive as everyone says." Alexander steps off the dressing stage now that Aries has finished his measurements.

There was a scheduling mix-up. Alexander was supposed to have his measurements done before the hunting trip, but his handler overbooked him. Now, Aries is behind in making his suit.

"Vampire politicians and royals across Europe all sing your praises—you have quite the resume," Alexander discerns.

Aries walks over to the table with his notebook. "I've been fortunate, your grace," he says, sitting on the stool. "I'll have the muslin ready for you to try on by tomorrow evening following dinner."

"It doesn't seem like good fortune to me," Alexander quips while walking in my direction. A smirk suddenly appears on his lips. "It's raw talent. Being ridiculously tall and good-looking certainly doesn't hurt."

"You are too kind, my lord."

"May I ask a question?" Alexander says. "I'm genuinely curious about something."

Aries turns on his stool so that he's facing us. "Of course."

"What is it like being a contemporary vampire? Moving throughout the world unbonded and feeding from whoever suits you at the moment. Focusing on your career and travel and the like because you find the concept of mating to be old-fashioned. Or worse, oppressive. I don't quite get how feeding works with that kind of lifestyle. Seems risqué."

Alexander's candor is flippant and the air in the room stiffens. There's a subtle tension in Aries's shoulders. "I take excellent care of myself, your highness. And we have many resources at our disposal."

"Like what?" Alexander glances down at the bench where I'm sitting and confidently holds out his hand, as if the absolute expectation is that I will take it. I have the urge to smack it away, but that would be rude and more trouble than it's worth. Reluctantly, I take it.

"What are the resources?" Alexander goes on as I stand by his side. "If you don't mind my asking."

He has put Aries in an awkward position with these invasive questions. Now, we both observe Aries. Like an audience that's paid money to see a show, we're waiting for his answer. I think Alexander is being impolite, but there's also a part of me that's curious.

"There are expansive networks of individuals who live similar lifestyles," Aries explains. His tone is stiff, much more formal than the usual ease and playful tenor that I've grown accustomed to. "We establish connections and look out for each other, your grace."

"Ah, brilliant," Alexander says, then lifts a honey-blonde eyebrow. "Do you get your sex this way as well, like network orgies—"

"*Alexander.*" Everything inside me clenches from humiliation. "That is totally inappropriate."

This amuses Alexander, because he turns, grinning and pulling me toward the door. "Whoopsies—looks like I've upset my little mister. Later, Aries. Let me know when the stuff is ready?" He throws a hand up in casual thanks, then drags me out of the room.

I try to catch Aries's eye before I'm through the door, but his back is turned as he works at his table.

When we're walking along the curtain wall with arched windows, I look at Alexander. "Why did you ask him that? It made him uncomfortable."

Alexander shrugs, still holding my hand tightly. It's raining and damp today, so his palm is clammy against mine. We're surrounded by a blur of slate gray from the sky and stones, but also radiant green from the rain-soaked trees and brush.

"I asked because I wanted to know," he says. "Some friends told me about him—how he's turned down purebred aristocrats in Paris and Rome because he values his 'free lifestyle.' Because he doesn't want all his eggs in one basket, so to speak. I found it surprising because I'm the opposite, I guess? I love the stability in feeding from only you. Who wants to feed from a different fucking vampire all the time? Not knowing where your next sip is coming from. It sounds like a nightmare."

In all my fantasies about traveling the world and studying photography in exotic places, I have never once considered this.

Who would feed me? How would I logistically stay alive?

Alexander has been my feeding source ever since my skin hardened. And I've been his. For years, our feedings have been routine and sterile—conducted under the supervision of some older vampire, strictly via our hands, up until this past week when our formal mating festivities officially began.

He fed from my neck for the first time during our awful bonding attempt. I was so stressed and humiliated. I've tried to erase that entire event from my mind. Now, the only thing I remember is that he bit me hard. Like he was too excited. Careless and selfish, as always.

If I were free... if I got my wish and was able to escape this place, who would feed me? How would I manage that? I don't know, but I'd take the risk.

"You might think it's a nightmare," I tell him, "but it isn't any of your business—and he definitely has his own reasons." Aries values his lifestyle and doesn't want to be addicted to a purebred. He has to protect himself.

Alexander stops abruptly and yanks my arm backward. The action surprises me and I'm irritated by his curt manner. "What is it?"

We're standing still with the gray gloom pouring all around us. In a rare moment, his voice is serious. "How do you know he has reasons? Did you talk to him?"

"I—*No*, it just makes sense that he would—"

"And why do you care so much about this designer that you're defending him... Do you like him?"

My breath catches. I swallow hard and swiftly shake off the shock of his shrewd observation. I ignore the heat climbing up my neck. "It's not about caring—it's about common respect and decency. You barely know him, yet you burst onto the scene asking about his sex life. It's vulgar."

He surprises me again when he steps into my space. I try to step back but he uses our still clasped palms to urge me forward until he catches my face with his free hand. His gaze is hooded and his voice is low as he looks at me. "This is why I chose you, Oliver. Because I knew that you would make me a better vampire."

"Is that my job? Your life coach and therapist?" I lean my head away, but he slides his palm down and grips my chin with his fingers.

"I really love it when you speak your mind like this. No matter how many times they tell you not to, you always do. You can't help yourself." His gaze is sleepy as he shifts closer, as if he's in a trance. "And your pretty eyes and these lips. Kiss me?" he whispers, aiming for my mouth. "Please?"

I wrench my chin out of his fingers and turn my face to the side so that the kiss lands on my cheek. I know that I'm supposed to be submissive to Alexander's will. Lord Blakeley and practically *everyone* has instructed me to please him and "make him happy," but I... I just can't. And what's more, I find myself feeling increasingly resentful of this expectation.

Alexander pulls up and I look at him from the corners of my eyes. Scowling. He huffs through his nose. "You're so damn stubborn. What's the problem, Ollie? Why don't you like me? Most vampires like me!"

With my nose upturned, I look him over and speak my mind since he apparently loves that. "Why *should* I like you? What's fundamentally good about you?" He's a prince. He's wealthy and attractive. But so what? What else is there? He's also rude, patronizing and dismissive of any boundaries. Completely selfish.

There's an odd moment where he just stares, blinking. I'm waiting for him to call me a nerd, a horse or boring. Maybe some new insult that perfectly fits this particular circumstance.

But he doesn't. He steps forward, still holding my hand and tugging me along.

"That wasn't very nice," he says, trying to sound breezy, but something in his voice betrays him. "They're expecting us in the study for tea. Let's go."

I don't say anything as I follow, and he doesn't say anything else to me, either. Not through afternoon tea with both of our families, nor at dinner later that night. Not even during breakfast the next day. Aside from polite greetings, there are no words, no names, no insults. He's silent the entire time.

This behavior carries over into the next day. Through every scheduled event, he's quiet and focusing his attention on everyone else around us. Maybe I should be concerned about this?

To be honest, I'm not. It's a relief.

Chapter Thirteen

A week later, the grand ballroom is alive with energy, light and elegance. A fanciful cocoon of uppity vampires swathed in their very best attire. This is the first formal ball as part of our traditional mating rituals—another rung in the ladder of Eden's antiquated practices.

Chandeliers glow and sparkle overhead like moons within their own universe. Their crystal hangs in teardrop shapes that slowly turn, reflecting and throwing spectral light against every surface.

The marble flooring has been polished to within an inch of its life. The surface is creamy with swirling and ornate golden patterns that look like symbols from a forgotten era. Another time when language and expression were represented in elaborate encryptions instead of meager words.

It feels as if every vampire within the South Eden aristocracy is here. The wealthy ones, anyway. Village chancellors and mayors. Some Central Eden vamps are in attendance as well, like Alexander's group of friends—looking expensive and snobbishly huddled together along the edge of the dance floor.

Aries is here, too. Presently, he's dancing with some woman in a slinky champagne-colored dress. It is taking everything inside of me to not hate her immensely. My feelings are completely irrational, but I think she's spending more time with him in this moment than I have in the past week.

Every day my schedule has been jam-packed with breakfasts, luncheons and family meetings. Soirées held in mine and Alexander's honor and village tours. The only time I've seen Aries was when I went back with Alexander so that he could try on the mock jacket. Aries had pants for me to try on as well.

With Lord Blakeley always watching—his foreboding, steely eyes constantly assessing my every move—I've played the part of a well-behaved mannequin on Alexander's arm for seven days straight and I am *exhausted*. The pressure is crippling.

Every night I have collapsed into bed, grateful to finally be alone and without intense scrutiny. Some nights I fell asleep in my clothes because I didn't even have the energy to shower and change into my pajamas.

Tonight, if possible, I want to dance with Aries. I haven't been alone with him since we kissed and I just... It would be really, really nice to be in his presence. That's all. I know that I can't ask for more. I don't even deserve that much, but I would give anything to—

"Ollie, straighten out your face. You look miserable." Sasha bumps my side, surprising me. I shake my head, looking away from Aries and the woman on the dance floor and stifling my immense jealousy.

These wild feelings suddenly take root—curling and tangling like a vine climbing up a stone wall. Intense desire and the ache of an inscrutable longing deep within my nature. It's overpowering. After two decades of my vampiric essence being utterly dormant, I'm not accustomed to these raw reactions.

"I smuggled a second pack of film inside tonight—for the camera I gave you. Camille said she'd stick it underneath your bed."

"Sash, you didn't need to do that. I haven't even used the first set you've given me. I haven't taken the camera out of the box."

"What the hell are you waiting for? You've got double the film now, so get cracking. Don't let Lord Heartless crush your creative spirit. Shall we dance?"

"Yes, alright."

Sasha takes my hand and pulls me onto the dance floor underneath the radiant lights. She leads, expertly guiding and spinning me until I smile helplessly. Until we're both laughing and breathless from the inherent jubilation that dancing brings. Her flared pants swish and my jacket flies with our movement—a tornado of fabric and color.

By the end of the up-tempo song, we're panting and grinning. I look around, narrowing my senses on the singular vampiric essence that deeply stirs me. The aura that I crave. I see him walking off the dance floor and passing a small group of vamps just as he dips out of sight and beyond a side entrance.

Intrinsically, I step in the direction of the door he's disappeared through. But I'm thwarted when a hand wraps firmly around my wrist, halting my progress.

"Did the two of you have fun?" Alexander asks, smiling as he holds on to me tightly. "May I have this next dance?"

"Haven't you already danced with him four times?" Sasha asks, her eyebrow raised in assessment. "Can't he dance with someone else, if he wants?"

"He can dance with whomever he pleases, but it can't be helped if my love for him is insatiable." Alexander winks as he pulls me away from Sasha and further onto the dance floor.

When we're in the thick of the crowd, he squares himself in front of me and lifts his hands, making it clear that he intends to lead yet again. Sighing, I take my position.

Alexander has been on his best "I'm a perfect and wholesome purebred prince" behavior this past week, too. He's so breezy and amicable at times with his sunshine-blonde hair and bright eyes that I physically feel myself shrinking in his shadow. As if I'm being crushed under the moral weight of his having everything he could ever want in his life and my having absolutely nothing.

"Your face looked different a second ago, when you were dancing with your sister," he observes, guiding us in a slow-tempo waltz. Everyone on the floor moves with the same flow and rhythmic pace, like the second hand of an oversized clock. "I'm jealous. Why can't I have that smile?"

"Because... my relationship with Sasha is different than my relationship with you. Why would I act the same way with you?"

"But we've grown up together, Ollie. Things have been strained because of all the strict rules, but we've known each other for a long time. You can't even manage a smile for me? Am I so horrible?"

"I never said you were horrible—"

"Then what is it? Tell me." Alexander swoops me around. I'm not expecting it, so I lose my footing and clumsily trip. He thinks this is funny, because he laughs.

His spontaneous movement, his statements and his affable demeanor suddenly irritate me. He always irritates me, so I tell him as much.

"Yes, we've known each other for a long time. But you haven't been nice."

"Haven't I?" He smiles. He's constantly grinning like this. Supercilious and teasing, like everything about me is a joke. Nothing I say matters.

"You're condescending. You belittle the things I like and you call me a nerd, short and a horse."

"I've never called you *short*," he interjects, chuckling. "I believe I said you weren't very tall, which isn't a lie."

"You tell me I'm uptight and that I need to relax, and yet you pressure me about sex all the time. Bursting into my room without being invited and trying to kiss me—always *touching* me."

For once, Alexander doesn't hit me with a quick rebuttal. We've stopped moving, like the center cog of the clock face while all the vampires dance and twirl around us.

I swallow hard, steeling myself. "It's shit and it's exhausting.

All of it, and I wish you and Lord Blakeley—*everyone*—would just leave me alone and let me breathe," I vent, feeling all the frustration and asphyxiated tension of the past week stuffed inside of my chest like swollen cotton.

Alexander stares with his mouth agape. His brow is creased in confusion. "I'm... I am not belittling you—"

"You are."

"No, I'm only teasing you! Ollie, I just want you to let your guard down. I want you to relax."

"Well, you're not funny and I'm far from relaxed."

My chest heaves as the music stops. The crowd awakens, disillusioned from their musical reverie, and slowly, they turn to watch us. Alexander smoothly bows, a polite show of respect given our sudden audience. "We'll talk about this later." He stands straight, then stalks off the dance floor without a word or second glance.

With us separated, the crowd carries on mixing, socializing and dancing of their own accord. Someone offers their hand for a dance, but I graciously turn them down as I leave the floor. I'm not sure if Alexander will tell Lord Blakeley about this—if my outburst will come back to bite me in the worst possible way.

Right now, I don't care. I've had enough of both of them, and my mind is singularly focused on the subtle vibration of Aries's energy. I exit the ballroom and enter the hallway.

The corridor is lined with elaborate sconces flickering and casting the space in yellow firelight. I receive a few polite bows as I move—vampires halting their conversations to offer a formal greeting. Desperately, my sincerest wish is that everyone would leave me alone.

"Your grace, what are you doing?"

Just as I turn down a narrow, darkened hallway, my father's primary manservant, Hudson, appears before me in his formal coattails and bow tie. "Why are you over here and alone?" he asks.

I start, taking a step back and remembering our encounter

two weeks ago. The room raid. "Hi, Hudson. I just wanted to take a walk... if that's alright?"

My resolve to find Aries weakens now that I'm faced with Hudson's stature and air of authority. In the past, he's always been kind to me. I've even visited his home with the viscount. When Hudson's son was born prematurely, I took his mate, Ji-Ahn, a bouquet of wildflowers.

But somehow, the start of this mating ritual and Lord Blakeley's tightening of the reins has strained our interaction. I don't know how to read him anymore.

"Of course, your grace. Please let me know if there's anything you need."

"S-sure. But I'm fine, thank you."

Hudson bows, then strides past me, not looking back as he heads toward the main ballroom.

When he's out of sight, I carry on toward the western library, an obsolete room full of outdated books that only a proper vampire Historian would likely appreciate. Why is Aries over here?

My footfalls are absorbed by the thick burgundy ornamental rug lining the hallway. The color is deep and time-worn, like fallen apples rotting underneath a tree. Ahead, the study has two large doors with intricate moldings carved in swirling trefoil patterns.

When I'm close, Aries's honey-dripped voice carries into the hall because one of the doors is ajar.

"My plan is to come straight there after this project is completed."

Outside, I lean closer to the crack, trying to listen. The door swings open and I jump, startled and blinking. Aries is there with his phone pressed to his ear.

"Yes, I think that's a fantastic idea. I have connections with a distributor in Budapest who might be able to help us. I'll give her a call tomorrow?" He steps aside, gesturing for me to enter. Sheepish, I slink over the threshold.

He closes the door, then wanders over to the heavy oak desk at the center of the room, carrying on with his conversation. "Of course. I'll let you know the result. Thank you again for the kind invitation. I do appreciate it." He sits on the edge, casually crossing one ankle over the other.

I wander, because I haven't been inside this room since I was ten. I'm taller now, but everything in here still feels massive. The heavy antique furniture, the bookcases lining the wall with their sturdy ten-foot ladders. This is one of the rooms that have been largely neglected because of our meager financial situation. Sasha calls us "castle poor."

The window behind Aries is huge—stained glass with our family crest designed in a weirdly evangelical style. Each panel of glass is its own distinct color, but in the night and with the moon full and high, they all glow, spilling rich, multicolored lights over Aries's wavy head and square shoulders. He looks like a fallen angel.

"Are you stalking me, young master?" Aries pulls at the satin lapel of his navy-blue jacket, which emphasizes the rich hue of his eyes. The inside fabric is silky, shiny and swirling with color—deep purple, green and gold, like the feathers of a male peacock.

As he slips his phone into a discreet pocket, I have a revelation. The outside of the jacket feels like the polite façade he exudes for us boring vampires in our antiquated aristocracy. But the inside is the real Aries. The drama, flare and confidence.

"Yes," I admit, stepping forward. "Please, just say my name?" God, I want him. My nature pulses and burns inside, both fiercely desiring and envious. Vexed but also ravenous. I want him, but I can't indulge and satiate my being.

Why does he deny me? it asks in a fervent, increasingly familiar whisper. *He is my choice.*

As I approach, Aries uncrosses his ankles and bends his knees. He rests his palms on the edge of the desk, leaning back and eyeing me seductively. "And if I don't? What will you do?"

I stop just outside of his gapped thighs. "I... I don't know." He's teasing me, but what could I possibly do?

He smiles. "Come here, please?"

Breathing, I step in between his knees and timidly slide my fingertips against his thighs. The fabric feels smooth and expensive. It makes my mind wander, thinking about how nice it would be to peel these pants off of him. Thoughts I've never entertained about another vampire.

Aries tilts his head. "Why are you following me?" His voice is low. Playful and sexy in a way that makes my groin ache.

"Because I haven't seen you this past week. I've missed talking to you."

"Is that all?" he asks.

Biting the inside of my lip, I hesitate, then decide to tell the truth. "And because I like you."

He closes the space between us and leans in, brushing our noses. My breathing hitches and my heart races. "Do you?" he whispers.

"Yes... very much." A trance-like state floods my mind as I close my eyes and boldly press into his lips. Needing to kiss him. I have to, because the urge is compelling, like the pull of a magnetic field. His palms are warm when he brings them up to hold my head.

Slowly, his fingers thread into the back of my hair as he parts his lips. The movement of our mouths fused together is easy this time, and the wet slip and sweetness of his tongue makes me light-headed. Lithe.

With this kiss, he could undress and lay me down, then have me in any way that he desired. I wouldn't object and I'd be forever grateful.

Aries lifts, gently, but the sensation is like being disconnected from the heat and pleasure of the sun. "You're unhappy here," he says. A statement. Not a question.

I smile weakly. "'Unhappy' is putting it nicely."

"You disagree with the way Eden operates. You reject this marriage, and yet, you remain compliant within this system. Why do you stay?"

His questions clear the sensual haze clouding my brain and body. I stand straighter. "I'm... not sure that I'm 'compliant,' necessarily."

"Then what would you call it? Is kissing me behind closed doors a satisfying act of rebellion—"

"*No.* It's not—It isn't like that."

"Do you know what I want for you?" Aries asks, settling back against his palms once more. "I want you to be free of this place. To live, explore and discover. I want you to step into the fullness of who you are and your power—unbound by precepts and anachronistic conventions. Confident in your truth and liberated from beneath the weight of your father's shadow."

My throat tightens as I curl my fingers against his thighs. "I want those things, too."

He leans forward as if he's about to kiss me again. I inhale sharply as he sweeps past my face and his lips brush my cheek. Aries's voice is as firm and deliberate as stone. "So, *what will you do?*"

"What can I do?" I ask, pulling away. "Logistically, I don't have any money or resources—I don't even know if I have a passport to leave Eden. And if I tried to run away, I... I can't..." My entire body shivers at the thought. Thomas tried to run away once. He tried, but it did not go well for him.

At all.

"It would be difficult to leave," Aries continues in my disturbed silence. "But isn't it harder to be complicit in this pageantry? Why have you let Alexander drag you across the ballroom all night, when it is clear to anyone with eyes that you are not enjoying yourself?"

"What do you mean by why have I *let* him? You're saying that this circumstance is my fault?"

"No." He leans forward, capturing my wrists in his palms. "That is not what I'm saying. Of course your circumstance has been fabricated by those around you—however, you don't need to make the execution of their agenda this easy for them, Oliver.

You have been bold and forthcoming with me. Why not be bold toward them?"

The ethereal light pouring in from the stained glass behind Aries encapsulates us as we watch each other in silence. My temples pound as the familiar, suffocating weight of humiliation bears down on my shoulders.

How must I look to Aries? Me, having my electronics and phone taken away. Alexander dragging me around tonight as if I'm his personal rag-doll. And then I have the nerve to follow Aries's essence across the estate, sniffing behind him like a lost puppy.

To someone like him—a free, contemporary vampire teeming with verve and confidence—I must... I probably look like an idiot. Like a silly and obedient fool.

"You say that you dream of freedom," Aries says, holding on to my wrists and looking into my eyes. "So *do* something, anything besides everything that they want. Simply try speaking your mind? Voicing your sincere desires or—"

Stepping back, I twist my wrists free from Aries's grip. A stark moment of tension sits between us before I shake my head. I can't breathe. "I'm sorry."

"Why are you apologizing?"

"I-I don't know... I should go back, I think." The embarrassment throbs like a wound in my chest. Suddenly, I feel so painfully pathetic and the darkness of it floods my being. Turning, I head toward the door because I can't face him anymore. What the hell have I been thinking?

"*Oliver.*"

Breathless, the familiar panic carries me forward and accelerates my steps. But the moment I wrap my hand around the doorknob, Aries collides into my back, enveloping me with his solidity, heat and fragrance and stopping my movement.

"Why are you running away from me?"

"Because I—I don't know!" My body trembles with shame. The heat of it flashes in my face, making tears well up in my eyes as I clench them shut. God. Before this moment, I don't think I've ever cried over anything in my life. When you're numb and raised to be a purebred robot, what is there to cry about?

My hand is gripped around the doorknob and I just want to escape. It's like when my eyes alighted that first time and I didn't want to face him.

Aries wraps his arms around my waist to hold me even tighter. His lips brush my ear. "Don't run away. Please talk to me?"

He waits, embracing me until my pulse slows. It's as if I'm being hypnotized by his nearness. His earthen, sweet scent is a narcotic, morphing my anxiety inside into a meditative calm.

I lose track of how long it takes, but eventually, I open my watery eyes and speak into the ambient silence. "I'm ashamed."

"Why?"

"Because I'm *always* ashamed. I always feel embarrassed, out of place and uncomfortable, and I don't know why I do what they say. I... I don't want my life to be like this, but I'm afraid, Aries! It's easier to be bold with you because you give me the space to do so. You don't make me feel like a bug you'll squash the second I speak my mind—the way Lord Blakeley has my entire life."

I take a deep breath before I go on. The words spill out like an exorcism of all my fears and doubts. "And how could I possibly survive if I ran away? What would happen if I refused to play along with this ridiculous charade? I'm so... *weak*. I complain, but I'm too scared to actually do something about it."

For a long moment, Aries doesn't say anything, and I'm glad. Admitting all of this aloud is strangely cathartic. I dream of being free, but I'm also afraid of the cost and consequences. I hate myself for that.

"I know what I am," I whisper. Aries snakes his arms around my waist a little tighter, melding his chest to my spine. "I'm just a silly, obedient poodle for Lord Blakeley and Alexander to fling around. Everyone knows and I don't usually care, but... I don't want you to see me that way."

"None of what you've just said even remotely describes how I see you, because you are none of those things, Oliver."

He's being kind, because this is who Aries is. "Then what am I?" I ask. Maybe I want him to prove me wrong?

"In my eyes, you are deeply intuitive and thoughtful. You are an intelligent and creative vampire who's been suppressed and told that you have no power, and that your desires are invalid. This manipulation is wrong. They have intimidated you to the point where you believe these falsehoods about yourself. They are lies, darling. None of it is true."

Dropping my hand from the doorknob, I wrap my arms around Aries's as he holds me. I want to believe him, and maybe deep down, I know that he's right. He's helping to unearth some irrefutable truth that's been buried under layers of shame, confusion and frustration.

"Why a poodle?" Aries asks suddenly. "Why that animal, specifically?"

"Sasha jokes that I'm Lord Blakeley's golden poodle. Alexander calls me a horse... among other things."

"Lies. Ridiculous lies."

He feels... *good*, behind me like this. Solid and powerful. My thoughts are like a snake slithering down into a hole and my nature is writhing around, licentious and warm. Demanding things and conjuring lurid images that I've never thought about or desired before.

Taking control of these wanton sensations, I wipe my face and turn within his arms. He gives me space as I rest with my back against the door and take a breath. "Believe it or not, I didn't follow you in here to have a mental breakdown. That wasn't my plan."

Aries grins, leaning with his palms flattened on either side of my shoulders. "I don't think anyone ever 'plans' to have a mental breakdown. They are impulsive events, by nature?"

"Right..." I say, chuckling. Lowering my head, I stare at the beautiful, satiny pattern inside of his jacket, then reach out to touch and pinch it with my fingertips. "I love this."

"Do you?"

I nod. "Yes. It's unexpected and... gallant? Classy. It's very you."

"Thank you, darling."

Grinning, I drop my hand. I also love that he's called me this twice. "I came in here because I wanted to dance with you. You've been dancing with other vampires all night. I was hoping you would ask me."

"Why haven't you asked me? If that's what you want?"

I don't say it aloud, but I was scared to ask him. Afraid of what Alexander would think or say, or maybe worried about Lord Blakeley's reaction. I lift my head and meet Aries's midnight-blue eyes. "Would you please dance with me?"

"In here? Or out there?" he asks, smiling playfully. "There's no music here, your grace."

"Out there, please? I would like to dance with you properly."

He leans, barely touching his nose to mine, and I instinctively close my eyes and part my lips. I inhale his scent but he only whispers.

"It would be my honor." He tilts and kisses me. Graciously connecting me once more to the energy source before we leave the room.

Chapter Fourteen

Aries and I walk arm in arm from the study, through the hall and back into the lavish ballroom soaked in creamy marble, shimmering gold and flecks of chandelier light.

Vampires turn and stare as we walk, watching our every move. My body trembles from fear—from the attention and potential rebuke from Lord Blakeley.

Outwardly, I haven't done anything wrong. By all accounts, I've simply asked one of our esteemed guests to dance with me.

But I've been surreptitiously trained to *not* take initiative. No one has told me directly that I shouldn't, but every time I have, I've been rebuked or punished in some way. So, in my head, I'm anxiously anticipating being admonished because I've dared to think for myself.

"Are you well, your grace?"

I glance up at Aries and his beautiful eyes are full of concern. Silent compassion. A flush of heat brightens my face and neck, but I push past it and guide him onto the dance floor.

"I'm okay." I am not. But I take a deep breath and decidedly ignore all of the eyes burrowing into us. I don't need to look around because I can feel them. "Will you dance with me?"

"Of course." Aries offers a polite bow. I'm waiting for him to lift his hands to lead, but he doesn't. So, we just stand there. Awkwardly.

"Um... aren't you leading?" I ask, confused.

"Well," he considers, raising an eyebrow, "you asked me to dance, so I assumed you would lead? Are you capable?"

Surprised, I chuckle. Of course I know how to lead, but no one ever expects me to. No one ever lets me. Not even Sasha. Whether it's because I'm shorter than they are or they think I'm a lapdog, I'm not sure.

Straightening my spine, I lift my arms to lead us. I don't feel particularly confident and Aries is so tall... Honestly, this is a little ridiculous, but I smile. As he takes my hands, he's grinning too. The moment we're connected, I guide him in the step, smoothly spiraling us into the current of the dance floor.

Aries follows my lead perfectly and I watch carefully as I guide him, making sure we don't crash into anyone or step on any toes. The musical piece emanating from the quartet is lively and energetic—more like a trot than a proper waltz.

But Aries and I rise to the occasion, moving with the melody as if we're birds soaring over a complex cityscape. My anxiety and fear dissolve and are replaced by the sheer excitement of having this handsome vampire in my arms.

Feeling audacious, I guide him into a turn, and the result is hilarious. He ducks down, folding himself under my arm like he's bending to avoid a head-on collision with a low-hanging tree branch. The motion makes us both laugh out loud but we carry on, somehow even more elated. Swept away by our momentum and this fantastic dance.

The quartet slows the melody, fading out the hectic rhythm. When it finishes, my chest is heaving but every part of me is wildly satisfied. Like I've run a race and won.

Applause breaks out—loud and cheerful. I look up and realize that nearly everyone in the room is watching us. I blink, utterly taken aback.

Aries wears a broad smile as he bows deeply. "That was absolutely thrilling, your grace. You are an exquisite lead!"

"Ah—thank you, I…" It's unnerving, having this much attention. In the back of my mind, I feel certain that I'll be scolded for this later.

"Bravo." The sound of Alexander's voice causes my anxiety to return. He's approaching us with a smug expression. "I didn't know you could dance that way." He looks to Aries, shrugging one shoulder. "I'm jealous."

"Your highness." Aries offers a neat bow, breezing past his remark. "Are you enjoying yourself tonight?"

"Well, I would be enjoying myself more if Oliver danced with *me* like that. If he seemed even half as excited to be in my presence as he is in yours. You'll have to tell me your secrets."

"Here ye! Attention, everyone!" Hudson's voice booms like a cannon over the crowd as he stands atop the lifted stage toward the front of the ballroom. "Lord Blakeley will give his closing address for tonight's festivities."

Lord Blakeley raises a hand, gesturing for me and Alexander to meet him and the viscount on the stage. As Lord Blakeley talks, I stand behind him twisting my hands and feeling short of breath, waiting for him to condemn me in front of all these vampires.

But he doesn't. His speech is straightforward and packed full of the expected aristocracy fluff. He thanks everyone for attending and he's *thrilled* for our clan to be formally united with the vampires of Central Eden. Of course he is—not to mention the elevated social status and huge financial dowry that come along with it.

After everyone has received champagne, he asks them to lift their glasses in a toast to our union. When his speech is finished, the guests lazily sip their drinks and mill around. Party's over. I'm still standing on the stage beside the viscount and Alexander when Lord Blakeley suddenly turns.

"You're certainly full of energy tonight, aren't you?" He takes a sip from his champagne glass, regarding me. I don't know how to respond to his comment, so I lower my head.

"If it's alright, I'd like to escort Oliver back to his room?" Alexander addresses Lord Blakeley and the viscount, then looks at me. "Is that alright? Are you ready?"

"Y-yes..." This is it. The very thing that Aries spoke of earlier. My perpetual compliance. How I make it easy for them to push me around.

Truthfully, I'd like to stay longer—to find Sasha and talk with her a bit more. Maybe... I could tell her about my conversation with Aries tonight and how I feel. I wonder if she would support me, or if she'd tell me that I was being an immature and selfish brat.

My throat is tight, so the words come out strained. "Well—no, actually, I... I'd like to find Sasha and talk to her if—"

"Talk to Sasha another time," Lord Blakeley commands, turning away. "Go with Alexander. You should be spending time with your *fiancé*, not causing a scene on the dance floor like some cheap and tactless entertainer."

"Charles, please..." The viscount's pale eyes shift nervously between me and Alexander. Lord Blakeley walks away, incontestably finished with this conversation. "Have a lovely night, you two," the viscount goes on, then follows his mate down the marble steps and into the crowd.

"Why do you need to talk to Sasha?" Alexander asks quietly. "Is it important sibling stuff?"

I sigh, defeated. "No. It's okay."

Did I deserve that? Is dancing with someone and actually having fun so detestable?

I walk toward the same steps that the viscount and Lord Blakeley just descended. Alexander follows. We leave the busy hall and head toward my wing of the estate.

The entire way, Alexander is silent. He doesn't try to hold my hand or link our arms. No touching at all. I'm glad about this, but admittedly, it's strange. In the way that I've grown accustomed to walking with a pebble in my shoe, but suddenly it's not there anymore.

Since it's quiet, I replay the evening in my mind. Primarily, the moments that involved Aries. Our conversation in the old study, my unexpected tears and then our lively dance.

It's incredible to experience a vast range of emotions and in such a short period of time. And to express them with someone who simply accepts them all. Whether I'm ashamed or insecure, blatantly horny and frisky with my eyes alighting, or having an emotional breakdown, Aries is stable like a rock. Patient and accepting me through all of my mess.

Once we've climbed the stone steps and are standing outside of my room, I turn to Alexander and offer a polite bow. "Thank you for escorting me here."

"You're welcome," he says. I'm waiting for him to make a plea to enter my room or say something rude. But he places his hands in his pockets and shifts his gaze toward the slim window set in the stone wall beside us. "Can I be clear about something?"

Here it comes. "What is it?"

His golden-brown eyes glint in the narrow stream of moonlight and meet mine. "About what you said earlier, after our last dance. I'm sorry that I've been unkind to you. Thank you for being honest with me."

We stare at each other in the warm darkness. I honestly don't know what to say.

"Good night." He turns and stalks toward the steps, but then pauses. "Next time we dance, will you lead, please?"

I nod. "Sure."

"I'll look forward to it. And your father was wrong, by the way. You didn't look like cheap entertainment. Not at all." He disappears around the corner. His footfalls echo softly as he descends the stairs.

Well... alright. That was different.

With Alexander gone, I enter the calming space of my room. Camille has been here, because my comforter is turned town and the oil lantern sitting atop my nightstand burns and flickers. This, in combination with the natural moonlight glowing through the square windows, creates a soothing ambience.

I take a long hot shower, luxuriating in the heat and solitude. When I'm finished, I'm emotionally tired but not physically. I need a mental distraction, so I get on all fours and peek underneath my bed.

Carefully, I pull out the boxes that Sasha gave me. Once I have the instant camera and film set beside me on the floor, I sit with my legs folded and open everything up.

I haven't been able to lose myself in nerdy camera things for weeks, not since Lord Blakeley had all of my equipment confiscated. Opening the boxes, I feel like a starved vampire who's been given a tiny vial of blood. Like an artist whose elaborate paint brushes have been stolen and replaced with a box of colored pencils.

After reading through the instructions to ensure that I don't make any mistakes, I load the film into the small hybrid camera. I'm flipping it over in my palms when I register Aries. Not stopping at his room at the bottom of the steps but climbing toward mine.

Soon, he knocks.

"Come in." My nature twists in excitement as he peeks through the crack in the door.

"Hello," he says.

"Hi." I'm sitting with the camera rested in the gap of my folded legs.

"I was worried about you. May I come in?"

"Of course. Why were you worried?"

He steps inside, then gently closes the door. "Alexander made that derisive remark after our dance, and then you left with him immediately following the toast and your expression was disheartened. Is everything alright?"

"Everything is okay—much better, though, now that you're

here." It feels like there are shooting stars inside of me from his nearness.

"Are you flirting with me?" Aries asks, stalking across the floor with his long legs.

"Maybe?" I grin. "As best I can."

"What is this?"

"A hybrid camera from Sasha. It's digital and instant but in the neo-classic style. I can take miniature photos. It's not very serious as far as photography goes, but still fun."

"That's very thoughtful of her. Shall we try it out and take a photo together?" He sits beside me on the floor, stretching his legs out and crossing them at the ankle.

"Really?" I would never have thought to take a picture with Aries, but now that he's suggested it, I'm elated.

"Of course," he says, inching closer. "Is it ready to go?"

"It is, I added the batteries so it's just a matter of learning the framing." I flip the camera and hold my arm out so that the lens is facing us. I'm estimating, but I won't know until I try. "Can you shrink down to my height so I can make sure that I have you in the frame?"

Aries chuckles. "Not 'shrink down.' You have long legs, Oliver." He relaxes back and leans so that we're cheek to cheek as we stare into the camera. The scruff of his low, neatly manicured beard is a little coarse but warm against my face.

"Yeah, sure." I shake my head, disbelieving. Still, his comment creates a small rush of pleasure that makes me smile. I sit up a little taller. "Alright, on three. One, two, three." The light flashes, then quickly fades, and I hear the camera working, processing to print out the small photo.

When it's done, it's still creamy white, so I set it aside. "Let me try one more while we wait. Is that okay?" Sasha loaded me up with film, so I can afford to take some risks.

"It sure is." He leans close again, and this time I angle the camera up slightly higher above our heads instead of straight on.

"One, two, three—" The flash pops just as Aries surprises me and turns his face, sneakily kissing my cheek.

"I figured we should have some diversity in our shots?" he says, brushing his lips against my skin. "You smell heavenly, Oliver. So light and sweet." His affection and words intensify the stirring of my nature. It makes my clothes feel scratchy against my flesh.

The camera spits out another undeveloped print. I set it aside. "I don't know if you did it in time, so... we could do just one more, but intentionally?"

"Mmhm," he hums, lifting a hand and cupping the opposite side of my face as he kisses my jawline. "Whenever you're ready." He moves up to my ear, sweeping his nose there, and it tickles. My lower half writhes because I'm getting hard and his oak and jasmine essence is overwhelming. I bite my lip and snap another photo, having no idea if my framing is right. Frankly, I don't care anymore.

The flash dissolves. A gentle whirring and humming ensures that another image is being processed. As it works, I turn my head, face Aries and kiss him on the lips. When the processing stops, I snap another photo.

The flash fades once more. Aries lifts from my mouth and whispers, "Do you think we got it that time?"

I don't answer him because I set the camera down, tilt my head and press harder into his mouth. I wrap my arms around his shoulders, and in a fluid motion, he lifts and drags me into his lap as we kiss and breathe each other. Tasting and wrestling with our tongues.

Aries holds me tighter, gripping my hips and smashing me into his groin. I can feel that he's aroused, too, and it is... marvelous. Absolutely divine.

The kissing intensifies—deeper and with a ravenous hunger we've not mutually expressed up to this point. I think we've been careful and polite, but in this moment... something between us changes.

His grip loosens on my hips and he pulls away from the smoldering kiss. Leaning his head back against the edge of the mattress, he looks up at the ceiling and sighs. "I promise you that when I decided to come up here, I only wanted to make sure that you were alright. My intentions were altruistic."

"It's fine if they weren't." Since I can feel him aroused underneath me, I take a chance and gently rock my hips into him. Just to encourage this heat and friction because it feels really good.

Breathing and feeling him like this, my nature pulses heavily inside. It flows up my spine and makes my eyes alight. I don't fight it as they glow to life.

Aries inhales through his nose. His chest rises as he watches me, but then he grips my hips to stop my movement. When he swallows, I see his Adam's apple bob in his throat. "I should go."

"Are you sure?" I ask quietly. "You don't have to... I would control myself if you wanted to stay. I wouldn't expose you to my aura—"

"I know, Oliver. I know that your intentions are earnest, but I..." He shakes his head and swallows again. Concerned, I uncoil myself from atop his lap. Even though it pains me and my nature is throwing a tantrum.

"I understand," I say, settling on my knees at his side. "I'm sor—"

"Don't, please." He cups my face with his palm. "No apologizing. I kissed you first... two out of three times."

I chuckle. "Are we keeping score?"

"Mm. Because I'm undoubtedly the architect of my own ruin. I keep starting fires, but I'm afraid of being burned."

Sighing, comprehending, I lean forward and kiss him once more. Softly and just a touch. He closes his eyes, exhaling.

"Now the score is even?" I say, smiling. "Goodnight, Aries. Thank you for dancing with me tonight, and for making sure that I'm alright."

Slowly, he opens his deep-blue irises and meets my burning gaze. "You're welcome, my alluring and sweet young master. Very welcome indeed."

Chapter Fifteen

After spending so much time with Aries the night before—our stolen kisses in the study and then again in my bedroom, coupled with our lively dance in the ballroom—I ride on a lofty and untouchable emotional high throughout the next day.

Well, nearly untouchable.

My mood is being challenged, because today, I'm forced to be in the presence of Alexander's extended family. There are no outside dignitaries or aristocracy members, because this is our time to sit and connect as a new unit—the combined Blakeley and Kendrick Clans of South and Central Eden. Finally, after centuries of complaining, moaning and much gnashing of our fangs, we'll become a royal family.

Everyone is kind enough, except for one of Alexander's uncles, who keeps making subtle but spiteful remarks about me. I honestly have no idea why, but sure. Let's have *one more* vampire who pressures and disapproves of me.

In the evening, dinner is served in a room that's been recently renovated. Lord Blakeley had it updated for the specific purpose of this occasion so that we don't come across as complete paupers, I guess? The banquet table is long and rectangular, set formally with beautiful creamy-beige tablecloths and shining silverware that gleams against the dim light overhead. All around, thick candles are strategically placed in sconces, their flames softly dancing in the reflection of the floor-to-ceiling west-facing windows beside us.

It's twilight, so the glass serves as a showcase for the rolling hills and sunset like a portrait—a bright rust-golden ball of fire dipping below the deepening green. It turns the sky just about every subtle color within the reddish-orange spectrum.

I'm focused on these elements, because they're much nicer than this rigid dinner.

"Your grace, you allowed Oliver to attend a semester at Carrington Elm University, is that correct?" Alexander's needle-nosed uncle addresses Lord Blakeley. For the second son in a situation that has little to do with him, he talks a lot. As if he needs to insert himself into the conversation to make himself relevant.

"Not a full semester, but yes," Lord Blakeley says patiently. "I thought it would help to diversify his learning experience—to allow him access to different environments in preparation for this wonderful arrangement."

That single week at Carrington Elm was incredible. Without question, it is the most art-centered and international school within Eden. It's one of the few schools that allow vampires from all stations—purebred, ranked and even lower-ranked—to attend classes and study freely. I received my bachelor's degree in economics from a different school in the southwestern realm, and my education was largely remote.

I begged and pleaded with the viscount to let me experience on-campus life at Carrington Elm—just as a trial, because it was truly my dream school. To my great shock, he convinced Lord Blakeley to approve.

Every moment of every day, I was guarded by someone from the estate. I was never left to my own devices. Having this constant shadow made me an interloper among my peers. A social outsider bound by stiff rules and pageantry.

Still, being around vampires who were allowed to think, exist and discover, the way the air hummed with autonomy, promise and higher learning... I could feel that energy against my skin.

I made a mistake, though, by sneaking away from my guard one evening to attend a study group. Just once, I wanted to feel approachable and normal. A little bit free to participate in an academic discussion, or maybe make a friend.

I was only gone for an hour, but when my guard couldn't account for me, Lord Blakeley pulled the plug on my academic adventure. Ended. Because I snuck out to take part in a study group.

Not a wild party. Not even a date.

"Hm." Alexander's uncle smirks with his spoon hovering over his crème brulée. "Is this school where he learned to make radical, public statements about the way our aristocracy is run? Did they teach him how to post photographic condemnations online?"

Lord Blakeley waves a hand as if he's the epitome of contentment and indifference. This derisive remark is nothing. "It's in the past. Oliver has learned from his mistake and has turned all of his attention to making this union a success."

Alexander's uncle scowls at me from across the table, as if he's won some psychological battle. "It is a good thing," he says. "Those photos were such waste of time and energy. Ridiculous."

"You're wrong," I blurt. The room stills. Everyone pauses to watch me, but I don't care because I'm fuming—at Lord Blakeley, and at this needle-nosed purebred talking as if I'm not sitting here. And at *everyone*, constantly making decisions on my behalf and pushing me around.

"I've heard that my photos have ended up in newspapers across Europe and North America," I defend, keeping my tone calm and even. "My photographs helped to convey an important point about the disparities in our communities. They have merit."

For the past two and a half weeks, I've been smiling and nodding, laughing at stupid jokes and being polite because that's what's expected of me. I've been respectful and have played my part nicely, but this is too far. Don't I deserve some inkling of respect in return? Am I the only one that's expected to behave with civility?

The table is silent with everyone looking between Lord Blakeley, Alexander's uncle and me. I don't care, though. I take a bite of my dessert.

"How exactly have you heard this? Considering your current Internet restrictions." Lord Blakeley's voice is accusatory and loaded. Now, everyone's eyes are strictly on me. Oh, shit... how do I explain—

"I told him about it, your grace."

My head whips toward Alexander at my side. His eyes meet mine in a quick glance before he goes on. "I... just thought he should know what the result of his actions were."

"That's very kind of you, Alexander," his uncle says, lifting his chin. "But *someone* needs a lesson in respectfully addressing their elders. It is truly unfortunate. These very, very unpleasant manners won't be welcomed in Central Eden. Is this the norm for vampires raised in the southern realm?"

"It most certainly is not." Lord Blakeley wipes his mouth with his napkin. "Oliver, we no longer require your presence this evening. Apologize to the Duke of Ealing before taking your leave. Now."

Being dismissed is perfectly fine, because it means I can get the hell out of here. Standing, I offer a shallow bow. "My apologies." As I turn to walk away, Lord Blakeley calls out.

"Leave your phone." I look back and he taps the table with his fingers.

Everyone stares tensely. Unspeaking.

Sighing, I pull the phone from the pocket of my blazer, then walk over to place it beside him.

"You and I will talk later," he says.

Humiliating.

My face is hot the entire walk back to my wing of the castle.

Even after I've entered my room and locked the door behind me, I'm still fuming.

Why am I constantly being disregarded? As if nothing I say or think has value. I'm like an alien in a strange place, even though this is allegedly my "home." These vampires are supposed to be my family—the creatures who care most about me. But they don't care, do they? I'm insignificant to them... No. To my family, I'm just a docile puppet for their exploitation. Nothing more.

After I shower, I put on a robe and dump myself across the bed to just lie there, feeling lifeless. Camille has been in here, because my bed is turned down, and the oil lamp on my bedside table is lit, casting a soft glow in the otherwise dark room.

I flip onto my back, staring blankly at the high-beamed ceiling and feeling miserable.

But then I close my eyes and intentionally breathe in deeply. Searching. I can smell Aries close by and the sensation is like being thrown a life raft. Like a ray of sunshine and warmth caressing my skin on a cold, cloudy afternoon.

What I wouldn't give to be submersed in his presence. Something about him is so comforting in a way that I've never known. That I didn't know I needed until the day I saw him.

A light tapping on my door makes me jolt upright.

It's Aries.

Mechanically, I scoot to the edge of the bed, then walk over to the door. I open it and Aries is standing there—tall, handsome and casually dressed in light-colored chinos and a beautiful black sweater.

"Hey," I say quietly, looking him over.

"Hello, Camille said you'd be out until late this evening and with your family?"

"I was dismissed. Is something wrong?"

"Not at all. She asked that I leave your suit in your closet when it was ready for you to try on again. There's still some detailed fitting to be done, but... I didn't expect you to be here."

I step back, opening the door wider. "Sorry. You can come in. It's fine."

He raises an eyebrow as he moves past me. "There's that word again."

"Ah, right." Lifting my hand, I rub it into my still damp hair. It suddenly occurs to me that I'm only wearing a bath robe.

Initially, there's a flash of panic, but then... my feelings mix and blur. Worry, messily tangled with heat, wanting and arousal. I'm naked underneath this singular swath of material. Just one layer between my flesh and his body. Easy access.

"Did the evening end early?" Aries asks, unaware of my horny state as he walks into my closet with a garment bag draped over his arm. "You said that you were dismissed?"

"No, it didn't end early. I was dismissed as in scorned. Rejected. My presence was no longer required."

His head pokes through the doorframe. "That doesn't sound positive. Is everything alright?"

"It's fine." I take a deep breath. I'm not going to dump my problems into his lap. Having him in here right now is more than I could have asked for.

Aries steps out of my closet after hanging the garment. "It doesn't seem fine. Would you like to talk about it?"

It would be nice to talk to him, but I shouldn't. It's not fair that he has to keep dealing with my issues and—

"Oliver." His voice is soft as he reaches out his hand. "You can always talk to me, and I will listen. I mean it."

Sighing, I step forward and take his hand. It's warm and sends tingles straight up my arm, dispersing all throughout my body. We walk over to the large ottoman at the end of my bed and sit together.

When we're comfortable, he turns to me. "Tell me what happened?"

"The Duke of Ealing brought up the photos I posted on social media. But he was being an asshole and insulting me. I didn't stay quiet, so I was reprimanded."

"You spoke up for yourself," Aries says. "Excellent. Good for you."

"Yes, but..." I slide my hand from within his, because sitting here with our palms clasped is doing questionable things to my nature and cock. I cross my leg at the knee and look up at the ceiling. "It would be nice if someone in my family spoke up for *me*. If the viscount or Lord Blakeley spoke in my defense, just once. It's like... no one cares. I'm in this room full of vampires who are supposed to be my clan. My allies. But nobody cares about me or my well-being—what I think or what I'm capable of.

"I care about them, though. Part of me wants to please them. I want their approval, even though I *never* get it. I'm just a tool and it's such an empty existence, Aries. What's the point?"

Aries takes hold of my hand again, threading our fingers together against his thigh.

"Your existence is not empty, because you are a complete, clever and striking vampire with much more to offer than you even realize. It's difficult now, but you don't know what will happen later. And... you're wrong."

I meet his gaze, confused. "About?"

"That no one cares. I care. Your sister cares, because she smuggles the necessary resources to support your hobby. You may not want to hear this, but I think Alexander cares, too."

I scoff, shaking my head. "Oh, he does not."

"He does. He's young, arrogant, and makes poor choices, but he watches you, intently, when he thinks you're not looking. He pays close attention. I know, because, well... I am guilty of the same behavior—sneaking glances at you and noticing your temperament. Wondering what you're thinking. You are a magnetic and complex vampire. Oliver. Please don't let the present circumstance weigh you down. It's stifling now, but later, things might change. They did for me."

Aries raises our entwined hands and kisses my knuckles. My nature bubbles like lava in my groin, and slowly, the heat of it crawls upward. They haven't alighted yet, but the sensation flashes behind my eyes like a warning. "May I tell you something?"

His dark eyes flicker up as his mouth hovers just above my knuckles. "Yes, darling?"

I take a breath and the words pour out. "You are the first vampire aside from Sasha to accept me—to sincerely listen and converse with me, candidly. The way you've appeared in my life, you're like an angel. Thank you."

He smiles, then presses another soft kiss to the top of my hand. "You don't need to thank me. I'm only returning the kindness and openness that you've shown me."

"Even still, you definitely don't have to, especially since... well, I'm making things complicated for you."

"Correct."

I laugh. "That was blunt."

"You are. This is a truth that we can't deny. However, you're also just..." He sighs, meeting my eyes. "You're very different."

"I'm strange." I grin. "Erratic."

"No. Unconventional. Completely unexpected."

Hesitantly, I slide my other hand over so that both of mine clasp his. "I know this circumstance isn't ideal, but I appreciate that you encourage me to have more confidence and speak my mind. I wish I could return the favor, somehow."

Shifting a little closer so that my knees brush his, I push myself to speak the words that I want to convey. Wanting to be assertive. "If there's anything that you want from me, say it and I... I'll give it to you."

He doesn't want anything from me. Aries has made that clear, and I know that this situation is impossible. But he also makes me feel alive. He generates these brilliant sparks in my heart, body and nature, and the sensation is priceless. Extraordinary.

Aries slides his hand from within my palms and draws back slightly. He takes a deep breath to where his chest rises and falls beneath his sweater.

"What's wrong?" I ask. I'm beginning to think that I've

committed some terrible faux pas, or that I've offended him greatly.

But then, I marvel. The deep, midnight hue of his blue eyes brightens. Intensifies. His irises burn so brightly that it steals my breath away and I gasp.

The color is deep and enchanting, like a winter night sky under a full moon.

Chapter Sixteen

Aries closes his glowing eyes, takes another deep breath and speaks on an exhale. "God help me. I can't believe this is happening."

Worried, I stand with a jolt. "What's the matter? Why?" I step into the gap of his legs and cup his face, mesmerized as my own eyes brighten in response. "Are you alright? You told me that you could control this."

"I have excellent control. Typically." He shakes his head, breaking free of my hands. "I am trying *very* hard to behave myself, but it's as if I'm being pushed to the edges of my sanity. You cannot sit here in a bathrobe and tell me that you'll give me anything I want."

"Even though it's the truth?" The luster of his irises is spellbinding. I can't look away from him. "Am I hurting you? Is this encouraging the addiction?"

"No." Aries's shoulders drop as he exhales. "It wouldn't happen this easily or quickly. You aren't hurting me... In some ways, it feels as if you would never hurt me—but I'm not sure if that's simply the allure of your nature or my being foolishly optimistic."

I want him. I want us to be closer and I want to touch him.

His eyes have alighted, which means he wants me, too. For certain, he reciprocates my desire, and resisting the inherent attraction between us is becoming painful.

"If I were free... if I were my own vampire, you wouldn't need to worry about being addicted. I would happily offer myself to you, Aries. Without hesitation." I don't care that I'm purebred and he's first-gen. I don't care that he's older, and I have no interest in being a pawn in Lord Blakeley's political goals. The only thing that matters is this moment and what my nature is telling me.

"You should not be saying these things to me, Oliver. You shouldn't..." He shakes his head as if the words escape him.

"Why?"

"Because this situation is... This circumstance worries me."

"In what way? I already promised that I wouldn't expose you to my nature. I don't care about my engagement, and I—"

"Not just those things." Aries raises his head. His jaw is set sternly and his eyes are razor sharp.

Concerned, I shift my weight. "Okay... I'm listening."

"Forgive me for speaking bluntly, but you're very sheltered. It feels as if I'm the first and only vampire outside of your isolated existence that you've ever had an authentic conversation with, and this... this makes me cautious. The chemistry between our natures is irrefutable. It is marvelous, but simultaneously, I'm not certain that I should act on it. Do you understand my hesitation?"

Standing in front of him, I absently pick the knot of my robe. Too many thoughts are zipping through my mind, along with the usual blush of embarrassment warming my chest and face. I stare over the top of his head, trying to understand my emotions.

"This isn't a rebuke," he says delicately. "I simply don't want us to fall into something that we might regret later."

I close my eyes, concentrating. Slowly, I comb through my heart, finding the words that I need to express. "I can't help my situation," I begin, then take a breath. "Because everything in my life is decided for me."

Steeling myself, I look down into his face. Aries stares at me with rapt attention. "In many ways, yes, you are the first, Aries. But being closer to you is also my choice. The first situation in my life where I could make a concrete, meaningful choice, and I... I want you. That is *my* decision. No matter what, I would never regret it. Never."

He may reject me in this moment. But that's okay. Because I've openly expressed my desires. No matter what happens next, that counts for something.

Sighing, Aries closes his eyes and lifts a hand. Using the knot of my robe, he pulls me closer as he leans and rests his forehead against the terrycloth material at my stomach. "You are tenacious, Oliver Blakeley. A discreet force to be reckoned with."

I raise my hands and thread them into the thick heft of his silky and dark waves. As I hold his head in my palms, I lean down. His hair is soft and fragrant against my face and nose. I breathe in. "I want you," I whisper.

In day-to-day life, I walk around embarrassed.

Nervous, frustrated and insecure.

I try hard to be inoffensive and colorless as I interact with other vampires because this is what makes my fathers happy. A living, breathing, well-behaved beige wall in every room I occupy.

Lately, though, I feel different. Aries has told me that my feelings are valid. So, I don't want to be colorless and meek anymore. I want to speak up and be bold. To at least try.

"Aries." I lift his head in my hands until his lustrous eyes meet mine. His full, beautiful lips are parted as his chest rises and falls beneath his sweater. "If we made love, would you regret it later on? Do you think I would be a mistake?"

Silently, Aries lowers his head. He unties the knot of my robe. When it's unraveled, he gently parts the material at my chest. He closes his eyes, leans in and places the softest kiss on my naked belly. I close my eyes, silently exhaling.

"No," he whispers, and his breath caresses my skin before he kisses the space just above my navel. "You are not a mistake, and I would never regret you." With his palms flat at my hips, he slides them around to hold my lower back. The robe falls open completely.

I'm naked and exposed to him as I stand with my fingers plunged within his hair. Every inch of me is hot with anticipation and nervousness. Excitement and immeasurable desire tingle from the top of my head and down to the soles of my bare feet.

He slides his fingertips up my lower back, tracing the subtle concave of my spine as he litters my stomach with kisses. I inhale and bite my lip as my hands rest on his shoulders, gripping the broadness of him because my knees are starting to feel weak.

Aries touches me. So gently and with such deliberate care. My eyes are bright and my shaft is fully erect. I felt emboldened a moment ago, but as I stand here naked, I'm realizing that I am very much out of my depth. Aside from the horribly uncomfortable mating session with Alexander in front of the council, I have never done anything like this with another vampire.

Aries's hands caress down my flesh until he cups my ass with both palms. Somehow, the curves of my cheeks fit almost perfectly within his large palms. It makes me tremble all over.

"How far do you want this to go?" he asks sincerely, raising his head to meet my gaze.

"As far as you'll allow? As far as you'll take me."

He breathes, laughing, and his bewitching eyes sparkle with amusement. "I've never met a purebred vampire like you, Oliver. And I am fairly certain that I never will again."

Aries stands from the ottoman. Startled, I step back to give him room. But in a fluid gesture, he bends, grips the back of my thighs and lifts me so that my legs are parted and wrapped around his waist. Quickly, I thread my arms around his shoulders, hugging him and bringing our faces closer together. He feels so good like this. Warm and tangible. Solid.

It's almost like a dream, but I've never dreamt about anything this sensual and exciting before. I don't think I have the imagination for it, so it must be real.

As he carries me, I lean in and kiss him softly, then brush our noses. He smiles, returning the affection before lowering me so that I'm sitting on the edge of the mattress. I'm thinking about how I want to undress him so that he's naked, too, but he surprises me when he stands between my thighs.

He bends down to catch my mouth and the passion bubbling between us is cautious but intense. Like water slowly boiling in a pressurized tea kettle. I grip his head with my fingers once more because I love holding him close like this—captured within my literal grasp. His palms stroke my sides and along my hips, making me squirm against the comforter.

Aries kisses into the concave of my neck, licking and inhaling my flesh. Closing my eyes, I lift my head to give him full access, wishing that I could give him consent to feed from me.

I would. If he wanted it.

"Your scent is perfect, Oliver. Delicious." Aries's voice is ragged as he shifts to his knees. He kisses down the center of my chest and his hands slide over the tops of my thighs. "It's torture."

"It doesn't have to be," I say cautiously. My breath hitches in my throat because my heart is pounding too hard. I'm hot, painfully aroused, and my suppressed energy is pulsing and burning inside my gut with a distinct hunger. A need for something more.

What I wouldn't give to nourish and fulfill him. To consent and allow him to have all of me—not only my physical body, but my blood and liberated essence as well. To show him how I truly feel so that there is no further question about my intention.

"Lie back," he whispers, then lifts to kiss my lips once more before I willingly tumble flat onto my back. He pulls my ankles up so that my heels are planted against the edge of the bed-frame —so that my entire lower half is splayed open to him. He kisses along the inside of my thigh, and my nature is starting to buck up against the hold I'm forcing on it. It's uncomfortable, but I can control it.

He speaks against my skin between kisses. "I need to taste

you… May I, please?" I inhale sharply and arch when Aries's tongue licks the underside of my shaft, then he uses his mouth to nip and suck at the flesh underneath before moving down even further.

"*Yes.*" The word escapes on an exhale as I grip and clench the comforter in my fists. I think I might explode from the pleasure and pressure.

Aries makes a hungry sound from his throat and his hands firmly hold my hips in an attempt to keep me still. But then his tongue dips inside of me and I reflexively arch my back hard against the bed. A soft whimper passes through my parted lips because I can literally feel the wetness of him licking into me and exploring my body.

In this moment, I am… a new kind of creature. Or at least a different one compared with what I've always been. My aura is repressed inside of my skin, and my lower half squirms and rocks in rhythm with Aries's mouth and hands because I need more—this wild and feral desire that I've never experienced.

Right now, I'm not like a beige wall. I feel electrified—neon pink and iridescent.

He teases and licks between my cheeks, driving me to the point of madness. Until I'm gasping and moaning in ways that I didn't know I was capable of. He moves back up, and I instinctively lift my head to see him. He grins roguishly before he takes my shaft into his mouth—the full length of me in one smooth and voracious movement.

His mouth is hot as he envelopes me and my eyes roll back as I drop my head against the comforter. I might pass out from the fire racing up and down my spine and this erotic sensation.

Aries moans and his mouth vibrates around my flesh as he slides his tongue against me, curiously tasting and relishing. He takes my shaft in deeper until I feel myself hitting the back of his throat. His fingers dig into my flesh at my ass and hips, slowly lifting me up.

He pumps in a seductive, slow rhythm. Intentionally, deliberately, he sucks and grips my body in his hands and everything inside of me reaches a delicate precipice—a hot and radiant pleasure. He thrusts me up and into the heat of his mouth, then drags my shaft down across his tongue, licking and pulling until my body can't take it anymore. Until I gasp, shudder and softly cry out as a bright, tingling sensation flows up my spine, to my brain and all through me.

My nature pulses hard and ravenous within my flesh, begging to be set free and wrap itself around this vampire that it yearns for. But I clear my head and separate the carnal pleasure from my vampiric desire—holding that part of myself inside because I can't... I refuse to expose him to the seduction of my aura.

Aries keeps his mouth on my cock the entire time. Swallowing with conviction and indulgence. When my body is limp and satiated, he gently lowers my hips and ass back down to the bed, then crawls up to hover over me. My breathing is labored and ragged because my heart, pulse and nature are thumping loudly like a drum.

He's calm, almost hypnotized as he stares. His eyes are still glowing. I can barely function, but I raise my head just enough to kiss his full lips. I want him naked, too, so I lift my hands to grip the bottom of his sweater.

But he stops me. He wraps one of his palms around my wrist before he whispers.

"I should go."

Despite my languid state, panic flashes inside my chest and my eyes widen. "What? Why?"

"If someone catches me in here, we—"

"They won't, Aries. I promise no one comes to my room until morning—and I've been dismissed, so I'm in exile right now. You're safe."

I don't want him to leave like this. It shifts the mood of what we've just done, as if it's something dirty or shameful. Something quick and tawdry that we need to cover up. I don't want him to feel that way, because I certainly don't.

"Please stay," I ask. "A little longer?" I hold his face with my free hand. If he really wants to leave, I'll respect his decision. But I wish with all my heart that he wouldn't. That we could at least have this night together.

Aries is quiet for a long moment, watching me. When he breathes out, it's heavy. His jasmine essence puffs against my face. "Okay."

My body unclenches as I offer a smile. "I held my aura inside. Do you feel alright?" It was uncomfortable, but I managed it. I'll keep him safe, no matter what.

"I feel fine, darling. Don't worry." Aries traces the line of my jaw with his fingers. I close my eyes. "The consequences of my actions are for me to deal with. You are superb, Oliver. And your eyes are enchanting—so pale blue but with flecks of bright silver. Like stardust."

I smile awkwardly as my face warms. Nobody has ever spoken to me this way.

"You taste like sex and flowers... peonies, specifically."

My eyes open as I shake my head. I can't stop grinning. "I don't know what that means."

"It means that you are delectable. Sweet perfection." Aries shifts upright, then grabs the hem of his sweater to pull it over his head. I sit up, too, shamelessly staring as he stands and reveals his finely toned chest and the sexy layer of dark silky hairs there. He unbuttons his pants and removes them, slowly.

My mouth is agape when he's finally naked and magnificent before me. Tall, gently sculpted and all beautiful, richly bronzed skin. God... I haven't had much access to movies or television shows, but I have a feeling that what I've just witnessed is far better than anything ever made.

As he climbs onto the bed, I shift my robe from my shoulders. Aries pulls the duvet and sheets further down before he lies back against the mattress, making himself comfortable.

I am beside myself. I cannot believe that this handsome vampire is naked and in my bed. How could I be so lucky? I am not lucky, typically, but this is an undeniable turn of fate. Maybe Venus is in retrograde, or some other supernatural occurrence that I can't possibly rationalize.

Eagerly, I crawl toward him. When I'm close, he lifts a hand and holds my face, then slides his other hand around my waist to pull me down on top of him. Our bodies align and the sensation is perfect—electricity sparking warmly between his skin and mine.

Aries draws his knees up so that I'm nestled comfortably against his groin. I'm swathed in his embrace as we kiss. Over and over—from this angle and that one. Gently, playfully, and then deeper and more intensely. Penetrating and exploring. Any way that two vampires can kiss, we experiment and indulge.

Just as my nature is painfully churning and twisting from the wonderful taste of him in my mouth, he breaks our connection. My eyelids are heavy as I try to focus. "Are we okay?" I ask, breathless. I never want this night to end.

"We are," he says, examining me in his familiar way. His hands lazily trace the length of my spine, then down further, flirting with the dip between my cheeks before sliding back up again. "You are astonishing to me. Too good and beyond my comprehension. Perpetually, I find myself overthinking."

"I can tell," I say honestly, shifting upward as I meet his gaze head on. "But I won't hurt you, Aries. I promise."

"I know that you would never mean to, but this is heretical. It goes against everything that I have stood for. You are purebred. You hold all of the cards in this situation. All of the power. You're also engaged, and these things are significant red flags. Even still... you're endearing and sincere. Traumatized and introverted. I don't know how to read this situation, Oliver. It perplexes me."

It feels as if we keep having the same conversation. Aries can't move past our obstacles, but I want to ignore them completely and focus on the here and now. This fleeting moment.

"I don't think I hold any cards or have any power," I tell him quietly. "I feel like I'm always at your mercy. Always waiting and hoping that you'll say yes to me."

"You have power. You just don't wield it in the typical way that purebreds do—which is excellent, in my opinion. It's partially why I'm drawn to you. These bewildering, complex layers of humility and empathy."

I place a soft kiss against his mouth. "You say such kind things. After the ceremony, I'll be relegated to arm candy. An empty, mindless shell."

"You could never be an empty shell. It's impossible." Aries moves one hand up, bending his arm and holding his head against the pillow while the other casually rests at my lower back. "Have you ever sincerely tried talking to Alexander? In the same way that you talk to me, I mean."

I frown. Alexander is the absolute last vampire that I want to talk about. "No. If I ever told him how I really feel, he'd use it as ammunition to mock me later."

"You could try." Aries lifts his head, touching our lips together in another kiss. "You've taken a chance with me. Why not him?"

"Because you're completely different. You're compassionate. You listen and... Before I even saw you, my nature was speaking to me in ways it never has for Alexander. Just the smell of you set me off."

"Hm..." Aries grins. "Love at first sniff? A rare phenomenon."

We both chuckle, but I shift, stretching my body and lying back down against the warmth of him. "Something like that," I say.

I think... this could be love? I don't know, because I haven't ever fallen in love before. When I imagine it, though, I think it'd be similar to this moment. Exciting and new. Soft, quiet and a little bit frightening. Exhilarating.

Falling is scary, but depending on where you land, it could be a magnificent ride. The landing might make every moment of the descent worth the fall.

Feeling bold, I swallow as I press my body against him. His hand slides up, caressing my spine once more. "Can I... do what you just did to me?" I ask. "I've never done it before, but I'd like to try." I'm embarrassed by this confession and my general lack of experience in life, but I've come this far. What would be the point of holding back now?

Aries smiles. "Thank you, but no, darling. You don't need to do that to me."

I pause, caught off guard by his quick refusal. "But I... would like to try—"

"No, Oliver." He shakes his head against the pillow. "I'm fine. I'd like for us to make it through this evening without me completely violating you."

"It's not violating if I want it. This sounds like you over-thinking again—like I'm the delicate young master and you don't want to sully me."

"Sully. That's the perfect word, actually."

"Aries—"

"Oliver." His eyes widen as he snickers. "You don't need to *do* anything. We're just enjoying each other. Relaxing, yes?"

Slipping from his grasp, I shift to the edge of the bed, then walk toward the en-suite bathroom. Who can relax when there's a delicious and naked long-legged vampire man with gorgeous bronzed skin in their bed? Is he serious?

It's true that I don't have much sexual experience, but I'm not useless. I don't want him to think that he needs to pamper me.

In the bathroom, I walk to the lower cabinets, crouch down and open them wide. I think it's still in here... I spot my objective, grab the small jar and head back into my bedroom. Aries is sitting upright in the bed with his back resting against the headboard. His arms are folded. "I sense much discontent from my young master."

"Shut up." I grin, climbing back onto the bed and straddling his thighs. As I rest down, he lowers his gaze, examining the small jar in my hands.

"Why in heaven's name do you have coconut oil?"

"It's my sister's," I answer, unscrewing the top. "She's obsessive about her skin and trying new beauty regimens."

"Is her skin very dry? Does she not feed regularly?"

"I don't know? She just likes to leave things here for when she spends the night. I don't get it, but everyone has their thing. Anyway, this will work, right? As lubrication?"

Aries narrows his eyes, amused. "Yes, but... what exactly are you lubricating?"

My cheeks are hot but I shrug my shoulders. "Us."

With the cap off, I scoop a small bit of the partially solidified substance out of the jar. I'm waiting for him to object or tell me to stop. To present another reason as to why we definitely shouldn't be doing this.

But when I flicker my eyes up, he's watching me. His gaze is hooded under his thick, dark lashes, and he's silent.

Good. Seems like I have his permission for this.

Chapter Seventeen

Coconut oil is lovely.

Despite the fact that it's fairly solid when I scoop it out, it melts into a slippery liquid as soon as it makes contact with the heat of my skin. Plus, it smells wonderful.

I know this works well as lube because I've used it before. Privately. But Aries doesn't need to know that.

Settled against his thighs, I shift closer and reach down and in between us. I wrap my palm around his shaft, enjoying the warm and buttery contact with his flesh. The scent of the oil mixed with Aries's natural essence is creating something like a dense cocoon around us—a tight, enclosed space where the outside world fades away from my cognizance. It's as if only the two of us exist in this hazy, sweet and sensual ecosphere.

He leans his head back and moans from deep within his throat. It's the simplest response, but knowing that I'm pleasing him sends an electrified jolt through my core. A rhapsodic and carnal thrill.

I am *not* a cold fish. I can do this.

Aries hardens in my palm, which is also encouraging. I want us to move together, but I'm not sure how to work it out from this angle. Plus, he's somewhat thick and large in my grasp and I don't know if I can hold us both with one hand.

"Is something wrong?" he asks. I blink and look up. Shit. I was so in my head about this that I stopped altogether.

Biting my lip, I shift a little closer. "No." I want to be confident, so I go for it, maneuvering both my shaft and his into my grip. It's... wow.

The feel of him against me as I stroke us both with the oil is marvelous. But now I have this insane urge to move my hips, and it creates another element of configuration that I need to resolve.

"Oliver."

"Yes?"

"Talk to me."

"I... would like to move, but it feels a bit awkward? I can't hold us both in my hand and do that at the same time."

He smiles. His eyes are soft and patient. "How about I hold us, then you're free to move?"

"I'm okay with that." I lift my hand, and Aries smoothly grips us both with his palm. The sensation makes my breath hitch as I grin. "Teamwork, eh?"

"They say that two heads are better than one."

"I couldn't agree more." I wrap my arms around his shoulders, then carefully scoot my hips even closer into him. When I do this, he grasps us tighter and my groin practically catches fire from gratification. Instinctively, I do it again, this time rolling my hips and settling with my thighs wider as I relax on top of him.

Every time I move, I'm rewarded with these firm tugs until I'm chasing them. Rocking and mindless—desperate for what Aries is doing.

He's hungry for this release, too, because his free hand at my hip slides down to squeeze my ass cheek, urging me to rock harder against him. I lean in to let my forehead rest in line with his. He tilts his head and kisses me fiercely—ravenous and deep. Shamelessly licking and tasting. I want to absorb every part of him. As much as I can.

I snap my head up from the kiss, because my nature is burning and I can't breathe. Lifting my face to the ceiling, I stuff the heat of it down, but continue rocking my hips at a steady pace.

I'm so captivated by him. His tenderness, trust and the goodness that he's given to me since the moment he arrived. I wish I could let my aura fan out so that he could feel it and understand. I want him to know, desperately.

With his face burrowed into the concave of my neck, Aries grunts, breathing raggedly and in a satisfied sound as his body trembles in my arms. I feel him spill over between us and that understanding—knowing that *I* caused that—in combination with his delicious body and this tempest of sensations pushes me over the edge as well. Closing my eyes, I hold him tight, reveling in the physical release.

My senses are so sharp in this moment, as if I can feel and smell and taste and see everything—like a wildflower in full bloom at the height of springtime, absorbing all the elements.

We hold each other. Aries's arms are wrapped tightly around my waist and we're warm, breathing in the silence. Nestled in the soft rise and fall of our placated bodies. Our mutual release is like a strange and sensual glue holding us together.

Lifting my head from the embrace, I keep my voice low. "Was that alright for you?"

He raises his head and his eyes are glowing cerulean. "Was it 'alright'?"

I blink, waiting. But he frowns. "Alright?" Aries unexpectedly lifts, and the surprise of his movement makes me yelp. He embraces me and flips our positions so that I'm on my back against the duvet. The shift makes my breath catch, but I laugh when I land softly onto the mattress and he's on all fours hovering over me.

"No," he says. "It wasn't 'alright.' It was fantastic. Heavenly." He leans down and kisses my mouth, then my cheek and forehead before moving down to my neck. I writhe and laugh from his frenzied affection. His voice is muffled against my skin. "You enchanting and tenacious creature."

My smile is so wide that my cheeks are starting to hurt. "Not like a cold fish, then?"

He lifts with his brow furrowed. "No. What in God's name? Why would you—"

"Nothing." I shake my head. "I don't know what I'm saying."

His brow is cinched in suspicion, but he leans down, dragging my arms up over my head and clasping our hands together. When he's flat against my body, he brushes our lips. I think my heart might burst.

"Where did you learn to move your hips like that?" he asks.

"I didn't know that I could. You brought that out of me."

"Mm," he sighs, fully resting his heavy body on top of me and nuzzling into my neck again, kissing me there. "I wish I could bring more out of you, my darling. The things I would do to you."

I draw my legs up, lifting my knees to cradle him. This is paradise. "We can do it," I tell him. "Everything. Anything." I shift my gaze to the side. His eyes are closed.

"We cannot. Because I'm not yours, and you are not mine."

"I'm not his, either."

"True. But you're not free, Oliver. You are not your own vampire."

I swallow and it goes down like cotton. "Please don't remind me of that, okay? Not right now."

He nods, but doesn't say anything else. I want to shake off the despondent feeling, so I change the subject. "Did you feel comfortable with my aura? I think I'm getting better at holding it in."

Aries slides one hand from mine, takes hold of my chin and turns my head to meet his gaze. "It was perfect. Thank you."

This warms my insides, helping to alleviate the shadowed feeling from a moment ago. "You don't need to say thank you. I want you to feel safe with me, Aries. To trust me."

He leans and presses his full lips to my nose. "Shall we sleep? Just for a little while."

Bringing my arms down, we realign so that I can hug his back as I relax my legs. The weight and scent of him are heavy and perfect. I didn't think I was tired, but within seconds, everything around me fades into a soft and contented darkness.

～

"Your grace?"

My eyes fly open and I inhale sharply. The light of the room is too bright. Glaring white morning sunshine. It's bewildering, but my body feels like a limp and very happy noodle enveloped in the warmth of my bed. Pulling the covers up and over my head, I groan. "Yes? What?"

"It-it's time to start the day." I can hear Camille opening windows and shuffling around the room. Why the hell is she doing that? She never opens my windows. "You're expected to attend breakfast this morning, and Alexander has asked if he can escort you down. He's waiting in the corridor. Right now."

I sit up straight with a jolt, looking to my right, then left. Aside from Camille standing near my closet and looking at me strangely, I'm by myself. Also, I'm naked. But to my great relief, my bottom half is covered by the comforter. I reach up and my hair is wild. "Alright... just, can I have ten minutes, please? Alone?"

Camille bows. "Of course, your grace. I've laid clothes out for you."

"Thank you." I flop back down in the bed, exhaling. When she leaves and the door is shut, I turn and nestle deeper into my sheets because I can still smell Aries on my pillows. It makes me tingly all over and I want to revel in this feeling. I stretch my legs out, then elongate my spine and breathe in deeply. Gloriously.

After one minute of indulgence, I pop up from the bed, strut across the room and take the quickest shower of my life. I wish I didn't even need to shower. I realize that I'm being crude, but I could walk around with his scent on me like this all day. Perfectly comfortable.

When I'm dressed, I open my bedroom door, and Alexander is leaning with his back pressed against the stone wall. His molten eyes meet mine.

"Good morning." I pull the door shut and move toward the spiral stairs.

"Good morning," he parrots, meeting my stride but falling behind as we descend toward the first floor. "How was your night?"

It was absolutely fantastic. Magical. Sensual and delicious.

I had sex.

Good sex.

The kind that makes people write erotic poetry to encapsulate the feeling of hot skin on skin. Two bodies moving together in a beautiful rhythm, slowly climbing toward the height of pleasure.

I wish Lord Blakeley would dismiss me from things more often.

"Fine," I say. "Yours?"

"Boring," he admits, sighing. "I was worried about you after what happened."

"There's no need. I'm alright." When we reach the bottom, I'm thrilled to see that Aries's door is open. I don't break my stride as we walk past, but I turn my head. He's not inside, but he's close by. I can feel him. Maybe he's in the rose garden—

"Ollie, slow down!"

We've just stepped into the outdoor corridor when I stop, confused. "Aren't we late for breakfast?" The sun is shining brightly today, and it's partly cloudy but warm. Birds titter and sing in surround sound, and the stone passageway is dotted with contrasting splotches of light and shadow.

"Yes, we are, but I want to talk to you."

"About?"

He tilts his blonde head and raises an eyebrow. "Yesterday?

Jesus, man. It was... well, it wasn't good. Why are you being so nonchalant about this?"

I shrug. "Lord Blakeley chastises me all of the time. This is my life, but... I guess it was the first time he did it in front of you? You may as well get used to it."

"It was the second time, because he was rude as hell to you at the ball, too. It's not something to 'get used to.' God... I was wondering why you never call him 'Father.' I'm starting to understand. Hey—how did you know that your photographs have been featured in newspapers around the world? Who told you that, because it sure as hell wasn't me?"

"Ah, I, well..." The memory of Alexander covering for me at dinner floats to the top of my mind. I had totally forgotten about it with everything that's transpired. "Sasha told me."

Alexander frowns and purses his lips as if he doesn't believe me.

Well, why should he? It's a lie. "Don't we need to go?" I urge him.

"I thought you'd be an anxious and nervous mess this morning after that awful scene. That you'd be humiliated."

I turn and take a step forward. "You thought you'd meet me first thing to rub salt in the wound? I'm sorry to disappoint."

"That's not why I came for you."

"Sure." I roll my eyes, but my breath catches as Aries turns down the hallway and stalks toward us. He's wearing a rich canary-colored dress shirt with the sleeves neatly rolled up to his elbows and dark khaki trousers. The deep yellow emphasizes the golden undertones of his skin, but it also brings attention to the fact that his coloring is off. In the bright indirect light streaming into the corridor, he seems a little too pale.

I'm concerned, but my heart does a somersault as he casually smiles and nods at both Alexander and me. "Good morning, my lords."

"Hello." I smile, and my nature threatens to radiate and flow. As he passes us, I see that his eyes are a bit dull, too. I have the strongest urge to turn and watch him walk away, but I don't. I stamp down my nature and continue forward.

Alexander is quiet the rest of the walk to the breakfast room. But when we're outside the double doors and I'm about to pull one open, he speaks from behind.

"You like him."

I pause, glancing over my shoulder. "Excuse me?"

Alexander's face is calm, as if he's just given me today's weather forecast and not made a razor-sharp accusation. "The designer. Aries. You like him. You're always so stiff and edgy with me, but as soon as he turns up, it's like you just... liquefy. Your whole demeanor softens. And you smile."

A flush of heat climbs up my neck as I yank the door open. "You're being ridiculous." I step into the room, but Alexander is close at my heels. His voice is low.

"You're a terrible liar, Ollie. Do you know that? What is it about him that does it for you? Why do you let your guard down around him? Tell me."

I ignore him because we're approaching the table, which is within earshot of my parents and his. This isn't good. I thought I was being discreet, but maybe what Aries said is true? Partially, anyway. That Alexander pays close attention. Closer than I realize.

When I step up to the table, Lord Blakeley addresses me without preamble. "I hope you spent last night reflecting on your behavior?"

Absolutely, without question, I did not. "Yes, Lord Blakeley."

"Do you have something to say to your family?"

Looking around the table, only mine and Alexander's immediate family are here. Alexander's relatives left the grounds last night and won't return until the official ceremony.

"My apologies for embarrassing you in front of our guests." I add a bow for effect.

"Do not speak out of turn going forward," Lord Blakeley commands. "I'll be keeping your device until after the ceremony so that we can avoid any other potential disasters."

I pull my chair out beside Alexander and sit down. "Yes, Lord Blakeley."

He lifts his mimosa toward his mouth, but then pauses. "Your phone buzzed this morning with a text message from the designer that I've hired to cultivate your suits."

God. Fucking hell.

I freeze and my heart practically stops. I forgot to tell Aries that my phone was confiscated again. In my panicked silence, Lord Blakeley continues.

"He asked that you try on the suit that he left in your closet. Why have you given him this mobile number? He should be addressing you through Camille."

"It-it's my fault. I'm only just upstairs from him, so it felt unnecessary to drag Camille from somewhere in the castle to play go-between."

Lord Blakeley's expression is flat. He looks at me as if I've said something utterly stupid. "My dear, silly child, that is literally her *job*." He leans, addressing Camille, who stands along the wall at the back of the room with the other personal assistants. "Please let Mr. Moralis know that all contact should be funneled through you going forward?"

Camille bows at the waist. "Yes, my lord."

When I turn back to the table, I'm relieved to see that Lord Blakeley has already leaned toward Alexander's mother to initiate a separate conversation. I exhale a sigh as I pick up my fork, but my relief is short-lived.

Alexander scoffs under his breath. "Ridiculous, am I?"

I don't say anything. Instead, I focus on my breakfast and thank God that Aries is the consummate professional.

Chapter Eighteen

After my father's inquiry about my (once again) confiscated phone over breakfast, the rest of the day drags on. Somehow, though, I don't mind.

Inside, I feel light. I don't think it's just the sex. That was satisfying, but it feels like there's something deeper at work here. More profound.

Someone has simply accepted me. All of me.

Nervous and anxious me, bumbling and saying the wrong things. Insecure me—trying not to be insecure me. *Naked* me. Emotionally and physically vulnerable me. Aries doesn't mock or say rude things. He just... talks and communicates calmly, like I'm alright. Like I'm not so ridiculous or uptight or a small horse.

I feel like I've suddenly grown wings and I can fly... No. More like, I've always had wings but nobody ever told me what they were for. No one ever showed me until now. Until him.

Today's event is a garden cocktail party for the local vampires directly under the southwestern realm. When things are winding down, Sasha comes over, slips her arm through mine and pulls me toward an unoccupied path. I look over my shoulder, and Alexander eyes us suspiciously.

"What's up, Sash?" I ask as we turn the corner and around a tall hedge covered in tiny white flowers.

"You tell me what's up," she says, guiding me within the inner trails of the garden. Our feet loudly crunch along the graveled paths. "What's going on with you?"

"Nothing. Apparently, there's a wedding happening in two weeks."

"Smartass." We step through an arched opening teeming with leaves and vines, then onto a grassy patch with rose bushes encircling us. Wall-to-wall green except for the splashes of vivid red. The sky overhead is full of billowing clouds shifting into sunset pink.

Sasha turns to face me directly, unblinking. "What is going on, Oliver James Blakeley?"

"Nothing," I repeat, avoiding her gaze. I don't want to lie to my sister. Before Aries, she was the only person that I could open up to. My lone confidant. But this... I can't share this. Not with anyone.

She folds her arms as if we're having some kind of stand-off. I don't say anything, because I have no idea what she wants. I'm assuming it's about Aries because he is obviously top of mind. But maybe she's wondering about something else?

Sasha exhales a sigh and shifts her body away. "I was hoping that you would be honest with me. I know I'm not perfect, but I think... You should know that you can trust me. I've shown you as much over the years."

My heart pulses in my ears. "Sasha, what are you talking about?"

Her eyes are shrewd. Serious. "Camille told me that when she came to your room this morning, you were naked, your hair was disheveled and the room... well, it had a very particular scent. Not just your subdued and soft essence, like usual. She said it was, quote, 'a little louder and muddled with someone else's.'"

My palm flies up and slaps against my forehead. Oh God.

"And she knows you weren't with Alexander because she'd

walked over with him," Sasha goes on. "What the hell were you doing?"

I can't breathe. Standing still, I shake my head, because I've completely ruined everything. I told Aries I would keep him safe. *Promised* him.

"Oliver." Sasha stares, waiting. I take a step back, but she steps into me, grabbing hold of my wrists. "Are you sleeping with Aries?"

Wide-eyed, frantic, I shake my head again. All of the goodness and contentment that I felt today is being siphoned out and replaced with a dark, inky dread. Thick and suffocating, like tar flooding my veins. "No, I... Please don't tell anyone. *Please*, Sasha."

I'm preparing myself for the worst, but my sister steps into me and wraps her arms around my shoulders.

"I would never tell our fathers *anything* about you," she whispers, resting her chin against my temple as she embraces me. "You're my Ollie! My sweet younger brother who dreams and contemplates and questions. Haven't I expressed how special you are to me?"

Slightly less terrified, I bring my arms up and wrap them around her waist, returning the hug. "You lecture me," I tell her. "Sometimes."

"That's what good big sisters do. And sometimes you are pretty whiny."

I open my mouth to object, but quickly realize that anything I say right now will absolutely validate her statement.

"I can't believe you've kept this from me," she says. "How in the world did this happen? How did it start? Who made the first move?"

"No one was supposed to know. Why does Camille tell you all these things? She told you when my aura flared out, too."

We separate, but Sasha grabs my hand and entwines our fingers. "Because she's my best friend, and after I married Elaine and had to leave the castle, I asked her to keep a close eye on you. I worry about Lord Heartless treating you like his golden show poodle and keeping you under glass. He's always been so strict with you. It's unreasonable."

I shrug. "He's strict with all of us."

"Yes, but much more so with you. He doesn't let you go *anywhere*. Thomas got to attend university until he tried to run away, and I went to the international vampire summits every year with Lord Pointless until my official bonding ceremony. But Heartless keeps the leash so tight with you. It's probably because you're the cleverest of us all. Too inquisitive and bold. You make him nervous."

I draw back slightly. "You think I'm bold?"

"Of course—when you're not trying to stifle yourself to appease everyone. You wrote that *Gallery of Stolen Artworks* essay, and then those photographs... The way you perfectly captured the excessive splendor of the fête contrasted with the housing conditions of the vamps actually living there. You challenge the status quo. Most of us aren't brave enough to do that."

"I was only observing what was in front of me," I explain. "Just putting two and two together. Why should I lie about what seems painfully obvious?"

"What's painfully obvious to you is completely invisible—or worse, irrelevant—to others. That's what makes you valiant, Ollie. Unique. Tell me... is Aries the reason your aura flared out at the banquet that day? Was it because of him?"

I look around. The sky is darkening and the garden lights along the path suddenly glow to life like magic. I'm comfortable opening up to her about this, but not here. "Yes, but—can we talk about this another time?"

She pouts. "Do you promise?"

Smiling weakly, I nod. "Yes."

"Perfect. I want this for you." She steps forward, pulling my hand. "It's a good experience and you need this, but I want to know how it started—all of the details. If your eyes alighted, too. Have they?"

Amused at her enthusiasm, I grin. "They have."

"Excellent. This is downright scandalous. Aries is so handsome—those long legs and that perfect tight and high ass. Nice going, sweetie."

"Please stop, Sash. No thank you."

"He's a bit old for you, though. Is he over a hundred? Can you handle that kind of vampire—one so worldly and progressive?"

I lift my chin because I feel incensed about this point. "He's ninety-five, and if our vampiric natures don't seem to care about those things, then why should I?"

She giggles, and as we round the corner back into the main garden, Alexander turns his head, watching our every move. "Touché," she says. "Can't argue with your nature. But what's the endgame plan? You know that this can only go so far, right? Regardless of what your nature says. Lord Blakeley would never accept this. Not ever."

"I know that, Sash. You don't need to remind me."

"I'm not trying to lecture you. I just... don't want you brokenhearted and even more miserable than you were before Aries arrived. Embrace it and be grateful for what it is."

We're close to the crowd, so I don't respond. The thought of losing Aries makes my chest tight—like a slow-moving shadow spreading all through me, darkening and corroding everything in nothingness and despair. I know it's inevitable, but I can't think about that right now.

Sasha unlinks my arm and seductively struts toward Elaine across the garden, dumping me in close proximity to Alexander. She's putting on a show for the onlookers and she's good at it—as if she's eager to be close to her proposed mate, even though it's been two years and they still haven't bonded.

I'm not nearly as convincing as I trudge over to Alexander. I probably look like I'd rather walk in a different direction. Or, I don't know, off a rooftop or into a pit of vipers. Wherever else.

"Have a nice sibling chat?" Alexander asks.

A waitress walks toward us, her palm lifted as she balances a silver tray of bubbling champagne flutes. Alexander has one in his hand already, but smoothly, he grabs a second glass and hands it to me. The waitress smiles awkwardly, curtsies and continues moving through the crowd.

"It was fine," I say, taking hold of the stem.

"What did you talk about?"

Is that any of his business? "Sibling stuff," I say, borrowing his phrase. I take a sip of champagne. It's dry and the fizzy sensation tickles my nose.

"My parents only had me, so I've always wondered what it's like to have a brother or sister. Seems nice."

"It can be. Sometimes."

Alexander takes a long sip from his glass. When it's empty, he stares down into it. "I wonder... if there's less pressure and expectation from your parents because there are more of you? Like, a table that can balance and hold everything with multiple legs instead of just one. It must be better than standing on your own all the time."

Mildly surprised, I look him over. "Well, not necessarily."

He raises his gaze from the glass and smiles. "I'll finally be two table legs after the wedding, at least? You and me."

Not knowing what to say, I take a sip of my champagne. I'm rescued from the odd moment when the mayor of Upper Avalon, a thin, gangly vampire with a head full of smartly trimmed brown hair, greets us with a deep bow.

"Ah, the handsome young couple," he says, grinning ear to ear. "My humblest congratulations to you both on your upcoming union."

"Thank you, Lord Darrick." Alexander smiles warmly, like a switch being turned on. His easy charm oozes like cream flowing over a coffee cup. "That's very kind of you."

"It is my honor," the thin vampire gushes with his hands clasped. "We're thrilled to be hosting the final celebratory fête within the southwestern realm next week. And thank you, your highness, in advance for the generous contribution to our housing development project—pending the completion of this lovely arrangement, of course. Thatched roofing just doesn't hold up like it used to in these changing weather patterns."

"We're happy to contribute," Alexander assures him. "We can't have our citizens living in tattered houses, can we?"

"We certainly cannot—we should take better care of our community."

"I agree, completely," Alexander says.

"Thank you, your grace."

I don't show it, but I'm surprised to hear about this—that there's a housing development project in the works for the Avalon community.

Evanshire's housing is bad, but Avalon's is probably even worse since that district falls under my family's realm. We don't even have enough money to properly maintain the castle, let alone village housing (except when money suddenly appears for renovations to impress other purebreds).

Considering all the controversy my photos caused, a project of this nature is unexpected. Why would Alexander choose to financially back this endeavor? It couldn't have anything to do with me...

Could it?

Lord Darrick nods, as if he means to end the conversation, but then perks up once more. "Are the two of you excited? It feels as if all of Eden is looking forward to this union! A new generation is taking charge."

I'm not good at faking it, but Alexander is. He reaches down and gently clasps my free hand at my side. He turns his head away from Lord Darrick to look directly at me.

"Excited doesn't even begin to describe how I feel," he says, focused as if we're the only ones standing here. "I've been waiting fifteen years to be mated with Oliver. I love him."

My eyes widen and I quickly glance away. A flash fire radiates up my neck and cheeks. For the love of God—what is he playing at? It's too far and he doesn't need to outright lie. Love? Nobody expects that within these rigid political arrangements.

"Ah," Lord Darrick marvels, clapping his hands in approval. "What a wonderful union this is—how happy the two of you will be. The Eden aristocracy as a whole will benefit from it greatly."

"Yes." Still staring and burning a hole into my side profile, Alexander squeezes my hand. "I have hope."

~

"My sister, Sasha, knows about us... Camille too, I suspect."

Much later, after the garden party has ended, I've been set free for the night. Aries gawks at me as I stand with my back pressed against my bedroom door. This is my weak attempt to prevent him from storming out.

He doesn't respond, just sighs, plunging his fingers into his dark brown waves. Again, I notice that his skin isn't the right richness of bronze. He's somewhat grayed. A touch paler.

Biting my bottom lip, I go on. "But they won't tell anyone. Honestly, it's better this way. They're like allies."

"Or co-conspirators in a crime."

"There's no crime being committed here," I defend. "Not realistically."

"And morally?" he asks. "Ethically?"

"Aries..." Pushing off the door, I walk over to meet him. I love saying his name and the way it floats effortlessly from my vocal cords. Past my teeth and through my lips with little to no hinderance. I can say his name on a breath, and only my tongue caresses the tail end like a whisper.

Setting my palms against his waist, I meet his gaze. "Do you regret last night?"

"I don't regret anything. But the situation is problematic."

"I know."

"And you're fearless. I'm finding that I am not nearly as brave as you, Oliver."

"It's not ideal that they know, but we—If Lord Blakeley or anyone found out, I would take full responsibility. I'd tell them that I manipulated you and used my aura. That you had no say. I'd take the fall for this."

Relief sweeps through me when he leans and brushes his nose against mine. "And who would believe that you'd be capable of such heinous misconduct?" he whispers. "As sweet and selfless as you are."

I caress my nose into him, reveling in the gesture and his warmth. "I would make it sound convincing—channel my inner villain."

Aries chuckles. "I doubt that you have one. You shouldn't offer to do that. It's like I have too much self-preservation, but you need more."

"We can meet in the middle and balance each other?"

He tilts his head, regarding me seriously. "Do you think we'd balance each other? That we're truly well matched?"

My heart skips and pulses harder. In a discreet way, he's asking if we'd be capable of forming a bond. If our vampiric natures are compatible enough to lovingly fuse and entwine themselves forever.

Two vampires with one uniquely joined essence.

"We could be," I say. "My sincerest wish is that we would have the time and space to find out." I lift and firmly press our mouths together, then wrap my arms around his neck and shoulders. Aries reciprocates, exhaling with pleasure and making my head spin.

Something inside of me feels different. Inhabiting this sensual space with Aries has manifested a new layer of existence. I feel... more confident? Relaxed and somewhat greedy.

Initially, I didn't think any of this was possible. I had accepted that my life would be forever void of authentic feelings like excitement and anticipation. No chance for true intimacy, love, trust or desire.

But Aries unexpectedly appeared on the horizon like a bright sunrise. He warms me all over and gives me every sensation. A comforting acceptance I've never known. This delight and reassurance that I feel... it gives me strength. I want to hold on to it. I want to make it into a fundamental part of my being and carry it with me always.

After a decadent string of tender but immersed kisses, he raises his head. His fingers are plunged into the back of my hair, holding me as he stares, unspeaking. He's always like this. Quiet in these stagnant pauses where he regards me. I can sense his scrutiny. "Overthinking?" I ask.

He scoffs. "Perpetually."

"You don't want to do this?"

He sighs and rests his forehead against mine. "I do. Very much."

"Then can we please stop having this conversation?" I tilt and kiss his mouth softly once more, then wait.

Meeting my gaze, he nods.

No more words are spoken, but the understanding and desire between us becomes clear as we undress—breathless and tugging at each other. When we're both naked, he whisks me up into his arms. I wrap my legs tightly around his waist and he carries me until we tumble onto the plush comforter. Our hands and lips move in sweeping brushstrokes of kisses and caresses.

My mind is aloft in a jasmine and oak paradise, practically drowning in the perfect scent of him. Aries rolls me underneath his weight, and I lift my hips into the heat and hardness of him, gasping and chasing a divine release as my essence fiercely pulses inside. It rages against my forced hold—hot, frenzied and making me delirious as I grind against him.

I need the completion of us. Unified in true ecstasy and climaxing together.

We don't stop for coconut oil this time because the wetness of our mutual arousal helps us in our pursuit. We play and adjust—feverishly tinkering with our connection and proximity, the gaps and curves between our vertically misaligned bodies until, finally, we get there.

The moment is just as magnificent as it was last night. My legs are drawn up as Aries relaxes down atop my stomach and chest, winded and satisfied. His eyes glow like a cosmic sky.

This is fulfilling, but inside, my nature demands more from him. Not just his body, but his essence and true core. I want everything.

My head swims in a rosy haze of desire as I lift my hands. I tangle my fingers into his hair and cradle his head as we catch our breath. *We want him*, my nature demands, vigorously pulsating all through me. *He is the one.*

The burn behind my eyes intensifies as I look at him, and more than anything, I want him to feed. To pull from me and nourish himself with my blood.

I close my eyes. The words pass between my lips in a whisper, like a midnight wind sensually gliding through a thick canopy of trees. Easily. Unfaltering.

"You have consent."

Chapter Nineteen

I've offered myself to him.

My blood and life essence are his for the taking, if he wants me.

The enclosed space between us feels too warm. The silence is deafening as Aries's relaxed and contented expression shifts into something sharper.

Confusion. Incredulity.

"What does that mean?" he asks.

"Consent to feed. If... you want to."

He starts, drawing away from me and shaking his head. "No, Oliver. Rescind it."

"But I want to hel—"

"Take it back. Now, *please*."

"I rescind my offer."

Aries sighs heavily and lays his head into the curve of my neck. His voice is muffled. "It's too far. I will not feed from you."

We're quiet as we lie together. I close my eyes and take several deep breaths to push back the fire burning inside. I don't simply imagine large snowflakes this time. Tonight, I need a blizzard. A complete white-out with low visibility and travel warnings. I plunge myself within the imagery until my head is clear and the intensity of my nature has dissipated.

After a long moment, I open my eyes and stare up at the darkened ceiling. "I'm sorry... that was selfish of me."

"You don't need to apologize, but please don't tempt me that way again, Oliver. There are some lines that we should not cross in this situation."

"I know, you already explained and I understand, but... when's the last time you fed, Aries?" I've tried not to ask. I've been avoiding it because it isn't my business. How often we feed and who from is a very intimate aspect of a vampire's life.

Even still, he's obviously underfed compared with the first day he arrived here. I wonder about his "networks" and whether he has someone in Eden who's willing to feed him. Our aristocracy isn't like the other, more liberal vampire communities across the modern world. I doubt that he has proper contacts here to aid him.

He rolls onto his back so that he's beside me, then rubs his palms against his face. "My young master is astute in his observations. Of course he is."

"I'm being serious. How can I help?"

After setting his hands on his stomach, he takes a deep breath in through his nose, then blows it out. "I'm fine, darling. You don't need to worry. I am overdue by a week, but I'll figure it out."

My body yearns to remedy this. Innately, I can sense that he's hungry and needs nourishment, so I want to give it to him. The equation is simple.

"The young master is incensed?"

Turning my head, I frown, but I'm half smiling. "Stop calling me that. No, I'm alright, I just... wish things were different."

"Rest assured, I feel the same way. Come closer, please."

I shift and lie against his side—into the taut, warm length of his elegantly toned body. When I'm nestled there, Aries lazily drags his fingers down my spine.

"I want to memorize you, Oliver. Your flowery scent, angelic eyes and the lines of your physique. The weight of you wrapped around my hips and the soft, breathless sounds you make when you come. I am determined to remember all of it."

Playfully, he strokes his fingers in between my cheeks, teasing my flesh before he grips my ass with his palm. Understanding, I lift my leg up and over his hip until I'm flush with the heat and thickness of his shaft.

He inhales, kissing my neck, and I'm simply euphoric. I want to memorize him, too, and being touched like this. Being adored in this tender, honest but ravenous way.

"I can't feed you, but... is my blood appealing to you?" I gasp as he swiftly drags me atop his body and settles onto his back, still licking and nuzzling my neck.

"Mm," he sighs, brushing his nose along my jawline and lazily grinding his hips into my groin. "Extremely." I find his lips and kiss him hard, practically smashing our mouths together. He exhales and it comes out like a growl—like somewhere inside of him the need is painful and he's unraveling underneath my weight.

When I pull up again, my lips and face are hot, stinging from the vigor of our affections. He says that my nature and blood are attractive to him, so I want to ask another question. "Aries?"

"Yes?"

"Do you think bonding would be oppressive? Because you'd lose your liberated lifestyle?" The rhetoric of mating and bonding has been drilled into my head since I was seven years old. This idea sits in direct contrast with my sincere desire to be free—like parallel roads, never crossing.

With Aries, and for the first time... I can see them aligned as a singular path. A winding lane forged from gold and flanked by rolling pastures filled with wildflowers. But am I being naïve? Is this unrealistic and the two cannot truly coexist? Bondage and freedom.

Aries draws his knees up, then rests his palms against the dip of my lower back. "No, I don't associate bonding with oppression. Your fiancé is wrong about that."

"In what way?"

"He talks about my lifestyle as if the underlying cause of my choices is fear—as if I'm afraid of bonding, and thus, I spend my years running away, traveling and working to avoid being mated with someone.

"But this is not the case. I live this way because it's truly what I enjoy. Design is what I'm good at, and it fulfills me. If I met someone in my travels that my nature responded to strongly enough to form a bond, I would accept that. Because at its baseline, bonding means that we are innately balanced and suited for each other. Our perspectives and deeper foundations would be harmonious, so we'd create a lifestyle that we both desire. That's what I believe bonding truly should be."

My heart is full as I lean in and press our lips together. "I agree," I whisper. Truly, everything that he said resonates within me. Profoundly.

"This is how it *should* be," Aries says. "But somewhere in the midst of our transitioning to contemporary vampiric society, we've lost our way. We became civilized, but rigid and rule-based. Burdening ourselves with obligations derived from greed, wealth, power, class and position. None of these have any place in forming true bonds. We're slowly realizing this now, though, and getting back to what matters."

I scoff. "Not here."

"True," Aries acknowledges. "Not in Eden. But across many other countries and aristocracies, things have changed. Vampires are free to choose and form quality bonds with whomever they are drawn to by nature. To explore and discover for themselves instead of being controlled. Alexander's statement that day revealed how susceptible he is to Eden's outdated rhetoric surrounding bonds and relationships."

"Oh, if we're complaining about Alexander, I have an entire list to divulge."

Aries laughs. "It isn't my intention to badmouth him. His comment simply emphasized what I had stated earlier regarding his immaturity. He needs more experience outside of his protective bubble. Having more worldly exploration would be good for you, too."

"I would like that. But I think you're being too kind about Alexander." Flattening my palms against his chest, I push myself upright to straddle his hips. His hands keep roaming all across my skin while he talks and it's driving me insane. "He mocks and antagonizes me like we're still children. All he cares about is impressing the vampires around him."

"You might be surprised," Aries says as his hands caress and grip my hips. I trace the lines of his stomach and he subtly writhes, hardening underneath me. "What you perceive as disdain could be a façade. Misdirected affection."

"That's enough," I say, throwing him a look that's meant to be serious but falls short. Trepidation floods my chest as another desire bubbles inside. My hands are resting near his shaft and he's definitely aroused. I want to taste him. Just *something* of him— whatever I can have.

When I asked yesterday, he told me no. Still, I take hold of him in one palm, feeling the heft and width of him. I'm not even sure if I can fit all of him in my mouth, but I want—

"Oliver, talk to me."

Heat warms my face as I inhale a breath. "Would you... Can I suck you? Please?" I don't want to meet his gaze, but in the silence that follows my question, I lift my head.

"Have you ever done this before?" he asks.

The blush intensifies, practically burning my skin. "No, but if you let me try—if you tell me what you like—*Ah*—" Aries pinches my hips and it makes me jump.

He drags himself upright, laughing breathily and holding my waist. His sumptuous eyes twinkle in the dim light. "God in heaven. Do you forget that you're purebred? That you're practically *royalty*, Oliver?"

"I'm not royalty, though. And what does that have to do with anything?"

"It is surreal to me," he says, shaking his head as he smiles. "I've never met a purebred that was so... unassuming. Even the kindest purebreds I've met still carry the inimitable air of their ancestry. And yet, you don't even exude that! Where is it? Where are you hiding it?" He looks behind my back, then lifts up my arm.

"I'm not hiding anything," I protest, yanking my arm down. Is he changing the subject to avoid my question? "And you shouldn't be surprised. I told you upfront that I'm a poor excuse for a purebred."

"Not at all." Aries pulls me closer into his body, then kisses my chin. "You are like a star shining brightly in front of me, but beyond my reach. I'm close enough to feel your warmth, but I can't ever hold you in a way that would truly satisfy me. Even if I did, I might be burned as a result."

Sighing, I slip my arms around his shoulders. "How many times do we have to talk about this? I'm withholding my aura—I would never hurt you and I'm not beyond your reach. I'm right here."

"But only temporarily. This spark between us is exciting for you now, given your circumstance. But it's inevitable that you'll forget me, in time. You'll move forward with your life and royal responsibilities. It's natural."

Frustrated, I take his handsome face in both of my palms. "I would *never* forget you. You keep talking as if you're the only one at risk of being devastated by this relationship, but you're wrong. You thinking that I won't be affected is bullshit." I take a breath, frowning. "Are you going to let me suck your cock or not?"

Aries blinks, speechless. After a few seconds, his expression melts and gives way to a relaxed smile as he bites his bottom lip. It throws me and softens the irritation tangled in my chest.

"Alright," he whispers. "You can."

I lift from his lap to readjust. "Then, tell me what to do,

please?" I respond. My voice is suddenly just as quiet. "How... how to make it feel good for you."

"Yes, darling."

~

Aries's cock is, well... large. I want to say it has a distinct girth, but that word makes me cringe while his cock definitely does not.

Having him in my mouth was an experience. A good one, with certainty. But also intimidating. When he finally spread his naked thighs and I was on my knees in front of him, I felt an unforeseen pressure, like I'd eagerly signed myself up to diffuse a bomb when I have zero experience in that area of expertise.

Aries was so patient as he talked me through it and... I don't know. Some people barrel into these situations, don't they? Confidently and blindly. To hell with any mutual understanding or, God forbid, conversation. The first bonding attempt with Alexander was this way. Like someone had unleashed a wild monkey onto my naked body.

But I really like that me and Aries talked as we did it. That he answered my questions. The whole thing felt comfortable. A careful exploration of pleasure. Of lips on sensitive flesh.

I'm also glad that he'd done it to me first, the other night. That experience served as a guide map for how I should approach him—how to cautiously take him in my hands, and how to use my tongue and lips to pull, tease and suck. Before he even came, he tasted so sensual and earthy to my senses—like a teaser for something even more delicious.

The end result was messy, though. He didn't want to come in my mouth, so he abruptly gripped the back of my hair and pulled me off of him. We argued about it afterward, because the sticky wetness of his orgasm landed on my face and neck. I didn't mind, but rationally, how is that any better than his coming in—

"*Oliver.*"

"What?" I look up from my breakfast plate and at Alexander

beside me since he's the one who called my name. He nods toward Lord Blakeley. When I scan the table, everyone is staring at me. "Y-yes?"

"Where is your silly little head today? Do you not hear me speaking to you?"

"Sorry... could you please repeat what you said?" I have no idea. The last time I was listening, they were gossiping about someone in Alexander's extended family. I zoned out and started replaying the details of last night in my mind because, well, being naked with Aries is much more interesting, isn't it?

Lord Blakeley rolls his steel-colored eyes. "No. I'll get my answer directly from the source. Camille, please ask our guest to join us?"

"Of course, your highness." Camille steps away from the wall of servants and assistants, then scurries from the room.

Nobody says a word and they all resume eating. Utterly confused, I flicker my gaze to Alexander, questioning. He's no help either as he offers a weak shrug, then stuffs a slice of toast covered in apricot jam into his mouth.

Would it have been so difficult to repeat whatever he'd said? Why does he show such disdain for me when I swear that all I do is whatever he fucking asks?

Ten minutes later, I get my answer. Setting my fork down, I mechanically look toward the entryway, because I smell him before I see him. We haven't fed from each other, but already, the scent of Aries is permeated inside of me, like a jasmine mahogany glaze covering my inner walls and senses.

Soon, he appears alongside Camille. He's poised, casual but handsomely dressed, and he's definitely paler than when he first arrived. Seeing him in the bright daylight and set against the dark pattern of his shirt somehow emphasizes this fact. Aries steps toward the long table full of my and Alexander's families and offers a deep bow.

"Good morning, your highness. You requested to see me?"

"I did. Have breakfast with us. My daughter's mate couldn't

join us today so you can sit beside Sasha." He gestures toward the empty seat next to Sasha, which is directly across from me.

Aries doesn't miss a beat. "Of course, your grace. It would be my honor." Fluidly, all long legs and self-assured stride, he moves toward the seat, pulls out the chair and sits down. Sasha's eyes meet mine in an obvious look that screams panic. I ignore her but adjust in my chair and take a deep breath.

Stay calm. Act natural.

What does natural even mean for me? Disinterested? Aloof? I can't remember anymore. There's no way that I could pull off either of those dispositions in Aries's presence. Given the things we've done in secret, my nature is too sensitive and attuned to him. Feigning neutrality in his presence is impossible when every atom and cell in my body is celebrating his nearness.

"How are the suits coming along?" Lord Blakeley asks. "The designs you sent for my approval were impressive."

"Thank you, my lord." Aries offers a polite nod just as someone from the kitchen sets a full breakfast plate in front of him. "Everything is on schedule. I'll have both gentlemen ready well before the ceremony."

"Good man. I'm excited to see the final result. It isn't often that we entertain such... progressive company. Aries—or do you prefer 'Mr. Moralis'?"

"Aries is fine, your grace."

"May I ask how old you are?"

"I'll be ninety-five this year."

"Astonishing. To be nearing one hundred but still unbonded. Please, forgive my ignorance, but I must inquire. How do you manage this lifestyle? Do you not worry about where your next feeding will come from, particularly when you travel to new locations such as this one?"

Around the table, everyone's attention is centered on Aries. Lord Blakeley has asked the question more politely than Alexander, at least. But it still feels uncomfortable and invasive—especially at a breakfast table full of strangers.

"Typically," Aries begins calmly, matter-of-fact, "when I travel, there are many others who enjoy a similar lifestyle, so it is not difficult to obtain a quality feeding source."

"And how do you find Eden?" Lord Blakeley asks this question with a devilish glint in his eyes.

Aries smiles, fluffing out his napkin before laying it across his lap. "Eden is much more conservative than I had anticipated. But I am well, your highness."

"*Ha.*" Lord Blakeley claps his hands. The elaborate ruby on his ring finger glistens in the morning sunlight. "I suspected as much. Your complexion is that of a vampire who's in desperate need of a good feeding—despite your admittedly very complacent outward demeanor. We shall take care of it. You are our honored guest, after all. Benjamin! Come here, please."

The viscount's primary manservant steps away from the back wall and smoothly approaches the head of the table. Ben is close to my age but older. He's first-gen, has a hefty, strong body and bright round eyes. Once he's beside Lord Blakeley, he bows. "Your highness?"

"Please feed our guest."

Ben nods, then purposefully steps toward Aries's side of the table.

"Ah—please..." Aries falters. I can see it in his eyes. The subtle blush of his pale, dimpled cheeks. "Your grace, I'm honored by the offer. But surely, I can wait until after breakfast—if Benjamin has time in his schedule?"

Lord Blakeley blinks as if he's startled by Aries's hesitation. He looks over at Ben and is clearly amused. "Well, do you have time in your schedule?"

"Yes, my lord. Of course." He bows, then hastily returns to the wall with the rest of our assistants and servants.

"I did not expect you to be shy, Aries." Lord Blakeley picks up his mimosa glass and brings it toward his mouth. "Are all contemporary vampires so... prudish?"

"We are mindful, my lord." Aries nods, then picks up his own glass and drinks as if he's finished with the conversation.

I watch this unfold and a new, unpleasant feeling gnarls and twists in my gut. It makes me lightheaded.

I do not want Aries to feed from Benjamin—not in front of me at this table, nor in private somewhere on the estate. How can... I cannot even imagine him being that close to someone else. To sink his teeth into his flesh and drink of him? Aries should be feeding from *me*. I've offered myself to him and he refused. Despite the fact that my nature is screaming to give—

"We're not so conservative, are we, my love?"

My train of thought is broken when Alexander grabs my hand and brings it up toward his mouth. The moment is like a psychedelic tailspin—utter confusion as I slowly witness his fangs elongate. Understanding with a shock of clarity, I snatch my hand away as if he's on fire.

"What the *hell* are you doing?" I exclaim, stunned. Has he lost his fucking mind? Yes, we've fed from each other in front of servants and assistants our whole lives, but never at a table full of our family members and a guest at a formal meal. Not ever.

When I glance around the table, everyone is looking at me as if I'm in the wrong. History has taught me how this will play out. Immediately, I shake my head, directing my attention toward Lord Blakeley. "I apologize, but please don't make me do this. *Please.*"

A long pause stretches over the table. To the point where I can hear myself swallow. My heart thuds heavily in my ears.

Lord Blakeley's voice is ice cold. "I have not 'made' you do anything—"

"Huh." To my surprise, a scoff pops out of me. It is laced with so much incredulity that my contempt is unmistakable. Lord Blakeley's eyebrows arch into his forehead as he draws back.

Apparently, I've surprised him, too.

"Alexander, we have not raised you to openly feed at a formal gathering. You know better than that," Lady Victoria

Kendrick cuts in from the opposite end of the table. Her demeanor is flippant, but I notice that Alexander sits up a little straighter. "If you wish to feed, take your mate somewhere private, please?"

The phrase "take your mate" hitches in my mind, making me feel sour. I'm not his mate and I have a name.

Without preamble, Alexander stands, loudly shoving his chair back from the table. "Yes, Mother." He glances down at me, frowning. "Let's go." He barks the order and walks toward the doors to leave the breakfast room. Everyone stares, waiting for me to move because there's no space to disobey him. There will be no discussion about this.

Annoyed, humiliated, I stand and slink behind him. Like an abused pet on an invisible leash.

"Meet us out front in an hour," Lord Blakeley says icily as I pass. "We'll be leaving for the tour of Ashbury. Do not be late."

My face burns from embarrassment. I refuse to look at Aries as I leave, because I physically can't. This circumstance is too demeaning.

"Did you hear me?" Lord Blakeley says, raising his voice.

I pause but speak without turning to face him. "Yes. I won't be late."

When I'm outside of the breakfast room and have shut the double doors, I notice that Alexander is ahead of me, waiting. I step closer, but he flips and walks with purpose down the corridor.

"Where are we going?" I ask, sighing and trailing behind.

"To your bedroom."

I stop dead in the middle of the hallway. "What? We don't need to go all the way up there to feed. You can feed here. Outside of the breakfast room is fine. Or in the study next door."

Alexander turns, striding toward me, and his brown eyes are filled with something like... I don't know? Hostility? I've never seen this expression on him before.

When he's close, I instinctively step back. But he invades my space, then points past me toward the double doors we just exited. "I am *not* going back in there with you."

"Why?" I ask, lifting my palms to create some distance between our bodies. His nose is inches away from mine. "J-just please calm down—"

"Because I refuse to sit there for another second, watching you fidget and swoon over that fucking designer!" His stare is intense. Accusatory.

I take another step back, shaking my head. "I don't know what you—"

"Bullshit, Oliver. Don't play me. You think I don't know you? I've been feeding from you since we were teenagers. I can read your aura and energy better than my own! You almost always run dormant and cold, but lately, the energy inside of you is bubbling and sparking like a damn volcano. And it sure as hell isn't because of me—so it's him. Stop *lying* to me."

Alexander steps away, huffing as he walks toward the wall beside us. He leans with his back against the stone, rubbing his face as his chest heaves.

I don't know what to say. In all my years of knowing him, I've never seen Alexander like this. Serious and upset. Usually, he's flippant and confident. Like the whole world is balanced on the tip of his pinky finger.

When I don't say anything, he drops his hands and looks at me. "Why? What... what does he do that I don't? Why do you hate me so much?"

I swallow. "I don't hate you."

"But you definitely don't like me. You never have. Seeing how you behave next to this Aries vampire, it's very clear to me now."

"It isn't just you, really—I..." Alexander and me, we don't talk this way. We don't have candid, real conversations, so I'm hesitant to try. His intention seems sincere, but I'm also waiting for him to flip this into a joke and call me a nerd or a loser.

Inhaling a breath, I steel myself. "It isn't just you, necessarily. I hate the circumstance. I hate being made to do things with no consideration of my personal wants, thoughts or feelings. It's demeaning and empty. Like I'm a puppet."

Alexander blinks, frowning as if I've given him a complex mathematical equation to solve. "But that's your role."

"Wow—"

"*No*, I mean... it's your station, Oliver."

"Maybe I don't want this to be my 'station.' Maybe I want something else! Something completely different."

"But what would you even want? This is who we are. These arrangements are the basis and core of our aristocracy. We don't have a choice."

"Wrong. You chose me—you at least had a say in this." I point between the two of us. This is a smaller, less relevant point in the bigger picture, but I want to make it.

Alexander shrugs. "Yeah, but you're the only aspect of my life that I've ever intentionally chosen. Everything else is told to me—or I'm pushed in some direction or escorted down another. But with you, I just... I don't know. I wanted you, Oliver. I've always known that."

How do I respond? How can I express that what I desire is far beyond him—or us or this. I want to get away from here. To be free and to make all my own choices. Is that so unfathomable?

I stand across the hallway from Alexander, picking at my hands and trying to find the words. He surprises me when he pushes off the wall, stepping closer.

"You don't hate me," he says, his eyes searching. "But could you like me? Could you try?"

"I... don't know if it works like that."

"Why can't it?" he asks, stepping even closer but more cautiously this time. His anger has diffused. "What if... you tell me what he does? What is it about him that makes you smile and stirs your nature? What about him turns you on?"

Heat flashes in my cheeks and I bring my palm to my forehead, stressed. I cannot do this. "Alexander, please stop, I don't—I don't think I can talk about this."

"Ollie." He wraps his fingers around my wrist, pulling my hand from my face. The blush is running all across my skin, and as I look at him, his face is flushed, too. His golden-brown eyes are soft. Almost pleading.

"I don't want to have an empty and fake bond with you. I need us to be real. Can you... Would you please *try*, with me? Not daydreaming about the designer, but looking at me and letting your aura flare because of me. Because I love you."

How can he say that so casually? What does he even know about me? I'm not sure how to respond to any of this and I feel inundated with emotions. I need to be by myself to process.

"I'd like to go to my room alone to think," I say, keeping my voice low to match the tone he's set. "I'll see you soon, for the tour?"

Alexander nods, still holding my wrist. "Okay, but... may I feed first, please?"

"Yes." I don't want him to feed right now. He's so close to my face and it feels too intimate. The way we feed is usually clinical. Distant to where I can shut my mind off and let it wander.

But there isn't any of that as he brings my palm up and licks my skin with a slow, intentional drag of his tongue. He bites down while staring directly into my eyes. As he pulls, his brown eyes alight, glowing fiercely in a radiant golden hue just before he shuts them and exhales a satisfied sigh. I look away, ignoring the warm and strange swish of feelings in my stomach.

This is uncomfortable. I don't know how to feel about it, but what I know for certain is that I'd give anything to have this experience with Aries. To nourish him back to health and have him pull from me.

But here I am, feeding Alexander—this vampire that's been forced on me against my will—while Aries is getting ready to slurp on Ben.

Life sucks, you know? It really does.

Chapter Twenty

"You're the bravest vampire I've ever met, you know that? Iconic."

Within ten minutes of getting back to my room, Sasha knocked on the door. She's pacing across the floor with the excitement of someone who's just left a major sporting event where her team won by a narrow margin.

"That scoff! The sound you made at Heartless when he said, 'We haven't made you do anything...' Christ alive. It was like a two-ton slap in the face. The weight of the world was delivered in that single-syllabic sound. Like, '*Don't you fucking dare—*'"

"Sash." I'm lying prostrate on my stomach on the bed, but I whip my head to the side, scowling. "Would you please lower your voice and calm down? This isn't a game." It must be nice to play the role of bystander, watching as someone else's life crumbles all around them. I press my face back into my pillow. I'm trying to smother myself but it's not working.

"How can I calm down when this is probably the most exciting thing that has ever happened to me?"

"That's... really sad. It's not even happening to you." The weight of the bed shifts, which tells me she's sitting at my side.

"And oh God—poor Alexander brooding through the entire thing. His narrowed eyes were darting between you and Aries like one of you stole his lucky penny but he couldn't figure out which one." Sasha laughs, slapping her thighs. "Ahh, what a time to be alive."

Unexpectedly, a laugh bubbles up from my chest. I turn my head to look at her. "You're insane."

"Maybe." She smiles. "It was a refreshing reminder of the Ollie that I knew as a kid. What happened after you and Mr. Purebred Prince left the room? And did you hear what Aries said?" She raises her chin to elongate herself, mocking Aries's confidence and smooth voice. "'We're mindful, my lord.' *Pow.* Another discreet slap across the face. Aries is like a fox. Watching him, you'd never know that the two of you were sleeping together... Are we sure that this isn't another elaborate fantasy that you've made up in your head?"

Lifting, I stare at her in disbelief. "Are you questioning my sanity?"

"No... well, a little?"

I roll my eyes and drop back down into the pillow. How could I possibly fabricate the goodness of his intoxicating scent? The mutual pull of our natures and the way my eyes alight. His compassion, patience and the way he validates things I've only ever thought about—things I've never dared to say aloud to another vampire.

"Well, Camille is the one who brought this to my attention," Sasha says, patting her hand in the center of my spine. "*You* tried to hide this from me."

"Yes, and your prudence is truly masterful. Good job at the breakfast table earlier."

She snickers, sensing my sarcasm. "Sorry about that. So, tell me what happened with Alexander?"

Flipping onto my back, I stare up at the high ceiling, examining how it arches elegantly to a point. The way the light from the window casts a hazy shadow on one side. "He told me that he wants us to have a 'real' bond. And that he loves me. Which is completely unnecessary."

"Why is it unnecessary?"

I turn my head to look at her. "You're not surprised by this confession?"

"You are? I think Alexander's affection for you has been fairly obvious since you were kids. You'd be totally in your own world, as per usual, but he used to pay such close attention to you—he would watch you watching the caterpillars."

"Excuse me?" I have no idea what she's talking about.

Sasha shakes her head. "You're impossible. Do you remember the first summer when they started bringing Alexander here to get you two acquainted? This was before the official decision was made, I think."

"No. Barely."

"Well, I do. You were such a chatterbox back then. That was before Heartless started his campaign to condemn you into silence and submission. Anyway, we'd be out in the garden with the nannies and you'd wander off, suddenly quiet and intensely watching some insect. A caterpillar, or maybe a bumble bee that had landed on the flowers. Alexander would sit and watch you, perfectly content. I always remembered that. It was sweet."

Exhaling a sigh, I roll over onto my side. "And yet he's dismissive when I speak, treats me like his pet and calls me names. What's 'sweet' about that?"

"I think... he wants your attention, but he doesn't know how to get it. How do you capture the attention of a hopeless daydreamer when you're grounded in the reality that they want to escape?"

Sasha pauses, regarding me as the silence settles between us. As if she genuinely expects me to answer this question.

"You're philosophical today," I tell her.

At first, she doesn't respond, like the wheels in her mind are busy and spinning. After a moment, her expression softens. "That's why Aries is so appealing to you—he's a liberated vampire living his life exactly the way he wants and traveling the world. An artist perfecting his craft. He's the embodiment of your wildest dreams, isn't he?"

Her words are like sharp stabs to my chest. My throat is tight, so I flip and turn my back to her. "That isn't the only reason why I like him."

"But that's it, isn't it? Maybe... and, not that I want to encourage your inability to accept reality—"

"Thanks for that."

"Maybe, if you were a free vampire, you wouldn't feel so desperate for Aries? You might find someone else even better suited for you."

"And if horses could fly, they might summer in the Maldives. You can play the 'if this then that' conjecture game with anything! *Ah*—" I yelp when Sasha slaps her open palm against my hip.

"Sassy. You're so restricted now, so you're probably just in need of *something*. Anything, you know? That's all I'm saying."

Lying still, I quietly consider her point. Is Aries just "anything" to me? Something exciting and shiny to play with? A vampire that checks all the boxes of my fantasy wish list?

Aries has come into my life at a distinct crossroads. I don't think this is a fluke, or even a passionate fling. In every interaction, he's conveyed something important, or unearthed some truth. I'm beginning to understand things about myself that, without his presence, I may never have known.

Sasha is partially right. Aries is the embodiment of my wildest dreams. But he also grounds me in a new reality. He opens my eyes to possibilities I had never once considered.

Turning my head toward her, I speak clearly. "You're right. His circumstance is appealing, but my feelings for Aries are rooted in something much deeper. Do you remember telling me about that purebred from Ethiopia? The one who made you feel like fire was rushing up your spine?"

Sasha smirks, folding her arms. "Of course I do."

"Aries makes me feel like that, except times a thousand. My nature, my heart and my mind, he sets everything on fire. All of it."

We watch each other for a tense moment, letting the words soak in. Soon, she stands from the bed. "That's beautiful, but... you do realize he's leaving in a couple weeks?"

Groaning, I flop back down onto the bed. "Sash, please—"

"And you're engaged to the most influential prince within our entire aristocracy. Speaking of, we need to head down. Heartless is still recovering from the 'scoff heard round the world.' Let's not add to the pile by being late for the Ashbury tour."

I sit up and start scooting off the bed. I should probably try to comb my hair and straighten my clothes since I've been flopping around like a depressed fish. I can't think about Aries leaving right now. I refuse.

"Oh," Sasha utters, standing near the door. "Camille said something funny to me, but don't be embarrassed."

"I'm already embarrassed." Walking toward the bathroom, I roll my shoulders. "It's my natural state."

"Right. Well, if you and Aries are going to keep, um... 'being rooted in something deeper,' you should do it in his room."

"Why?" Inside the bathroom, I pull out a brush, eyeing the wild flop of cinnamon-brown hair in the mirror's reflection. The sporadic, odd strands of blonde likely bleached by the late-summer sun.

Sasha peeks her head inside the doorframe. "She said that when she comes to wake you in the morning, she can tell when you two have been doing things in here, because, quote, 'the air is all sticky and sweet, like vampire sex.' She said you'd be better off doing it in his room, since the scent won't be quite as suspicious considering he's a free agent."

I drop my arm, staring at her through the mirror with horror and disbelief.

She grins. "Honestly, I envy you. Sounds like you're having an excellent time. Just... try to remember that this romance is transient? I'll wait for you in the hall."

The Ashbury tour was a mix of boring, neutral and uncomfortable, like any other official village visit. Townspeople fawned over us, giving our family praise and congratulations on my and Alexander's upcoming union. Alexander asked for permission to hold my hand while we walked the village gardens, which was new.

He's never asked for my consent to touch me in the past. Usually, he just grabs my hand like it's his birthright. I don't know what to think about this sudden shift in his behavior, but... I welcome the change.

By the time I return to the east wing of the estate, it's evening and the hallways are patterned with shadowy candlelight flickering from the sconces. The moon is high and luminous, causing silver light to pour through the corridor's arched windows.

When I approach Aries's room, I'm grateful that his door is shut because shame rushes over me as I recall the spectacle at breakfast this morning. Lord Blakeley shouting at me, then Alexander demanding that I follow him out of the room like I'm his naughty pet that accidentally peed on the carpet.

And, of course, Aries feeding from Benjamin.

I stalk up the winding staircase toward my room. I'm such a morose idiot—like a wounded animal caught in a trap with no chance of escape.

What does Aries see in me? Pathetic.

After I've taken a hot shower and am sitting on the edge of the bed in my pajamas, I still feel wretched, but also... insatiable. Today's disappointments sit like a weight in my chest, but my heart and nature yearn to be in Aries's presence. To feel his magnetism against my skin—the warmth of his nature, his scent and the soothing sound of his voice.

Almost involuntarily, my body springs into action. Before I

know it, I'm standing, barefoot, and walking toward my door. I move out into the hallway and down the stone steps until I'm in front of his room. The ground is cold beneath my feet despite it being a warm night.

I breathe. His woodsy and jasmine essence beyond the door is like an incense. A swirling and striking entanglement of spices that summons my nature. If he's asleep, I don't want to disturb him. It's selfish of me, but I place my fingertips to the textured wood and whisper his name. "Aries?"

"Come in." His voice is low beyond the barrier but alert. Awake.

Pushing the handle, I step inside and am met with the comforting *woosh* of his scent and goodness, like entering a portal and being transported to the most perfect summer evening. An orange, twilight sunset and woodsmoke. Emergent stars and the impending hush of night. His essence radiates this way to my senses. A distinct mood unto itself.

He's sitting upright in bed, shirtless and with a single lamp glowing brightly on the nightstand. A hardcover book rests in the fold of his right thigh. His left leg is outstretched with his pajama pants pushed up his calf. The covers around him are messily turned down. He smiles, warm and welcoming. "Hello, darling."

I smile. "Hey."

"How was the day?" He closes the book, then pats the space beside him. An invitation.

I walk over, but as I settle onto his bed, I notice his coloring is warmer, more bronzed and healthier than it was at breakfast this morning. It isn't just the lighting, because I can also sense the subtle change in his essence.

A hard lump lodges itself in my throat and I look away from him to distract myself. "Long. Tiresome... You fed."

He's quiet. Only for a moment, but it stretches on like a dreary, lonesome road as I wait.

"I did."

My skin prickles all over, and for the first time, my nature *hurts*. Sharp stabs piercing my back and spine, pushing through to my chest and stomach. Clenching my eyes shut, I take a deep breath.

"I can't feed from you, Oliver. We discussed this."

"I *know*. I know you can't. Just... give me a minute." Inhaling, I focus, stifling this pain in my nature that I've never felt before. Like betrayal. Indignation twisting into impossible knots. Logically, I understand this situation, but my body doesn't give a damn about what my brain is telling it.

Aries is silent while I work through these new feelings. After a few minutes, the pain fizzles out and my insides cool. The hurt is still there, but an echo. Much less intense. I lie back against the headboard and exhale.

"The desire of a purebred's nature can be profound," he says, finally breaking the silence. "To deny it without suffering takes immense skill and control. I don't want you to be in pain because of me." Aries slips his hand into mine, entwining our fingers and squeezing.

I open my eyes and turn my head toward him. "I'm alright. I'm fine now, and..." I pause a beat to gather my thoughts. "Even if it's painful, being close to you and considering everything that you've shown me, it's worth it. Does that make sense? Or do I sound like an insane vampire?"

Aries leans, touching his forehead to mine. "It makes sense." He kisses me with a lush press of our lips, just once, before he lifts his head again. "I think you're stronger than you give yourself credit for."

I chuckle. "Am I? I didn't feel particularly strong today."

"You are. But you're miserable here. In this place."

"I am."

"Have you ever sincerely expressed your discontent? Have you tried talking to your fathers about it?"

Hopeless, I shake my head. "Absolutely not. They wouldn't care. Well, maybe the viscount would, but it's doubtful."

"What about Alexander? Do you feel that he would listen to you?"

This question catches me off guard for some strange reason. Alexander might listen, but his behavior is confusing lately. "I don't know, to be honest."

Aries sighs heavily. "Could you run away? Simply disappear?"

With his hand still fastened in mine, I look up at the ceiling. "I've fantasized about this a million times—running away, I mean. Lord Blakeley doesn't have any power or reach outside of southwestern Eden, but escaping without support feels impossible.

"I don't have any money. I'm not even sure if I have proper identification or a passport to travel with. What would I do for work to support myself? Logistically, I don't know how I could pull it off."

Lowering my chin, I stare at the ivy-covered window across from the bed. The leaves flutter in the nighttime breeze like black slips of paper. Occasionally they reveal the glimmering, moonlit lake just beyond the glass.

"I could help you, Oliver. You wouldn't have to do it alone."

Surprised, I turn my head and our eyes meet. His offer is genuine.

The entire scenario of him helping me flashes across my mind like a tumultuous movie reel. I'd leave here, only to fling myself into his arms and be totally reliant on him. Depending on his money and resources like a spoiled pet. I'd go from poodle to poodle. Only the location would change.

I would hate myself for that. It's not the future that I would want with him.

"I appreciate your offer," I say sincerely. "But if I left here, I'd want to do it of my own accord—by my own will and effort. Then, I'd like to work, study photography and maybe travel?"

I'd perfect my craft until I was worthy enough to stand in front of Aries again. Not as an isolated and naïve vampire with no experiences, but as his equal.

"Those are brilliant aspirations," Aries says. "Truly, I hope they come to pass. But know that there's nothing wrong with accepting help along the way. We all need help, sometimes."

I'm listening, but his words trigger a recurring memory. "My brother, Thomas, ran away once," I offer. As a rule, I'm not allowed to talk about Thomas. With Aries, though, the rules don't seem to matter.

Aries blinks in surprise. "Really? I didn't see any stories about that when I researched your family."

"That one didn't make it to the papers. It lasted for about three days, but it was kept secret. He went missing at university—just vanished from his dorm room. He'd evaded his security guards, packed his things and was gone. Long story short, they found him. He'd tried to elope with a purebred girl he'd met in one of his classes. I don't know where they found him, but after they dragged him back home, he disappeared a second time."

"A second time?" Aries asks. "What does that mean?"

"We didn't see him around the estate for months. Lord Blakeley carried on as if nothing was amiss. The viscount was very anxious and tight-lipped. Everyone was eerily silent, and me and Sash were too afraid to ask what had happened. Then one day, Thomas just reappeared at breakfast. He was as pale as a ghost, his skin had scabs and he was rail thin but well dressed. The only words he spoke were 'Yes, sir' or 'No, sir.'

"Even now, he won't come to the estate unless he's formally mandated to do so. This pomp and circumstance for the wedding —the garden parties, banquets and village tours? He refuses to take part. But if Lord Blakeley specifically requests his presence, he shows up."

"Good God. What did your father do to him?"

I shrug. "I don't know, but my brother changed after that. Thomas and I were never close like me and Sash, but we used to talk at least, sometimes. He likes nature the same way that I do, so we'd trade books or go on walks together through the woods. But he's a stranger now. He only offers the bare minimum communication, then goes back to Upper Avalon until he's summoned again."

"He's traumatized." Aries sits back, exhaling another heavy sigh and running his free hand through his hair. "They broke his spirit."

"Maybe. I think the reason Sasha and me weren't allowed to formally attend university is because of Thomas. Things got harder after he ran away. I've never been anywhere outside of the estate without an escort or guard, like a prisoner."

"You are, in some alarmingly tangible ways," Aries says. "If you change your mind, know that I'm more than happy to help you. It would be my honor."

Hearing him say this is more than enough. A deep comfort to my mind and heart. "I know. Thank you. What are you reading?"

"Ah." Aries perks up, touching the thick book resting atop his lap. "This is Auguste Racinet's *Le Costume Historique*. I'm researching for my next assignment. Some light reading." He wiggles his eyebrows. The book is anything but light.

"For the production of *A Midsummer Night's Dream*?" I ask.

"Yes, you remembered," he says with his eyes sparkling. "I am embarrassingly excited. The elements I'll have at my disposal—vibrant silks, elaborately draped fabrics and heavy brocades. Gauzy wings, floor-length capes, prosthetics and horns. The sheer drama. It'll be a Shakespearean paradise."

"This is your passion," I recognize. I've never seen him so animated or enthused. "Not boring suits for outdated vampire ceremonies."

Aries winks. "We all have to start somewhere, and this event is far from boring—thanks to you."

"Hm." Leaning forward, I kiss him, just a quick touch of my lips to his. "I should go back to my room."

"Or you could stay?"

"I've interrupted your reading. I don't want to be a burden." I'm still embarrassed from earlier today. The ridiculous display between me, Lord Blakeley and Alexander weighs heavily on my shoulders.

Aries grips my hand a little tighter. "Reading was a diversion. Truly, I wanted to know if you were alright, but I couldn't decide if I should come to you. Please stay, my young master."

I draw back with my nose upturned. "Stop calling me that."

His gaze is frisky. "You don't like it?"

"No."

"Are you sure, my young lord? I am but a humble servant to your needs. To your sweet and delicious essence that resonates like moon-dust and sugared peonies." He inches forward, grabbing my waist and pulling me toward him. I writhe, half balking at his absurd description but half turned on by his playfulness.

"*Stop*," I protest, laughing and giving very little resistance. "You know it's not like that."

With my waist in his grip, he wrestles me down onto the bed as he settles on his knees, trapping and straddling my thighs. "Isn't it precisely like that?" he says. "I find it sexy."

"But I don't see you that way. You're not my servant. And you're always stressed about the difference in our rank, or me manipulating you with my aura, which I would never—"

"Oliver. Early on, I might have made some unfortunate assumptions based on your station and circumstance that I should not have. Now that I know you better, for heaven's sake, you don't even..." Aries pauses, then shakes his head. "Darling, where vampiric bloodlines are concerned, you are my superior. This fact cannot be denied. However, if *I* choose to lean into and embrace this truth, the power between us becomes aligned. It is stabilized. Do you understand?"

I stare up at him like he's crazy. "No."

He leans down until his face is inches above mine. His voice is low and seductive. "You will, in time. Sleep here tonight, with me. We'll make sure that you're back in your room before sunrise?"

My response is muffled because as soon as I part my lips to

answer, Aries is there, covering my mouth in a desirous kiss and dipping his tongue into me.

Soon, I forget about everything. The constant pressure and disapproval from Lord Blakeley, the confusion and weirdness surrounding Alexander.

All of it disappears.

Chapter Twenty-One

Lighthearted music fills the air and the sun shines golden and warm in a partly cloudy sky on the day of Upper Avalon's celebratory fête. Royal purple and striped navy blue and silver tents beautifully line the village green. The colors represent Alexander's and my families' crests, respectively. Scalloped awnings flutter in the soft breeze as each vendor showcases some unique form of amusement.

There are several tents that offer challenging games of wit or strength for prizes. A tent for wine and whiskey is packed full of vampires, then there's another for "bloodied" candy apples and treats. One vendor offers to do a free aura reading to determine the fortitude and deeper essence of a patron's vampiric line.

I enjoy fêtes. Stiff banquets and balls are boring. It goes without saying that I'm not a fan of combined family meals. But something about the cheerful, simplistic nature of a traditional village fête usually makes me smile.

Not today, though. Today, a weight is sitting at the pit of my stomach. Heavy dread and discontent. I can't shake it.

Tomorrow, we're all leaving for Central Eden. Both Alexander's family members and mine will be there for five days, doing yet another full-blown tour of breakfasts, banquets, balls and garden parties. This time, the festivities are for the amusement of the Kendrick Clan's local aristocracy.

I'm not looking forward to it for many reasons, but primarily because Aries won't be with us. He's nearly finished with Alexander's suit, so he's been instructed to remain at the castle until we return. At that time, he'll do a final fitting before his assignment in Eden is over.

It's the beginning of the end.

Every time I think about it, I feel like my insides are being raked out until I'm hollowed and raw. I can't face it. I know that I have to, but it's stirring an anxiety and sadness inside like I've never known. The distress is burrowed so deeply that I don't know how to manage it.

All I can do is pretend that it's not happening. Which isn't the healthiest response.

As we stroll the green, Alexander walks beside me with his palms clasped behind his back. He smiles and speaks to every single vampire that we pass. Sometimes, he initiates a friendly conversation.

I do not, but I nod politely. For the past week, he's been... I'm honestly not sure what he's been. More respectful toward me? Well mannered? His behavior has shifted again. It makes him a little easier to be around, if I'm honest.

"Hey, isn't that your brother?" Alexander nods in the direction diagonal from where we stand. I look, and Thomas is there, sitting alone on a bench just off the brick-lined path and in between two purple tents. I wasn't sure if Lord Blakeley would require him to attend this event. Considering it takes place within his mate's realm and where they reside, it would have been odd if he wasn't here.

"Do you want to talk to him about sibling stuff?" Alexander asks. "I can wait here."

I'm not sure that I do. Seeing Thomas feels like a superstition —or rather, some kind of ominous omen, especially when I'm already unsettled about our impending departure to Central

Eden. The air and mystery surrounding my brother feels dark because of my childhood memory of his disappearance then horrifying reappearance.

However, I'm an adult now. I should probably act like one and say hello. "I'll be right back," I tell Alexander, then walk toward the bench.

When I'm close, I half expect him to see and greet me first. He does not. As I approach, he's staring off into space. I'm within a couple feet of him, and he doesn't even notice me. "Hey, Thomas."

His head doesn't move, but his pale gray eyes shift at the sound of my voice. There's no warmth in his expression. No familiarity or affection. "Hello, Oliver. Congratulations on your engagement."

"Thank you..." I pause because he looks off as if the conversation is finished. I could walk away, but I gesture toward the seat beside him. "May I sit?"

"If you wish."

Gingerly, I sit on the edge of the bench with my palms set against my knees. Thomas and I are literal opposites within our family's genetic spectrum. He's taller than me, and his skin and eyes are pale like Lord Blakeley's. My complexion and natural, unlighted eyes favor the viscount and our southern Eden coastal roots—a warm, sun-kissed skin tone and bright oceanic-blue irises. "How are you?"

"Well, and you?"

I shrug. "I'm just okay. Where is Lord Ashford?"

"At home. My presence here is mandatory but his is not."

I have no idea how Thomas feels about his mate, Lord Ashford. I've only met him a handful of times and he's very quiet. Reserved. The two of them were pushed together through yet another political arrangement. They officially bonded within the first three months of being married, though. Three months is record-breaking according to Eden standards.

Maybe they actually like each other?

"Did Lord Blakeley require you to be here?" I ask. "I'm sorry if he did."

Thomas flickers his gray irises in my direction. "Why should you apologize for his actions, Oliver? You have no say in this circumstance, either."

"Yes, right..." I'm tempted to apologize again, but I hear Aries in my head, telling me that I apologize in excess.

"It's funny that after all this time, you still adamantly call him Lord Blakeley," Thomas says, watching me from the corner of his eyes. "I can't ever recall you saying 'Father' to address him."

"Because the word 'Father' should be demonstrative and endearing. It's reserved for someone that a person holds dear and maybe even trusts. Why would I call him by that name?"

I'll never call him Father. "Birth conduit" or "Overlord Blakeley" would be even more appropriate.

To my surprise, Thomas laughs. Not outright. Just a quick huff of breath through his nose as he shifts his gaze toward the green. "You were always the smartest, Oliver—out of the three of us. You are right to feel that way about him. Spot on."

Thomas stands. I'm assuming the conversation is finished, but he turns his lanky frame to the side and looks at me.

"May I give you some unsolicited advice?"

"Yes," I say, meeting his intense, unemotional gaze.

"Never trust a word that vampire says. Nothing. Do you hear me?"

I nod, unmoving. "I do."

He turns and takes a step, but then pauses again to look over his shoulder. "Another thing. If you're clever enough to get away, don't get caught. *Never* return to that castle." Without another word, he stalks across the grass.

I stare after him with my mouth agape and my pulse beating in my temples. If the dread inside of me was like a misty rainfall before... after this conversation? It's a thunderous hailstorm.

～

The heavy black veil of night beyond my window shifts into a moody blue. Still dark but warmer. Tinged by the subtle golden glow of the rising sun.

Everything is tranquil and soft. Birds chirp and fill the air with their cheerful song—like fingertips lightly grazing the high notes of a piano.

Aries's breath huffs against the back of my neck. His heavy arm is draped over my hip and his chest is melded to my spine.

I haven't slept. I didn't want to.

Sleeping felt like a waste of valuable time. How could I risk being unconscious in the presence of this creature that I may or may not ever have again? When any hope of a future together is so precarious and uncertain.

So, I've lain here all through the night, simply absorbing his presence and shrouded in his scent. Savoring the calming heat of his skin against mine and the steady beat of his heart.

Aries and I have fallen into a routine over the past week. Following dinner every night, Alexander insists on escorting me back to my room. Thankfully, he hasn't brought up "practicing" anymore. He hasn't tried to touch or kiss me, either. Once he's gone, I shower, put on my robe, then spend the night in Aries's room. Sometimes, if I take too long, Aries ends up in mine.

We indulge. We kiss, caress and embrace. We push ourselves to the brink of passion and we come. He's only let me suck him once more since my first try, but he does it to me *every* night. I think this is unfair, but I don't argue it. Aries is hesitant about letting me do it, so I'm happy with what I can get.

Withholding my aura while we make love has gotten easier, but a vital part of myself is being denied each time. It's like... having an incredible orgasm but not being allowed to make a sound. Everything inside of me wants to scream. To exhale, moan and relish the feeling of our entwined bodies and how he makes me feel. I want to express my innate gratification with his essence and make my intentions clear.

But I mute myself. Making love with him is wonderful, but

I'm severely restrained because I don't want to jeopardize his health by overexposing him to my nature.

My thoughts are distracted when Aries shifts his heavy leg over me. It makes his cock rest in the curve of my ass. I inhale, tensing as my heart-rate doubles.

Quietly, I've contemplated this in the deepest recesses of my mind. But I've also been too shy to ask him about it. We've been comfortably exploring each other. which, this much I'm truly grateful for. That he's entered into this private, sensual space with me despite his rational and valid apprehensions.

But he's never made a move to suggest that he wants more of me. Aside from me asking to suck his cock, we haven't talked about anything. He never initiates our sexual advancements. It always comes from me.

Why? Knowing Aries, I suspect that it has to do with his usual logic—I'm a purebred with "ancient blood." Younger. Inexperienced. He wants to respect these things and not overstep whatever invisible social or moral boundaries exist between us.

We've already crossed multiple lines. Why pick and choose about holding back now?

"Are you awake?" I ask quietly. My body naturally arches into him, grazing his shaft.

"Mm... I should go." His voice is groggy and full of sleep, but he doesn't move. Several seconds pass and he remains lazily wrapped over me like the most divine quilt.

"I wish you wouldn't," I say, dazed as I arch more. I close my eyes and revel in this gentle, teasing sensation. The length of him rubbing against the dip of my ass. This delicious friction.

My breath catches when he clamps down, gripping my stomach so that I can't move.

"God in heaven—would you stop squirming?" he groans, but kisses into the curve of my neck. I lift my chin against the pillow, wishing with every inch of my soul that he would bite me. For his fangs to elongate, break my skin and pull to his complete satisfaction.

I'd give anything. Everything.

"I might be okay if you stopped rubbing your ass into me," he argues in between kisses. "How am I supposed to leave when my young master is behaving with such enticing unrestraint?" As he leans down to lick me, his hand slides lower. Soon he grips my shaft and I push into him again, clenching my eyes shut and inhaling sharply with my lips parted. I can't speak.

"I'll see you next week when you return," he says softly. "But... perhaps I should satisfy you once more before we separate? If you wish?"

"I..." The fire inside swells and fiercely rushes up my spine—wanting to push outward and be free. I force it down because I need to concentrate. I have to say this. Otherwise, it won't be said. "Aries, could we... would you..." I swallow. How do I vocalize this?

"Yes, darling?" His grip tightens on my shaft and he playfully runs his finger along the tip. "Tell me what you need."

"*Ah*—" Straining, I bend my leg so that his grip falters and I trap his hand. He pauses. I take a breath and the words rush out. "Could we do this with you inside of me? Could I please have that?"

The appeal is there, sitting stagnate between us. Shifting my head, I blink up at him.

Aries stares down at me for a long moment before he sighs.

"Oliver."

"Yes?"

"The sun is coming up."

"I know."

"Which means I need to go back to my room before Camille arrives."

"Sure..."

"And me being inside of you isn't something to be done hastily."

"No?"

"No."

"Oh…" It's awkward. I look away because I don't know what to say. "I'm sor—"

"Don't do that," he says, turning his head and considering for another moment. "Why didn't you express this last night?"

"Because I've been nervous about asking, I think."

"Hm." He considers, working his jaw as he looks at me. "May I ask a potentially inelegant question?"

"Yes?"

"Have you done this before? Perhaps with Alexander or some other vampire?"

"I haven't… Does that matter?"

"Yes," Aries says, his face softening. "It absolutely matters." He climbs over me and stands from the bed. "Where is that oil that you used before?"

Hopeful, I sit up slightly. "In the bottom cabinet on the far right, just behind the shampoo." A messy, emotional mix of excitement and nervousness swishes around in my chest. He strides, naked and god-like, into the bathroom. Does this mean we're doing it? Is he giving me what I want?

"I can't give you what you want," he says, returning to the bed with the jar of coconut oil. "Not completely."

"Oh."

"You've never done this before and Camille will be here soon. We don't have much time."

Looking over at the analog clock high on the wall, I estimate. "Well, we have some time. But if you don't want to do this—"

"It isn't that I don't want to." He sits along the side of the bed, holding the jar against his thigh. He's silent for a moment. "I just… don't think that I should be the first vampire to touch you this way. Who am I to be doing this with you?"

I draw back, frowning. "What does that mean? 'Who am I?' You're *my* choice, Aries. You're the one that I want to do these things with. Doesn't that matter?"

This is absurd. He already holds the title for so many of my "firsts." He's the first vampire that I've ever wanted to indulgently kiss—the first that my eyes and nature intensely responded to. The first that I've ever willingly made love to. Offered my blood too.

Everything with Aries is a first, so why should this be any different?

What's more, I would choose him for my remaining firsts. I've never had my aura pulled while someone fed from me, and I've heard that can be pretty earth-shattering. Nor have I ever bonded with another vampire. If I thought he was willing, I'd want these things, too.

He turns his upper body, facing me. "Of course it matters."

Sitting all the way up, I lean forward, resting my forehead against his temple. "I want to know how this feels, with you."

Aries chuckles. "You might not like it."

"Well, if I don't like it with you, I probably won't like it with anyone."

He tilts and presses a swift but luscious kiss to my mouth. "I think you have too much faith in me. Would you lie on your back, please?"

Grinning, I scoot and rest back down against the bed, thrilled as my nature burns and twists.

"I'm only going to stretch you with my finger, so you'll know how it feels and whether or not you might enjoy it," Aries says, positioning himself in between my knees.

"That sounds fine." Already, there's pressure in my groin and lower back. My body and nature are aroused from simply talking about this.

"You should know that anyone who does this to you quickly and without properly stretching you is either desperate, callous, ignorant or selfish. Likely all of the above."

"Noted. See? I've chosen my 'first' well."

Shaking his head, Aries picks up the small jar, examining the label. "You and this oil. I'll never be able to smell or see a coconut again without thinking of you."

My smile is devious as I writhe. Perfect. What else can I do so that he won't forget me? What can I do so that he remembers me whenever he breathes air?

Unscrewing the cap, he grins. "My sweet coconut prince."

I laugh, shaking my head in disapproval. "I'm not a prince."

"You're my prince. Coconut and peonies."

"Is that a good combination?"

"It is for me," he says. "You're perfect. Edible." He lays his palm flat against my stomach, which only intensifies the heat stirring there. Promptly, my eyes alight and my aura burns and pulses in my core. I stamp it down.

With one palm heavy on my belly, he wraps the fingers of his free hand around my shaft. I inhale sharply and arch because it's like being plunged into a warm, slick and tight ecstasy. The moan that passes between my lips is so loud that Aries shushes me as he smiles.

"My sweet insatiable prince. I've barely touched you." He grips me again, harder, while simultaneously rubbing my stomach with his palm. The fire of my aura crawls up my spine but I fold in my lips to keep myself quiet, humming in response to the pleasure radiating through me. Like my body is in a frenzied and electrified state.

Strangely, my incisors pulse. A low throb backdropped against everything else that's happening. That's new. I'm due to feed on Friday. This fact rushes to the forefront of my mind like the flash of a camera.

"I want you to touch yourself," Aries says, recapturing my focus. "Can you do that for me?"

I nod. He removes his hand from my cock and I take over. The sensation is not as euphoric as Aries's larger, firmer grip, but not bad. I know how to please myself, at least.

As I hold and pump, my shaft is already slick with coconut oil. Aries lifts up, resting on his elbow and hovering over me while his free hand strokes lower between my thighs. His fingertips trace the sensitive curves and flesh beneath my shaft, then dip and tease between the heat of my cheeks. The sensation is so gratifying that I gasp. Aries seizes the opportunity and covers my mouth in a kiss, slipping his tongue against mine and stimulating every part of me.

"Relax your body," he says, sitting up from the plush kiss. "But talk to me as we go. Tell me how it feels."

Nodding against the pillow, I want to answer him, but the wildfire spreading and curling underneath the surface of my skin prevents any logical speech from forming. I feel like I'm on a cliff and mere seconds from tumbling over.

"Lift your hips for me?" His voice comes out husky and masterful. I do as he asks. The next thing I know, I'm still on my back, but being dragged halfway into his lap and slightly inclined against his thighs. All of me is exposed to him. Wide open.

The moment his fingertip gently pushes into my ass, my hand freezes on my cock and I clench from the shock and foreignness of it.

"You're tensing," Aries says patiently. "Are you alright? Should we slow down?"

"I... No..." He urges my frozen hand aside, reclaims my shaft and grips me. I inhale, then blow it out. "It's just... new." If anyone else tried to do this to me, I honestly think I'd kick them with the heel of my foot. It's so strange, but carnal and intimate.

Intentionally relaxing my lower half, I let my legs fall open. I close my eyes and mentally and physically allow the intrusion. No. I welcome it. The reality of Aries's hands on my body—in my body. Touching me and exploring.

"Yes, darling... just like that." His voice is sensual and soothing, like an invisible element flowing over and stimulating my skin. It makes me relax and submit to him even more.

His finger pushes deeper, slowly pulsing as it moves. I take another breath and the sensation gradually morphs from foreign intrusion to wanton indulgence. From blind darkness to prolific sunrise.

A hedonistic desire blossoms from an unexplored corner within me. Aries's hand grips my cock and his finger delves deeper. I feel myself slipping into a kind of mental haze as my nature radiates hotter inside my body.

"Are we still alright? Talk to me."

I hear his voice but I can't respond. His finger pushes up against a wall and the pressure is... teasing but intense. He hits the spot a second time and I clench and gasp. I don't know if I can hold it together.

"Oliver?"

I can hardly breathe—hardly focus as I form the words. "I—We... Maybe we should stop..."

"Are you in pain?"

"*No.* I don't think—I can't—*Ah.*" He drags his finger back a little and I arch and clench my alighted eyes shut. I think... I might literally explode.

"Let it out."

My eyes flash open from shock and my breathing is labored. I shift my head to look into his face. "Are you sure?"

"Yes. Relax, Oliver. Let your aura rest."

Without another word, I do just that. I exhale, and slowly, the desire, heat and excitement melt from within. The sensation is like holding sand in my clenched fist, but then I relax my fingers. I open my palm and the grains stream and slip free.

Except it isn't just my hand. My body and nature open and are liberated. Weightless. Like magic, the energy of my essence glows all around my frame in a pale, silvery blue. It's enchanting and warm. Incomprehensible.

Aries parts his lips and inhales deep. His chest rises. His eyes alight and burn brighter than ever. I'm about to ask if he's okay, but his finger suddenly pushes within me again. It cuts off my ability to think and speak.

He touches the wall deep inside. Over and over. It's too much. Too good. I can barely breathe because of this wild flood of sensations. I close my burning eyes and give in to it completely, melting like hot candle wax in his hands.

My aura radiates more intensely as I come. Relentless and

joyful. Free from my imposed bondage. After a long moment of blissful tension, my entire frame goes limp—my arms and legs tremble and my fangs pulse aggressively.

Aries pulls out from inside and grips my body as if he's holding me steady. Or maybe he's at risk of being swept away by the force of my energy as well?

Slowly, the intensity of my aura dissipates. It fizzles out and I inhale a breath as I stare up at the ceiling. Holy shit...

Delirious, starving, I run my tongue along my teeth and realize that my incisors have sharpened to points.

"Oliver?" Aries watches me with shimmering deep-blue eyes. There's an expression settled in his face that I can't easily read. Disbelief? Shock?

Embarrassed, I reach and grab the pillow beside me to pull it over my face. My voice is muffled. "I'm alright." Am I? God help me. Every nerve ending feels charged with a thousand volts—screaming at me. I've never wanted to feed so badly in my entire life.

"Are you alright?" I ask, feeling my face and every other inch of my skin flush with heat. "I didn't manipulate you, did I? I didn't try to." Gripping the soft material in my fists, the pillow does little to cool my flesh. Suddenly, the makeshift protection is stripped from me and I gasp in surprise.

"Darling, what are you doing?" Aries asks, resting the pillow at my groin as he examines me with glowing eyes.

"Ah, well, I don't really know... exactly."

"Your fangs are out."

"Yes, right—but you don't need to feed me, obviously. I'm okay." This is awkward and slightly inappropriate. Evocative. Facing him openly with my fanged mouth is a clear indicator that I want to feed. From him, specifically. Plus, I'm purebred and that only creates additional, complex layers. That he should submit to my will and desire.

"I'm fine," I repeat, slowly shifting and drawing my leg up to unwrap myself from around his hips. "I just, hmm... I wasn't—"

"Oliver, how... how can you feel this strongly for me?" Aries asks, making me pause. "I don't think I understood. I thought, perhaps you were just... that truly, this is..."

He blinks, then runs a palm through his dark hair. His eyes are searching as if he can't find the words. Or maybe he knows the words but doesn't want to say them.

I fill in the gaps. "You were thinking that I'm young, and that this is just a chance meeting—a phase in my life. Once I'm properly bonded with my prince, I'll forget about you. You thought I would move on, right?"

Aries inhales a shaky breath and rubs his palms against his face. He doesn't answer, but he doesn't need to. Being exposed to my nature, he knows better now. He understands the truth.

"I keep telling you that it isn't like that, Aries," I say softly. "My feelings for you are..." I shake my head and take a breath. "I'm sorry if I overwhelmed you."

"You don't need to be sorry," he says, dropping his hands. "I asked you to let it rest."

"You did, but—"

"But nothing," he says. "It was... beautiful. Profound. Truly, you... You're the antithesis of everything I've known a purebred to be. It's as if the cosmos was determined to prove me wrong when it brought you into my life."

Pushing myself upright, I settle against my palms but with my legs still haphazardly gaped on either side of his body. I grin. "The cosmos and I have successfully colluded against you. Do you feel differently now?"

"I'd be a fool if I didn't." He leans down, brushing past my lips and kissing me on the cheek. Likely to avoid my fangs.

He lifts, meeting my gaze. "Do you feel stable? Are you in control?"

My body is still zipping with energy and I want him badly. Wholly. In every way. But my mind is clear, so I nod. "I am."

Aries cups my chin with the hook of his index finger, then raises his thumb to my lips and softly traces the shape of them.

"With my being first-gen, you know that I carry remnants of human DNA within my blood."

"I know that," I whisper against the pad of his thumb, entranced. Paralyzed. "You don't have to keep reminding me."

He sighs. The oakish-jasmine scent of him wafts against my face. I close my eyes. "For this reason, I might taste unpleasant to you. It's possible that my blood isn't strong enough to satisfy your palate and biological needs. Especially considering that you're accustomed to ancient purebred blood. Feeding from me could weaken your vampiric energy, or create health defects."

"No." I shake my head, resolute. "It won't."

He chuckles. "You're certain?"

Slowly, I open my still alighted irises and look at him, because I want to be clear.

"I am." Cautiously, I open my mouth. We maintain eye contact as he slides the tip of his thumb between my lips. I meet him with my tongue.

"Just a taste," he says, allowing it to slide further inside. "You have consent."

My heart pounds twice as hard but I don't hesitate. Smoothly, I take hold of his wrist to keep him steady, tilt my head and pierce his skin with my teeth. The smallest drop of his blood hits my palate and I suck his thumb. I close my eyes, exhaling and concentrating. Tasting and memorizing.

His essence is warm and buttery as it slips down my throat. Bright, but lively—like something spiced. Ginger or sweetened pepper.

I want more. To drown in him and have his flavor overwhelm my senses. If I had more, I could taste deeper and truly dissect. I could know and savor his undertones.

But I can't have him that way.

Not now. Not yet.

Opening my eyes, I slip his thumb from between my lips, breathing. Stifling the painful hunger inside.

"Am I unpalatable?" he asks, watching me vigilantly. "Perhaps I taste watered down?"

I sit still, considering for a moment. "You taste like liquid gold. Like life-giving energy. Honey, light and ginger. Like love." As we stare at each other, my fangs slowly retract. We're swathed in a silence that feels like soft cotton. Warm and protective. Enclosed.

Aries takes a breath and the trance is broken. "You've made it so painfully clear that you desire me, but what am I supposed to do, Oliver? What would you have me do?"

I shake my head. "Nothing. Thank you for trusting me. I'm grateful to you, Aries. I really am."

He turns, looking out the window and noting how far the sun has climbed over the horizon.

"You need to go," I tell him. "Camille will be here soon."

When he whips his head back toward me, there's uncertainty in his eyes. Hesitation. Lifting my hands, I hold his face. "I'm okay."

"You are not."

"But I will be, I promise. You've shown me so much. How can I ever be the same? How can I blindly go along with their plans anymore? I can't. I won't."

"What will you do? If you try to escape, I can help you."

"No." Lowering my hands, I find his between us and clasp his palms. "I want to do this. To stand up for myself and carve my own path, but... maybe we'll meet again? If I'm able to become free of my circumstance, somehow, would you be willing to see me? I don't need a promise or anything, I'd just really love to—"

I gasp, breathless. My words are cut off because Aries bends, takes hold of my head with both palms and kisses me, hard. Quickly, I shut my eyes, exhale and try to meet his rhythm. The intensity of his affection leaves me spent. Liquefied and molten.

When he raises his head, his face is flush. "Yes," he says. "Because I would give *anything* to meet you again—free from this place and circumstance." Smiling, he brushes his nose into mine. "And yes, it's a promise."

Relief sweeps through me. Effervescence, love and warmth flood my body as I lift my arms and pull him into a secure embrace. "I'll miss you this week," I whisper.

He kisses the tip of my nose, then looks me in the eyes. "I'll miss you, too, my sweet coconut prince."

Chapter Twenty-Two

It takes Aries several minutes, but he picks his clothes up from the floor, re-dresses, kisses me at least four more times in between, then finally leaves my bedroom.

I'm soothed and contented in his wake. The most wonderful tropical storm has swept through my bedroom—across my body, my bedsheets and even within me. I feel ravaged but delightful. Exhausted but fulfilled. Liberated.

The morning sun pours in through the windows and skylights, warming my flesh as I lie flat against the rumpled mess of sheets. Lifting my arms, I stretch, extending my limbs from the tips of my fingers, through my shoulders, spine and hips, and all the way down to my toes.

I finally let my aura breathe.

And I *tasted* him.

It was only the tiniest drop—a crumb or mere morsel where blood is concerned. But the memory of it is stark. Peppery and bright. I'll never forget his flavor. Not for as long as I live.

Shifting, I throw my legs over the side of the mattress. In my blissful and naked state, I open my bedside drawer where I keep the polaroid pictures that I took of Aries and me.

There are three photos sitting in the drawer, but... didn't I take four? I pick them up to examine them more closely. There's one of us both smiling at the camera, side by side—nice, but a little sterile. Another with Aries kissing my neck and me biting my lip, and the third is us kissing head on. My favorite. All the angles are perfect. Good for me.

There was definitely another one, though. The second shot that I took is missing. Maybe I dropped it between the bed and the nightstand?

Time is ticking, so I set the polaroid photos back inside the nightstand drawer. I'll look for the missing one later. I'm grateful for these pictures. Because now, the image of Aries won't be strictly concealed within my mind. I'll have physical references of him to divulge in. Images of the two of us together.

First, I open up all the windows to let the cool morning air inside. I do this after Aries spends the night in here, because I will never forget Sasha's remark about vampire sex smelling, quote, "sticky and sweet." Gross. But not gross if you're the vampire doing it, I guess? Not at all.

When I'm in the shower, I'm still riding the epic high of my night with Aries. I don't want to think about how I have to spend the next five days in Central Eden. At least Aries has equipped me with lots of memories and scenes to replay in my mind during the trip.

Dropping my arms, the hot water sprays my face and body. I close my eyes and a heavy weight settles inside my chest.

What am I going to do about this wedding? I can't go through with it anymore, can I?

After everything that Aries has shown me about myself, how can I keep playing this hollow game of purebred puppetry and arranged bondings? What if there's something more that I can offer to the world besides being Alexander's pet? Shouldn't I fight to find out?

But how do I escape? Where would I go?

Outside the shower, I'm cleansed of Aries's scent and essence, but a distinct sadness has blanketed my heart. Dried off, I'm slipping into my robe when something hits me.

Rather, someone.

Alexander's essence and presence are suddenly too strong. Confused, I step forward and yank the bathroom door open.

Alexander is sitting on the edge of my disheveled bed in a robe and his pajamas. He isn't looking at me, though, because he's examining something in his hands. Slowly, I realize my nightstand drawer is open beside him. Before I can mentally connect the dots, he lifts his head.

"You're actually fucking him, aren't you? This designer?"

Dead silence.

My brain has gone into shock because there's too much to process at once. Why is he in here this early in the morning? And more importantly, why is he sitting on my bed when I didn't invite him inside? Why has he gone through *my things*?

"Are you fucking him?" Alexander flips the polaroid around —and it's the one of me and Aries kissing straight on. "Answer me."

"What are you doing in my room? Who told you to come in here—"

"Don't evade the question, Oliver. Is that what matters right now?"

"*Yes*," I say loudly. Agitated. Furious. "Because you don't respect boundaries! How dare you come in here and go through my things?"

"How dare you fuck this first-gen designer when you're supposed to be bonding with me? How dare you *kiss* him when you barely even let me hold your hand?" Alexander's voice had been shrill, but then, he chuckles in a bitter, ugly sound. "I can't believe this horse shit. I thought you were just having your little wishful fantasies about this guy, but you're actually fucking him —and he's into you, too."

"Is that so hard to believe?" I ask, feeling my throat close from the hurt of his statement. From the stress of this moment. "That someone would want me? That another vampire might value me?"

Alexander stands abruptly, making me start and step back as he throws the picture down onto the bed. "*No*, that's not hard to believe, you prick—because I want you! *I* value you."

I shake my head. "You do not."

"How don't I?" He lifts his palms, dumbfounded. "I've told you over and over again that I want you—that I'm sincere about you, and that I've been waiting for this fucking ceremony since we were twelve! I've been waiting for you, Oliver."

"You haven't," I tell him, standing my ground. "You told me before that you've slept with other vampires—that 'everyone cheats' and that's how we work the system. You made fun of me for not having any experience." I take a breath and my chest heaves as I lift my hands, gesturing toward him. "All this, you reacting this way, is because I'm not your innocent and obedient little poodle that's been kept under glass especially for you anymore. You being upset about this is unfair. Hypocritical."

He scowls. "It's not. You're wrong."

I huff, amazed by his inability to see the logic in this circumstance. "Of course I'm wrong. Because I'm always the one who's naïve and stupid, right? I'm a nerd and a cold fish—"

"*No.*" Alexander turns, snatches the photo from the bed and stalks toward me. He thrusts the image at my face. His movement is so forceful that I flinch and step back, alarmed.

"You're wrong," he repeats, holding the picture of Aries and me kissing directly in front of my nose. "This is different because you *love* him, Oliver. You are in love with him. I slept with other vampires, but I didn't love them. What I did was just... It was meaningless experimentation. Practice, if I'm being honest. I've only ever loved you. *That* is why I'm hurt. That is why I'm upset."

Alexander stares at me with glassy brown eyes. Truly wounded. I never pay much attention to his aura, but I do now. His frustration and sadness are palpable. I don't know what to say.

He drops his arm and shakes his head. "There's no space for me now. I know that I get on your nerves. I realize that I've been immature, but I... I had hope that, given some time, maybe you could grow to like me—maybe even love me someday. When I've finally pulled you away from your father and you have more space to breathe. But it's done now, isn't it? There's no chance for me."

He lifts the picture in his fingertips and stares at it. "You'll *never* be like this with me. You won't ever be this... comfortable or happy. And I'll always be comparing whatever you do to this godforsaken picture. This stupid polaroid where you look so fucking blissful. I've never seen you look like this, but *he* has. He's probably seen everything of you that I've been dreaming about for the past ten years and it's bullshit!"

Alexander walks to the side of the bed, but he drops down onto the floor, letting go of the photo as he draws his knees up. He plunges his fingers into his blonde hair, massaging and making the usually perfect swoop of it wild.

The silence in the room is heavy after our shouting match. I walk over to the ottoman at the end of my bed and sit down, processing my mixed feelings about this situation.

How easy is it for him to play the victim? Am I supposed to feel guilty for falling in love? For meeting someone kind who treats me with dignity and respect? Someone suave and handsome who tells me that my thoughts are valid, and who genuinely considers my wants and desires. Am I supposed to feel bad about that?

Because I don't.

"I don't want to fight with you," Alexander says, breaking the silence. He looks over at me. "Aren't you going to say *something*?"

I consider for a moment. "Are you going to tell Lord Blakeley?"

He scoffs, upturning his nose as if I've just offered him something truly offensive. "No, I'm not going to tell 'Lord Blakeley,' you twat. Is that what you want? For him to have yet another reason to humiliate you in front of me and anyone else within earshot?"

"No," I admit, folding my arms. "That's not what I want."

"Your father is a jackass. I've always thought that my dad was a silly dinosaur, but holy hell. Your father is flat out cruel. He barely respects you as a purebred. He treats you like... I don't know—"

"His puppet?" I offer. "A glorified prisoner to do his bidding?"

"Yeah. It's wild. I know that we have responsibilities and all, but fuck him belittling you *all the time.*"

"You belittle me, too." I cast my eyes to the side, watching his reaction and waiting for him to deny it. To blame me for his behavior.

"I'm sorry," he says, meeting my gaze. "I mean it. I apologize. Really, I hadn't noticed until... Seeing the way he talks to you at these events, and then you perking up anytime that goddamn designer is in the room, it made me realize... I really got it wrong with you, didn't I? I thought I was being funny and casual, but I was just... I was mimicking his behavior."

Deflated, I shrug. "That's how it is in Eden. It's how we treat each other. Thoughtlessly. Callously."

"But you're not part of that, Oliver?" he asks. "You think that you're perfectly innocent?"

I open my mouth to respond, but immediately close it. Am I callous? Until this moment, I never thought so. Hearing the hurt in his voice a few seconds ago and the way it surprised me, I felt a twinge of remorse. I'm not sorry for anything that I've done with Aries, but I don't want to fight cruelty with cruelty.

Alexander leans his head back against the bed, sighing and closing his eyes. "I'm not an unkind vampire. Just... maybe a bit stupid, apparently."

Despite myself, I chuckle through my nose. I don't say anything because I can't argue with that.

"Do you love him?" Alexander opens his eyes and turns his head against the mattress, watching me. Serious.

The conversation is softer now. Calmer. "Yes."

"Why?"

"Why does anyone love anyone? Reasons. Feelings."

"Tell me the reasons. Tell me the feelings."

"You don't want to hear this," I say. "We don't need to do this. We don't do this."

"What do you mean?"

"Talk candidly and honestly. We never have."

Alexander sits upright and folds his legs as he faces me. "We could try? I'm serious, Oliver. Tell me why. I would like to know."

My spine stiffens as I cross my leg. "If you call me some stupid name or insult—"

"I won't! Look at you. See? This is what I mean. Your arms are folded, your legs are crossed and you're as rigid as a board. Totally closed off from me, like always."

"You've never given me a reason to *not* be rigid around you! Suddenly I'm supposed to bare my soul?"

"No, Ollie. You don't need to do that, I just want... Could you try to relax, please? I only want to listen. I promise."

Breathing, I roll my shoulders as I unfold my arms. I set my palms at the edge of the ottoman. Before I start talking, I want him to answer my original question. "Why did you come in here this early? You're not even dressed."

"Because I felt the essence of your nature flare outward this morning. It was so unusual to feel it radiate strongly like that. Part of me was afraid of what I might find, but I wanted to know."

Seriously? Was the strength of my nature that profound? That Alexander would sense it from across the estate? Does this mean that other vampires may have felt it too?

"Were you with him this morning?" Alexander asks. "Is that why?"

I roll my shoulders again. I'm really not comfortable answering these kinds of questions. "I was having lurid dreams."

He scoffs. "Liar. You're such a terrible liar."

"A minute ago, you asked me why I like Aries—"

"I asked why you love him."

I take a breath. "He talks to me openly and candidly. He listens and respects me—"

"He's first-gen and you're the purebred son of the lord who's hired him—of course he's going to listen to and respect you."

Pausing, I stare at him without speaking.

"What?" he asks. "It's true."

"Right. So, if you're going to cut me off and demean and negate everything I say, then I don't want to talk about this. I *won't*."

Alexander meets my gaze for a moment, considering. "This is where I go wrong, isn't it?"

"You like to cut me off. You enjoy telling me that I'm being stupid or naïve in some form or fashion. This is why I don't bother talking to you. Why should I waste my breath?"

"Alright, I'm sorry. I get it."

I roll my eyes. "Stop being sorry and just listen without judgment for once. Stop being so fucking self-centered."

Alexander nods. "Aries is not self-centered, then?"

"He isn't," I confirm, refolding my arms. "He's thoughtful and patient. He considers me and he *listens*. He does not demean or belittle me, and it isn't because I'm the purebred son of his employer. It's because he respects me as a vampire—as another living, breathing entity. He doesn't want anything from me. There's no selfish ulterior motive behind his actions."

There's another pause when I finish, but this one seems intentional. Alexander is listening and processing.

"May I ask a question?" he says.

"Go ahead."

"Has he asked to feed from you? Or has he tried?"

"No. Never." This detail is none of his business, but I want to tell him that I even offered myself and Aries refused.

"Well, that's good," Alexander says. "I've heard that there are first-gens out there who will do whatever it takes to latch themselves to a purebred to feed from them. There's even a whole black market that deals in purebred blood. They sell it for astronomical prices."

"That's dark. I've never heard of anything like that."

"There are a lot of dark things beyond the walls of Eden, Oliver. Trust me."

"It's not all flowers and sunshine within the walls of Eden, either." Of course there are a lot of things that I don't know. But Aries has nothing to do with that. "You're suggesting that I'm being naïve again. That he's only interested in me because he has ulterior motive."

"No, I'm just sharing valuable information that might be relevant to you."

"Whatever."

"I'm being serious. Your father has kept you so isolated that you're cut off from a lot of things. If we were together, you'd have more space to learn and do what you wanted... At least, that was my plan, anyway. What are we going to do, Oliver? What do you want?"

Here he goes, asking me questions that I'm not certain I should answer truthfully. "You don't want to show Lord Blakeley these pictures?"

"I already told you that I'm not doing that. Your father and my mother are both so... outdated. They don't need to know about this. But what about me and you? Can we possibly make this work? Do you even want to?"

It feels as if I'm being pushed into a corner. A few minutes ago, I had room to think about my circumstance and try to figure it out on my own. I didn't know what to do, but I felt as if I had time. Suddenly, there's no time and I have to make a decision, now.

I set my palms against my thighs as if to hold myself steady. I'm afraid to admit this to him, but I don't have a choice anymore. "I want to be free and independent. No more vampires telling me what to do, where to go, how to dress and orchestrating my entire life. I want to arrange my own life. Make my own choices."

Alexander is quiet, but it feels good to have spoken these words—my truth and sincerest desires. He's right in some ways. I don't know what awaits me outside the walls of Eden. Whether it be black blood markets or shady vampires with ulterior motives... I can't imagine. But I'm willing to risk it if it means leaving this golden cage where everything is artificial and forced.

"How do you plan to do this?" Alexander asks after a long pause. "How are you going to get this freedom and independence?"

"I don't know."

He looks toward the window, thinking. "May I ask you for a sincere favor?"

"What is it?"

"Can we get through the next five days together in Central? Can you just... try to be open and honest with me like this? Then we'll decide what to do. Maybe we talk to your father or... something. I don't know." He shifts his gaze to meet my eyes. "But first, five days. Is that fair?"

I've already been stuck in this awkward situation with him for the past fifteen years. Part of me thinks, what's the harm in five more days? Admittedly, him knowing the truth already feels better than upholding all the lies and pretending I want this.

Even still... "I'm not going to magically fall in love with you because you've decided to be nice to me for five days. To be clear."

"I didn't say that you would, you twat. I can't believe you just said that."

I shrug. "You asked me to be honest. Here it is."

"I already regret it," he huffs, shaking his head. This makes me laugh.

"Fine," I say. "Five days. I'll behave myself in Central."

"No." He whips his head up to look at me. "I didn't ask you to 'behave yourself.' I asked you to be honest and *real* with me. There's a difference."

"Alright. I'll be honest with you. Dea_." Alexander's shoulders relax and he nods with relief. I raise an eyebrow because I'm surprised. "You've... taken all this pretty well."

"What do you mean?" he asks.

"I don't know. I'd expect you to scream at me and call me even more names than usual."

He frowns, looking insulted. "And what good would that do? What could I possibly achieve by pushing you even further away than I apparently already have?"

Well, that's shockingly self-aware. "Fair point, I guess..." As I watch him, my incisors pulse in a subtle reminder. I sigh. "Since you're feeling generous, may I feed, please?"

He looks up, blinking his golden-brown irises in innocent bewilderment. "We're not due until Friday."

"Yeah, but I'd like to do it now, if that's okay? We don't always have to abide by the strict rules laid out for us, right?"

Alexander shifts to his knees. I'm confused, watching as he crawls the short distance between us, then kneels in front of me. He sets his palms against the ottoman on either side of my hips. "Your wish is my command."

"Since when?" I frown. "You're being weird."

"I'll allow you to feed early if you feed from my neck instead of my hand."

"Is this how the next five days are going to be?" I ask. "If you do this, then I'll do that? Petty deals? Tit for tat?"

"No. I would just like it if you fed the right way for once. You can have my hand if you really don't want to... God, Ollie."

The problem with feeding from his neck is that I have to fix the inside of my head. If I'm thinking that he's an annoying and arrogant jerk that gets everything he wants (like usual), all of that will pour right into him. I'm not a huge fan of Alexander, but I don't want to make him suffer. Well, not any more than I probably already have.

Rolling my shoulders, I take a deep breath. "Just give me a second." I try to let go of the animosity while searching for a reason to make my thoughts more pleasant. Kinder. After a few more breaths, I'm ready. "Alright."

Alexander sags his robe from his shoulders, then unbuttons and spreads his pajama collar until his neck is exposed to me. He lifts his chin in offering. Placing my hands on his shoulders, I lean down and gently bite into his flesh.

He tenses initially, as if preparing himself for some malign influx of energy. But as I feed, his frame relaxes under my palms. I think about the fact that he's accepted my truth fairly quickly. Easily. And that he's willing to nourish me despite the circumstance. I am grateful for these things, so I let it pour into him.

When I'm done, I lick the wound clean. I feel better. Less depleted but not totally satisfied. Letting my aura fan out with Aries's scent all around me and his finger inside of me... something in my hunger shifted. Desperately, I'm craving a decadent treat—a rich piece of double chocolate cake. Instead, I've had to settle for an apple. Nourishing, sweet, but it doesn't quite hit the spot.

Alexander's eyes are closed as I look down at him. "Are you alright?" I ask. I tried to make it nice, but I'm not sure how it felt on his end.

He opens his eyes and they're glowing golden. "Yeah," he says, sighing. He bends, resting his forehead against my exposed knee.

"Alexander?" I tense when I feel his lips brush and kiss my skin. I almost push him away, but he lifts his arms, cradling my hips as he turns his head and rests so that his ear and cheek are pressed against my thigh. His fists grip the material of my robe.

"Just five days, Ollie," he says quietly, closing his glowing eyes. "Give me five days to let you go, alright? *Please?*"

I swallow hard, but relax my body. I keep still and don't shove him.

"Okay. Five days."

Chapter Twenty-Three

Comparing my family's estate to Alexander's is like comparing a heavily draped horse-drawn carriage to a Lamborghini.

The contrast is bizarre. It always has been.

The Kendrick estate is composed of speckled, sandy-colored brick and clean lines. Glass windows, recess lighting and polished natural surfaces. It stands in jarring contrast to what I'm accustomed to—ancient tapestries, high, echoing cathedral-like towers and stone walls. Hard edges, cold rooms and dreary, dank corners.

Alexander's home estate, while luxuriant in its design, feels more alive, somehow?

Secretly, I've always liked visiting this house. I've been here many times through the years for routine social visits and various celebratory or political events. This will be the first time I've stayed for a whole week. Central Eden is only two hours away from our estate, so we typically go back home after our scheduled engagement.

We arrive early in the day, which gives us time before lunch is served in the dining room. In the foyer, after our parents wander ahead of us and are out of ear shot, Alexander turns to me, smirking. "We could follow them to the drawing room, but... with you being such a nerd, you'd probably rather sit in the library until lunch is ready?"

"Yes," I confirm, sensing his jest. "And since you're averse to 'nerdy' things like books and knowledge, I'm assuming I'll be alone, which is a plus."

Alexander chuckles. "Sorry, but you won't be. I'll take my chances today and join you. I won't touch anything, though. Some of that gross knowledge might get on me."

"God forbid." I sneer. He laughs, taking my comment in stride as we walk down the hallway.

The library has large picture windows, which makes it brightly lit, rain or shine, and perfect for reading. I imagine, anyway. I've never had the privilege or privacy of enjoying a book here.

Maple furnishings gleam in the sunshine. Stately moldings line the sage-colored walls and the space is equipped with cozy tufted chairs, a couch and a large desk. There's a spiral wooden staircase leading to the upper level, which hosts more bookshelves and a marble chess set placed atop a table between two armchairs.

It smells like timber and worn paper pages. Dusty hardcovers, but with a tinge of something earthy and sweet. Maybe patchouli?

"Buffyyy." Alexander sings the word as he bends, sweeping his long-haired calico cat up from the bottom step of the staircase and into his arms. He cradles her like a baby and kisses her face. The teardrop shape of her nose and mouth is white, but the patches covering her eyes are mismatched blobs of orange and black. She looks like she's wearing a mask. A feline bank robber ready for a heist.

"Why did you name her Buffy?" I ask, stepping past him and moving toward the couch. "What does that mean?"

"Because of the TV show," he says, still holding her as he plops down on the couch beside me. "The one the humans made about vampires—*Buffy the Vampire Slayer*?" He looks at me, waiting for some kind of recognition. I have none.

I shrug. "I don't know what you're talking about."

"God, Ollie. What the hell?"

"Why would you name your cat after someone who might slay you?"

"Why have they kept you so damn sheltered?"

"For you," I say plainly. "Because I'm your prize."

He huffs. "Some prize. You don't even know about *Buffy*. What good are you?"

"Exactly. I'm totally useless. You should get rid of me."

Alexander's body tenses. His face is serious. "That's not what I meant. It was just a joke."

"I know, I know." Shaking my head, I lean, rubbing my palm atop Buffy's head. She lifts her chin, welcoming the affection and purring loudly. Silence falls between us as I pet her. The room is cozy. Insulated and secluded.

I think this is the most at ease I've ever felt around Alexander. It's... nice. Surprising.

Glancing to my right, I see a laptop computer on the desk. Ever since our honest talk this morning, I've been thinking more seriously about how I could escape. Particularly, what I would do and where I would go if I even managed it. I need to do some research, but the lack of electronics has put me at a disadvantage.

Buffy flips in Alexander's arms, purring and resettling on his lap. Swallowing, I take a chance. "Would it be alright if I used that computer?"

He glances up at me, absently stroking her fur as she makes biscuits on his thigh. "Sure."

"Is it password-protected?" I stand and move toward the desk. "Is it monitored by your security?"

"God no. Why would we do that?"

"All of my devices were monitored... except for my phone, but that's gone now." The moment I touch the space bar, the screen comes to life. He was telling the truth because the desktop icons are just there. No password needed. I sit, taking hold of the mouse and navigating to the Internet.

"For the record, I never asked anyone to keep you under glass for me. I don't know whose idea that was." Alexander's voice drops to a grumble. "Not that it did anything, considering you're sleeping with someone else right under my nose."

I pause, turn and meet his eyes. He stares back at me from the couch with his arms folded. Buffy hops onto the floor at his feet, then starts cleaning her face. "What?" he asks. "I can't say it aloud? It's the truth."

He's right. It is the truth. But what do I say? I turn back to the computer without speaking and resume my search. I don't know what I'm doing anymore. All I know is that I need to get out. I need to find a realistic path to freedom.

Alexander stands from the couch and moves toward me. "Are you upset?"

"No."

"Why aren't you talking?"

"What am I supposed to say?"

He's at my side when he shrugs. "I don't know. That you're sorry? That you apologize?"

"But I'm not sorry," I say, looking up at him in earnest. "I've been apologizing for everything, every day of my entire life, but with this? I don't regret anything that I've done." We stare at each other in an emotional stand-off. I don't move or flinch. Neither does he. Eventually, I turn back to the computer and carry on.

Alexander sighs. "You're a bold creature, Oliver Blakeley. Fucking formidable."

I keep typing, but I realize that Alexander is the third vampire to make this declaration. Sasha said I was brave. Aries called me tenacious and said I was stronger than I realized. Maybe I don't give myself enough credit?

"What are you doing?" Alexander asks.

"I'm just… wondering what I could do to earn money if I became free. Or where I could live. I need resources because I've never actually taken care of myself, so I think I would need some sort of help. Especially with feeding." This time, Alexander is silent for a beat too long. I look up at him. "What is it?"

"Formidable," he repeats. "I can't believe you're sitting here and looking up ways to run away—right in front of me."

"You told me that I could be honest. I thought we'd talked this through."

"That doesn't mean I totally accept it. That I'm going to aid and abet you in this insane pipe dream!"

I drop my hands from the keyboard and exhale a sigh. Why did I think that he understood me? "Right. I'm sorry—"

"Ah God, just don't, alright? *Fuck*, Ollie." He turns, rubbing his palms against his face as he sits against the edge of the desk. "Don't go all obedient purebred robot on me."

Sitting here, it feels like I'm damned if I do and damned if I don't. Just when I thought we'd come to some sort of consensus.

"You—you probably won't need resources or whatever," Alexander says, massaging the back of his neck with his eyes clenched shut. "If you decide to leave, they'll banish and strip you of your title, but you're still purebred, you know? They'll set you up decently. That's what they did with my cousin Leoni when she refused her mating arrangement."

Leoni. Why does that name sound familiar? "Did they?" I ask. "In what way? What happened?"

Alexander sighs, dropping his shoulders and opening his eyes. "Like I said, she refused her arrangement, so her mother banished her to the outskirts of Eden. She has a cottage there and she gets some support. But her life is really simple. She's an outcast. A social pariah. She probably prefers it that way, though, knowing her."

Something in me brightens. I'd definitely prefer that kind of arrangement, too. "Do they provide a feeding source for her?"

"Don't know. I haven't actually spoken to her since it happened. I just heard about it from my father. My point is, you don't need to have everything figured out. You'll probably still be looked after in some significant ways."

I sit back against the chair, considering. Truthfully, I don't know what will happen if I formally refuse this arrangement. It's illegal to enforce corporal punishment, so that isn't a realistic fear. Still, the memory of Thomas that day, and even more recently, the things he said... it makes me wary.

Never trust a word that vampire says. Nothing.

"Your father is a wild card," Alexander goes on in my contemplation. "He may just banish you, or... I don't know. It'll probably help if I corroborate this decision—if I say we've both decided it and that it's not just you."

I lift my head, hopeful. "Would you be willing to do that?"

He looks away. "I don't know yet."

"Well, thank you for considering it... and for telling me about your cousin. It's helpful."

Alexander pushes up from the desk. "Yeah, yeah. Let's head to the dining room for lunch. You can use the computer whenever you want this week. Feel free."

Feel free. Odd choice of words. It makes me laugh. "Thanks."

"I mean it, Ollie." Alexander stops and turns to face me. "If you want to come down here in your spare time and read, use the computer, whatever, it's okay. You're not a prisoner in this house. Not around me."

I appreciate Alexander's intent. I do. But even my being in this house isn't my choice. What he doesn't understand is that my life is a prison. I exist, therefore I am a prisoner.

"Thank you," is all I say. There's no use in ruining the mood again. We're standing on shaky ground as it is.

With each passing day, I grow more detached from this life. My patience for it sinks lower and lower. A heavy stone drifting and descending to the bottom of the ocean.

All week long—through brunches, dinners, meetings and neighborhood tours—I've played my part. I've been amicable and kind. Listening and observing more than talking.

Something about our candid conversations lately has caused my perspective of Alexander to shift, just slightly. As we perform our duties together, for the first time, I'm not annoyed. I've always thought of Alexander's sparkly public façade as fake—his bright, buoyant smile and affable demeanor.

But now that I'm paying closer attention, something in his manner feels... sort of genuine, maybe? He's good at navigating social situations and vampires' expectations of him. Much better than me, anyway.

In my quiet moments at night and when I'm alone, I think about Alexander's cousin, Leoni. From what I can understand about her situation, she isn't entirely free now. The figurative chains still grip her ankles, but the links stretch much farther out than they did before.

Alexander did some digging and told me that she lives in a cottage on the edge of eastern Eden with a servant. She has no direct master and no forced mate—no pressing duties or vapid responsibilities.

It isn't exactly the life I want, but it's a step in the right direction, isn't it? I don't care about my title, inheritance or public image. I just want my own life and the freedom to make it up as I go along.

On our final night at the Kendrick estate, Alexander's family throws a splashy and glitzy ball. The villa where the party is held sits back from the main house and is flanked by majestic spruce, pine and fir trees that reach high into the deep blue overhead like skyscrapers.

Where my family's ballroom is predominately composed of marble floors and dramatic chandeliers, the space here matches the modernity of the main estate. Floor-to-ceiling windows offer a full view of the surrounding forest. The hardwood floors gleam underneath an incredible instillation across the entire ceiling that looks like glowing white icicles. Like illuminated stalactites spanning a glamorous cave.

In the back corner of the room, there's a lifted stage with a grand piano. Alexander is there, sitting silently on the bench with his hands resting in his lap. His eyes are focused on the keys. The twinkling ceiling lights have been turned down low and it feels as if everyone in the room is holding their breath. Watching and waiting.

Alexander lifts his hands and rests them atop the keys. There's a brief moment of pause before a soft but full melody swells from the impressive instrument. It fills the space. Elegant and calming, but... beneath the composition's layers, there's something else. He plays and the music is weighted with emotion—romance and reflection. Wonder and sadness. Heartbreak.

As I listen, something in my chest tightens. I can't explain why, but it moves me. It's palpable and can't be ignored.

When Alexander lifts his hands and the final note echoes through the room, there's another distinct moment of pause. Someone interrupts the silence with applause, then the rest of us join in. The spell is broken but the sentiment lingers. Alexander stands, smiling in his camera-ready way as he bows. When he steps off the stage, he tries to make his way toward me but is swallowed up by a small crowd of vampires showering him with accolades.

"Did you recognize the piece?"

I turn, and Raphael, Alexander's primary manservant, is standing beside me. He's young, but older than Alexander and me by a decade, I think. His maroon-colored eyes are sharp. The lights in the hall brighten, highlighting the gingery warmth of his short hair.

"I didn't," I admit. "I'm not very good with recognizing classical pieces. Which one was it?"

"*Rêverie*, by Debussy," Raphael says, lifting an eyebrow. "That wasn't the piece he originally chose for tonight."

"Really? I had no idea." I wasn't even expecting him to play the piano this evening.

"What made him switch to something so melancholy?" Raphael asks. "He was supposed to give a dedication before playing the piece, but he didn't. Why has he drastically altered the program? This is a celebration, isn't it?"

Nervous, I twist my hands and see Alexander making his way

toward us. "I... don't know, but it was beautiful. I haven't heard him play since we were kids. He's drastically improved since then."

"He has," Raphael says. Maybe I'm paranoid, but his gaze feels intense as he scrutinizes me. Disapproving. "He's been practicing for a very long time because he wanted to surprise you. Specifically, for tonight, to celebrate your wedding."

"Hey." Alexander approaches us with his forehead crinkled. "Is everything alright? What are you saying to him?"

Raphael shrugs, suddenly indifferent. The gesture reminds me of a naughty child with a stolen toy behind their back. "I'm not saying anything. Don't get your undies in a bunch." Raphael shifts his attention toward me, then offers a shallow nod. He walks away, disappearing into the crowd and leaving the two of us alone.

"What did he say to you?" Alexander asks. His eyes are filled with panic. "What were you talking about?"

"We were just talking about your performance. It was wonderful. I didn't know you'd gotten this good at playing the piano." I'm always surprised at how casual Alexander's relationship is with his manservant—another thing I find enviable about his estate versus my own. Lord Blakeley would never accept this kind of informal behavior.

Alexander shrugs. "It's not a big deal. Well...it was supposed to be a surprise, but—I told my father I didn't want to do the performance anymore, and that it might make you uncomfortable. He wouldn't listen and... whatever. It's nothing."

A quick-tempo song cuts into the awkwardness of our conversation. Alexander takes a deep breath and shakes his head. "Anyway, will you dance with me, please?"

"Yes, sure." Taking hold of my hand, he guides me onto the main dance floor. The vampires here aren't moving in the same clockwork, uniform rhythm that I'm accustomed to. Everyone does their own thing. It's nice.

Alexander steps in front of me. "Will you lead?"

I chuckle. "Again? I've been leading all night. If you're trying to make a point, it's been made."

"I'm not," he asserts, smiling. "There's no hidden objective. It's just more fun when you lead—you're *good*. You like to do it, right?" He opens his palms between us, offering them to me.

"I do. Alright." I take his hands and guide him into the flow of movement.

Leading gives me an inkling of control. Not control over Alexander, but influence over a brief circumstance when I usually have none. For a few minutes—the span of a sprightly dance—I can choose whether to move left or right. To turn or remain linear. How fast we move or how slowly. Whatever I decide, it just happens. No questions asked.

It's pathetic of me. Valuing something so trivial. Something so transitory as a dance. But I do, because I don't have much else. The only other circumstance where I have any sense of control is when I'm manipulating my aura with Aries.

Being able to withhold or relax and liberate my vampiric nature—exploring this deeper essence of myself in a trusting space —it's magical.

By the end of the night, I'm exhausted. Usually, after a ball like this, I'm worn down from faking interest in dull conversations. Fake greetings and fake smiling. From strictly withholding my sincere thoughts and offering the most banal and expected responses.

Tonight, though, I think... maybe I've actually had fun? Even as Alexander holds my hand while we walk back to the main estate, I'm not displeased or recoiling from his touch. Everything feels kind of pleasant. Easy, for once.

"Did I ever tell you that Ashwin challenged me to a duel over you?" Alexander asks as we climb the stairs toward our separate rooms. "After I officially chose you as my mate, she squared off with me at a banquet. We were *ten*. I said, 'Nobody duels anymore, get the fuck out of here.' She was dead serious."

I frown because this story is absurd. This is Alexander's explanation as to why Ashwin kept asking me to dance and checking to see if I needed anything, like she was my own personal waitress. "I've only seen Ashwin three times in my entire life, including tonight. How bizarre."

"She was into you. Still is, apparently."

"I can't imagine why."

"That's part of your charm, Ollie. That you have no idea how alluring you are." We stand together in front of my door. Isolated in the cool hallway lit by soft white recess lights lining the ceiling. Alexander faces me, still holding my hand. "Thank you for tonight."

I chuckle. "What are you thanking me for? I didn't do anything."

"You've been much more relaxed this week, and we had fun together. You feel lighter or something. It's really nice."

Maybe it's because he knows the truth about how I feel, so I don't need to hide or pretend with him anymore? Or maybe it's because I'm contemplating my liberation as a possibility? A reality. Not some far-flung made-up fantasy in my head but something tangible. Achievable.

Alexander squeezes my palm. "May I feed? It's Friday."

"Ah, right." Letting go of his hand, I lift my wrist to unfasten my cufflink. "Why didn't you say something earlier? We should have done it this morning."

"It's not a big deal," he says, staring. "I'm fine, but can I..."

I'm struggling with the clasp for some reason. "Can you what?"

"May I feed properly, please? From your neck, I mean."

The air is suddenly thicker between us as I breathe. Alexander's gaze is soft but unwavering. I swallow hard, dropping my hands. "When you fed from my neck at the first mating confirmation, I think... you bit me too hard. Can you not do that?"

"I won't... I didn't know, I—Maybe I was too excited? I'm sorry."

"Yeah..." I reach up, scratching my head. I take a breath and start unfastening my bow tie and collar. He's silent as I work. Watching. It makes me nervous. If he bites me softly this time, it should be fine, I guess. "Alright," I say once my collar is undone.

His eyes shift and warm, glowing in vivid gold as he steps forward. I almost step back because I just... I don't know. He's suddenly so intense and it makes me anxious. He slips the fingers of one hand into my hair at the back of my head as he leans into my neck, then rests his free hand at my waist. He licks me, sighs, then bites into my flesh softly like I asked.

Initially, his thoughts are warm. Harmless and affectionate. But as he drinks, his intent shifts as it pours into my being.

He loves me, but more than that. There's inscrutable desire. He wants me to be *his*, and without warning, a wild current of tangled, frustrated and fiery emotions dominates my senses.

"Alex—" I gasp because everything has intensified with a snap —like a surge of electricity before a blackout. His fist clenches in my hair and the hand on my waist wraps around to embrace my body tightly against him. He feeds even deeper, as if to consume me. Somehow, I feel him inside, mentally and emotionally reaching within my core. Grabbing at my nature and taking hold. My essence shifts from his manipulation and the sensation is so *wrong*.

This thing inside of me that I am only just learning how to navigate—he's pulling at it. Trying to take and control it for his own pleasure.

"*Alexander*, stop!" The second he lifts his head, I push him as hard as I can. An unfamiliar rush of pressure and intensity emphasizes my movement. He flies backward, slamming hard into the opposite wall. Alexander tumbles and falls onto his knees, leaving an indentation of his frame in the corridor.

My eyes have alighted, but it's completely different compared with what I feel with Aries. I'm not aroused or at ease. Not filled with wonder and joy.

I'm furious. Panic and stress pulse through my veins like a tumultuous storm. My body trembles as I fall back against the door and slide down. On the floor, I curl my arms around my bent knees, trying to regain control of myself. Of *my* nature and body. Everything inside of me is in chaos from this external, foreign manipulation.

"Oliver—"

Alexander's fingertips brush my arm and I jerk, pressing myself further into the door and smacking his hand away. "Don't touch me! *Why* would you do that? What the hell are you thinking?"

"I'm sorry—*Shit*—I'm so sorry, I just... I don't... God. Fuck." He's on all fours and staring at me with bright eyes. But he sits back, rubbing his palms down his face. "*Fuck.*"

"You're an idiot, do you know that? A selfish and egotistical idiot. We've never even talked about you pulling my aura before. Why the hell would you try? What's the matter with you?"

My body quivers violently as I shout at him, so I slink my arms around my knees again, trying to hold and put myself back together. "If you had bothered to ask, I would have told you *no* and saved us both from this horrible experience."

Alexander is silent, his palms rubbing into and destroying his perfectly styled hair. His eyes are closed and he has a trickle of my blood on his lip. He takes a deep breath and blows it out. "I wasn't... It wasn't my intention to do that. I just... lost myself. I got carried away and I'm sorry. I apologize." He drops his hands, opens his eyes, and slowly, they burn out.

My eyes are still burning. Angry. "I don't forgive you. It doesn't matter how much you 'want' me, you can't just do things without asking! I don't have *anything*, Alexander. No phone, no more cameras or equipment—even these stupid clothes are chosen for me. *Nothing* is mine, except for my aura and nature, and you tried to release it without my consent? You can't even let me have that?"

I'm surprised when hot tears gather in my eyes. I blink and they pour out. Another moment that feels like it's against my will because I don't want to cry in front of him. Shaking my head, I bring my palms up and swiftly wipe my face. "I fucking hate this."

The hallway is silent. I want to leave, but I barely have the energy and control to stand. After being pulled at so forcefully, my nature is tightly curled into itself, like an armadillo that senses danger and shifts into a hardened ball.

Slowly, my body stops trembling and my eyes return to normal. I breathe deeply, in and out, trying to regain a sense of calm. Alexander sits across the hallway, not saying a word. I couldn't care less about him in this moment.

When I'm more composed, I set my palms against the floor on either side of my hips, thinking I might try to stand. I still feel gross and upset, but I don't want to keep sitting here with him staring at me.

"All this week, I've been thinking about you," Alexander begins. His voice is quieter now. Hesitant. "Well, I... I think about you all the time, Ollie. For years, since we were kids, you've occupied so much space in my mind. But this week, I was thinking—I was hoping that maybe this situation with you and Aries could be a turning point for us? A wake-up call for me, a good experience for you... that maybe he came into your life so that *we* could have a better life together and really start to see each other. To make this arrangement work..."

Alexander had been staring down at the floor, but he looks up, meeting my eyes. "I've ruined that chance, haven't I? Officially. It's over."

"Even without this, you still don't understand. What I want —it's not about Aries. It's not about being with him or you. He showed me how badly I want to be free to live my own life and understand myself. For you this is some weird love triangle or couples therapy exercise. For me, this is about having the right to make my own choices. If I'm here with you, I'm stuck inside this choice-less bubble. Period."

"It doesn't have to be that way, Oliver," he says, pleading. "You could be with me and take pictures—have all the equipment you want and pursue your goals. We could even travel if you wanted. *Whatever* you wanted, I would do, I would give you…" He pauses, his cheeks flush as he shakes his head. "Up until a few minutes ago, we had fun this week. We could be good together, in time."

"Why do you have to own me? When you fed from me just now, everything flowing from you screamed 'mine.' Like possession. Why couldn't we be friends and do those things sometimes? Why do I have to be legally and biologically chained to you?"

Alexander huffs, smiling weakly. With his unkept hair and the dried blood on his lip, he looks like a maniac. "Well, like you said, because I'm selfish. Because I love you and I want you near me. I want to be the one that makes you happy."

"You want me to be your pet poodle. You'll let me take pictures and play. You'll make sure I have a really sweet life, so long as you can keep a tight hold on my leash. I don't want that. Fuck that."

"That's not how it is, Ollie. God…" He breathes, rubbing his palms down his face again, as if he's at a loss for words.

"And anyway, I'm obviously not a very good poodle. I'll just keep pissing on the carpet and not doing what you want me to do."

"Stop calling yourself a poodle. I hate it. It's not funny."

I smirk. "Well, we finally agree on something."

Alexander meets my gaze for a moment, then looks away, down the empty hallway. "We agree on other things."

"Like what?"

"Like your freedom." Slowly, he pushes himself up from the floor, then comes to stand over me. His palms are outstretched. "I'll help you, Oliver. Let's talk to your father together. And… I'm genuinely sorry that I hurt you. That wasn't my intention, and clearly, I make for a pretty horrible lover and have a lot to learn. Would you *please* forgive me?"

I hesitate for a moment, then put my palms in his. It doesn't ever feel like Alexander is deliberately trying to hurt me. Maybe

Aries was right in observing that he's immature, but I don't know. This could also be his character? Either way, I'm not willing to gamble with him and find out.

Someone else can have that honor.

He pulls me to my feet and I dust my pants off. "Yeah, alright. But don't ever expect to feed from anywhere but the tip of my pinky finger for as long as we're in this mess. At arm's length."

To my surprise, he nods. "That's fair... Maybe we can do bags? I could have it arranged?"

"That would be fine with me. I like that idea."

"Alright." Alexander sighs. "By the way, when did you get so strong? What was that?"

"What was what?"

"The way you pushed me." He turns, pointing to the damaged wall. "*That.*"

I shake my head and open my door, because I don't know what that was. Hopefully, I never have to experience that awful feeling again. I'd rather it remain a mystery.

"Goodnight, Alexander."

<h1 style="text-align:center">Chapter Twenty-Four</h1>

The main gates to my home estate slowly drag open. They stand tall and imposing in black wrought iron contrasted against a steely sky brimming with clouds. The metal swirls intricately, curling into an elegant pattern with golden leaves sprinkled throughout. Our family's crest is featured in the center, so it splits as we drive inside.

Immediately, something is wrong. I've been using my senses to feel for Aries as we've gotten closer. It's like when I was a child and Chef Maru would promise freshly baked madeleines for lunch. I'd walk toward the kitchen, expecting the warm, buttery and vanilla scent to waft through the air.

I'm anticipating Aries's essence in the same way—for his discreet but luscious jasmine aura to hit me in the face, comforting and wonderful.

But there's nothing.

It's empty. Cold.

My nature churns with anxiety and confusion.

"I've been waiting fifteen years for your eyes to alight for me." Alexander sits at my side in the backseat of our private town car. Our parents' cars are ahead of us as I stare out the window, bewildered and half panicked. "They finally do, and it's because you're furious with me." He chuckles, then sighs. "That's so on brand for us."

"That's because there should never have been an 'us' to begin with. You can't force two vampires to be together."

He scoffs. "Tell that to every fucking vampire across the Five Royal Houses of Eden who've been forced to mate for centuries. I guess they didn't get that groundbreaking memo... Are you alright? Your nature feels farther away than it ever has, even though you're sitting right beside me. It's like I can barely sense you."

Closing my eyes, I sit back and breathe. "It's nothing. I'm alright." Since last night, my aura has been a tight fist in my gut. Dormant, like how it was before Aries. Only after I met him did it start to stretch, move and flourish. Cautiously seeking and desiring to please itself.

"Something is obviously wrong. If you don't want to tell me, that's fine..." He pauses, then speaks a little lower. "I really am sorry for what happened yesterday."

"Yeah, I know." I turn my head and open my eyes, deciding to be honest. "I can't sense Aries. Can you?"

"Hm..." Alexander purses his lips, then leans past me, focusing on the view of the castle beyond the window. He's quiet for a long moment. "Nope. He should be here, though. Our final fitting is tomorrow."

Sitting back, I rub my temples. What the hell is going on?

"Should we talk to your father tonight?" Alexander asks. "I think sooner is better. Maybe after dinner when everyone parts ways?"

I inhale deeply and blow it out. This is it. It's really happening. "I think that's a good idea."

"Right, so... what are we going to say?"

"The truth," I explain. "That I... I refuse this arrangement and I want to be set free. I'll relinquish my title and nobility. If he doesn't want to support me, that's fine. I'll accept banishment and figure it out."

Alexander folds his arms as if he's taking on my tension and anxiety. "I don't think it'll be that simple. Not to put pressure on you, but refusing this marriage means that your clan's admittance within the Royal Order will be annulled. No royal title, no dowry, no seat on the governing board. Something about your dad is just... I don't know. He's not going to shrug this off and say, 'Easy come, easy go.'"

He's absolutely right. My muscles tense and my pulse accelerates from the truth of it. This is not going to go well. Plus, that relentless, eerie memory of Thomas keeps haunting me, along with his warning to not trust anything Lord Blakeley says.

"I'm afraid of him," I admit. For some reason, saying it out loud feels therapeutic. "I'm scared of what he might do, but I want to try. I have to."

Alexander sighs and absently runs his fingers through the sunshine-blonde swoop of his hair. "I didn't realize how different my situation was from yours. Up until this event, I always thought we had a lot in common and that our lives were similar. That's why I chose you. I thought it'd be easier for us to get along."

I shake my head. "Aside from our age and us both being pure-breds, nothing about our lives is similar. Your parents are kind to you. One of mine is silent while the other is a controlling, manipulative viper. Every other facet of our lives diverges based on that singular point."

Looking down at his hands, Alexander nods. "You were pretty carefree when we were kids, but I noticed that as we got older, you seemed more uptight and robot-ish. I never understood why, but after the past few weeks, it all makes sense. It's no wonder you want out of here."

"Well, thank you."

"You're welcome..." He raises his head to meet my gaze. "Can I just say that all this time, you've been treating me like I'm the bad guy—but I'm not, alright? My parents would *never* ask that you be restrained and controlled for me. We're not like that."

I shrug. "You may not be the bad guy, but you're not a good guy, either."

Alexander pokes my upper arm. I jump away, startled. He grins. "Then I'm a *neutral* guy, you twat. Not black or white. Gray. And a hell of a lot more interesting."

"You wish."

He chuckles, and the mood in the car lightens as we pull up to the front of the house. The moment I'm out of the car, I walk up to Camille. She's standing in the long line of servants assigned to receive us upon our arrival. She stayed at the castle for the week because they have their own full staff at the Kendrick estate.

Camille bows as I approach. Already, I notice that her expression is off. Harried. "Your grace, welcome back home."

"Thanks, Camille. Can I talk to you?"

"Of course."

I turn back to Alexander. He's standing behind me, still near the car. "I'll see you at dinner?" I call out.

He nods. "Sure."

Turning, I link my arm in Camille's, which completely shocks her, but she goes along with it as I pull her inside. From the corner of my eyes, I catch a glimpse of Lord Blakeley examining me, but I don't care.

"Your grace, wh-what are you doing?"

I'm practically dragging Camille down the corridor toward my wing of the castle. By now, unquestionably, I should sense Aries somewhere on the grounds, but I don't. It's making me feel panicked and queasy.

When we're far enough away, I let go of her. "Where is Aries? Why don't I sense him?" We're in the outdoor passageway of arched windows that separates my wing from the main estate— close to where his room is located, but there's only emptiness. Deafening quiet to my senses.

Camille's shoulders rise and fall in a breath. Her entire expression shifts. "I'm sorry, Oliver—"

"Where is he?" She's never called me by my first name before. I turn, walking in the direction of his room. Camille trails behind.

"Lord Blakeley dismissed him yesterday once he finalized your and Alexander's suits. He told Aries that if any final, small adjustments needed to be made, they'd have a local tailor handle it. Aries is gone."

"*What?*" I turn and rush toward the tower. Within seconds, I round the corner to the short hallway where his room is, just before the stairs leading to mine. The rosewood door is already ajar, so I press my palms to the cool surface and push it open.

Empty.

Only overcast light and dust motes. Stillness and silence. Everything associated with Aries is gone—the dressing stage has been broken down. No table full of fabric swatches, scissors and thread. No sewing machine or male dress form. Slowly, I step inside. Dazed, as if a lovely dream has been ripped away. As if it was never a reality at all.

"I'm so sorry, Oliver." Camille stands behind me, her voice solemn in the weighted emptiness of the room. "Aries was... He maintained his usual decorum, but I could tell that he was upset to leave so suddenly. But... if you go upstairs, your suit is in your room. He told me that he left something for you in the jacket pocket."

I turn, only meeting her gaze for a moment before flying past her and up the stone steps, taking them two at a time. When I burst inside, the suit is there, hanging on a freestanding silver hook situated toward the end of my bed. It's like a beacon as I draw nearer. A lighthouse in the dense fog of distress and disbelief clouding my brain.

The color of the material is a regal, evocative shade of blueish gray—rich and elegant in the shadowy light pouring in through the windows. I touch the lapel. Dark satin. Cool and soft. Something catches my eye and I pull the jacket open.

At first, the lining simply looks pink. But it's creamier and more complex. The softest shades of rose and blush. When I look closer, I realize there's a large pattern of the most beautiful, ethereal-looking flowers. Peonies, partially bloomed and lithe, like delicate clouds drifting over an island sunset.

My eyes threaten to water as I gently stick my fingers into each pocket, searching. The moment I touch the smooth folds of a paper note, my throat closes.

Sitting on the ottoman, I hold the note for a moment, breathing. Everything is silent. A thin ray of sunshine breaks through the clouds, warming and casting golden light on my face.

Carefully, I unfold the note.

I sit for a long moment, staring down at his eloquent handwriting, then back up at this suit made by his artistic and arresting sensibilities. Made just for me.

I love this suit. It is the most incredible, personal thing that anyone has ever given to me. But I don't want to wear it. Not for its intended purpose.

Slowly, I bring my knees up, setting my feet onto the ottoman so I can wrap my arms around and hold myself together yet again. Regret washes over me in spades as the stream of sunlight disappears once more behind the thick blanket of clouds. It leaves me cold and despondent.

I didn't even have the chance to tell him that I love him.

All day long, I'm lifeless. As if my soul, or at least some vital part of me, has simply vanished. Maybe I'm overreacting, but it hurts. Having him snatched away without warning. Without a proper goodbye. I've been dreading the reality of us parting for so long, and now it's just... done. A clean cut from a guillotine.

"I'm nervous as shit about this, Ollie." Alexander paces in front of me as I sit slumped on the couch of the waiting room outside Lord Blakeley's office. His hands are in his trouser pockets as he shakes his blonde head. "I don't have a good feeling about it at all."

"It's now or never." What have I got to lose at this point?

The door to his office swings open, showering us in a stream of ghostly yellow light. "His lordship is ready to see you both." Hudson appears in the open frame, gesturing for us to enter.

"Thanks, Hudson." I stand, and as I step forward, Alexander is at my side.

"Hey," he says. His voice is low. "Give me your hand, please?" I don't argue and simply slip my palm into his. We walk into the office together.

The office is as old-fashioned as Alexander's house is new and modern. There are battle weapons and antlers mounted on the stone walls. The color palette is noticeably limited to the deepest shades of forest green and brown. Lord Blakeley sits in his large velvet tufted armchair. A vibrant fire crackles beside him, throwing ominously dancing shadows across every surface. He is the perfect cliché of an old, outdated and power-hungry vampire.

"The two of you wished to speak with me privately?" His leg is crossed and his hands are folded calmly atop his thigh as he watches us, unaffected.

I open my mouth, but Alexander steps forward with his hand gripping mine. He bows his head in reverence. "Lord Blakeley, I know that Oliver and I have been betrothed for many years now."

"Indeed, you have. The two of you seem to be getting along very well, lately."

Alexander hesitates and looks at me. "Yes, we are, however..." He turns back to Lord Blakeley and takes a deep breath. "I love Oliver very much. And truly, I want what's best for him. I think... we need more time. Specifically, *I* need more time."

I'm shocked and confused. My mouth is agape as I shake my head. "No—"

"My esteemed young prince, what in God's name are you talking about?" Lord Blakeley asks, his dark brows furrowed.

"I've hurt Oliver, multiple times, because I'm... well, the truth is, I need to grow—to become a better mate and partner. So, I'd like to call this arrangement off until I can do right by him. As it stands, this isn't a good idea for either of us. But I'm still committed to the business deals and arrangements between our clans. I'm happy to fulfill those contracts, since this is primarily my fault."

Both Lord Blakeley and I stare at Alexander with a distinct pause, utterly taken aback by his declaration. I understand what Alexander is doing, but this isn't what I want. He doesn't need to cover for me. I take a step past Alexander. "Lord Blakeley, I want—"

"Prince Alexander," Lord Blakeley says coolly, as if I hadn't spoken at all. "Will you please give me some time alone with my son? I'd like to speak with him privately."

My chest constricts as Alexander looks at me with panicked eyes. Ignoring the stress, I nod. "I'm okay. Just go." His gaze says that he doesn't believe me, so I squeeze his hand. "I'm fine."

Exhaling an audible breath, he turns and bows to Lord Blakeley once more. "Your grace." He lets go of my hand, leaves the room and closes the door behind him.

A strange, icy stillness hangs in the air. The tension is high, like a wolf and a rabbit staring at each other across a winter tundra. Waiting to see who makes the first move.

Casually, he looks away as if he's bored. "This is your doing," he says, breaking the silence. "You've manipulated him into this."

"I-I haven't. That's not—"

"You are, without question, a constant disappointment to me, Oliver." He shifts his head and stares with cold gray eyes. "No matter what I do to provide for you—feed, educate and clothe you, selflessly hand you immeasurable opportunities—you are ungrateful. You are useless and offensively selfish. Why are you insistent on ruining this opportunity? This historic moment for our family."

I blink, feeling as if I've been physically assaulted instead of just verbally. My throat is dry and I can't seem to swallow as the emotional guilt washes over me. I feel myself shrinking down, because the weight of his words are heavy on my heart. They make me second-guess myself, and a tiny, well-conditioned voice inside says, *He's right. You are useless. Why can't you ever do anything right? You're so selfish.*

I have an urge to apologize. It's my natural inclination to do so, but I pause. I inhale a deep breath and recall Aries's words to my mind. He tells me to stop apologizing. That my feelings and thoughts—my wants, hopes and desires—aren't wrong. I shouldn't be remorseful of these things.

I'm afraid of this vampire. My "father."

But I stand straighter and speak slowly. "Yes, you've provided for me, but... only to groom me for this relationship with Alexander. For *your* self-interest and goals. Nothing you've ever done has been for my benefit. Please don't pretend as if taking care of me has been some kind of parental and loving self-sacrifice. I think we both know better than that."

The silence is palpable, but I don't break his gaze. To my surprise, Lord Blakeley smirks.

"This has been my greatest challenge with you, Oliver. You're too clever. You are the sharpest tool in my arsenal, but simultaneously, the most difficult to wield and control."

"I'm not a tool for you to use," I say, finding my confidence as he stands. The shift in his position makes me start, but I press on. "I'm not a puppet. There are things in life that are much more important than money, power and royal titles."

"Such as?" He sits at the edge of his desk with his arms folded, waiting.

I scan my brain, quickly organizing all the things I want to say. All the things I could express to him in this moment. "Creativity, inspiration and self-discovery. True love and friendship. The freedom to simply exist and make my own choices! In twenty-two years, I haven't had any room to *breathe*—let alone live or learn about the world and understand myself."

After taking a deep breath, I exhale, then say what needs to be said.

"I don't want this arrangement with Alexander. I refuse it. If I'm so useless, selfish and ungrateful, then let me go. Be done with me. I want to leave this estate and this family. I want to live my own life."

There it is. I've said the words and my chest heaves. My limbs shake as I wait for his response.

His face is expressionless. The crackle from the fire feels uncomfortably loud to my ears. The heat stifles my skin.

"No."

I'm anticipating more, but that's it. The word is simple and cuts through the air like a blade. He doesn't change his posture. Doesn't blink. It's a curt and strange response given everything I've said, so I can't help but repeat it. "No?"

"No. I will not release you from this arrangement with Alexander. I will not let you leave this family. Request denied."

Taken aback, I shake my head. "You can't make me do this—"

"Of course I can." He smiles unkindly. Hollowed and without warmth. "I can, and I will. The Blakeley name will finally be chronicled in the historical record as a member of Eden's governing board. Our family will become royalty with ties to the most prolific and powerful clan in our aristocracy. We'll inherit Alexander's dowry. And you, my selfish and arrogant little vampire, will give me all of this, whether you like it or not."

I can't believe this. How he can sit here, so unaffected, and say these things. Disbelief swells in my chest, shifting into rage. "We don't need to live like this anymore! Aren't you paying attention to the outside world? We're in the modern age and Eden is peaceful. We haven't been at war for *centuries*. Alexander said he'd still help our realm with whatever we need. We don't have to abide by these weird mating rituals anymore. Most aristocracies abandoned these practices decades ago and they help each other as a community. We could do that, too!"

There's another long pause where he says nothing. Unblinking. Like a stone sculpture of a pigheaded and antiquated vampire.

He sighs. "Silly vampire, I do not care about the 'outside world.' I care about our title, position and the dowry. You will do as I say."

We watch each other, and I realize that we don't speak the same language. It's as if we're from two different cultures and we're failing to properly communicate. I can't find the bridge to meet him halfway, and he doesn't even believe in bridges. He has no interest in them.

"I won't." I take another deep breath. My voice comes out firm. Unwavering. "I'm not mating with Alexander. That's not what I want."

He doesn't move. "And you're certain?"

"I am. I refuse."

"Interesting. Are you willing to sacrifice the designer's life for this decision?"

I draw back, frowning, because the statement feels like a slab of concrete being thrust into my abdomen. "*What?*"

Lord Blakeley adjusts and folds one knee over the other. "He's still here," he says casually, as if he's telling me the weather forecast. "Aries. The one you've been whorishly consorting with behind my back for the past few weeks.

Another flagrant show of your selfish, disgusting nature. He's very weak, presently. His essence might be difficult for you to discern."

A million thoughts zip through my mind, so fast that I can barely process any of them in combination with the stress, fear and humiliation. "Wh-where is he? Why is he weak—What have you done to him?"

Panic races through me. God, please no. I promised Aries that I would protect him, no matter what. This cannot be happening.

"If you want him to be safe, you will comply with my wishes."

"Let me see him *now*."

"After the wedding and ritualistic ceremonies are complete, I will release him. When you have married Alexander, I'll allow you to see your first-gen whore."

The fire pops behind us, throwing warm shadows across the floor and walls. Ghostly shapes that dance and make my hands tremble as I clench them into fists at my sides.

I lift my chin. "You're lying."

Lord Blakeley narrows his eyes in a discreet movement. "Excuse me?"

"You're a liar. Aries isn't here. Even if he was passed out somewhere, I'd still be able to sense him. This is your last-ditch effort to manipulate me, but it isn't working. I'm tired of being controlled by you. I'm done with this. All of it."

Thomas warned me, and I'm grateful. I'm leaving this estate, right now. I'm walking out into the garden, through the woods and across the lavender fields, and I'm never looking back.

I turn and step toward the door. There's no use in talking to this vampire anymore. I'm wasting my energy.

I reach for the door handle, but my entire frame jolts with searing pain. A heavy, burning sensation rushes all through me in a way I've never experienced. The worst of it is in my throat. My hands fly up to my neck because it's cutting off my air passage. The pain and fire are crippling as I fall to my knees and bend over. I can't... I can't breathe. What's happening to me?

"Silly little vampire, you have no idea who you're dealing with."

Lord Blakeley's shoes appear in my limited field of vision as I stare at the floor, gasping for air that isn't there because my throat is simultaneously filled with fire and closing in on itself.

My vision blurs as I gag and cough, desperate for oxygen. Is he trying to kill me?

"You should not waste your energy this way, your grace. Let him be." Another voice... Hudson? I fall over onto my side. I can't breathe.

"A little more. This one has been defiant for far too long. I've allowed him to get away with too much. He's overdue for this lesson."

Hearing his callous words, my eyes alight. Rage and incredulity clamor inside my core, violently swirling and radiating.

Painstakingly, I lift my hand from my fetal position on the floor. The surge of furious energy courses through me, then explodes with a forceful shot.

My nature releases and a vulgar rumble of noises follows. A shout, expletives and a hard *thump*. Lord Blakeley's shoes and ankles disappear from my sight. The constricting burn in my neck and body eases and I gasp loudly as I roll onto my back, desperately sucking in air and clenching my watery eyes shut.

Everything hurts. My throat is raw, but I can breathe now.

I can't believe... He intentionally used his powers to discipline me. To *hurt* me. Using our vampiric powers for torture, intentional violence or discipline has been forbidden since the end of the war, when all five houses signed the peace treaty. If he's gone this far... I don't want to know what else he's willing to do.

My next objective is to stand. I need to run away or get help, now. I shift upright to my knees, still wincing, aching and feeling the burning sensation all over my body.

"*Ah—*" The painful fire enraptures me again, taking control and making me immobile on my knees. There are tears in my widened eyes as I stare at Lord Blakeley limping forward with his hand outstretched.

He holds me in place with his powers, except he isn't closing my throat this time. The internal blaze shoots through my torso, but I can breathe as he stands over me looking disheveled. His eyes burn silver and crazed, like a vampire that's lost his fucking mind. A monster from a disturbing nightmare.

"How dare you?" he hisses angrily, baring his fanged mouth. "You *will* obey me, Oliver. You will give me what I desire."

The clenching within my throat returns and I fall over. The second round is even hotter, more unbearable and painful.

I want to fight. I need another surge of energy, but it doesn't come because all I can feel is heat and searing pain. The lack of air and overwhelming fear.

I want to be free from this place. From this situation, this life and this cruel vampire standing over me.

But the only freedom that comes is blackness, because I can't tolerate the pain anymore.

Chapter Twenty-Five

Everything is dark.

Cold, hard and damp.

The air is musty. Stale as it hovers with the scent of raw earth and old, dried blood. It stinks and makes me gag. My hand flies up to my throat from the searing pain and I wince when I swallow.

Slowly, I register that I'm lying on my side. Is this stone? Dirt? Where the hell am I?

My skull pounds and my body aches across every inch of my flesh. Within every layer of muscle down to my bones. I tumble onto my back and try to breathe softly as I hold my neck. With my eyes closed, I fill my lungs with the disgusting air because there's no other choice. I need to breathe.

I don't think I can move, but when a loud squeak registers just beside my ear, I fling my body up and scoot away. The scramble of my legs, hands and ass against dirt and stone is loud in the eerie silence. Almost immediately, I slam into another hard surface and a new reverberation of pain slices through my shoulder. I cry out.

My voice echoes.

No one comes.

The squeaking sounds titter faintly all around. Both close by and at some inconceivable distance as I sit still, rubbing my shoulder in the darkness. When the pain diminishes, I reach over, examining what I hit.

Bars. Metal but rusted. Rough and frigid against my fingertips. I look up and the ceiling is low. The space I'm in is small, as if it were made for a large animal. There isn't enough room to stand upright.

Still breathing, I set myself against the wall beside the bars. The ground feels filthy, gritty and damp. I'm glad I can't see it and the scent is unbearable.

I'm sitting in a dungeon. He put me in an actual fucking cell. Absurdly, I chuckle through my nose. For years, I've been comparing my life to a prison. This feels like some kind of cruel karmic joke that's finally come into manifestation. It's right that I should end up in a literal prison at some point. Poetic, even.

How long can he possibly keep me down here? I can't marry and bond with Alexander if I'm in a disgusting dungeon cell, can I? Does he plan to invite the other royal houses down here for the ceremony? A destination wedding no one saw coming.

I laugh to prevent myself from crying. Truly, my life has never felt so preposterous, and that's saying a lot.

Unbelievable.

～

Clack.

Delirious, I start, and my eyes open slowly as a series of new sounds litter the black, mouse-ridden stillness. A door closing or opening. Heavy footsteps echo softly in the silence. I can't tell if the person is coming toward me or leaving. I passed out again while leaning against the bars, as if my body had slipped into a state of self-healing torpor. I'm tired, but my nature is slowly regenerating and attending to the injuries and abuse that my "father" inflicted.

Breathing in the stale air, I concentrate. It's not as terrible as it was before I fell asleep. When you're in the farmhouse long enough, you cease to notice the animal-shit smell, I guess. I push past the traces of dried blood, rat feces, wet soil and mold to focus on whoever is coming or going.

It's Hudson.

Without question, he's coming closer.

I don't know what to think. Part of me is relieved that it isn't Lord Blakeley, because his face and essence are the last things I want to contend with right now. Seeing him would throw my body into a state of post-traumatic stress and shock while I'm still trying to recover.

But Hudson's presence doesn't put me at ease, because he's the overseer's enforcer. He administers whatever punishments or verdicts Lord Blakeley hands down.

Apprehensive, I scoot into the farthest corner of the shallow cell. I draw my knees up and wrap my arms around my shins, curling into myself. I joked and snickered earlier, but now, my pulse races and beats hard in my temples as he approaches.

I'm frightened. I don't want to be hurt again, and being tortured by Lord Blakeley's aura... It was crippling. Terrifying. No alleged "parent" should ever do something so cruel, dark and menacing to their own offspring. Or anyone, for that matter.

When Hudson appears on the opposite side of the bars, he's too tall and I'm too far back in the corner, so he has to squat down to see me. I'm so tense I think I might snap as I stare into his eyes. God, I really don't want him to hurt me. Please...

"Your grace, are you alright?" he asks, tilting his head. Unexpectedly, he produces a flashlight and shines it toward my face. The sensation burns my irises and I wince. "My apologies," he says.

Keys rattle in the darkness. Then, there's a distinct *click*, followed by the groan of the metal bars swinging open. "Can you stand?"

Quivering, cold and mistrusting, I draw farther back into my corner. "I—" My voice comes out hoarse and dry because my throat is still wounded. I attempt to clear it and swallow, but it doesn't help much. "Where are you taking me now? What's happening?"

Hudson crouches down to my level. "I'm going to show you the way out of here. There's a plan in place, but time is of the essence. Can you stand up?" He holds a large palm out in offering.

"A plan?" I ask, looking at his face, down to his palm and then back up. "What do—"

"Yes," he says with urgency. "Will you trust me?"

I hesitate. I don't know if I trust Hudson, but what other choice do I have? This might be another elaborate scheme that Lord Blakeley has cooked up, but I'll go with it for now. I place my hand in Hudson's palm. Carefully, he guides me out of the cell.

"How long have I been down here?" I ask when I'm standing and unstable. Thankfully, he keeps a firm hand wrapped around my upper arm. "What time is it?"

"You've been down here for two nights. It's four in the morning on Sunday."

Holy shit... Have I slept that much? Time flies when you're half dead, I guess. "Okay, but what did you mean?" I ask, rolling my shoulders in a weak attempt to address the stiffness there. My brain is foggy and I have a pounding headache. There's a slight, annoying tickle in the back of my throat. I need to feed. "You said that you're showing me the way out?"

Hudson shuts the metal bars. "I'll explain as we go. We have some ground to cover."

"You're going to let me escape? As in leave the castle altogether?" I ask, somewhat hysterical. "You're helping me?"

"Yes. That is exactly what I'm doing. Come with me." He turns, shining the flashlight down the path and stalking forward. Scrambling, shocked and confused, I follow him.

"Why are you helping me?" I ask, struggling to keep up with his stride. It's difficult because my limbs and head are still aching from the fight, but adrenaline has taken over. Hope pushes me forward.

"Because I disagree with your father's choices and I refuse to take part in this merciless cruelty. Not again."

"Again," I repeat, immediately understanding. "He did this to Thomas, didn't he? Is this... Did Lord Blakeley keep Thomas down here?"

Hudson is quiet for a moment, as if he doesn't want to answer. Or he's refusing. I'm not sure which. "Hudson?" I prompt.

"Yes, this is where your father kept Thomas. For three months."

I stop dead on the narrow, dark path and wrap my arms around my torso because my stomach lurches in anguish. "Three months of this?" Easily, I recall Thomas's shallowed cheeks that disturbing morning at breakfast. His dried, scabbed skin. His misery.

If he was forced to spend three months down here, I... I can't imagine. It's unfathomable. Unforgivable. "Did anyone feed him?"

"Lord Blakeley only allowed us to feed him when he was near starving. Even then, he was strictly given lower-level blood—second-gen and below. It made him violently ill the entire time. I am... deeply ashamed to have participated in that abuse. Until this day, I carry the weight of my decision to be obedient and the subsequent harm it caused Thomas. I won't let this happen again."

"Was this his plan for me, too?" I ask.

"Yes, but this situation is different from before. Times have changed, drastically. Lord Blakeley wants to rule with an iron fist because it is the way he was brought up. But the social and political landscape outside of Eden and across the world has shifted. His actions toward you are inexcusable. If anyone discovered what he did to your brother..." Hudson shakes his head. "I cannot even imagine the consequences. I will not be part of this again. It was wrong the first time and it's wrong now. Come, my lord, we must keep moving."

Nodding, I step forward. We walk, passing cell after decaying cell as the dark, narrow hallway gently curves. It feels as if we're inside the belly of an iron snake.

"The outside world has mostly abandoned these antiquated practices," I note, wanting to continue this discussion. To hear more of his opinion. "But it feels like I'm the only one who thinks that this... this pageantry—this restrained lifestyle of forced bonds, silly banquets and meaningless titles—is a thing of the past. It's something we should have abandoned decades ago."

"You are not alone in your observations, my lord. Many of Eden's smaller houses can no longer maintain a full staff of servants, because lower-ranked vampires are leaving this aristocracy in droves, searching for a more independent existence. Even some younger royals, like you, are rebelling."

"Leoni in eastern Eden," I say mechanically, remembering Alexander's cousin who refused her arrangement.

"And Santiago Torres of the west. He casually left his estate one day and never returned. I heard that he sends letters from unmarked addresses. I, too, am questioning whether or not to raise my child here. We cannot continue in this oppressive lifestyle."

It's such a relief to learn that I'm not alone. That I'm not crazy—or selfish or silly. Aries taught me that my thinking is valid, but hearing this? Icing on the cake.

Stepping up beside him, I look up into his face. "Hudson, can I just disappear? Is that possible for me, too?"

He slows, coming to a halt and meeting my gaze. "The difference between you and Santiago is that he had been planning his escape for months. I'm told that he established connections on the outside, so that when he made his move to escape, he had a safe refuge. We have hastily devised a temporary solution for you, however... do you have any outside connections, your grace?"

We? Are there more vampires than Hudson involved in this

plan to help me escape? Biting the inside of my cheek, I consider. "No... well..." Shit. I'm not clever at all, am I? Because if I were, I would have spent my free time thinking this through and planning something in advance.

"What about Aries?" he asks.

Heat unexpectedly flares in my cheeks and I grin. God. Does everyone in the castle know about this? "Maybe?" I say. Reaching into my pocket, I caress the small paper rectangle of Aries's note. After I read it earlier, I folded it up tightly and have been carrying it with me like a talisman.

There's no doubt in my mind that Aries would help. I have full confidence that if I reached out to him, he would rescue me—gallantly and stylishly as he did so.

But that's not what I want. I need more time to think about it.

"For the interim, we're stashing you at a support house that my friend Roland is renovating, just outside of Nantshire. I've already spoken to him and his mate and made the arrangements. Your presence there will be of the utmost secrecy."

"Wait, Roland?" I ask, surprised. "Is he the same vampire that showed me the derelict houses in Evanshire? The ones I photographed."

"He is. I've known that vamp for a long time and he was impressed with you. Roland and his partner are in the process of opening a new blood clinic in Nantshire to help the lower-ranked and human-vamps in Eden. It'll be the first of its kind in our realm. He was able to buy the property sometime after your pictures were featured in all the news articles. The outpouring of support for the project was fantastic."

"Really? That's incredible." This is exactly what Eden needs. Novel ideas. Inclusive and benevolent projects that push us forward and into the modern era.

"Listen," Hudson says, resuming our trek through the dank labyrinth. "Once I show you the way out, you'll need to walk through the western woods while it's still dark. If you move along the stream, eventually you'll reach a dirt road. A car will be waiting for you at the edge where the brush meets the lane. I apologize for the nature walk, but having a car pull up to the front of the house at this hour is too risky. Someone might hear the engine and the tires on the gravel."

"Alright. I know the woods' edge and where the stream runs. Is there anything else?" That area is rough terrain, but I'll manage it. Anything is better than spending another millisecond down here.

"I'll guide you out of the dungeon, but you'll have to go alone," he says, picking up his pace. "I'm supposed to be doing rounds right now, and if I don't show up at my post—"

"But, wait," I say, stopping as I consider. "What about that—if I disappear, how will you cover for my escape? I don't want you to end up down here in my place."

Hudson grins broadly as we stand in the hallway. He shakes his head. "You've always been my favorite of the children, do you know? The most kindhearted. I hope you know that you deserve much better than how Lord Blakeley treats you."

A warm blush ignites my cheeks. "Ah, well, I... Thank you for saying that. But I'm serious, I don't want you to be punished because I got away."

"Lord Blakeley won't know that you've escaped for some time. He never once came down here to see Thomas—he only requested updates. I'll have some time to figure out my story. Plus, you need a head start."

"Hold on." I turn, then step up to the metal bars of a random cell beside us. "Did you tell him which cell I was in, specifically?"

"No, it wouldn't matter. It's not like we were picking a room at The Four Seasons."

I snort. "Okay, good. I don't know if this will work, but..." Blowing out a breath, I wrap my palms around one of the thick, cold bars. The texture is rough and gritty, but I clutch it hard, closing my eyes.

I'm still woozy and tired, but I need my energy to flourish. I channel that same inner fury and hurt from before. I think about Lord Blakeley ordering for me to be dumped into a literal cage. Like I'm an animal—as if he hasn't done enough to control and manipulate my entire life. The way he weaponized his vampiric nature against me. Twice. Without any hesitation.

Slowly, my eyes warm like fire in my head as my nature springs to life. It blooms, concentrated in my hands, and I pull with all my might.

At first there's nothing, but I put even more effort into it and grit my teeth. Wrenching. Fuming.

Soon, the metal groans from being manipulated in its hinges. Then, it's done.

Shaky, I stand straight and dust my palms against my thighs. I take another deep breath and roll my shoulders.

"My God," Hudson says with his hands on his hips. "Impressive."

My eyes are still alighted, but I try stepping in between the bar I've bent and the vertical one beside it. I can fit through the space I've created without much of a struggle.

"Now it looks like I escaped on my own," I explain. "It won't be your fault."

He smiles. "Brilliant. You're very thoughtful, Oliver. And like a miniature Incredible Hulk."

I scratch the back of my head. "I don't know what that is." Why am I miniature? I resent that, somehow. Hudson is probably seven feet tall, so who isn't "miniature" to him?

"It doesn't matter," he says. "Thank you, your grace. Ah—I meant to tell you, my mate dried out the bouquet of wildflowers you gave her."

My heart brightens at this unexpected news. "Really?"

"Yes. The arrangement was beautiful, so they've become the new centerpiece on our kitchen table in the cottage. She loves them. That was thoughtful of you to visit us, and we will truly miss your presence. It has been a pleasure watching you grow to find your own strength, voice and purpose."

"No, I should be thanking you—for not listening to Lord Blakeley and doing all of this for me. I don't think I could ever thank you enough." Seriously. What could I do to repay him for this?

Hudson turns and resumes walking. "I almost laughed when Lord Blakeley said that Aries was down here. I was listening outside the door, and it was difficult to come in with a straight face."

"Really?" The hallway curves more sharply as we walk. Suddenly, the shallow cells are replaced by larger, open chambers with the same low ceiling. I notice heavy chains and cuffs on the walls and ground. Abandoned and rusted like a tormenter's former playground. Disgusting. I had no idea that all of this was underneath the castle.

"Aries is an outsider," Hudson observes. "A widely celebrated one. Renowned. There's no way Lord Blakeley could have kept someone like that down here for long. The last thing he wants is the focused attention and scrutiny of the outside world."

"Does he know that our ways are outdated? Could he possibly have some self-awareness that the rules we abide by would be shunned by other, more modern aristocracies?"

"He does," Hudson confirms as we move faster. "But these very old purebreds... they're resistant to change, aren't they? They see evolution and modernity as some personal attack to their core identity. As if embracing new ideas and ways of living leads to some distinct loss of their perceived, innate value. Forgive me for saying this, your grace, but I think it's bullshit. As a species, we are meant to evolve and grow. Things should not always stay the same."

Despite our grim surroundings, I smile. "No forgiveness is needed. I agree on all points."

Hudson glances over his shoulder, mimicking my grin. "Which is exactly why you should be free, your grace. Let's pick up our pace and get you out of here. You're long overdue."

Chapter Twenty-Six

Outside of the dungeon and into the woods, the night air is still cold, but dry. A steady, frigid breeze caresses my face like silk as I traverse through the brush and along the bank of the narrow stream. Hudson handed over his flashlight to aid me in my journey, but he also warned that I should only use it when I have to, lest someone from the estate notice a bright beam shining in the woods at four in the morning.

The wind is icy, but a noteworthy improvement from the stale dungeon air I've been breathing for the past forty-eight hours. Down there, the air was stagnant. Lifeless.

The tangle of woods at this hour feels alive in comparison. Wild, breathing and brimming with possibility. Fallen leaves crackle underneath my feet with each step. Twigs snap from the force of my weight. This, along with the wind rustling the trees overhead, is my soundtrack to freedom.

Along the way, I pause occasionally. When I do, the sound-track shifts and quiets. A new, subtle melody crescendos—birds whistling and singing to welcome the impending sunrise. The hoot of an owl. The hushed babble of water running over rocks in the stream beside me.

In these moments, I breathe in deep, filling my lungs with the early-autumn air. I want to remember this moment forever.

By the time I reach the edge of the forest, the clouds are deep gray, but tinged with pink and gold as they float overhead. The dark of night has warmed to where I can finally see my watch face without the help of the flashlight. It's taken me an hour to get through the brush.

As I approach the road, I see a car parked with someone inside, just like Hudson promised.

Breathless, invigorated, I jog toward the car and wave my hands. The car starts up—a baby-blue Volkswagen Beetle humming to life. Camille sticks her head out of the driver-side window and calls out.

"Oliver! There you are! For God's sake, you took a long time."

I'm beside myself as I approach the car. Camille eyes me with one brow lifted. "What the hell? Were you birdwatching? Hurry up and get inside, we need to go, you slow poke."

Bewildered, I stare at her. "Did... Who sent you for me?" I ask, suddenly cautious.

"Is this a bloody test?" she quips with her nose upturned. "Hudson sent me, of course—get in! Get inside before someone sees us." Without another word, I rush around to the opposite side, pull the door open and settle into the passenger seat. Within seconds, we're driving off and into the sunrise.

"Are you alright? Are you cold?" Camille takes one hand off the steering wheel to tinker with the dashboard. Seconds later, soft heat radiates and warms my icicle toes. She reaches between us. "Here, this one is for you." There are two thermal cups in the holders and she hands one to me. I wrap my palms around it and am met with the most soothing heat in my life.

"Thank you—this is... It's unbelievable. Just give me a second to catch up. You and Hudson are in on this?"

"Not just me and him. This was a team effort."

My brain is a scattered mess as I process that. "Wait—there are more vampires at the estate who know about this? About me escaping?"

"Oh, for sure—there's me and Hudson, and also Benjamin and Chef Maru. We all agreed that I should be the one to leave with you, since I've been wanting to get the hell out for ages now. But preparing everything without seeming suspicious was tricky. If I suddenly disappeared and stopped showing up for my shifts, the dyspeptic diehards on the staff would have reported it to your father."

Multiple aspects of her statement throw me. For starters, I've never heard Camille talk like this. Not ever. "You've been wanting to get out?"

"God yes. Hudson finally gave me the green light." She turns, beaming at me for a second before facing the road once more.

"The green light?" I ask, taking the bait. "For what?"

"To motherfucking quit! I have *hated* working under your fathers and all those snobby, old-timey, geriatric and cobweb-crotch vampires. To hell with them!"

Wide-eyed, I sit frozen with the thermos between my palms. My mouth is agape. "Then, why did you stay?"

"Because of you. I promised Sash that I'd look out for you. She's my best friend and you're a good vampire. You definitely needed an ally in that godforsaken castle. But, turns out, you had more than one." She shifts her eyes and winks before looking out the windshield again.

Unbelievable. I take a long sip from the thermos, flooding my senses with the heady, flowery oil and bergamot of the earl gray inside. Satisfied, I sigh as the hot liquid scothes my throat. "Benjamin too?" This surprises me.

"Of course. He's loyal to the viscount—not that other asshole."

"So, how did you all pull this off?"

Camille smiles, as if the simple memory of the tale pleases her. "Well, *I* wanted to just leave and break shit on my way out the door. Possibly shout some obscenities? But Hudson vetoed that idea. A bit too grandiose for his taste—perfect for mine, though.

"Chef Maru suggested I break or spill some dish during breakfast service, since Lord Blakeley swiftly reassigned me to the kitchen right after you mysteriously disappeared. We all agreed on the chef's plan. I spilled and dropped the entire pitcher of orange juice into the Duke of Ealing's lap."

I balk and jerk upright. "You spilled juice all over Alexander's horrible, needle-nosed uncle!"

"Yes, sir. A real prick, that one. He's lucky I didn't have the coffee."

I sink down into the seat, utterly satisfied. "That was very thoughtful of you." What a fantastic morning I'm having. The dungeon wasn't great, but this? Perfection.

Camille chuckles. "You're welcome. He had a right fit, of course. Then Benjamin—God bless his acting skills—screamed and sanctioned me to my quarters for the next week. With all the fuss the duke made, Lord Blakeley easily agreed to it.

"Immediately after I was dismissed, I packed up everything, then waited until dinner service to make my move. While everyone inside was preoccupied, Hudson let me out the main gate. It all went smoothly!"

Listening to her story is truly humbling. Also, I owe Ben a sincere apology. I am definitely guilty of sending some bad vibes his way over feeding Aries. I never even considered that he was forcibly ordered to do so by the overseer.

"I've been wanting to quit ever since Lord Blakeley raked me over the coals for those pictures you posted—utterly fantastic, by the way. We were all so proud of you for speaking up and publicly highlighting that issue, but we couldn't say anything." She reaches down and grabs her thermos. "I didn't quit after that, though, because Hudson told me to hold out. He didn't want me to leave, then be replaced by some old fart who religiously drinks from the fountain of Lord Blakeley's piss and would stifle you even more."

"That's... graphic."

"That's how some of them are. Loyal worshippers. Anyway, Hudson kept saying that we needed to be watchful in case you wanted to escape. That we should help if we could. It's like he was waiting for a sign." She glances at me, bringing her thermos to her lips and wiggling her eyebrows. "We sure got one, didn't we? An astrological sign. Sexy Aries."

Leaning my head back against the seat, I close my eyes. Humiliating. "Is there anyone who doesn't know about that?"

"I think Lord Blakeley suspected, but only put two and two together the morning that you left for Central Eden. You had some rather, um... distinct energy bursts early that morning. I guess it could have been you and Alexander but... let's be honest. We *know* it wasn't you and Alexander." She laughs loudly and it fills the small car. "Mr. Perfect Purebred doesn't seem like the type to give someone that kind of raw pleasure, does he?"

In a drastic gesture, she gasps, which makes me start and sit upright. Nervous, I glance around. "What is it?" Is someone following us? The jig is up?

"Before I forget, look in the glove box. Your phone is in there. I swiped it on my way out. Fuckers. There's a suitcase of clothes and some things for you in the backseat too. I couldn't take too much but I grabbed what I could."

Cautiously, I open the glove box, and there it is. My real phone. When I pull it out and tap the screen, it's fully charged.

"I don't know how long it will be before Lord Blakeley has it shut off, but you should text the golden prince and tell him you're alright," she says.

I pause, confused. "Alexander?"

"Yes, Alexander. He's pitching a bloody fit back at the castle! Livid and blatantly questioning Lord Blakeley about where you've disappeared to. It's brilliant, honestly. Masterful. I've never seen anyone just openly confront and provoke Lord Blakeley like that—in the presence of servants and everything. Zero fucks about decorum and all that rubbish. The rules have been blown out the window. I guess he's got some fire in him after all? Good for him."

Admittedly, I am surprised to hear this. "Maybe... I'll text him when I get to the safe house." Alexander has already helped me a lot—more than I deserve. I want him to know I'm okay, but I need to think for a minute. Everything is happening so fast.

"Maybe? Despite his shortcomings, I've always pegged him for being genuinely devoted to you. Your ride or die, so to speak."

I frown. "What does that mean? Who's dying?"

"Never mind. Welp, it's your choice. It'd be easier if he knew, though. Then he could, like, help and feed you. We don't have a long-term plan for your escape, but Alexander has connections beyond Eden and might have some ideas? Feeding-wise, you've never had anything below purebred, right? Unless you had a sip of Aries..." She cuts her eyes in my direction as if she's waiting to hear some juicy gossip.

Could I even call what I had a sip? I bypass that question altogether. "What's your plan? Are you going back to the castle at all?"

"Hell no. I've got my clothes back there, too. I've been hoarding cash since I started assisting you. I'm catching the next flight to Paris. Au revoir, assholes."

Laughing, I lift, pulling my talisman from my pocket and unfolding the paper to reread Aries's words. *We made a promise.* We did indeed.

"Can we keep in touch?" I ask.

"That's a given. You and Sasha will need to come visit me someday soon—if I can finally convince her to stop fooling around and walk away from Elaine." Camille takes another sip from her thermos. "Speaking of, text your sister. She's waiting to hear from you."

"I will. And I look forward to visiting you in Paris. Wow."

Part of me wishes that I had Aries's phone number. I had it saved in the temporary phone that Lord Blakeley gave me. Not my real one.

Another part of me is glad that I don't have it. Camille probably has his contact information. I'll ask her for it later, just so that I have it.

I don't want him involved in my mess. This chaos that is my life right now—physically fighting with my evil birth conduit and being imprisoned in a dungeon. Traversing through the woods and being smuggled off to a safe house. It's a lot, and I have no idea what will happen next.

When I see Aries again and talk to him, I want to be independent. Self-sufficient and stable to a point where he doesn't feel the need to swoop in and save me. My hope is that I can stand on my own two feet and meet him at his level. Two liberated and worldly vampires choosing each other—intentionally coming together as one because we are well matched. Because we know it's right.

Not by force or codependency. Because of love.

Well, for better or worse, the first major step is done. I've officially escaped.

"Here you are, you're grace." Tall, lanky and with warm brown skin, Roland moves toward the bed and sets a pile of towels and linen atop the bare mattress. "If you need anything at all, just let me or Kathryn know. We're truly, deeply honored to have you here—what an incredible turn of events."

I couldn't agree with him more. What would have happened if I hadn't confronted Lord Blakeley? If I hadn't stood my ground and forced his hand. Would I be asleep in my tower in the castle right now? Curled up and crying my eyes out about how miserable my life is? Grudgingly complying with his plans for me?

What if Alexander hadn't barged into my room that morning and found the pictures? That's the moment that triggered all of this.

Alexander... God. I need to make a decision about him.

The area surrounding the safe house is lush and woodsy. A

perfect environment for respite. However, the house is in rough shape. Broken or missing shutters and worn paint plague the outside. Squeaky floors, doors and outdated furniture pollute the atmosphere inside.

Even still, there's something cozy about the ambience. A delicate, quiet peace. The house has amazing character. Once they get it fixed up, I have no doubt that it'll be a huge success.

My room is on the second floor. It's spartan but decent with two twin beds neatly tucked in opposite corners. A writing desk and chair made from warm maple wood sit just beneath a large picture window. The glass offers a bright ray of natural sunlight and a view of the dense woods. The cottage has multiple rooms like this one, plus a large old-world kitchen, a potential medical office and outdoor space for recreational gardening and lounging.

"Thank you so much for letting me stay," I tell him in earnest as I sit on the desk chair in front of the window. My clothes are too filthy to sit anywhere else. "I know this is unexpected, and I don't have a plan yet for my next move, but I appreciate it more than you can imagine."

Seriously, the kindness I've experienced within the past few hours. First Hudson, then Camille and the other estate vampires, now Roland and Kathryn. Why should I be so fortunate?

"Your grace—"

"Please, just call me Oliver."

Roland nods. "Oliver. It's alright. You don't need to have everything figured out. That's what we're here for, to help other vampires in need who might be lost. You're our first official guest! And, truly, this house wouldn't exist if it hadn't been for you. Those photos led to a level of exposure that I never could have fathomed."

"I'm really happy to hear that."

"You're welcome to stay for as long as you need, and we'll keep your presence here a secret. My only concern is that we don't have access to blood that's high enough to properly nourish you. Our donors thus far are typically lower-ranked vampires. Unfortunately, I don't have purebred, or even high-quality first-gen nourishment to offer and sustain you."

I wave my hands. "Ah, no, it's alright. Maybe I can try some new blood? I won't know until I test it." I smile, wanting to reassure him.

He shakes his head with a grave expression. "Nooo, I'm very sorry, but you *cannot* suddenly introduce blood into your system that is predominantly comprised of human DNA. Your body will suffer greatly. This isn't something for you to play around with."

God. What the hell am I supposed to do? "I'm fine for now. Let's not worry about it."

"Oh, I'll worry about it, your grace. A lot." He rubs his fingers into the top of his short hair. "Let me discreetly ask around."

"Thank you. I'm so sorry to burden you like this." I'm tired of being helpless. I'm twenty-two years old and it's like I've done nothing to fend for or take care of myself my entire life. I know it isn't healthy to beat myself up over this, but it's difficult not to.

"We'll get it figured out," he says, heading toward the door. "I apologize for the state of the room and... well, the entire house."

"Don't apologize. It's great. There's a lot of potential here— it'll be fantastic when you get things fixed up and officially running."

"*If* I can make that happen." He smiles weakly, shrugging. "We got a lot of initial support to buy the property. Having the funds to renovate it is another matter. Unless some miracle occurs, I'm afraid I might have bitten off much more than I can chew. Anyway, I'll let you get settled. The bathroom and shower are just across the hall."

"Thank you," I say again. "I'm sure something will work out? If I can help in any way, let me know."

"Thank you, your gr—Oliver." He grins, then turns and leaves the room.

When the door is closed and I'm alone, I slouch and run my fingers into my hair.

I'm free, but...

What the hell am I doing?

What am I *going* to do?

Where do I even start? How do I survive?

I haven't fed since last Monday. I told Roland that I was fine because I didn't want to create added stress. But it's almost been a full week and I feel the irritation of hunger in the back of my throat. A dry, painful and itching sensation that I am not accustomed to at all.

I'm fed so regularly in life that it rarely ever gets this far. The blood is always just... there. I don't think I've ever been deprived of this basic need before.

Not having it is terrifying.

Sitting up straight, I shake my head, then slap my cheeks. "Keep it together, Oliver. You can do this." I have to stay calm. Freaking out helps nothing.

First, I need to shower and dispel the grimy dungeon dirt, rat feces and old blood from my skin and hair. I stand from the desk chair and walk over to grab the suitcase that Camille packed for me. After laying it flat against the creaky wooden floor, I unzip it.

The moment I flip it open, Aries's handmade suit is staring me in the face. Neatly folded, elegant and hauntingly blue. My hybrid camera, the extra film and the three photos that I took of me and Aries are tucked in the corner just beside the suit. My latest writing journal is there, too.

Without warning, I burst into tears. Happy ones—but nervous, too? Relieved? I'm such a mess lately. A volatile roller coaster of emotions. I should message Camille and thank her again.

I wipe my eyes with the backs of my hands as I return to the desk. I reach over and grab my phone from the surface, and as I sit down in the chair once more, I tap open the messaging application. I navigate, looking for Camille's name, but then pause. Another name catches my attention first.

Alexander.

In the silence, I stare at his name while biting the inside of my cheek. The achy tiredness beats all over my body like a hard base-line. The soreness in my throat is dry and inflamed, and even my retracted incisors are steadily throbbing.

Is it fair for me to call Alexander and ask for his help when I've fundamentally betrayed him? We were supposed to be married in a few days. Bonded for life. Surprisingly, he seems to have genuinely wanted that outcome. All this time, I thought his behavior was an act. An elaborate show for the wide audience of our snobbish aristocracy.

Now? I know that he was sincere.

Regardless, I've said "no thanks" and run away. I've told him as much to his face. To add insult to injury, I've been sleeping with another vampire behind his back for the past month.

With what nerve can I ask for Alexander's help now? And why should he help me? I obviously don't deserve it. There's no way.

Swiftly, I flip my phone face down onto the desk, then take a deep breath. I can't do that—I shouldn't burden him with the choices I've made. I'll figure this out, somehow. There has to be another way...

Right?

Chapter Twenty-Seven

"We need something like an investor or spokesperson, you know? Someone with power and influence to support this project." Kathryn sits back against the chair in a huff, folding her arms over her empty dinner plate. Her tightly coiled hair is parted on the side and artfully styled in chunks. She looks as if she's wearing an elaborate crown. "That's the only way we'll ever truly get this clinic off the ground."

"But that would take a miracle," Roland adds, standing from the wooden table and gathering our plates. I get up as well, collecting the silverware to help. "Because—Wait, you—No, your grace! You don't need—"

"Let me help, please?" I ask, offering a smile. "It's the very least I can do." I've only been at the safe house for a few hours, but Kathryn and Roland have already shown me such sincere kindness. I still can't believe how lucky I am to be here.

Roland nods, but exhales a sigh. "Excuse me for being frank, but this is so freaking weird. Having a purebred here and... acting like it's normal."

I chuckle. "Some of us are capable of normalcy, believe it or not."

"You hardly touched your food," Kathryn chimes in, concerned. "Are you sure you're feeling okay?"

Trembling and trying to conceal it, I wave a hand. "I'm fine, never mind me. Roland, you were saying? It would take a miracle?"

"Yes," he says, casting a suspicious glance my way. "It would take a miracle to find a vampire in Eden with capital and influence that's also willing to help us launch this development. To help us change the narrative surrounding ranked vampires—that it's good for *everyone* to support those who are in need, and not shun them for being different or 'lesser.' But there are no vampires like that in Eden."

"Except maybe you?" Kathryn smiles.

"I'm honored that you think so," I admit. "But I've never had any 'power' or 'influence' to speak of—especially not now." I can't even figure out how to feed myself, and the dry itch at the back of my throat is becoming unbearable. Also, my incisors are pounding. I feel like hell, which is why I couldn't eat. "What about outside of Eden?"

"We've accepted some external support, but Roland and I have decided that it would be better to have someone on board from the inside," Kathryn says. "Having a purebred or ranked vamp from an outside aristocracy intervene in such a provocative endeavor will seem like an attack—like someone coming to Eden and meddling with our culture. We don't want to create strife. We want to slowly change minds."

"That makes sense," I tell her, walking over to the sink with silverware clutched in my fists. As I approach, Roland is there. He looks me over yet again.

"Forgive my saying this but... you look a little gray."

"I-I'm alright, don't worry—I'm just tired. It's been a crazy couple of days." Jesus Christ. Is my vision getting blurry? "I think I'm going to lie down for a while."

"Let us know if you need anything," Kathryn calls as I leave the kitchen and head back to my room.

Upstairs, I stop at the bathroom. When I look in the mirror, my skin tone is indeed worse than it was even a couple hours ago. My eyes are dull and lifeless. I'm really getting anxious now. But I don't know if...

I can't ask him. I can't.

Into the evening, I pace back and forth across the creaky floorboards of my room, still thinking and researching on my phone. All the while, the dryness in my throat flares and aches to the point where it's physically uncomfortable to swallow.

My entire body shudders as I sit in my pajamas on the side of the bed. Fear is manipulating and tangling my thoughts into a dark web, because I keep remembering the damp stone walls crowding every side of me. The horrible smell of dried blood and the squeak of invisible rats circling the perimeter. Waiting and excited for a fresh meal.

Inside my core, my nature is depleted. Hollow from the dangerous combination of overuse and a lack of sustenance.

I can't go on like this. There's no other choice.

Giving in, I pick up my phone and text Alexander.

[Hey...]

With my hands quivering, I try to decide what I should say next. How I should make this ludicrous request of him that I don't deserve. Before I can type anything, though, he responds.

[Ollie?]

[Yes.]

[Where the fuck are you?]

I hesitate and absently chew my bottom lip. I need him. I have to trust him and he's already shown me that I can. More than once. Exhaling, I type my response.

[At a safe house just outside Nantshire. No one knows
I'm here. I ran away.]

A new message comes through almost immediately.

[Send me the address.]

I don't know the address to this house, so I tinker and figure
out how to send him my exact location instead. Five seconds later,
he texts again.

[I'm on my way.]

Within an hour of messaging him, I can feel Alexander
approaching the house, because his essence always radiates
brightly. Like he's never once thought about tempering or stifling
his aura.

Why would he, though? He's a proud and happy purebred
prince whose parents have let him have friends and go to parties.
He's allowed to travel and watch TV shows called *Buffy*. I bet his
father would never attack and throw him into a dungeon.

I feel ashamed that I couldn't even make it one whole day on
my own. Not only did I have Hudson, Camille, Ben and Chef
Maru conspire to free me, I have to drag Alexander into the mess
as well because I'm too scared to suffer again.

When I finally hear Alexander coming up the steps, I inhale,
then blow it out slowly, because I never know what to expect with
this vampire. Soon, there's a light knock on the door. "Come in."

Kathryn peeks her head in first. "Your grace, Prince Alexander
is here."

Alexander enters the room wearing a camel-colored trench
coat with a high collar, a matching fedora and dark glasses.

I burst into a fit of laughter. Surprisingly, it feels good. I don't know, but the sight of him is utterly ridiculous. "Are you here to solve a mystery? It's dark outside."

"You're one to laugh," he spits, whipping off his sunglasses and stalking forward. "Do you think this is a joke? You look like utter hell."

"Well, I've felt better. What's with this outfit?"

"Never mind me. How long have you been here?"

"Since this morning."

"Why have you only texted me just now? What the fuck, Oliver?" Behind him, Kathryn clenches her teeth and slinks out of the room, sensing the impending explosion and saving herself.

I exhale and lift my palms. "Listen, please... don't shout at me. It's been a really hard couple of days and I'm depleted. I don't want to fight with you."

Alexander's golden-brown eyes sweep over me in assessment, and it makes me a little self-conscious. He walks over to the desk near my bed, pulls the chair out and sits down.

"I didn't come here to fight with you," he says, frowning and running a hand through his hair. "But I've been racking my brain and worried sick about you ever since that night in your father's godawful study, trying to figure out what happened—or what I could do to help you."

He drops a hand and looks directly at me. His expression is pained. Or maybe disappointed. "I know you don't like me, Oliver. I've made a lot of mistakes with you, and I get that. But could you at least have the decency to look at me as an ally? As someone who sincerely cares about you?"

"It wasn't like that," I explain. "I didn't think it was fair for me to ask for your help after everything that's happened. And I wanted to try handling this on my own."

"Well, it looks like you're doing a shit job."

Half-heartedly, I chuckle. "Yeah, well..." My throat and fangs ache so badly, and they're pulsing even worse now that he's here. It's like my body knows that a proper and nutritious meal is sitting in front of me.

I once compared Alexander and Aries in my mind, saying one was like an apple and the other a decadent piece of chocolate cake. I didn't want this apple before. Now, I'm desperate for it. I'd *love* an apple, please and thank you.

"Tell me everything," Alexander says quietly. "How did we get here?"

I explain what happened after he left the study, sparing no details. Saying it aloud feels good. I've noticed this about myself in the past few weeks. I've spent the bulk of my life holding everything inside—my thoughts, feelings and even my vampiric essence. Letting out my words, my experiences and emotions has become euphoric. Therapeutic.

Alexander listens intently and doesn't interrupt. He doesn't take his eyes off of me. When I'm finished, he sits back in the desk chair and folds his arms, visibly bewildered.

"Wow," he says. "Your father is truly diabolical. But also, comical? Like he's determined to play the part of a spiteful villain in an old-fashioned movie. Twirling his mustache and cackling after tying someone to the train tracks. It's fucking unbelievable."

"It was crazy," I concur. "Horrific. I could barely register the situation when I was in it, because everything happened so fast. Now that I'm here, though, the reality of it is sinking in." It's also getting harder to concentrate because I'm so anemic and hungry.

"Should I tell my mother and father what he's done?" Alexander asks with his arms still folded. "The fact that he used his powers on you is forbidden. Him putting you in a dungeon afterward makes it even worse. I could bring this information before the Royal Order and he'll be tried and accused. There's no way he'll ever be eligible for a royal title after this behavior. You'll have to give your testimony and face him again, but... we shouldn't let him get away with this."

Looking off, I lift a hand to rub my fingers against the top of my scalp. If I did this, not only would I have to confront Lord Blakeley a second time, I'd also have to explain how I got away, which means involving Camille, Hudson and Benjamin. I don't know if I—

"Don't decide now," Alexander cuts in, as if he can read the distressed state of my thoughts. "Just, think about it. The option is there, and if you want him punished, I'll facilitate the process."

I nod. "Thank you for this offer, but... I doubt that anyone on the governing board would even take my side. I'm not important enough to any—"

"You *are* important, to me," Alexander asserts, then sighs, considering as his gaze shifts and catches the bright stream of moonlight radiating through the window. "Eden has its problems, but I think, maybe someday, we can change? I know that you hate it here, but I have hope in our aristocracy. We can do better."

He might be right, but I'm not sure if I'm willing to fight against this antiquated and stuffy system that's definitely rigged in favor of vampires like Lord Blakeley. Vampires like Alexander who hold all the cards.

"You feel that way because you're a vampire with power and influence," I tell him honestly, recalling Kathryn's earlier words. "When you're like me and you have nothing within a static system, it's difficult to have hope."

Silent, Alexander looks down at his right hand rested atop his thigh. My gaze falls there as well. He's staring at the two golden bands wrapped around his ring finger. I'm fairly certain that he's worn those rings since we were teenagers.

"This is... yet another reason to dislike me, right?" he says softly. "My 'power and influence'? You think of me as being the same as your father."

"No, I don't. I was just... That's not what I meant."

He sets his palms against his knees and pushes up from the chair. He avoids eye contact. "Sure, Ollie, if you say so. Anyway, you can't stay here."

"Why?" I ask. "Roland and Kathryn have been very kind."

"Because this isn't a place for purebreds."

I frown and narrow my gaze. A moment ago, I felt bad for

pointing out his obvious privilege. But now, he sounds like a classist snob. I'm about to tell him as much, but he holds his ringed palm up.

"Not like that," he says. "Literally, they aren't equipped to feed you, plus, you'll eventually draw unwanted attention from the townspeople. Word will get out, and I doubt that Roland and Kathryn want to be wrapped up in this situation and pitted against your evil-ass father. I'm sure he'll take great pleasure in campaigning to shut this house down and making their lives hell the moment he knows you're here."

Alright. He has an excellent point. "Okay," I sigh.

"I have somewhere that's better for you. Farther out."

Drawing back, my shoulders tense. "I'm not staying at one of your houses."

"It's not my house, you dummy. Does that make any sense considering we're trying to hide you? Would you just trust me for once, please?"

Calming my mind, I take a deep breath and nod. "Yes, sorry. Alright."

Alexander turns and his long trench coat shifts with him as he moves. "Rest for tonight. Tomorrow morning, I'll drive you out to my cousin's house near the eastern mountains. Only Raphael will know about it, because if I don't tell him, he'll somehow know that I'm keeping secrets and will drive me insane. But I trust him more than anyone. Don't worry."

"Your cousin Leoni?" I ask.

"Yes, Leoni. I've already called and spoken with her, so we're good." Alexander turns to leave and I stand, feeling woozy. I don't know if I can keep my sanity through the night. I look up, and Alexander is near the door, watching me.

"Do you need to feed, Oliver?"

"Yes."

"Then why don't you say it? Why don't you ask me?"

"May I please feed, Alexander?" I step toward him. He leaves the door, meeting me halfway.

"You may." He offers his palm. Without hesitation, I take it and bite down.

While his blood fills my mouth and nourishes me, his voice is low. Flowing over me like a spell. "Listen, I... I'll do anything in my power to help you—but you have to tell me that you want it, okay? I'm not going to force myself on you anymore. Does that make sense?"

This feeding is so deeply fulfilling and warming to my body that my eyes naturally alight as I pull. If possible, I never want to feel like that again. Wretched. Cold, afraid and famished.

When I stop drinking and open my eyes, they're still burning. But I meet Alexander's gaze sincerely. "Yes, it makes sense. I appreciate you letting me feed. Thank you so much for coming to help me." I lick his palm to clean it, then let his hand rest softly against my nose and face. I close my eyes, grateful for his warmth and familiarity after such a jarring and tumultuous couple of days.

Alexander snatches his hand away and my eyes fly open. He's blushing. Bright, rosy red, and his eyes are alighted and golden. "Well, don't suddenly be all sweet to me, because then I'll get confused. I'll come back to get you in the morning... you twat." Flustered, he turns, yanks the door open and leaves the room.

Slowly, my body stops trembling and the ache at the back of my throat fades. Just disappears, and I can swallow again, functionally. Normally.

I feel better, but still fatigued as I drag myself over to the bed and crawl underneath the sheets. As I stare up at the ceiling, my body shifts into torpor again, but gently this time. Soothed and fed. I sleep, soundlessly, but my mind is a showcase of vivid dreams.

Not of dungeons, searing pain or dangerous, silver-glowing eyes. But of hope and possibility. Of my life splitting and forking along two divergent paths. One flashes with images of everything I've dreamed of—freedom, travel and creativity. Love and acceptance like I've always yearned for.

The second path is... new. Unexpected, but not cold. Not the restrictive, loveless and forced union that my waking mind has always conjured. This novel life is warm but very slow. Gradual, like water heating in a tea kettle. I can't see any of the images clearly, but I can feel that when this life begins to boil, it thrives. It shrieks fiercely, powerfully, and turns the world around it—the air and the environment, *everything*—upside down.

When I wake up the next morning, I open my eyes slowly and inhale a deep, smooth breath before I blow it out. Aside from the birds singing beyond the window, it's quiet. The sun shines buttery and radiant through the window and I'm warm and comfortable in the bed.

My body is healed. My nature is serene, curled up and pampered like a contented house cat in my core, and there's no pain anywhere. Not even in my throat. This is Alexander's doing. His blood. I won't deny that, and I'm grateful.

I know what I want. For as far back as I can remember, I have been dreaming of my freedom and independence. This desire is entrenched, and since I've come this far, I'll do whatever it takes to achieve it. There's no turning back now.

But this unexpected dream? This second path. I can't ignore that it stirs me. An intense vision of a prospect that I've never once considered.

Maybe, if things had been different, Alexander and me, we wouldn't have been half bad. If I'm honest with myself, the warm sensation pulsing in my chest tells me that we could have been great. Powerful and aligned, like nothing the vampires of Eden have ever seen before.

I won't choose that path, though. I can't, because there are too many layers. In my heart, the reasons are like violent shards of broken glass—too much trauma, oppression and burden. There are so many painful memories associated with Alexander and the life that Lord Blakeley neglectfully forced on me. That path... it would be like going back and combing through the wreckage of a devastating fire.

Yes, the foundation might be intact and suitable for a new

start. Maybe, far beneath the charred debris and rubble, there's hope. A chance for Alexander and me to rebuild.

Regardless, I want to walk away.

This is my first official day of complete freedom from that unbearable life, and I... I am choosing to move forward.

I have to.

Chapter Twenty-Eight

The landscape of Eden is truly beautiful. Our territory is a generous island surrounded by the sea, yielding all sorts of rich resources and vegetation. To the east, the terrain is lined with craggy mountains that become tipped with snow through the winter and into early spring. To the south, where my clan is from, there are sandy beaches and lush coastlines. Artistic sunsets that paint the sky in golden hues.

Alexander drives with confidence, deftly guiding us through condensed and charming country towns one moment, then on narrow roads flanked by vast, breathtaking valleys the next. As he focuses on the road, we engage in casual conversation.

Gradually, I have become painfully aware of how much I've envied Alexander throughout our lives, and how my bitterness has contaminated our relationship.

Of course, I've always felt resentment—usually in the form of offhand jokes laced with cattiness inside of my head. But after that dream last night and his willingness to help me despite all I've done, I'm slowly unpacking my complex feelings toward him.

We were born in the same stifling and archaic aristocracy, but his existence is so different from mine. His house is more comfortable, soft and modern. The way in which he carries himself—with this assured air of freedom and contentment—feels foreign to me. I can't imagine navigating Eden with such assertion. It's always seemed unfair. Why should he have this life when I don't? Why should he have everything that he wants, including me?

"I don't want you to report Lord Blakeley because I don't want vampires to feel sorry for me," I say, continuing our current conversation. We've been driving for almost two hours. The landscape is rural now that we're close to the mountains. "I'd also rather not have my actions and the actions of the vamps who helped me scrutinized. I just... want to move past it and never see him again."

"Alright, I understand what you're saying. Personally, I would like to see Lord Blakeley held accountable for what he did to you. He can't be properly reprimanded if we don't tell your side of the story."

Folding my arms, I puff out a breath. "Just make sure he never gets a royal title or a seat on the governing board. That will be punishment enough for him, I promise."

Alexander chuckles. "Your wish is my command. I'll see to that."

"What is his excuse about why I've disappeared? What is he saying?"

He shakes his head. "That you've 'fallen ill' from the stress of the wedding. He's insane. Nobody is buying that."

"What about your parents?" I ask, wondering what he's told them if he's only exposed the truth to Raphael. "Do they believe Lord Blakeley?"

"They're just relieved that I've stopped openly calling your father a fucking liar and am back to being on my best behavior. Let me worry about them."

A long beat of comfortable silence rests between us as I gaze out the window. We pass a stretch of brush that's perfectly organized in symmetrical, parallel rows. Maybe it's a vineyard? Looks like we're getting closer to Leoni's cottage.

"What about the other thing I mentioned?" I ask, interrupting the silence.

"What other thing?"

"The blood clinic. Roland and Kathryn needing support."

Alexander shrugs, blinking innocently. "I hope they get it."

I narrow my eyes. "Are you being obtuse on purpose?"

"Listen—this clinic sounds great. Truly. But I don't stick my nose into controversial things, you know? I'm just like... the fun-loving mascot of Eden. I show up wherever my parents tell me to and make balloon animals. Messy things like 'blood clinics' are not my bag."

"Bullshit." I turn my head, frowning. "You've happily stuck your nose into this mess between me and my father?"

"This is different."

"How so?"

"Because I—" Alexander shakes his head, visibly bristling as he rolls his shoulders. "Because it *just is*."

Sitting back against the seat, I stare forward and give him a second to compose himself before I speak once more. "What's the point of being a lovable mascot with power and influence if you don't use it for anything important? I can't do anything about the problems of Eden, but you definitely could."

I know this now, because I dreamt it. Deep down, I have this unequivocal sense of exactly what Alexander is capable of. Whether he knows it yet or not, I'm uncertain.

Alexander sighs heavily as he slows and maneuvers the car into a long graveled driveway. "Just... get off my back, Ollie, alright? Leave me alone, please."

"You stood up to my father and upset the polite social norms for me. That's great, and bold. Defiant in a way I really respect. But what about the other vampires in Eden that have terrible situations? That's all. Think about it." I watch him, waiting for his response. But Alexander looks through the glass of the windshield intensely, as if driving suddenly takes his full concentration, even though we're crawling along at a snail's pace.

"Can you really make balloon animals?" I ask, just to lighten the mood.

"No. And I *hate* that rubbery squeaking sound that they make when the balloon is being contorted. It makes my skin crawl." Alexander shivers and I snicker.

The gravel road bends just before a small, cozy-looking two-story cottage with white shutters comes into view.

"We're here," he says, pulling the car up to the front and stopping beside a set of shallow steps that lead to the porch and front door.

Each side of the cottage is flanked by giant, sprawling hydrangea bushes in the most vivid violet color I've ever seen. On the opposite side of the cottage and driveway, healthy vineyards stretch as far as my eyes can see, like an ocean of green. The mountains rise up in the distance, imposing against the blue sky. The sun casts its rays in golden beams across the entire scene, like a radiant blessing from the gods.

I'd love to have a camera good enough to photograph this landscape. What a dreamy place to live every day.

"Hola, Puercoespín. Tengo mucho sin verte," a cool, teasing voice calls out from the front of the cottage as I close the passenger-side door and look up.

A purebred with a wavy dark brown bob cut just below her chin is there. Her thick bangs are like a seductive shadow over her vibrant brown eyes. She walks to the porch railing, setting her palms against the banister as she leans and addresses Alexander. "Estoy feliz que llegaste bien. ¿Cómo te fue el viaje?"

"Hey—it was alright." Alexander is busy pulling my suitcase out of the backseat. Can he understand her? Why is she speaking Spanish? I rush around, meeting him on the driver's side.

"I can get it," I tell him.

"It's fine." He waves and picks up the suitcase. "You need to take it easy. Oliver, this is my cousin Leoni. Leoni, this is Oliver."

"The famous Oliver of Southern Eden," she says, grinning

and stepping over to meet us with her hands stuffed in the pockets of her brightly patterned coveralls. "It's a pleasure to finally meet you."

Am I famous? In what way? I have so many questions. "You too. Thank you for letting me stay."

As we reach the plateau of the porch, Leoni blocks Alexander's path, which makes me pause just behind him. There's an odd moment of silence before Leoni's hand darts out and does something to Alexander's side that makes him yelp and practically crumble.

"*Leoni.*"

"Eso es porque solo me llamas cuando tienes necesidad, baboso." Leoni steps aside, winking at me. "I had to get him at least once. His weak spot." She chuckles as Alexander nurses his waist and steps past her.

"His what?" I ask. I can't keep up.

Leoni blinks. Her eyes are almost the same color as Alexander's. Actually, they might be a mirror image? But her irises register differently set against her auburn features and compared with Alexander's blonde ones. "His side, you know? How he's extra sensitive—"

"Oye, ¿podemos entrar y ser normales por cinco segundos?" Alexander is obviously annoyed as he holds the door for me and Leoni. "Detente por favor. Él no sabe nada."

"Why? Haven't the two of you been engaged since you were seven?" Leoni says, walking past Alexander and into the house. "How could he not know that about you? *I* know that about you —and all your other 'unprincely' little characteristics."

"Yeah, well, it's complicated," Alexander says. As I pass him, I study his face. His expression is agitated and he intentionally avoids my gaze.

What the hell?

∼

"So let me get this straight. You've never worked before. Never gotten your hands dirty or done any type of proper manual labor? You've been 'princing around' your whole life?"

Leoni stares at me in disbelief. As if she's genuinely confused about my presence in her beautiful cottage and what I could possibly offer. I'm starting to wonder myself.

I rub my palm against the back of my neck. "Um, technically, I'm not a prince, but... I'm—"

"You called and asked if I needed help with the vineyard." Leoni turns to Alexander, who's sitting in a sunken armchair and glancing around as if he's considering buying the place. Like he's impressed and he'll make her a very nice offer. "I said yes, and this is what you bring me? A runaway purebred prince who's never worked a day in his life?"

Alexander shrugs. "Yeah, but he's good for it—aren't you, Ollie?"

"I am," I say, straightening my spine. "I haven't worked before, but I'm not afraid to. I'm willing to earn my keep and I'll abide by your rules." I'm nervous. Leoni is petite but regal, with her arms folded and her leg casually crossed as she regards me. Her skin tone is like toasted cashews and seems to glow in the reflected sunlight bouncing off the walls of the cozy room.

"Ollie is the smartest, kindest vampire I've ever known," Alexander says, folding his ankle over his knee to make himself even more comfortable. "Trust me. He'll be a great fit for you here."

I take a step forward, meeting Leoni's eyes. "I promise that I won't be a burden to you, and I'll do whatever it takes to help. If you give me a chance, I'll show you." I don't know what it is, but something in the atmosphere of this house feels right.

I've never been this far east in Eden before. I've only seen the mountains of our aristocracy from a great distance, like a far-off metaphysical wall representing the boundary that encompasses my secluded life.

Leoni's house is near the mountains. We're surrounded by them, so both symbolically and physically, I'm pushing against my pre-established and long-sustained restrictions. Her cottage is small, more utilitarian than the excessive and opulent grandeur I'm accustomed to, but I like this about it. The space feels personal. Deeply intimate.

I can grow and learn here. Something inside of me knows that this is where I need to be. This is the next step.

Leoni smirks as she listens, but when she looks past me at Alexander, her eyes are affectionate. "You're a real sap for falling for a creature like this."

"What's wrong with being a sap?" Alexander asks. "There are worse things."

She folds her arms, grinning. "Well, I can't make this decision on my own, anyway. We'll have to see what Danny thinks. He should be back from town any second—"

Behind us, the front door clicks open, then pushes wide. In the golden stream of afternoon sunlight, a first-generation vampire enters the room carrying a large basket full of vegetables —tomatoes, onions, broccoli. Some dark, leafy greens and sweet potatoes, just at a glance. His hair is very long but pulled back in a sleek, shiny and dark braid that reaches to the center of his shoulder blades. It falls forward like a rope as he drops the basket inside the door.

"Ah," Leoni says, popping up from her seat and walking over to meet the new vampire. "There you are. I was just talking about you."

"Good things, I hope?" His voice is casual and cool. Meditative. He wears a blue T-shirt with a graphic of a man looking through a pair of binoculars. The words around the image read, *Oh look! Nobody gives a shit.* There are dirty gardening gloves hanging over the edge of one of the large cargo pockets of his gray sweatpants.

I'm not sure why, but he's difficult to read. His aura is muted.

Almost non-existent. He's definitely first-generation, but the energy emanating from him is so weak. It's as if he's barely there.

"Daniel Lim?"

I turn, and Alexander is on his feet, his golden-brown eyes wide with some expression that I don't easily recognize. Gazing back to the door, Leoni and this Daniel vampire seem just as confused as me. He's lean and towers over Leoni's shorter frame.

"Do I owe you money?" Daniel says, offering a detached smile. "You said my name like I owe you money."

"No." Alexander steps forward, staring as if he's in a trance. "I just... I haven't seen you since I was eleven. My God... what's happened to you? Are you alright? I didn't know you were here, too."

Alexander is visibly awestruck, but the air in the room stiffens. I don't know Leoni and Daniel at all, but I can read the shift in both of their demeanors very clearly—especially Leoni's. Daniel tries to play it off, narrowing his lilac-colored irises. "Who are you, exactly?" he asks.

Alexander draws back, blinking. "You don't remember me?"

"Should I?" Daniel raises an eyebrow, unimpressed.

"Danny," Leoni cuts in, admonishing. "Stop it. I told you about this last night. Alexander is here to stash his fiancé away from his evil father."

"Oh yes," Daniel says. "Our runaway purebred. Fantastic. Welcome. Pleasure to meet you both." Without waiting for a response, Daniel reclaims his basket and disappears into the kitchen. We stare after him and the unexpectedly frosty vibe he's left behind.

Waving her hands, Leoni gestures us toward the door. "Outside, please? Let's go outside on the porch." Confused, me and Alexander follow her lead.

There are two wicker rocking chairs and a small matching bench situated on the porch overlooking the majesty of the vineyard, sky and mountains. Both me and Alexander step toward the chairs to take a seat, but Leoni speaks up again.

"Alright, Ollie can stay. Puercoespín, you need to leave."

Alexander's posture stiffens. "What did I do? What the hell was that in there?"

"Listen, it's a long story, and Danny has a thing about purebreds. Too many of us are encroaching his space, so I'll do you this favor and help Ollie, but you gotta go, cariño. ¿Luego hablamos?" She makes a gesture with her hand, urging him to go as quickly as possible.

"A thing about purebreds?" Alexander frowns. "You're pure-bred and he's living with you?"

"Except for me. Again, long story."

Alexander rolls his eyes and sticks his hands into his coat pockets. "Fine. Whatever. But I have to come back with a nurse soon so that they can make feeding bags for Oliver and me."

"Er, sure... no problem," Leoni says, taking hold of his shoulders and physically guiding him down the steps and away from the house. "Call me and we'll arrange it."

Obedient, Alexander heads toward the car, but then glances over his shoulder. "Message me, Ollie, if you need anything?"

"I will, thanks," I respond, waving. Soon, his shiny black sports car heads back toward the main road.

Leoni examines me with her manicured eyebrow raised in confusion. "Why do you two need feeding bags? Aren't you engaged?"

He didn't tell her. Alright, understandable. It's complicated.

I take a breath and nervously clasp my palms in front of me. "Well, not anymore. I called it off—that's the reason why we're in this mess with Lord... er, my parents."

"Wait—you've dumped Alexander?"

"W-well I wouldn't put it like that?"

"¡Ay nooo!" Leoni sighs as she moves toward the wicker bench and plops down. I sit in the rocking chair beside it. "Now I feel bad for shooing him off. Shit. I'll call him later. This is a much bigger mess than I thought."

An awkward gap of silence forms as she processes what I've

said. Somehow, I feel the need to cushion this revelation. "Alexander accepts my feelings, though. We're alright."

Her gaze flickers over to me as she sits with her arms folded. "Maybe. Or he's putting on a good show to make you feel comfortable. He's good at that, you know? Making everyone else feel comfortable and like everything is fine when he's not. Well, I guess you probably *don't* know that."

This makes me pause. Is he only pretending to accept my decision? I'll tuck this away for further examination, later. "I didn't know that Alexander spoke Spanish."

Leoni's brown eyes widen, then narrow in suspicion. "Did you two never spend any time together, ever? Was Alex just making stuff up when he gushed about seeing you?"

"No, well, we spent time together—just, always supervised? We didn't have many opportunities to talk candidly growing up, and I, um..." Can I tell her that I wasn't interested at all? That I hated the entire arrangement and wanted nothing to do with it or him?

It feels rude, so I'll leave that part out.

"You don't know about his Achilles waist, you don't know that our grandparents, his mother and his uncle—my father— were born in Mexico but immigrated here as children... What *do* you know about Alexander?"

"Um... he plays the piano and has a calico cat named Buffy?" I offer, wincing. Jesus. "Why do you call him 'puercoespín.' What does that mean?"

Leoni sighs, shifting her focus to the expanse of the vineyard stretched before us. "Porcupine. And because of what I just said. He puts on a show of being tough and unaffected, but he's a little softie underneath the façade."

Contemplating, I let the silence settle between us. It's starting to feel like she knows a much more complex version of Alexander than I do. The version I've refused to see all these years. But how could I, given our circumstance?

"Anyway," she says, unfolding her arms, "if Alexander says that you're reliable, then I believe him. But give Danny some time to adjust, alright? Major trust issues there."

"Sure, no problem," I assure her. Of course, I want to know why, but it's obviously not my business. "Really, thank you for letting me stay here. I'm not useless. I promise that I can pull my own weight."

"I didn't say that you were useless. I may have implied, but I didn't say it. Regarding room, boarding and compensation, I know your situation is dire, so you'll work the land in exchange for living here. If you're very capable, I'll give you a small cut of the house allowance I'm allocated each month."

I nod a little harder than I need to, but I want to show her that I'm listening and engaged. "Yes, that's very generous and fair. Thank you."

"The house rules are simple," Leoni continues. "No lies, no servants, no drama. Let's break them down. Rule number one—no lies. Danny and me are always honest with each other. If we're having an off day, need some time alone or one of us does something that the other doesn't like, we say as much. No hard feelings.

"Second rule—no servants. We clean up after ourselves, share responsibilities with regard to house chores and generally help out where it's needed. I cook, do meal planning and prep for one week, then Danny has a week. We alternate like this so that the burden is never just on one person. It also helps us so that we're not looking at each other every single day like idiots and having the 'What should we eat?' conversation. I hate that."

Leoni is purebred, but Daniel is first-generation. In any purebred house in Eden, he would be designated as some sort of servant. I'm really happy that this isn't the case here. It's just further confirmation that I'm in the right place.

"Are you alright with this?" Leoni asks. "The three of us operating as equals?"

"Yes, of course."

"Good. Can you cook?"

"Ah, I... well, I've never tried outside of our chef letting me help him bake sometimes, but I'll absolutely learn and do my best."

"Well, that's all I can ask for. The last rule is no drama. No pomp and circumstance, no balls, banquets or gossip. Our house is a peaceful refuge for both of us, and we don't want any of the garbage from the Eden aristocracy invading this space. We both put up with it for a long time. But no more."

"I feel exactly the same way about Eden's practices," I tell her. "All of this sounds perfect."

Leoni stands from the bench and stretches. "Glad to hear it." When she drops her arms, she lifts her chin. "Smells like we're having curry for dinner. Let's go inside? Just tread lightly and you should be fine."

I'm nervous as I stand. "Okay, will do." She leads, and I follow her back into the house, which is indeed overflowing with the scent of fresh curry, turmeric, sautéed vegetables and coconut milk.

In the kitchen, Daniel is at the counter. Olive-green cabinets and drawers frame him where he stands, and the space is complemented by a trail of healthy, leafy vines winding their way across the top of the cupboards. They trickle down, reaching like tendrils over the window above the large sink.

There's a rice cooker and a large pot on the stove. Both are billowing with steam and mouthwatering fragrances. A large wooden chopping board covered in an assortment of vegetable scraps sits in front of him.

Daniel turns to glance at Leoni and me as we walk toward a round wooden table with four mismatched chairs—one is sky blue, another rose red, the third is sunflower yellow and the last one is the same olive green as the kitchen cabinets. It's eclectic, richly colored and smart. A cheerful and pleasant space.

"Dinner is almost ready," he says calmly as he turns back

toward the counter. "Why the hell am I cooking for two perfectly healthy and capable purebreds?"

"Don't do this," Leoni encourages him. "We talked about this, and it's your week to cook. Do you want me to take over?"

Daniel sighs heavily. "No. But for the record, I feel some kind of way."

"Noted," Leoni says, then winks at me. She mouths, "He'll be fine."

After dinner, we move into the sitting room to continue our conversation. Well, I should say, my and Leoni's conversation, since Daniel hasn't said much at all aside from expressing his displeasure with cooking for us.

Leoni cradles a steaming cup of tea as she sits in a large armchair. Daniel is on the floor with his legs folded. Beside him, there's a basket full of what looks like colorful balls of yarn. He works diligently, wielding two long wooden needles entwined with red fabric.

"There used to be an entire staff at this house, working my family's vineyard," Leoni explains. "One by one, though, everyone started quitting." She takes a long sip of her tea before continuing. "Soon, there was no one left to run the place. It'd been abandoned for six months by the time Danny and me got here."

"What happened?" I ask, holding my own spiced apple tea in my palms as I sit on the couch. This sounds like the makings of a ghost story.

"Times have changed, and they were tired of being servants to our family—tired of being treated like second-rate citizens in Eden. This phenomenon has been happening more frequently across the aristocracy."

"Hudson, the lead servant at my family's estate, recently told me that as well," I offer. "He said that some smaller houses can't maintain a full staff anymore. My handler, Camille, officially quit after she helped me escape. She dropped me off at Roland's safe house in Nantshire, then caught a train to Paris."

Leoni smirks. "Good for her. Ranked vamps are getting sick of this bullshit—these strict roles and dogmatic ways of existing. Me included. And you too, obviously. Otherwise, you wouldn't be sitting here."

She already knows most of my story because of my impromptu interview during lunch. I'd like to know more about her, and Daniel, too, but I'm not sure how receptive they'll be. I'll give it time before I start probing.

"Why did you dump Alexander?" Leoni says, sitting up a little straighter and obviously not nearly as concerned with probing as I am.

The question feels so direct. It makes my heart skip. "I didn't dump him. I just... I don't think Alexander and I were meant for each other."

"He certainly doesn't feel that way," she says, point blank.

"I know, but... we were forced into this traditional arrangement. We've always been starchily supervised and managed by the older vamps around us—everyone telling us what to do and how to interact. It was suffocating and I really... I want something entirely different for my life, and I met someone who helped to validate those feelings."

"Someone?" Leoni asks. "Someone special?"

I nod. "Yes, he's... Well. To me, he's everything good. He's patient and thoughtful. Accepting of me like no one has ever been. He genuinely listens when I have something to say, and I listen to him, too—his stories about his travels and his concerns. He's the first vampire to tell me that my thoughts and feelings were valid, and I... Meeting him has changed my life for the better. No matter what happens, I'll always be grateful to him for that."

Leoni exhales, then shrugs a shoulder. "Well, he sounds nice. Sucks for Alex, though... Christ. Welp, lucky you for finding another purebred that's capable of such compassion."

I shake my head. "Ah, no—Aries isn't purebred. He's first-generation."

Unexpectedly, everything goes silent. It's as if an invisible current had been flowing within the room, but then halts. Leoni blinks, then her light brown eyes flicker over to Daniel, who's stopped knitting altogether. He stares down at the red fabric with his pale irises, unmoving.

"Wait," Leoni says, staring intensely. "Your someone special is a *first-gen* vampire?"

"Yes. Is that so strange?"

"In Eden?" Leoni asks. "Yes. Hell yes, it's strange."

"You say that he's 'special,' so are you serious about this vampire, Aries?" The sound of Daniel's assertive voice surprises me as I meet his concentrated stare. "Or was he just a convenient, emotional comfort to you? Like a therapy dog."

"*No*, it wasn't—it's not like that at all. I love him. Very much."

"And you'd want to be with him, publicly? Not just behind closed doors, but bonded with him, drinking his blood and permanently entwining your natures?"

I shift in my seat and grip my teacup because I'm nervous under the weight of his vehement questioning. "Of course. That is, if he'd have me? I... I offered myself to him, but he refused me because of my circumstance—which was understandable. My hope is that once I'm free and can stand on my own, he'll accept me."

Another pause settles between us. I can't read the mood, but some nuanced emotion is being exchanged between Daniel and Leoni as they look at each other.

Breaking the silence, Daniel shakes his head and huffs with incredulity. "Unbelievable." He drops his needles and fabric into his lap, then smooths a palm over the top of his dark hair.

"Danny..." Leoni's tone is cautious but pleading as she leans over the arm of her seat. "See? I told you it's possible—"

"Don't." He stands, then places his needles and tuft of red

yarn into the basket. "Do not, Leoni. I'm going to bed." Daniel stalks out of the room. The quiet is deafening in his wake.

"Did I say something wrong?" I ask quietly.

"No," Leoni assures me as she stands, walking over to Daniel's abandoned basket. "We just need to give him time. This is good for him to hear. It's excellent." She leans down and carefully picks up the bundle of red yarn. "Sorry, little crab. Your dad is upset, but he'll calm down and finish you later, I promise."

Chapter Twenty-Nine

Within a few weeks, I feel more settled into life at the cottage with Leoni and Daniel than I ever had in my existence leading up to this point. It amazes me. My world has been completely turned upside down, but in the best possible way.

Leoni is a purebred with an agenda. She's driven and determined to make friends with the vamps in the surrounding communities. Her mission is to, quote, "right the wrongs of our asshole ancestors." When we're not all working together in the vineyard, she's off somewhere at a community market or local event. Constantly networking.

I'm so impressed by her resolve and fearlessness in achieving her goals. It inspires me to try and put myself out there, too.

So much so that I've started looking into photography apprenticeships and part-time work outside of Eden. I've even started filling out some applications for university programs that focus on technical photography skills. The biggest roadblock is that I don't have any kind of passport or identification. I need that to leave Eden, but... I have to start somewhere. One thing at a time.

Sitting at the kitchen table alone, I pull my new smartphone from my pocket and tap the screen. Sasha sent me this one shortly after Lord Blakeley had my original phone disconnected. Apparently, he realized I escaped a few days after I arrived here.

No one is searching for me, though. I was scared that I'd see reports about me missing in the news, and that Lord Blakeley would stop at nothing to drag me back and exact his revenge for my disobedience.

But Alexander told him to leave me alone. And so, he has.

Seriously? I'm trying hard to mend my jealous feelings toward Alexander, but it's getting ridiculous. Lord Blakeley has never once listened to or respected a single word I've said. Alexander could tell him to jump up and down while meowing like a cat and I bet he'd do it.

Absently, I navigate to the social media app where I regularly stalk Aries. Every single day, I do this, because I think about him all the time. He exists to my mind, heart and essence like sound. Always present in some form or another. Rarely is it ever truly silent. The intensity of it may change depending on the moment, place or circumstance—whether it's the soft hush of the wind or raucous, lively music.

Love is like this, I think? Never ceasing.

I have his phone number because Camille gave it to me the day she dropped me off at the safe house. But... I don't know.

When I scroll through his feed, he just seems so completely out of my league. There are glamorous photos of vivid, colorful fabrics and materials. Impressive theaters and noteworthy people. He was in New York a month ago, then Miami, Shanghai and Tokyo after that. Now, he's in Vienna working on some opera house project. He always looks so stylish, handsome and immaculately put together.

We made a promise. We did, and it means the world to me. But I'm starting to wonder what he even saw in me. With everything that's happened, our time together is starting to feel like some far-away dream, because there's no way a vampire like this would want a useless scruff like me. I'm finally getting better at cooking spaghetti when it's my week to feed everyone. Meanwhile, Aries is traveling the world and mastering his art. The gap is too wide.

Shaking my head, I flip the phone over so that the screen is face down on the table. I take a deep breath. As I blow it out, I speak aloud. "Stop it. You'll get there someday." I won't give up.

"Are you ready?" Daniel peeks inside the kitchen, dressed and ready to work.

"Yup," I say, standing. I intentionally leave my smartphone on the table since it's a cruel instigator for my dejection and anxiety. I follow Daniel outside.

Sometimes we do gardening work in his greenhouse, but today, me and Daniel are spending the afternoon in the vineyard. The wind is brisk, rustling the drying leaves around us. But the sun shines bright and clear. When I turn my face up toward it and close my eyes, it warms me all the way through. A perfect autumn day.

There's so much that has to be done on the vineyard and we are severely understaffed. Pruning is the biggest task, which helps to improve the stability of the vines and makes them stronger for winter. I'm not great at identifying the parts that need to be removed, so I typically work side by side with Danny. He seems to hate me a little less, now, I think?

He's quiet and mostly keeps to himself. I notice him being softer with Leoni, but otherwise, he has a steady routine that he rarely deviates from. Yoga on the back porch first thing every morning, then breakfast. After that, he works either in the garden or in the vineyard. Once or twice a week, he'll disappear for almost the whole day.

I haven't asked where he goes. Even if I did, I don't think he'd tell me.

When we're done for the day and return to the cottage, there's a package sitting on the mat at the front door. Sometimes Daniel and Leoni have mail because they order things from the local villages, but I never do. So, I'm surprised when Daniel picks up the box, then turns and hands it to me.

"It's addressed to you," he says coolly.

"Me?" I take the package in my hands, bewildered. "I didn't order anything." Swiftly, I examine the label. It doesn't have a return address name—only that it's from "Canon." Canon... as in, the camera company? What in the world?

As soon as I'm inside the cottage and have my shoes off, I walk briskly to my bedroom in the hallway just behind the stairs. I love this room. My first favorite element is the colorful quilt that covers the edge of the bed. Daniel knitted it as his first big project. My second favorite element is the beautiful view of the mountain range from the window. Waking up to it every morning makes me smile.

I sit at the desk in the corner and set the box against my knees, peeling at the taped edges until I can yank open the flaps. I'm excited but also very confused as I part the paper inside. There's a box within the box and—

"Holy shit..."

Carefully, I pull the second box from inside. I'm literally holding a Canon EOS R digital camera. A very expensive and high-quality photographer's camera. The best I've ever had my hands on, anyway. It also includes a 24–105 mm lens. God...

Is this some kind of mistake? I set the camera and lens boxes on the desk, then dig around in the packaging it came in. There's a card. I open it, and the message inside is typewritten.

My Darling Oliver,

Congratulations on your newfound freedom.

Love always,
Aries

"How?" A startling rush of emotions makes my throat close.

How does he know where I am? And he... Does he still think about me? Somewhere in between his international travels and glamorous lifestyle, does the memory of us and our brief but passionate romance cross his mind?

I have to say something. Frantically, I look around for my phone. I remember that I left it in the kitchen, so I burst out of the room to retrieve it, literally running past a confused Daniel as I make my return trip.

When I'm back, I softly close my bedroom door and lean against the wood. I stare down at my phone and his contact info.

Should I call him? He doesn't have this phone number, so he won't recognize it.

I should text him—but what? He's probably busy...

Dropping my hands at my sides, I lean my head back and close my eyes, thinking. Why is this so hard?

"Stop it." I raise my arms, look at my phone and type out a message. Biting my lip, I make sure I spelled my name right before I hit send.

[Hi, Aries. This is Oliver...]

That's all I've got. Maybe I should ask if he has time to talk? Or maybe we could schedule a day and time—

My phone buzzes in my hand. Ringing. I look at the screen and it's Aries calling. I take a deep breath even though my heart has lodged itself inside my throat. I answer the phone.

"Hi..." I say, closing my eyes and resting my hand on my navel to calm my nature down.

"Hello, darling," he says sweetly in his creamy, dark-chocolate voice. "I've missed you."

"I've missed *you.*"

"Why haven't you reached out to me?"

"I don't know... because I wasn't sure if you'd still want to be bothered with me. Things are up in the air and—I'm not anywhere near where you are in life and your achievements and

I… I wanted to be better when I talked to you again. More independent, I mean. I'm not good enough yet. I can barely make spaghetti!" My voice is harried as the speech pours out, like word vomit.

There's a brief pause on the line. "What does spaghetti have to do with anything?"

Chuckling, I lift my palm and rest it against my forehead. "It's just something I'm dealing with right now." Saying all of this out loud, I suddenly realize how ridiculous I sound.

"Oliver, you are good enough, *right now*. There is no 'yet.' At our foundation, your nature speaks to me, and mine to you, yes?"

I nod, dropping my hand. "Yes. Of course."

"That is what matters. The fact that our very souls connect. Everything else is bullshit—conditional and volatile. Do you understand what I'm saying?"

"I do." I wander over toward the edge of the bed. I've missed this so much. Hearing his voice and having these forthright, honest conversations. These discussions that strike directly to the heart of the matter. I only get this with him, and it's deeply comforting. Like walking into an emotionally safe space.

"I understand what you mean," I go on, sitting on the colorful quilt. "I just… I look at your social media all the time and you're so elevated and refined. Successful. I wonder what the hell you saw in me. Or if I imagined the whole thing."

"You look at the very carefully crafted instrument I use for advertising my work and compare yourself to it?" he asks rhetorically. "Please don't."

"I know—"

"I mean it. Please stop. That is my resume for my job. It means nothing in the larger scope of my life. But you? You mean *everything*."

Holding the phone against my ear, my mouth is agape and my heart practically doubles in size. I'm about to tell him that I feel the same way, but his smooth voice flows over the line once more.

"I love you, Oliver. No matter what, I want what's best for

you. If you're avoiding me because you are enjoying your freedom and have moved on, I can accept that. But if you are falsely deeming yourself as inferior solely because you haven't checked enough 'achievement' boxes—that, I cannot accept."

When I swallow, it goes down thick. "I am enjoying my freedom, but I could never move on from you, Aries. I love you, too. I want... I want to be with you."

"Then be with me, when you're ready. I'm here, darling. To hell with spaghetti."

A warm sense of relief washes over me. I take a deep breath, smiling. "I've been applying for internships abroad."

"I know. Sasha told me."

Surprised, I sit up straighter. "She did? How—Did she give you my address, too?"

"Yes, because I reached out to her on social media to ask how you were. Since she was made privy to our circumstance, I figured I'd be candid with her. I tried Camille first, but her phone was disconnected."

"She quit. She left Eden and lives in Paris now."

"Yes, Sasha told me that as well. We talked at length. You sister divulged all that's transpired over the past month, including the confrontation with your father. I was... surprised that you didn't attempt to contact me at all."

There's a perceptible hurt in his voice. A sadness. My heart aches with the realization that I've caused it. "I wanted to talk to you, *so* badly. But I also didn't want to drag you into this mess. I really imagined myself as being stronger and better the next time I saw you. I wanted to be your equal." Plus, crippling insecurity. But I don't say it.

"Because of the difference in our bloodlines, we can never be equals," he says pragmatically. "Even beyond that, I can never be a great photographer, and you might never design clothing. Inevitably, there will always be areas where one of us ascends and the other falters. But we can be balanced. Our unique natures—our minds, hearts and temperaments—can be well matched."

Nodding, I grin. "They can. I think we are."

"I agree. And what's more, I recognize that you have been exposed to much trauma and disparaging admonishment in your life. The insecurities created from this likely reside deep within you. The impact might wane over time as you become more liberated. Regardless, I accept you, Oliver. All of you. Always, you can talk to me. When in doubt, please tell me what's on your mind?"

If he were in front of me, I would kiss him. Hard. I'd wrap my arms around his shoulders in an embrace so tight that he'd physically feel the depths of my love and gratitude. If he allowed me to, I'd rest my aura so that there'd be no further question in his mind.

I can't do any of this yet, but I'm looking forward to that moment. "I'll be honest about how I feel from now on, and once I get my proper IDs and can leave Eden, I'll come to you. We made a promise?"

"We did indeed."

Flopping back onto the bed, my smile broadens. I can't wait. "Thank you for the camera. I've never had a professional-grade lens. I'm excited to try it."

"An artist needs his proper tools. I'm happy that you like it."

"I love it," I say, exhaling a contented sigh. "How are you doing? Is everything okay with your body and nature?" I only exposed my aura to him once, so I doubt that he's been deeply impacted by me. Even still.

"I am well, my darling. But I'm looking forward to the day that I can gaze into your celestial eyes. When I can kiss the sweet pout of your beautiful lips."

From head to toe my nature glitters inside, wildly euphoric. Bubbling with anticipation.

"Me, too. I want those things and much more, Aries. So much more."

I can't see him, but I can hear the handsome upturn of his mouth into a wry grin. "Whatever the young master desires, he shall receive."

~

Later in the week, Alexander visits the cottage in his same camel-colored wool trench coat. His thick blonde mane is handsomely swept back and his attire is smart—all signs of his having left an important engagement.

"It's nice to see you," I tell him honestly as I sit in the plush armchair opposite him. A low coffee table occupies the space between us and a healthy fire burns in the hearth. It makes the sitting room glow with auburn light.

After he arranged for our blood to be medically bagged, Alexander stopped coming to the cottage. It's a lengthy drive from his home estate in Central, and he doesn't have any real reason to come out here unless it's for a bag exchange or drop. We still talk a few times a week, though. Our relationship is probably better than it's ever been.

"You too," he says. "I have good news." He shifts, reaching into the large square of his coat pocket. When he pulls his hand back out, he's holding a small bundle of documents. He leans, handing the packet to me from across the table. The motion creates a gleam of light and the two golden bands on his right hand sparkle.

I marvel at the documents as I reach. "Is this what I think it is?"

"Your birth certificate and passport," Alexander says, sitting back against the armchair. "The viscount sends his regards."

Blinking, astounded, I shift my focus from the documents up to Alexander's face. "You met with the viscount?"

"Yes, and it was obvious that he was the one who convinced Lord Blakeley to yield to my proposed arrangement. That hard-ass barely spoke to me during the meeting—no more niceties. Only his ridiculous demands." Alexander rolls his eyes.

Ridiculous demands? This gives me pause. "What exactly did you have to agree to in order to get these things?"

He shakes his head. "Don't worry about it. What matters is

that you have them now, right? You can finally leave Eden if you want. It's what you've been dreaming of."

He's right. This is definitely what I want, but... something in his smile seems off. Maybe forced? I often remember Leoni telling me that Alexander puts on a good show to make everyone comfortable. A quality of his that I always perceived as fake and self-serving. I never thought he might be acting that way for other people's approval or benefit.

"Are you okay?" I ask somewhat abruptly.

He pauses, blinking his molten eyes in surprise. "What do you mean?"

"I mean, are you really okay with everything? With the arrangement between you and Lord Blakeley, with doing all this for me."

"Of course I am. I would do anything for you, Ollie. Anything. It's just how it is." Still grinning, he takes a visible breath, then runs his fingers through the top of his hair, mussing the perfect swoop of it, and those rings catch the light once more. "So, what's your plan? Will you... Are you going to see Aries straightaway?"

He's tried to ask me about this nonchalantly, but it doesn't quite land. I shake my head. "No. I want to take some time for myself—to challenge myself in a new way. Maybe get a job somewhere? I've been looking into proper photography programs at universities across Europe. I don't know yet."

It's strange. When I was secluded and pressed underneath Lord Blakeley's thumb, I had all these whims about what I would do and where I would go if I were a liberated vampire.

Now that Alexander has literally handed me my freedom, it's like there are too many options—and logistically, how do I choose the right one? More importantly, how do I avoid ending up shriveled and starving in an alley somewhere because I no longer have a steady feeding source?

Alexander folds his arms and casts his gaze toward the flickering fire. "I don't think you need to go to school. You're already pretty damn good at photography. You've read a ton of books on it, and you obviously have an eye for angles based on your social media account—plus you have the photos from Evanshire that were used in multiple international news outlets."

"Do you think that actually counts for something?" I ask.

"I do," Alexander confirms. "At least three wire media services circulated those photos. That's no small feat. I think you need professional experience and connections. Something like an internship? The pay wouldn't be great and you'd have to figure out your own housing, but would you be okay with something like that?"

"Would I be okay? Are you serious? That would be phenomenal. Like learning underneath a true professional in the field—on actual assignments?"

"Maybe?" Alexander says, grinning. "We have connections with a European fashion magazine, and I also have a friend that's a freelance photographer. She mostly does nature and landscape stuff. I can talk to her first and see what she says?"

The thought of working with a professional photographer sends a new kind of thrill up my spine. Holy shit I am excited.

"You keep doing all of these things for me, but there's literally no way that I can repay you. I don't have anything, but—"

"You don't need to repay me. Ollie," Alexander says sternly. "Just... let me do these things for you, alright? It makes me happy to help you, so let me have that at least. Please?"

Alexander's imploring eyes are glassy in the firelight. The air is warm but soft as it hovers between us.

It's amazing. What happened to the teasing, arrogant and flippant vampire that I was engaged to? The one who called me a nerd, a horse and a cold fish. Where has all that silly teasing and bravado gone?

Lately, the lens with which I view the world has widened. I was suffocating when I was living in the castle. I couldn't breathe, and the lack of air was my primary focus. My existence was that of a caged animal with a singular thought ringing in my mind—over and over again, every day, like an emergency alarm.

I don't want this. I need to get out.

At the cottage, though, I can finally breathe. Now that my mind and body are no longer in crisis, I'm able to scrutinize my environment and the people in it more thoughtfully. Sitting here and looking at Alexander, I notice that his aura feels dimmer compared with what he usually projects. As if he's quietly curled up inside of himself.

I take a deep breath. Maybe this is presumptuous, and maybe it has nothing to do with me, but... "Can I tell you something, honestly?"

He meets my gaze, nervous. "I hope so?"

Huffing in a laugh, I clasp my hands in my lap. "I've always been jealous of you, Alexander. Bitterly. You seemed content growing up. Carefree and genuinely happy in a way that I couldn't understand. Between that and Lord Blakeley constantly pressuring me over our engagement, I resented you. I disliked you."

Alexander scoffs. "You *hated* me."

I nod. "I did. But what I hated more was the circumstance. My anger toward you was largely a byproduct of that."

The space suddenly feels too warm as we watch each other in the weighted silence. His brows furrow and his cheeks flush in the orange light.

"Even still," he says, shifting his gaze toward the fire, "I didn't help the situation. I was stupid... and immature. I was unkind to you. You were right to hate me."

"But I don't hate you," I say clearly. I lean forward a little, into his field of vision, to make sure he's listening. "Not anymore. I appreciate you, Alexander. For everything that you've done—for accepting my decisions and for standing up to Lord Blakeley when I disappeared. You've kept feeding me and even found me a safe shelter. The words seem insufficient, but thank you. For everything."

The log in the fireplace shifts, pops and crackles. Alexander stares into the hearth, unmoving.

"You don't hate me," he says quietly. "But you don't love me, either. There won't ever be a chance for us, because I can't compete with *him*. He's the one who holds your heart. He was there for you when I wasn't."

I stare at his side profile, remorseful but knowing what I have to say. "Yes." It's more complicated than that. And it feels like there are a million unspoken words between us. But this is the bottom line.

We slip into yet another tense moment of pause. My heart pulses in my throat as I wait for his response or reaction. Anything.

He doesn't speak. Not right away.

Slowly, he stands. He doesn't look at me.

"Are... you okay on blood bags?" he asks. "I should have asked you that before I came today. Sorry. That was stupid of me."

"I'm good," I say, acquiescing to this shift in our conversation. "Are you alright on bags?"

"Yeah." He turns, then hesitates. "Well, we should probably do a few extra before you take off somewhere—so you have time to find a new source and you don't feel panicked or rushed."

"That sounds like a good idea. I'd appreciate that. I'll make extras for you, too."

He sticks his hands inside his coat pockets. "Thank you."

"Of course."

Alexander walks toward the door, and I stand to follow him. We're silent as he steps into his shoes. He still refuses to meet my eyes. He checks his watch, then turns toward the door.

Somehow, this feels like goodbye. I don't know how or why, especially when we've just agreed to exchange more blood bags. Even still, something in the energy and air between us has markedly shifted.

"Alex—"

"I called Roland yesterday, like you suggested," he says, facing the door with his back to me. "I told him that if I can, I'd like to help with the safe house. You're right. It's a good idea."

"That's great news. What made you change your mind?"

He steps aside and cracks the door open. A cool waft of autumnal evening air graces the skin of my face and neck. "I don't know... It might be nice to do something different with my time. Maybe I need a change."

"Lots of change for both of us. I think it's fantastic that you're going to help him and Kathryn. It's very brave of you."

"Hm." He pulls the door open wider and steps through. "Message me if you need something."

Feeling oddly panicked, I follow him and step into the frame. As he approaches the steps, I call out into the twilight, "Is it possible for us to be friends? Is that selfish of me to ask?"

Alexander stops on the bottom step and turns to the side. His shoulders rise and fall in a deep breath. "I don't know yet. I'll let you know what my freelance photographer friend says. Good night, Ollie."

"Good night..." He goes, and I watch from the porch, standing in the wash of dusky sunset until his little black sports car disappears down the lane.

I don't love him, but something deep down tells me that I could have.

If my life had been different.

Summer

Chapter Thirty

Nine months into my newfound freedom, I have learned many valuable lessons. The most important one being this: life is a funny thing.

I find that when I trust my instincts and take intentional action, life eventually gives me exactly what I need, when I need it. Even when something seems bad, embarrassing or unfair, if I'm patient, the tide shifts in my favor. My apprenticeship with Alexander's professional photographer friend, Sylvie, has shown me this time and time again.

A misplaced camera lens during a shoot in Hong Kong led me on a frantic hunt through the concrete maze of the city. As I weaved between the indomitable skyscrapers and endless barrage of neon signs filled with foreign fonts, I found a tiny photo shop. Over the course of a month, the owner of that shop saved us not only once, but three more times before we were all invited to the most incredible feast of dim sum at his home before our departure.

In Thailand, a rather touchy client unexpectedly canceled a shoot, despite days of preparation and planning. This led us to a spontaneous trip to Phang Nga Bay, where glassy canals reflect the sky as they curve and flow through seemingly endless trusses of rainforest and bulging mountains. The scenery reminded me of a place where dragons with lustrous scales might nest and raise their young. I learned a ton about shooting broad landscapes (like I've always dreamed of) and took some of my best photos there.

Finally, Kyoto brought us inclement weather, which delayed our schedule by three full days. But after the rain, and within a week's time, the cherry blossom buds transitioned into a million powdery pink bursts. Everywhere I looked, the trees had been swathed in cotton candy and vibrant green overnight. It gave us the best possible backdrop for our project, and I couldn't help but remember Aries's description of it as I sat underneath the ethereal canopy. I missed him the most then. In that moment.

When I met Aries and started falling for him, it felt like a cruel cosmic joke. Here was this incredible vampire that made me feel alive for the first time in my life, but I was stuck in an impossible situation.

Turns out, meeting him and submitting to my feelings—letting myself fall in love—was the best decision I could have made. For myself and others around me, because my choices had a ripple effect. On Sasha, who's formally and mutually parted ways with Elaine. On Hudson, because he and Ji-Ahn left Eden with their son and moved to Seoul. Even Camille is loving her new life in Paris.

Ending our engagement was the best thing for Alexander, too. After I found out how much he'd done for me (much more than I had initially realized), I made it a point to go back and set things right.

I can honestly say that we're friends now. Genuinely.

As far as Aries is concerned, I don't know if I've affected his life nearly as much as he's changed mine. I recognize that this isn't something that requires a balance—a sternly equal give and take.

Being in love, it isn't like that. That's not how it works. Me endeavoring to compensate for everything he's instilled within me —the way he's empowered me—well... I can never reimburse him for those things. Trying will lead to our ruin.

This became clear after Aries gifted me the expensive camera, which served as a kind of priceless instrument in the success of my apprenticeship. The literal cost of the camera isn't what matters. It was his intent. He paid attention and knew exactly what I needed, then sincerely provided support.

Maybe I can't afford to buy him the most expensive sewing machine that he's always dreamed of—and I have a feeling that he wouldn't want that from me anyway. But I can meet him with the same intent. With the same sincerity, honesty and loyalty. We can be balanced.

I'm on my way to see him now. To do just that.

The evening that I land in Italy, the sky is a rich, clear and deep blue. The kind of blue that seems like velvet to touch and is unique to the summer moon. The air is warm and makes me feel a little stifled in my suit. As I ride in the taxi, I marvel at the city through the glass.

Brightly lit boulevards are filled with stylish people and charming restaurants offering bistro tables for sidewalk seating. Whenever we pass a cross street, I peek down the lane and am surprised to see even more people bustling in and out of any and every shop imaginable. Quaint bakeries, bookstores and pharmacies. Specialty shops with quirky names and enticing signage.

In the distance, a second city—which is literally called Città Alta, or the "upper city" in Italian—hovers above us. Elegant buildings and stately, colorful homes are perched atop a luscious and green hillside. A stone wall encapsulates all of this, like the fortress of an old kingdom long perished.

"Ah—Mi scusi, può accostare qui un attimo? Vorrei andare dal fioraio?" I see a vendor with a cart full of flowers up ahead. It gives me an idea.

"Non c'è problema." My taxi driver waves a hand, then maneuvers toward the flower stand.

The plan is for Aries and me to spend the week together in

Bergamo. After tonight, Aries will be in between work assignments. He needs to make a decision about where he'll go next, and he has some promising options. I haven't told him yet, but the terms of my apprenticeship have recently changed. Now, I have more flexibility.

I don't want to hinder him in any way, but, deep down, I want more than just a week with him...

I want everything.

His blood and essence flowing through me. Nourishing me and deeply entwined with my own. And I want to sustain him, too, so that he never needs to search for another feeding source again. No more "expansive networks" or Benjamins. Just me. Reliable, consistent and *good* for him. I know that I would be. I can feel it.

Aries once told me that he wouldn't be afraid of bonding if he was innately balanced with someone. That if he found another vampire whose perspective and deeper foundation were harmonious with his, he would submit to it.

Isn't that what we have? During my apprenticeship, I loved traveling and discovering new places. It's what I've always dreamed of, and truly, every day I wanted to pinch myself. But how much better would it be for Aries and me to travel and experience new places together? It's what we both enjoy and our natures call to each other. I just... I don't want to hold back anymore.

Soon, we arrive at the Teatro Donizetti, which is one of Bergamo's primary opera houses. It stands imposing and lit with warm spotlights emphasizing every inch of its creamy stone façade—every clustered column, scalloped ledge and arched venetian window.

As I step out of the taxi with my bouquet and rolling suitcase, I can't believe I'm here. In Italy and finally meeting Aries again, face to face.

Already, I sense him, despite the crowd of well-dressed humans and vampires, each with their own distinctive perfumes, odors and auras. Aries's sumptuous essence cuts through all of it like a blade. Like an electric charge to my body and senses. It makes my nature dance and the hairs on my arms stand on end.

My plane was delayed. I'm late, but still right on time for the show. Aries has left a ticket for me at the box office. This is the last night for the production that he's designing for, so he warned me that he'd be busy backstage until the end of the performance.

"Ah, you must be Oliver—young lover to our Aries." A first-gen vampire that looks relatively young herself watches me through the ticket office glass, haughty.

"Um, excuse me?"

She stands, briefly tapping and whispering to the vampire beside her. A second-gen whose eyes brighten with interest before he smiles and waves. This is getting weird.

The young first-gen woman leaves the box office. Soon, she steps through the main doorway to the building and gestures for me to meet her there. She's refined in her burgundy jacket, black tuxedo slacks and shiny wingtip oxfords.

When I'm in front of her, she looks me up and down, then grins. "Is this an Aries original?"

"What? Oh—my suit? Yes, Aries made it." Self-consciously, I smooth my blush-colored tie. This suit was meant for a wedding, but Sylvie said she thought it was appropriate for an opera house as well. Especially in this case, with it being the first time Aries and I have seen each other in almost a year.

"Lucky you. It is perfection, per his usual work. Follow me, your grace? I'll store your luggage in our cloak room until after the show, if you please." We drop the luggage off first, then I'm guided up a flight of stairs, past several humans and vampires alike, who nod politely when we make eye contact.

"You're pretty famous around here," my guide says as she stops and draws back a heavy red curtain. "Everyone is excited to meet you."

"Everyone?" I ask. Why in God's name?

"Yes." She gestures for me to walk through the gap that she's created. "We'll be having a night out to celebrate the end of the production. I hope you'll join us?"

"Ah, sure. Wow." I'm perched high on a balcony just near the stage. The theater twinkles with bright lights, smooth marble surfaces and golden accents. Red velvet chairs and ornate moldings. The ceiling is a dome fashioned to look like the blue skies of heaven with wispy clouds and angels.

"Premiere box seating for our special guest. Welcome, and please enjoy the performance." She bows, then disappears as the curtain falls. I glance back at the auditorium in awe, impressed at the architecture and design. That someone I know—someone that I love—is part of this.

Still holding the bouquet, I sit in the tufted chair, taking everything in because it feels unreal. Aries's essence serves as a gauzy overlay for the scene, gently caressing my nature and making my heart beat with anticipation.

I turn and look behind me because suddenly, he feels even closer. The velvet draping to my balcony is pulled aside. In the same moment, I lose my breath.

Like a vision in my most fulfilling dream, he's there. Tall and elegant in his dark maroon suit, Aries holds the curtain with one hand. Backlit by the hallway lights, he stares at me with his beautiful midnight-blue eyes.

Abruptly, I shoot up from my seat and set the flowers on the cushion, because every nerve in my body is electrified. Christ. He looks even more striking, long-legged and Greek-god-like than I remembered.

"Hi," I say, but it comes out hoarse because my heart is in my throat.

Without a word, he lets the curtain fall and stalks toward me. I barely have time to lick my lips before he's on me with his large warm palms cupping my head. His long fingers thread within my hair and his mouth covers mine.

Our connection is soft, at first. Slow and intentional. But as I exhale and grip the satin lapels of his jacket, he presses into me with an overwhelming desire. This kiss reminds me of cream. Like a fresh strawberry set atop a whipped swirl, when the weight of it sinks deeper and deeper until it's completely submerged.

It feels as if he wants to taste the very core of me. To understand my soul.

My eyes burn behind closed lids as I moan. His scent is delicious and swathed around me like a jasmine cloud. My nature churns and sparks, threatening to release its full weight after so many months of dormancy. Aries's hands still grip my head, but I pull back from the luscious kiss and take a breath. When he opens his eyes, they're alighted like sapphire.

"I take it you missed me?" I whisper, smiling.

"Mm..." He leans, rubbing his nose into mine and closing his eyes. He kisses my cheek, then my jawline, before caressing his lips toward my ear. "You came to me."

"I said that I would. We made a promise."

"I'm grateful." He laces his arms around my waist. "I'm honored."

Lifting to my toes, I wrap my arms around his shoulders as he pulls me tightly into him. Warm, firm and so soothing.

How have I been without him? How can I ever be again?

"You don't need to be honored or grateful," I say, holding him tightly. "Thank you for waiting for me."

"I would wait forever, darling. You look delicious in this suit. I hope I'll get to peel it off of you later tonight."

Heat burns in my cheeks as I pull him in, even closer. "You can do more than that."

"Excellent. I have to go back downstairs, but I wanted to see you. I couldn't wait any longer." He unwraps me from his embrace, and I take the opportunity to quickly grab and present my flowers in their brown paper wrapping.

"Congratulations on a successful run," I say. "You did it." I've kept up with some theater and entertainment magazines online because they often post articles about Aries. He's unquestionably making his mark in the costume design industry.

He takes the flowers, brushing my fingers as he does so and sending tingles up my arms. He pulls the bouquet up to his nose and inhales deeply. "Peonies from my love. Thank you." Aries dips and kisses my lips once more. "I'll come back here for you once the performance is complete. Wait for me?"

He backs up toward the curtain, watching and grinning in that suave way I've missed. That elegant confidence.

"I'll wait for you," I tell him. "Always."

Immediately following the show, Aries guides me backstage to his office, which also functions as the wardrobe closet. I wander around the romantically lit room in awe, marveling at all the intricate costumes and luxurious fabrics hanging on freestanding racks and bust forms. I also take note of the giant, impressive vase filled with pink peonies set on the table just inside the door. The room is perfumed with their sweet scent, but gently intermingled with Aries's earthier essence. Looks like my bouquet choice was spot on.

We have dinner with everyone at a fancy restaurant near the theater, but Aries's apartment is situated in Città Alta, overlooking the sprawling lights and sparkle of the lower city. The mountains around us are dark, heaping shapes, but there are flecks of light scattered throughout from neighboring houses and buildings. "This view is beautiful."

"Wait until the sun rises," he says, moving toward the double doors, which are heavily carved and laden with iron accents. "The view will take your breath away." He unlocks one side and pushes it open. I peek past him and see an intimate courtyard drenched in moonlight.

"You take my breath away," I admit, following him inside. It's embarrassing for me to say these things, but it's how I feel.

"I've missed you. Truly. Achingly." He tilts his head to kiss me and I lift, meeting him and wrapping a palm around his neck. I don't know what's happening inside of me, but it's almost painful, how badly I want to be closer to him.

When we were together before, I was always restraining myself. Worried, apologizing and insecure. Constantly being polite. I don't want to be shy and hesitant anymore.

A lot has changed in the year that we've been apart. I know that I still have a long way to go, but I can take care of myself now —cooking, cleaning and picking out my own clothes. I've worked really hard as an apprentice, which has allowed me to earn more independent assignments. I've been able to save money so that I don't need to rely on anyone else financially.

My nature feels as if it's about to implode because it's so tired of me suppressing and denying it. Can I have him and be free now? Is he still afraid of being addicted to me, or can I finally indulge these desires and this hunger I feel?

The answer feels like "no" when he suddenly pulls away from the kiss, and I sigh. He must register my discontent because his brow furrows as he cups my face.

"What is it?" he asks. "You seem restless, suddenly. Are we alright?"

"It's nothing," I lie. "We're alright."

"Hm..." He takes hold of my hand and pulls me through the moonlit courtyard full of leafy plants bowing and swaying gently with the nighttime summer wind. The sidewalk beneath our feet is cobblestoned and we pass a trickling, artsy fountain. The small pool of water reflects the stars above in the clear sky.

This place is much more picturesque in person compared with the images he's sent me. The villa is owned by the opera house, but they're hosting Aries here as part of his contract.

"Have you decided whether or not to renew your position here?" I ask as he unlocks a second door. This one is framed by a cluster of vines teeming with waxy leaves.

"I have not. I'm weighing my options."

"The offer from the theater in Milan is a bigger opportunity, right? Teatro alla Scala is world renowned."

"Yes, but as you know, I don't do this because I wish to chase fame. There are more important things for me to consider." He turns to glance at me as the door clicks open. "Shall we have a glass of wine? You were so popular at dinner tonight, I feel as if I haven't had a moment to truly soak you in for myself."

"Sure," I say, trailing behind him. He flicks a switch and the space glows in low, well-placed lighting so that the atmosphere feels calming and insulated. Natural and rustic with modern influences.

The high-beamed ceiling is painted eggshell while the walls are dark wood. White accents and furniture brighten the room—two plush sofas separated by a round coffee table. A thick beige rug is set against the worn wooden planks of the floor. The centerpiece of the space is a fireplace made with what looks like boulder stones.

What gradually becomes more apparent to me is that there are vases full of peonies artfully but strategically placed all throughout this room, too. There's a giant vase on the coffee table. Another on the kitchen counter, then a third on the sink, near the window. Even here, just beside the door on a small entry table, sits a fourth vase. All of the bouquets are fresh and fragrant, as if they've recently been replenished.

I think... I may have underestimated how much he likes this particular flower?

As he steps inside with my gift bouquet in hand, he removes his shoes and places them on a rack, so I do the same.

"Red wine or white?" he asks.

"Red, please." I walk further into the open space toward the couch. "You really like peonies. There are so many..."

"I do, indeed," Aries quips, making his way over to the kitchen. He bustles around underneath white spotlights like he's a chef filming a TV show.

"Have... you always liked them this much?" I stop in the middle of the room and glance up to my left. A wooden staircase leads to a cozy-looking loft with a bed. There, too, on the night-stand, is a large vase full of puffy pink flowers.

This is starting to feel strange, because he didn't request all these flowers when he stayed at the castle in Eden.

"Define 'always'?" he says, chuckling and uncorking a bottle at the counter.

He's laughing, but I'm not as I look over at him. "Aries, are you addicted to me in some way?"

There's a moment of pause as he pours the burgundy wine and half fills one of the glasses. He concentrates, making sure that he doesn't spill. "'Addicted' is a strong word."

"Okay, but are these flowers because of me? Has something within you shifted since you left Eden?" My anxiety flares up as I watch him. This situation was his biggest fear the entire time we were together. It was the reason I held back and learned how to restrain myself.

Was all of that for nothing? Have I still managed to hurt him?

Aries sets the bottle down and takes a breath. "Let's talk. We need to talk, yes?" He abandons the wine, moves around the counter and stalks forward. When he's close, he takes hold of my hand and urges me toward the couch.

"I'm guessing peonies aren't just your all-time favorite flower," I say, worried and feeling a flood of guilt.

He smiles, meeting my eyes. "They are now. Let me preface this with assuring you that I'm fine."

"Okay..."

He sits back comfortably and takes another deep breath. His shoulders rise and fall. "After I left Eden, I'd get... I'm not sure. Tremors? Shaky in a subtle way that's never happened in my life. It wasn't crippling, but sporadic and unsettling. I find that if I have these flowers around, the scent of them calms me. Because, admittedly, they remind me of you."

I squeeze his hand harder as my throat closes. "Why didn't you tell me this?"

"Why would I tell you? It isn't detrimental to my health, and I've found a way to manage it."

"But you always tell me that I can talk to you—to *please* communicate and be honest with you. Why haven't you done that with me? Why doesn't it go both ways?"

"It does—but what would you have done if I'd told you about this, Oliver? Not accepted a fantastic apprenticeship that's allowed you to strengthen your craft while traveling all across Asia? Not made new friends and connections? Would you have rushed to be here with me, so that I could hinder you?"

"You'd never hinder me, Aries. Not ever." I clasp his hand with both of mine as I stare into his eyes, because I want him to understand. "We can't be balanced if I'm the only one being honest and openly communicating."

"I know that, darling. I just... I don't want you to feel obligated. You've spent your entire life restrained and duty-bound." He lifts his hand and kisses one of my knuckles, then rests his nose there as his eyes flutter closed. "Now that you're free, I want you to enjoy your life, uninhibited and unburdened. My intention is to support you in whatever you want. What *I* want is for you to be happy and live in the fullness of who you are."

My pulse is beating so hard that it thrums in my ears. I take a deep breath, pushing past the fear of rejection and anxiety and saying what's in my heart. "What if what I want is you? To live in the fullness of who I am—to be uninhibited and unburdened, but *with you*, Aries."

His eyes open and his deep-blue gaze locks on mine. The air around us feels stagnant. I swallow, wanting to fill the silence because my heart can't take it. "Can I have that?"

"I'll be a burden to you."

I shake my head. "You won't."

"I will. If we're together and I'm feeding from you, I'll be dependent upon you, Oliver. You won't be able to go too far, or stay away for too long without me, do you understand? You'll always have to consider me in any assignment or travel plans you make."

"I'll be dependent on you, too," I rationalize. "It goes both ways."

"Yes, and you'll be restricted and encumbered again. Just as you were in Eden—"

"No. Eden was different because I had no choice there. The restrictions were forced on me. But I'm *choosing* you. And you would never be a burden, because all you've ever done since the moment we met is set me free. All you've ever done is open my eyes, encourage and lift me up. It's like—you've given me wings, Aries! You could never restrict me because that's not who you are. That's not who *we* are. And I'd be thrilled to consider you and have you depend on me. I'd be honored that you chose me as your feeding source."

My chest heaves from the rush of emotion—from the intensity of my words and my nature clamoring inside, wanting him to understand. Still holding my hand, Aries shifts and sits straighter with his feet planted on the floor. His jaw works and his expression is bewildered. Almost... nervous.

Suddenly, I understand.

"But if you're not ready to depend on me," I say quietly, "then this is a different conversation altogether."

We sit and the silence shrouds us once more, but he doesn't let go of my hand. He stares, intensely focused on the large glass vase of pink peonies set in front of us.

"Are you still afraid of being addicted to me?" I ask. "To my blood. You're already affected by me, so you're afraid of being pushed over the edge?"

"Not afraid... cautious. Once I feed from a purebred, there's no turning back. I'll be forever conditioned to you, and I won't be able to feed satisfyingly from another ranked vampire again. Right now, I can feed from almost anyone. But once I have you..."

I nod, listening. He explained this to me before, when we were in Eden. "I understand. If you aren't comfortable, it's okay.

But... do you know that I wouldn't leave you or change my mind after you fed from me? I wouldn't betray you. You can trust me."

"I know you wouldn't. I trust you."

"Do you even want to feed—"

"*Yes*, Oliver. Of course I do." Aries pulls my hand so that I fall over and into him. He catches me, then brushes his lips against my temple. Slowly, he caresses down past my ear and toward my neck.

"Some nights, I lie awake, hot and restless—aching, because the thought of feeding from you consumes me." He opens his mouth and flattens his tongue against my flesh, licking the sensitive curve just beneath my jawbone. Dear God. Him doing this sends a violent shiver all through me.

I close my eyes, breathing and controlling my nature. I've made my desire for Aries clear. Now, I have to give him the space to choose how far he wants to go with me. I won't push my will on him, because it's his body and nature that will be forever altered. Not mine.

"You don't need to make the decision now," I say with my eyes still closed, concentrating on stifling my nature. "But if I give you consent to feed, will you ask me to rescind it, like you did back in Eden?"

Aries breathes in a laugh—a warm puff against my neck where he's licked. "This is like dangling a mouse in front of a snake."

"I want you to know that you can have me when you want me. When you're ready. You have consent." Hesitating, nervous, I smile as I glance down at him. "Squeak squeak."

"Sweet Mother of God." He pulls away while pressing his palms against his face as he sinks, slouching into the couch and laughing. Taking advantage of his position, I lift and throw my leg over him to straddle his hips.

As I settle on my knees, I grab his wrists with both hands. "You never rescinded the consent that you gave me when we were in Eden together. Are you comfortable with me biting you?" I can sense that the invisible, rigid and omnipresent barrier that typically exists between two vampires is absent from Aries. Like a glass wall that's been lifted—both ways, now, since I've formally given him my consent.

I pull his palms down so that I can view his handsomely chiseled jawline. His perfectly full lips and dimples.

"Yes," he says, opening his eyes. "You can feed. You still have consent."

"May I have something else? I know I'm asking for a lot, but..." I shift my hips into him. He bites his lip and groans as he exhales. Something in that small gesture is extremely satisfying. "We have time tonight, right? We're not in a rush."

"Not that I'm aware of."

I lean, kissing him softly on the lips before meeting his sultry gaze. "Will you make love to me? And not just with your finger this time, but all of you? I want to know how it feels when you come with your cock inside of me—how much you come and how wet it feels."

Aries leans his head back and closes his eyes. Already, he's aroused and hard underneath me. "When did you start talking like this?"

"Today. But sometimes, like you, I lie awake at night, just thinking about you being inside of me. Is that okay? Does it make you uncomfortable?"

Sliding his hands up the sides of my thighs to my hips, he wraps his palms around my ass, then playfully lifts me into him. "It's more than okay. Let's get you out of this suit, shall we? You're getting it wrinkled."

Chapter Thirty-One

The way Aries undresses me—removing the stylish materials he's handcrafted specifically for me, his muse—is like a labor of love. Piece by piece he takes the beautifully lined jacket, shirt, tie and trousers and sets them aside.

When I'm completely naked in his loft bedroom, his behavior shifts. His movements are less like a careful, prideful task, and more like intentional acts of worship. Relishing and savoring. The way he touches and teases—his lips softly tracing the curves of my calves and thighs, then up to my stomach, chest and collarbone. His fingertips dimple the flesh of my hips and his palms caress around to hold and squeeze my ass.

For most of my life, I've been disregarded. My existence has been that of a political tool. I've been called useless, selfish and ungrateful, as if my very being and presence in this world mean nothing.

Aries corrects this narrative. He communicates with me and listens. His kindness, his patience and the intensity with which he touches and kisses me... He reassures me that I am indeed something. Not just "something," but *someone* valuable and worthy of being treasured.

A person worthy of giving and receiving love.

He kisses me, and I can feel that his mind... No. His essence. His very being is centered on me. Alive and present. Not thinking of the day or what tasks might await him tomorrow. Aries is celebrating and cherishing this long-awaited moment: the two of us naked and enveloped in the cool folds of his downy comforter.

When I can't take it anymore, I set my palms against his chest and push myself upright. I shift so that I'm on my knees with him behind me and take hold of the headboard like it's a pair of handlebars. "I want to feel you," I tell him, arching my lower back and pushing my ass toward him.

"Whatever my young master desires." Aries's voice is husky as he pulls away for a moment. I hear him remove the cap on the coconut oil that he secured from his nightstand drawer earlier. Soon, he meets me, grabbing my torso and urging me upright.

He's warm and solid with his chest pressed against my spine. His shaft is hard as it caresses and dips between my cheeks. The lazy sensation is so sensual and good that I exhale a moan. At the same time, my aura flexes and threatens to seep out. I inhale, pushing it back down—

"You don't need to restrain yourself." Aries wraps his large hand around my waist, then warmly settles his palm at my navel, as if cupping and encouraging the core of my aura. "I want to feel you, Oliver... everything. I trust you."

Lacing my hand over his, I tilt my head back and rest against him. This embrace and his words alone are like a sweet, honeyed ecstasy pouring over my mind and heart. "Are you sure?" I ask, breathless.

He leans into the curve of my neck. The softness of his full lips tickles my skin when he answers. "Yes, darling. I'm sure."

I close my eyes and allow my nature to unfurl, letting it seep, move and radiate all through me and outside of my flesh. My body melts into his embrace and the sensation is sublime. True liberation.

"Mm..." Aries drags his nose up my neck and into my hairline, breathing and caressing my belly. "You're perfect," he whispers. "Like a delicious dream."

Delirious with the joy of this release and being ensconced within the jasmine heat of his embrace, I smile and bite my bottom lip as his free hand slickly crawls between us to part my cheeks.

"If this is uncomfortable for you at any moment, please tell me? I can make you feel good in multiple ways. We don't have to finish this way if it's too much." Aries's voice is a smooth, satiny whisper near my ear. He kisses the concave of my neck, gently pushing his fingers inside of me. My aura and eyes burn even brighter as I grip the headboard. I don't want to orgasm too quickly, like I did before.

"I want... I want to finish," I manage, breathing out and arching into his fingers to drive them deeper. I must have surprised him, because the hand on my stomach caresses higher, resting in the bow of my rib cage.

"Slowly, darling," he coos. "My cock is... a bit more to take. It might be uncomfortable."

"Let me try," I say, turning my head. I catch his gaze and he leans, seductively kissing me over my shoulder. Discreetly, he slips another finger inside. The pressure of it intensifies, but it doesn't hurt. I lift from the kiss and breathe, relaxing my lower half and shifting my hips with the pulse and rhythm of his intrusion.

I let him work and stretch me in silence, but as my aura intensifies, I notice his subtle resistance to it. As if my essence is hitting a solid object instead of permeating it. Flowing around instead of into and through him. I don't know if it's because he's very focused, or maybe he's afraid to indulge in me, but the more I give myself over to what he's doing, the more I notice his defiance.

"I'm ready for you," I tell him, glancing over my shoulder once more. "May I have you, please?"

"Yes, my love," he says, pulling his fingers from me. I inhale and gap my thighs wider when he spreads my cheeks again. A moment later, the tip of his cock rests against my flesh. "You'll tell me if it's too much?"

"Yes," I say, arching my lower back and breathing. "But I want you to enjoy this, too."

This makes him pause. "Of course. You're perfection to me, Oliver. Truly divine." He finally urges himself inside and my breath catches from the initial fullness and shock of his tip. The heat, hardness and slip of his flesh penetrating mine. Naked, oiled and delicate skin embracing skin.

"Are we alright?" he asks, only partially inside. He rests one hand at my hip, waiting for my response.

"Mm," I breathe, closing my eyes and urging myself back, wanting to feel more of him. Needing to take in more.

"Oliver—" Aries gasps and I feel his strong body hitch. He trembles where he had been calm and steady before.

This is exactly what I need. More of this.

Aries barely has time to recover before I repeat my movement. Using the headboard as leverage, I gently push my hips back and into his frame, taking him in deeper and breathing as I move. Without question, he is thicker than his fingers, but I can handle him. He feels excellent, and closer in a way I've been wanting for a very long time. My aura rests in a heavy haze around us, and I can sense Aries slowly submitting and becoming malleable to me as he wraps his other hand around to grip my cock—fusing our bodies together.

With my nature released this way, he can feel my sincere love and fidelity. My truth. That I would never abandon him. He can trust me and I trust him, completely. And he could never be a burden to me, because that word doesn't even exist anywhere inside of my being.

I'm doing the work and steadily rocking my hips back, driving his shaft into me, slowly, over and over again. Aries breathes heavily while saying my name in my ear, telling me I'm beautiful. He leans into the curve of my neck as if he wants to feed, but he hesitates. Still afraid.

I'm not, so I take his wrist and drag the hand rested on my hip up toward my mouth. Shifting my grip, I lift his pointer finger and slip it into my mouth, sucking it while still rocking my hips.

"God—Oliver, *please*..." Aries is losing himself in me—in my essence and what I'm doing. What we're doing with our bodies and natures intimately entwined.

Willing my fangs out, I bite the tip of his finger and the fragrant, oakish and jasmine flavor of his blood fills my mouth. It pours down my throat and soothes me so deeply, so inherently, that I sigh in a satisfying moan and truly indulge.

The pleasure of his blood, his presence and his body inside of mine rushes over me like a perfect storm. Aries's grip on my shaft freezes and then he's with me, shuddering and spilling over warm and wet inside of me. Gasping with his hand fixed and trembling on my cock.

I love us like this. Erotic, sticky and breathing. Entangled and embracing as we come down from something we've done together. Love that we've made.

As Aries holds me, I take his finger from my mouth, flip his palm around and bite into it again because I'm greedy. I want to feed properly from his neck, but since he isn't ready to feed from me, I can't take too much. I shouldn't be too selfish.

He's patient, waiting as I finish feeding before he removes himself from my body. Lazily, I turn and flop back against the side of the bed that hasn't been stained with my release and squirm cozily against the plush comforter.

Aries leans over me. His hair is mussed from my fingers and our foreplay, and his expression is relaxed. Satisfied. "I don't remember the young master being so frisky. You've always been bold, though."

Shrugging, I lift my hands to caress and hold his face. "Thinking back, I don't know who or what I was in that castle. I know it wasn't even a year ago, but it feels like eons. God... I was under so much pressure and stress. I didn't have the space to be 'frisky.'"

He grabs my hands, then brings them both to his mouth, playfully kissing my knuckles. "You have the space to be and do whatever you choose, now. I was wrong, though. You're not a mouse. More like a tiger. And I think I'm the one in danger of being devoured."

I trace his lips with my fingertips. "Not in danger. I'll protect you."

He takes hold of my wrist again. "Will you?"

"Fiercely."

My heart-rate doubles as he parts his lips and takes my finger into his mouth. Timidly, he bites the tip. I don't move or say a word, because it feels like a butterfly has landed on my shoulder. Aries closes his eyes, tasting. When he finishes and opens his eyes, they're alighted and stunning, which makes mine burn even brighter.

"Even if I don't properly feed from you, I think... I might already be too far gone. You're only here for a week, Oliver."

"Well, actually..." I grin, feeling somewhat guilty for withholding important information. "Do you remember how I told you that Sylvie was considering splitting up the remaining jobs between the two of us?"

"Yes, because you impressed her so much with your talent and work ethic on your assignments together. How could I forget?"

I sit up to rest on my elbows underneath him. "She's decided to split the assignments by location. She's going to do the remaining jobs in Asia, but she's entrusting the ones in Europe to me. We only had two shoots in North America, and we already did those together before we separated and I came here. Dividing things this way, there's more time in our schedules, so we can both breathe and establish a home-base..."

A hushed moment of pause passes between us as Aries registers what I'm saying. He smiles. "Which means... you now have the flexibility to live where you want in Europe."

"Yes."

"Why didn't you tell me this earlier?"

"Because I didn't want you to feel pressured," I assure him. "And I made the decision without asking you, so I wasn't sure how you'd feel about me following you around."

Sylvie knows all about Aries, since I spoke of him fairly often in our downtime. On long layovers and casually over meals. Sometimes during those idle moments of waiting for elements and people outside of our control. It was her idea for us to split the remaining work, and I'm forever grateful to her for it.

Another funny way that life has given me exactly what I needed. "If you don't want me to stay with you," I go on, bracing myself, "then I'll—"

"I want you to stay, Oliver." Aries's eyes are so rich and haunting in the soft moonlight. The single candle he's lit flickers wildly on the bedside table. The low light casts sensual shadows across his face and body as his gaze pierces mine. "Will you please stay with me?"

A smile spreads across my lips because the delight I feel in this moment is warm and full. So powerful that it might overflow from within.

I inhale deeply, saturating my senses with his fragrance as my chest rises, then falls. "Yes, I'll stay with you. I'm more than happy to, Aries. I'm honored."

Aries is right about me being frisky. This new, unexpected personality trait. Because after I wake up first beside him, I proceed to stroke my hand down his abdomen while kissing his neck and shoulders until he wakes up, slightly disoriented and very aroused.

The morning sunlight is like liquid platinum as it streams through the tall windows, flooding the cozy loft with light and hiding nothing as I climb onto his hips and start grinding against him.

"You don't need to be impaled by me every time we have sex," he says, laughing and taking hold of my hips. "If you enjoy this, you could have me, too."

"What if I like being impaled by you?" I ask honestly. "I enjoy having you this way. Is that bad?"

He raises an eyebrow, considering. "No, of course not. I just want you to know that we have options."

"Well, that's fine. But we've only done it once. I want you in me again."

So, I have him. He fusses at me to use the coconut oil and I do, but when he asks to stretch me, I wave him off. I tell him I'm still stretched from the night before. He says that's not a thing.

Slowly, focused, I work myself onto his cock, then ride him until he's incapable of protesting. Until he's writhing, entranced and breathless. Vanquished. I love the way he feels inside of me and that I can please him. Watching his eyes alight as he reaches the height of pleasure, and feeling his solid, sculpted frame satisfied and shuddering underneath me... it's glorious.

When I climb off of him, I decide that I'm in the mood for pancakes. "Do you have flour and fruit? Like strawberries or blueberries? Maybe syrup?"

Aries's dark brown waves are in a chaotic state. Even messier than the night before. He rolls over onto his side, takes a deep breath and smiles. "I... think so?"

"Do you want pancakes? I'm really good at making them if you have the ingredients. I like to add cinnamon because it gives them a nice earthiness." I'm sitting on the edge of the bed, and when I stand, my legs are wobbly and my ass is throbbing, but in the best possible way. I head over to my suitcase and slip on a T-shirt and pajama pants.

"Not spaghetti?" he asks. "Your specialty."

I laugh. "I can make spaghetti if you want? Can we have it for dinner, though?"

"Sure... How can you even move right now?" He watches from the bed with disbelief. "I'm adding a new character trait to the list—insatiable. My insatiable and frisky tiger. My long-legged tiger prince."

"Alright, that's enough." I laugh, standing. Utterly ridiculous. "I'll let you know when breakfast is done. Coffee or tea?"

"Coffee, please? And thank you. When I am no longer incapacitated, I'll come down and help you."

Chuckling, I lean over and kiss him on the lips. Once, then again. When I stand straight, I glance at his bedside table and notice a tiny picture in the center of an elegant glass frame. Bending, I look closer.

It's us. Me, with my eyes wide in genuine surprise as Aries kisses my cheek.

"You kept this?" I say, pointing to the second polaroid that I took of us. The missing photo.

"I did," he admits, stretching his spine and lazily drawing a leg up. The sheets shift and his naked thigh and hip are exposed. He looks edible and I'm very tempted to crawl back into bed with him. "I needed a memento."

I don't say anything as I meet and kiss him once more. Softly and sincerely. Why is he wonderful? It's like I've won some kind of cosmic lottery. What are the chances that he'd come into my life, given the way I'd existed up until that point?

I never thought I would say this, but thank you, Lord Blakeley, for hiring a designer for my wedding.

Beaming, I head down the wooden stairs toward the rustic, glamorous kitchen.

Turns out, he does have all the ingredients that I need, and more. It feels as if he went grocery shopping before I came. We've talked a lot about how much I enjoy cooking, so, as always, he was paying attention.

As I gather the food on the counter and search through cabinets for the proper pans, bowls and utensils, I notice how completely contented and at ease I feel. Not that I didn't feel comfortable living with Daniel and Leoni, and traveling through Asia with Sylvie.

But this... Occupying space with Aries feels like an enhanced and new layer to my life. An added, fundamental goodness. Like dancing in the rain, but then the sun comes out and the raindrops glimmer in the radiant light as they fall. A rainbow appears, coloring the brilliant blue of a partly cloudy sky. All these elements fuse together to create something truly special. Something magnificent.

Being with Aries is like this. And now, he's asked me to stay with him. I don't know how long it will take for him to truly accept and feed from me, but it doesn't matter. We're here, and I'm willing to wait for him—

"You're distracted."

"*Jesus Christ*, you scared me."

"What are you so absorbed in right now that you didn't notice me coming down the stairs? These pancakes? You really are a serious chef. My long-legged, frisky tiger chef."

Aries stands behind me, shirtless and sexy in sweatpants and nothing else, just as I was attempting to measure flour in a cup. He surprised me, so now there's white powder everywhere.

"I'm just content," I say, sweeping up the mess with my palms. "Why? What's the matter?" He places his hands on my waist, making me pause. When I feel him lean into my neck, my nature churns with anticipation. Internally, I tell it to calm down out of habit.

"I gave it some thought," he says, kissing my temple. "And I... I would like to accept your generous offer."

I freeze. Blinking and holding my breath. "Okay..."

He bends, brushing his lips along the curve of my neck. "Would you like me to pull your aura, Oliver? May I feed properly?"

Closing my eyes and lifting my chin, I can barely respond. The last time someone tried to do this, it was terrible and unwarranted. But this moment is nothing like that. Everything inside of me is screaming for it. For him to put his mouth on my flesh and pull to nourish himself. To take of his will.

"Yes," I say quietly. "Please."

He licks me and a hard shiver rattles my spine. Like an earthquake rooted and internalized in my groin. Aries softly bites down into my neck, then sucks and wraps his arms around my waist, gluing me to his hard body as he feeds.

Aries's thoughts pour into me, and they're not what I expected of him based on what I perceive on the surface. He almost always radiates a cool confidence. A vampire that's strong and capable. Someone who knows how to take care of himself.

But as my eyes alight, Aries's thoughts are warm and... timid. Again, I'm reminded of a butterfly—a swarm of them floating through me, so lovely and light. Hesitating.

He loves me. He thinks I'm the bravest and most remarkable vampire that he's ever met. Aries pines for me, truly, but he's scared to depend on me. He's afraid, but he's pushing through the fear because he trusts in our connection. He wants to rely on me, or at least to try.

Aries's desire is soft and coaxing. It tugs, but gently waits for my response. For my acquiescence. I close my burning eyes and submit to his desire. I relax back and let him take it from me.

The joy of my nature swishes like a glittering fire from deep in my core—up my belly and chest, swirling around my spine and to my head until it rushes outward. Warm, hazy and blueish silver like the night sky flooded with stars. My knees give, but Aries's grip is tight around my waist. He doesn't let me fall.

Every fear... every worry, insecurity and anxiety, it all eases. With this release and connection to Aries's mind, a new understanding solidifies between us. Somehow, I can sense him more deeply. Clearer than I could before, as if he's given me access to a sacred place.

Aries lifts his mouth, licks me and leans into my temple. "Are we okay? Was it alright?"

"Yes..." I say, breathless and slouching.

"Can you stand?" he asks, chuckling. I'm unsteady, but I do.

Holding on to the counter with my flour-covered hands for leverage.

"You're not saying anything?" he says.

I turn to look at him and blink in surprise. His cheeks are flushed with deep crimson. "Now you know how much of a coward I am. But I... I want to do this, Oliver. I want you. I love you and I think you're audacious and intelligent, courageous and loyal—I admire these qualities in you, but I just... I don't know why I'm so afraid of this."

Lifting my hands, I place them on his cheeks so that his eyes are focused on mine. "I love you, too, Aries. We can go as slowly and take as long as you need. Alright?"

He nods, and I can see tears forming in his ethereal eyes. "Alright." He leans down and kisses me.

We kiss, and nothing else matters. Where we decide to go next, whether or not we're capable of forming a bond, or the fact that I've now gotten flour all over his face and in his hair—those things aren't important.

What matters is us being balanced and honest. Us being liberated vampires, trusting, listening and understanding each other. Making our own choices.

Together. Me and Aries.

Exactly two hours later...

Chapter Thirty-Two

"Oliver, I'm not a pogo stick. You can't keep hopping on and riding me when you feel like it."

"What's a pogo stick? I don't even know what that is, so how can I treat you like one?"

After a hearty, romantic breakfast and a very explorative and sensual shower, we're clean and sitting on a daybed in the courtyard, surrounded by leafy palms and wildflowers.

"I don't know if I can keep up with my frisky tiger." Aries leans over, pulling my folded leg loose so that I slouch and fall back against the cushion. I laugh as he lies down, covering me with his body. "Christ. Can I just cuddle you for a while? I need a minute to recover."

I grin underneath his weight. He's so warm. "It's exciting," I admit. "Finally being with you like this. Isolated and free." No clandestine meetings in my bedroom or stifling my nature... not that I did that very well toward the end, apparently.

"I agree," Aries says, wrapping his arms around my waist. "But we have time to learn each other, darling. We don't need to figure this out and have a sex marathon within the first twenty-four hours."

I chuckle again, nuzzling my face into the curve of his neck above me. "I need to tell you something."

"Mm?"

"Before I met you, I never wanted to have sex—or be kissed or touched at all. When I fantasized about my freedom and life of travel and exploration, I was always alone. I didn't think I was interested in romance or sexual intimacy. When I was forced to be in that space with Alexander, I hated the thought of these things. It made me so uncomfortable."

"The primary phrase there is 'I was *forced*,'" Aries says. "I think it's perfectly natural to be repelled by something when you're pressured to do it against your will. This logic holds across any scenario, but especially in physically intimate acts like feeding and lovemaking."

I nod, sliding my palms up his spine. "You were the first vampire that truly made me feel comfortable. You didn't have to talk to me the way that you did, but you were sincere. You listened like no one else ever had. Without judgment, ridicule or rebuke. You made me feel safe."

The wind picks up, rustling the brush around us as the sun shifts from behind a puffy cloud. It smells like oak, jasmine and sunshine when I inhale deeply. It is paradise. "Aries?"

"You're going to make me cry again," he says, shifting and kissing my nose. "You say such beautiful and honest things. It makes me crumble."

"In a bad way?" I lean into the concave of his neck once more, breathing. I want to feed deeply from him. The yearning is almost painful, but I know we should take it slow. I need to calm down.

"In a good way," he says. "I had... well. There were grievances that I'd built up after I left the aristocracy in Mykonos, but you've eased that burden. You've given me something that I didn't think I'd ever have again. A subtle but important sense that I've been missing for so long in my travels."

"What is it?" I ask, because I genuinely have no idea.

He kisses me on the forehead and between my eyes. "A home. A stable place to rest—somewhere I can finally let my guard down and feel safe. You feel like home to me, Oliver."

The words are like an incantation, making my emotions well up and my eyes alight once more. Aries senses the shift in my essence and glances down, smiling. "I also love that you're so easily sparked."

"May I feed?" I ask. "Properly."

"Yes, darling. You may."

I lift my chin to breathe his skin, then swiftly bite into his neck. My aura pulses outward and I don't restrain it because I want him to know how grateful I am. I want him to understand my heart in its entirety and full capacity—more than words can express.

Aries is delicious as I pull. Divine, richly sweet and earthy. Unlike last night, his nature is malleable with mine as I feed. Accepting and welcoming of my nature's embrace and intention.

Something in our energies shifts and I open my eyes.

Softly, cautiously, his nature manifests as deep blue, misty like an airbrushed sky as it melts and twists with my silver light. Merging as one.

I stop feeding because the spectacle of it is mesmerizing. Breathtaking and mysterious like the northern lights. Aries watches, too. His eyes are alighted in awe as our natures entwine.

After a moment, they float down and over us like a feather-weight blanket. Heat and goodness tingle against my skin, then seep inside my core and spine.

My nature adjusts, settles, and it feels... different. Enhanced. I can sense Aries within me, giving me strength. Offering assurance and love.

He looks down to meet my gaze, and I notice that his eyes have changed. They're blue, but with an inner glint of silver now. My essence has manifested inside of him.

I was willing to wait for him to accept and form a lifelong bond with me. Even if it took weeks, months or perhaps years.

Apparently, that isn't our story.

Looking up at him, I smile helplessly. "Hi."

He laughs, bending and sweetly brushing his nose into me as he closes his burning starlight eyes. "Hello, my darling."

357

-The End-

Acknowledgments

Thank you to Madeline, Shepa and Lindsay for being the best beta readers there ever were and giving me the hard feedback that I sometimes don't want to hear. To my parents, Roy and Ann, for always believing in and supporting me in my creative and whimsical endeavors. And a special thank you to my Patrons who supported and traveled with me on the journey of writing Oliver's story.

Rafael Rodriguez
Ryan
Alek
Naely Liriano
Nathalia
Spencer King
Sarah Rukhsana
Shadow & Moonlight
Alexa
Celina Hofstadt
Dare
Kate
AmoraBleu
Nadine Kennedy
Kay
Julie Lapierre
Nora
Nea
Lilu_7_

Mary Jay
britturble
Kaylina
Koray
Bree Dalton
Teddybearjinx
MissDaddy
Zahra
Julia
Ashley Beierwaltes
asia khem
Lauren
Janette Derucki
Verenisse Marron
Paige McLarty
L
Erin Arthur

About the Author

Karla Nikole is passionate about thoughtful stories with diverse, queer and adult themes. Her books are centered in fantasy, consent, communication, mental health and romance. She is also deeply inspired by travel and cultures, and has lived in Japan, South Korea, Prague, Milan and the South of France. Her debut trilogy, *Lore and Lust: A Queer Vampire Romance*, has been featured in multiple book subscription boxes, is carried in-store by bookshops across the U.S., and has been translated into multiple languages worldwide for readers to enjoy.

instagram.com/karlanikolepublishing

9 7 9 8 2 1 8 2 9 8 2 6 5